DESOLATION

Pathfinder Media Group
Harrisburg, Pennsylvania, USA
media@pathfinderops.org
legacyofsorrow.com

Desolation – Volume III of The Legacy of Sorrow

LEGACY OF SORROW

Disclaimer:

All characters and events portrayed in this book are fictitious. Any similarity to real persons, living or dead, is purely coincidental, and not intended by the author.

The content of this book or series may cover controversial or sensitive topics to include assault, violence, addiction, loss, trauma, SA, suicide, or other potential triggers. Readers' discretion is advised.

ISBN (KDP Paperback):
ISBN (Kindle eBook):

Though these books detail a long and bloody war, I've been through battles of my own as this series was written across more than a decade and a half of my life. For those who stood by my side, those who believed I could finish the fight, and for my readers who face their own battles, this story is for you.

Few know death.
Fewer know him the way that I do.
The way we danced and laughed and sang our nights away
like eager lovers…
But I've betrayed him.
Not of my own choice, death has always courted me, yet was
always found wanting.
And now – again – I have left him at the altar.
But he waits, ever-smiling and ever-patient.

This deception, this engagement with my own end,
This endless darkness and the thing that dwells within…

He is the architect of my desolation.

TABLE OF CONTENTS

SEVERAL YEARS AFTER
THE EVENTS OF SORROW

TREMOR
KRYSTAL

There was a long pause, like the deep breath before a plunge into frozen waters, before the pain finally came to infect my body. All my long life, I had not known true pain until the certain fact came to my mind, despite its madness in my state of apparent death: I was, in some form, alive. The darkness that shrouded both my eyes and my sense of awareness was unparalleled by even the blackest night, fading all rational thought from becoming useful and only serving to keep me aware of the same burning torment I felt that I suffered for eons. Time passed. Whether it was seconds or millennia, I was unsure, but the trickling grains of each blistering surge of agony kept the sands of my internal hourglass moving forward, and until the pain would subside, I knew I was still alive. Ghosts of images formed themselves in front of my eyes: fading and fleeting pictures of nonsensical environments, irrational surroundings, and impossible atmospheres. In my comatose slumber, I was torn apart and repaired time and time again until I was sure that it was nothing more than a terrorizing nightmare. This was my hell.

Repeatedly, I found myself nearly lucid, flailing without hands to grab some imaginary support or take hold of consciousness, although both eluded me. I thrashed, screamed, felt my hands on cold metal bars

without end or purpose. I cried. I fell. Until I was spent of my life's energy, I fought and confronted these twisted visions of nightmares, until at long last, there was a convoluted, isolated semblance of thought.
I was...cold.

***

I lurched forward from a lying position, quickly confronted by a brief fall and the unforgiving surface of a tile floor before coughing profusely. My eyes roamed as I panicked, my perception of vision being nothing more than a field of black with endless depth and pitch. My eyes wandered without purpose, flickering back and forth in order to find a distinction that didn't exist among the nothingness. I gritted my teeth, senses far from recovered, and sucked in gusts of painful air while listening to myself sob.

How am I alive? Where am I? Who's there? Please help. It hurts. What happened to me?

The flurried, rushing waves of questions and misplaced thought made me dizzy and nauseous as I croaked inhuman, hoarse bouts of air, alternating between crying and trying to scream for help. My throat was tight, keeping the flow of oxygen constricted and irregular. I hesitated for a moment, holding my breath and regulating my breathing.

In. Out. In. Out. In...Out...In...

Distinctive shapes made their way to my brain as I lifted my head from the floor, staring at the blurred leg of a metal piece of furniture. My reflection gazed back at me, a hazy image of a pale woman with cerulean hair. I glowered at the image for longer than I expected, looking at each small feature of the face that stared back at me. It was somehow different than the image of my familiar face: not unrecognizable, but changed in the most subtle of ways. My eyes were set in a darker blue than I had come to know, a strong ocean current running through them in curiosity. My hair, while unchanged in color, was lengthened by almost a foot and clung in angry clumps around my uncovered shoulders. I looked older, somehow, the slightest pronunciation of my features removing a small degree of apparent teenage youthfulness and replacing it with an image of maturity. In some small way, it reminded me of Alice. A white tank top covered up enough to protect my modesty, but did nothing against the unforgiving cold of the room.

Despite not being able to isolate an origin, my body roared in immense pain. My frame was sore in every muscle imaginable, making every small movement a struggle. I stood up slowly, my head turning to look around the room while my skull tried its hardest not to rupture. Alice's largest and most intricate intensive care unit had been fashioned in the style of a hospice room. While medical instruments and machines crowded the space immediately around me, I noticed an array of personal effects. Painting upon painting covered the walls in Violet's signature style, dimly lit by the only light in the room.

The lamp's glow flickered more than it should have, a clear indication of either neglect or fault. A large man's coat was draped over a chair next to my bedside, an artifact I picked up and guided over my shoulders to conserve warmth. As I slid my arm into the left sleeve of the leather jacket, a sharp pinch forced the realization that I was connected to an IV line. I withdrew my arm and looked at the skin around the flexible plastic port. In spite of my ability to heal more quickly than most humans, track marks and scar tissue indicated I had undergone dozens, if not hundreds, of needle punctures from some sort of medical procedure. My breathing grew heavy, the shadow of memories or dreams overtaking my saner thoughts.

Flashing red lights. A rumble, growing closer. Darkness. Cold. Fire. Burning. Everything burning.

"I died." I whispered, coughing as the words left my mouth. My throat felt laden with knives that dug into my flesh with every breath I drew. Making a hasty decision, I followed the IV line to its silver pole, inspecting the clear, nearly empty bag closely.

Factor Five. Manufactured and sold by Raven Biopharmaceuticals. Raven…?

My trembling increasing to border on epileptic, I ripped the line from my arm and sat back down on the edge of the hospital bed, my hair gripped in tight fistfuls against my scalp.

What the hell is happening?

I snatched a bottle of water from the nearby table and broke the seal on the cap before drinking all of its contents in one long, appreciative gulp.

"Okay…" I whispered, lifting my head to look around the room again. "I'm definitely in the city. Back in Aerael. How…did I get here?" I decided to move into the mindset of solving a mystery, peering around to obtain clues about my situation. Aside from the apparently-frequent visits to the hospital room from familiar members of my family, I couldn't discern any solid facts about why or how I was still alive, nor why I was alone. I stepped off of the bed carefully, my legs weakened by some period of neglect, and wandered to the open medicine cabinet. "Saline, blood, plasma, platelets, dextrose, morphine…" My eyes lingered on the latter, but continued to move along the shelf to my own surprise. "Diazepam… Factor Five." I picked up one of the clear bags labeled with the unmistakable logo of our enemy's legacy and inspected it closely, reading the administrative instructions and dosing chart. "This is Alice's medicine. With Raven's logo." I whispered, turning it over in awe.

For Vampyre Use Only. IARC Group 1: Carcinogenic to Humans.

The hiss of my numb lips forming simple syllables was captured by the softness of the room, shrouding the area I occupied in unsettling silence. Even after the city had emptied during the peak of our conflict, its citizens were returned and its mechanical workings had resumed. No subtle indications of life in any meaningful capacity gave rise to hope or confidence. I set the bag on the shelf, realizing I needed to keep investigating, and that the room would only provide so many clues. Tossing aside blankets, sealed envelopes with well-wishes, and trinkets of recovery, I managed to find a small pile of burgundy scrubs, apparently left by my sister. The stitching was thick and rough as I slid the pants over my legs, a coarse fabric indicating they were of the same kind that were specially crafted to resist her torrid body heat. Deciding to throw the jacket over the scrub top, I was finally insulated against the seeping chill of the dim room. My feet were still bare and cold, but a lack of available covering made for the mild discomfort to be both trivial and unfixable.

My neck struggled to turn my head toward the door: a metal slab with nothing but a small window to peer into the hall outside. I approached it, looking into the profound darkness that plagued the other side of the door. Faint and murky rays of soft light illuminated the empty hall of the hospital just enough to see it was abandoned in its entirety. I lifted my hand, sensation still distant in my fingers, and grasped the handle of the door tightly to open it. With a quick jerk, the handle snapped and fell to the floor in a loud clatter of frozen metal. I looked at my hand, covered in a thick layer of frozen blood. A deep cut made its way down my palm, the sharp metal from the remains of the handle having dug into my skin. Growing anxious, I held my untarnished hand to the lock, freezing it with my Vampyre-gifted ability and throwing my shoulder into the frame. It failed to give in, the door normally opening in the opposite direction of my impact.

No. No, please…How am I going to get out?

I clenched my fists, pounding on the door until my hand made its way through the glass window, thankfully failing to cut me as the handle did. I reached through carefully, gently turning the lever on the other side and opening the door into the room. A warm breeze of musky wind crossed my face, drawing the cold air of the room into the hall. I stepped forward, moving slowly and deliberately along the concrete walls of the familiar structure. Like ghosts, I could visualize the nurses and technicians of the well-lit infirmary, pacing through each room to keep the system running smoothly. Instead, a still and dark warmth stalled my feet as I approached a familiar sight. One of Alice's trauma rooms had been reorganized since my incident with Kara, the memories of an otherworldly pain sparking a grimace as I stared into the black. I leaned into the door frame, closing my eyes for a moment to remember things as they were.

Why is everything…different? Abandoned? We won our war.

I returned to my slow winding through the hospital, stopping in the atrium as the glass front of the structure opened into a grim omen of wretchedness. My mouth agape, the crisp salt of tears found their way to my lips as I left the infirmary and stood in the main hall of the city. Its lights were nothing more than the dying ember's glow of an effort to stay alive, casting deeply-drawn shadows over the emptiness it attempted to illuminate. A dismal, dusty darkness pervaded the air with no movement or joy to cleanse its forlorn aura. Every door and opening to the establishments and recesses of the city were bathed in a hellish atmosphere of abandonment and sickness. I was paralyzed with true and deep fear, coveting a release from the vision that sprawled in front of me.

Faintly, I could make out the browned edges of dried blood on the wall across from me, mottling the concrete in an asymmetric pattern of splotches and splatters. It was nearly too easy to spot, the arboretum that previously divided the main hall into two distinct halves now bearing the jutting edges of dead trees and lifeless vegetation. I could almost smell the history of the hall in its dank, stale air that saturated my tongue with dust and damp earth.

"What the hell..." I wondered briefly if that was my true destination, deliberating the likelihood of an afterlife before a quiet, soft scrape from farther down the hall assured me that I was correct. Some demon moved a distance from me, hidden entirely in the long shadow of an everlasting night. Its hooved feet slid in long steps, striking the ground with a tap and a long scratch with each stride. It was light, only the quickest and faintest echo of reality making its way to my ears. I looked around in a frenzy, my hair whipping across my nose as the search for a defensible weapon began. I moved back toward the front of the hospital, locking my eyes with the black depth of my threat's origin. It grew closer to the edges of the light, nearly in the visible range of my eyes.

A single tap, a scratch, and a moment's pause repeated itself in my ears, spiking my already surged veins with an unparalleled adrenaline out of raw terror. Realizing I had no choice, I slammed my elbow into the glass wall of the infirmary, shattering it into hundreds of large shards that fell to the ground in a treasure trove of wounding instruments. I withdrew my hand into the sleeve of the leather jacket and picked up the largest I could find, nearly six inches long, and held it toward the darkness as a threat. Shaking in the most violent of ways, the makeshift knife seemed to perform its duty diligently, the pattern of approaching footsteps faltering, then falling completely silent. The muscles in my throat were shuddering in tears and quiet, sharp breaths, cutting off my ability to utter a war cry or warning against the thing that stood just inside the edge of darkness, watching me.

"Way to break the last intact building." A feminine voice erupted in an unexpected statement as I jumped, the shard slipping from its weak hold in my jacket and falling to the ground.

That voice sounds familiar, but…different.

"H-…" As I went to call out, my voice squeaked a fearful whimper and instigated the last of my fortitude. "Who are you?" I cried in a tearful whisper. A single, calf-high black boot exposed itself to the light as she took a step forward, the glimmer of silver buckles adorning the suede shank. It was followed quickly by the rest of the leg, tapered athletically into a slim thigh and narrow waist. I recognized my friend immediately as her torso and head made their way into visibility, covered in a much smaller leather jacket than the one I wore and a small array of ear piercings that weren't present the last time I saw her. Violet took another long, slow step, her boot scuffing the ground in lazy strides as she made her way toward me.

"I…" She began, her lips twitching into an uneven smirk. "Am Prince Charming." She stopped in front of me, my body still reeling in waves of uncontrollable nausea that made its way into my throat. "What's up, sleeping beauty?"

"Vi?" I whispered, a choking sensation in the back of my throat triggering an episode of intense vomiting on the floor to my right as she took a step back and chuckled. I could barely make out the edges of her boots as my tears blurred my vision to a monochrome haze, but I refused to let her out of my sight. Setting my shock aside and accepting gratitude, I embraced her in a tight hug, my chest heaving with the effort to stop crying. She returned the gesture hesitantly, lightly patting my shoulder until I felt nauseous again. I pulled away, fearful of another round of sickness.

"That happy to see me?" She chuckled. I was doubled over, panting heavily as she spoke. Shaking my head, I spit repeatedly and wiped my mouth on the corner of the scrubs, quickly standing upright to look at her face one more time.

"I just...I can't believe it's you. I mean, I can't....I'm alive. How? And what happened to...everything?" I gestured around frantically as she shrugged, grimacing.

"Trust me when I say that I can't explain everything in a short amount of time. You're going to have to be really patient, but we'll get you up to speed." Despite the dark, rock-and-roll look and carefree attitude, she was clearly happy to see me, a soft smile gracing her face. "Walk with me." She extended a hand, which I took gratefully, as we stepped closer to the middle of the hall to avoid the glass scattered around the floor. "I know you're going to have a trillion questions, but I need you to avoid asking them right now. I have answers to things you haven't even thought of yet, but there has to be a certain...order to everything." She continued.

"Is there anything you *can* tell me right now? I mean...Vi, I have so much going through my head. I thought I died." I tried to calm my nerves as we walked through the hall, approaching the wall of shadow that darkened the area of my former living space.

"You did." She returned quietly. A note of bitterness tainted her voice before her eyes darted over to me. I could make out her chocolate-colored irises tainted with anger as they peeked at me through jet-black strands of hair far longer than they used to be. "When that lab went down...the whole building collapsed. We didn't expect....well..." She withdrew a small flashlight from her pocket as we entered the hallway of rooms, shining it on my door and indicating that I go inside. Without the light, the hallway was so dark that even my enhanced vision couldn't distinguish much else from the shadows. "Jalix and Kara, along with your sister, went to visit the lab's rubble before they tore the site down. Right after your funeral." We stopped in front of my door, my heart pounding as she revisited the story of my survival. She looked up at me, her long hair falling over half of her face and laying in loose strands down her back as it brushed against the leather. "They laid down flowers, and as they were saying their goodbyes...those flowers froze solid. Alice knew you were still there. Eric pulled some strings to let us dig and Tony got his engineering team to get through the rubble. And we found you." Her voice threatened to break, but held steady by anger or determination. "I don't know if you did it on purpose, or whether it was a defense mechanism, but when they finally cleared away the steel and concrete, they found a six-foot-thick block of ice with you trapped inside. You had some burns, and when they finally broke it open and chipped everything away, you were comatose. But you were definitely alive. Alice didn't leave the infirmary for the next six months, refusing to let anyone else take care of you."

"So my body just...shut down?" I asked in awe. Violet chuckled again, biting her lip and pushing open my door.

"Welcome home, Krystal. To what's left of it."

The door swung open without a creak or squeal, allowing the flashlight's luminescence to flood the undisturbed room. Aside from the reek of abundant mold and the clear decay it set into my furniture, everything was undisturbed and left untouched since last I had seen it. Seeming to be just days ago, my eyes lingered over the plush blue comforter Kara and I had sat on, now worn through with holes and coated with dust.

"How did all this happen in just six months? I mean...the whole city...." I peeked into my bathroom, the ash of a dozen incense burners littering every flat surface they could. Even my garbage can still held the clear plastic casings of discarded needles. I rubbed my arm in remembrance, but no familiar craving for a blissful high set in.

"You were out longer than six months, Krystal." Violet remained unmoved from my doorway, only shifting slightly to shine her flashlight around wherever I roamed. "But like I said, we'll explain everything soon."

"We?" I asked hopefully. "Alice? Kara? Is everyone okay?" She clicked the flashlight off, unforgiving darkness swallowing my eyesight. I could hear her delicate chest heave in a quiet sigh.

"Please...just wait. Okay? I want to tell you everything that happened, but I have half of it written down and the other half is going to take hours to tell you. If you really want answers, we'll give them to you. But..." She clicked the flashlight on again, held limply at her side in a slump of agonized deliberation. "It's going to be like becoming a Vampyre all over again. You're not going to understand, and you're not going to want to." She fell quiet for a moment, turning back toward the hallway we came from. "But you're not going to have a choice."

"I can handle it, Violet. I've handled way worse. As long as everyone is okay-"

"Then follow me." She began moving without waiting, prompting me to tug the jacket closer to my chest in the chill of the still air and trot after her, my bare feet hardly touching the ground as I caught up. We turned back into the main hall, heading further into darkness with only a cone of harsh light to lead the way. She shined the light over several familiar establishments, the café appearing long dead and the fast food restaurant left in a state of pure chaos. Once again, I could spot the faint outline of blood smears, a poor attempt to wash them away fading them into the concrete walls.

"Where are we going?" I felt like it was a safe question, choosing to focus my energy into the next immediate moment and not prying into the past or future.

"Archangel. It's…home, for now." She looked around as we neared the nightclub, the main half of the city still eerily quiet. "If you can't tell, most of the city went to shit, but we made this place our own. As much as we could, anyway."

She keeps saying we. Who else is here?

I bit my tongue and continued to walk, placing one shaky foot in front of the other before the oak doors appeared before me, its hinges re-drilled into a new spot in the wall after the night Kara had gotten married and the crowd had destroyed them.

How is this so long ago? It just happened yesterday, from my point of view.

The musty smell of humid soil died down as she cracked the door open, a dryer and cleaner odor similar to that of a tidy kitchen pushing its way into the hall.

"Just don't ask questions. Mkay?" Violet smirked, her eyes wincing for a moment in a mixture of mischief and anticipation. Even behind the happiness, some aura of absolute burden clung to her eyes. I nodded once, hoping it would speed up the process of the door opening into whatever answers I had yet to ask for. The interior of what I remembered to be the nightclub was warmer, drier, and surprisingly transformed from its previous purpose.

As I looked into the nearest corner to my right, a bed and nightstand were accompanied by two small bookshelves and a dresser. The ensemble created a makeshift bedroom, however open to the rest of the room with the exception of a series of blankets hung to act as a large curtain. Strewn throughout the sparse furniture were a mix of firearms and art supplies, both having seen some slight age from lack of use. In the opposite corner, a similar construct stood without the artistic utensils and differed by a large man sitting on the edge of the bed, facing the doorway. The lower half of his face was obscured by a thick, dark beard with natural tinges of blonde and accented with eyes of smoldering coal. I took a step into the room, the ambient light from small lamps finally drawing me to an elated conclusion.

"Val?" I gasped, my chest heaving in inconsistent flutters. I walked over to him slowly, his body forcing itself to its feet and studying me as I approached.

"Get some sleep?" He smirked, his voice quiet and low while his eyes sparkled with a similar happiness to my own. I trotted the last few steps and wrapped my arms around him. The entire experience seemed surreal, someone I had known and cherished seemingly back from the dead.

"How?" My voice was muffled against his chest, but for a lack of fresh tears, was distinguishable.

"Can't kill a cockroach." He mumbled, rubbing my back gently as I let myself reunite with the thought of another friend coming back into my life. "Kara's alive too. Alice is still around and kicking...somewhere. We'll talk. Just walk around for a minute and get your bearings." While his advice came from a place of caring, I feared for my own sanity if I had to hear one more time to wait on rational conclusions. The thought of my sister and Kara being safe and alive was enough to get me to heed his words, taking a step back and beginning to pace around the former nightclub.

It worked. We rescued her.

The room had been stripped of its business purpose, the bar now a place for bath towels and shared toiletries while the shelves reserved for booze now held cleaning supplies and small bags of nonperishable food. I dragged myself toward the stage, its lights dark and likely to not be used again. One of my friends had clearly gone to work on the wooden platform, transforming it into a center for trivial electronics and a computer desk.

"You guys want me to get my bearings and calm down, but I really can't do that in this environment. Everything is…foreign. Weird. I'll stay calm, but…I need filled in. What the hell happened while I was out?" I was torn between a loss for words and attempting to spit out every word that crossed my frantic mind. "And how long exactly was I out? Violet said it was over six months, but-"

"Nineteen years." Val's low voice rumbled across the room, freezing my heart in place and weakening my knees to the point of no return. "Almost twenty, now."

No. No, no, no…

Leaning against the stage as my vision dimmed to a blackened tunnel, I felt Violet's thin but muscular arms swoop under my own and hold me upright long enough to lean the majority of my body weight into her.

"Easy…" Violet whispered, placing one arm around my waist. "Don't pass out us just yet."

"No, I can't-…Guys, I-…" The sharp grinding of my throat finally won over, once again inciting a gasping, choking series of painful sobs.

This isn't possible. It's genuinely not possible.

"You're alright, Krystal. You've got a lot of healing to do, and your body's been through a lot. Things are going to seem worse than they really are for a little bit. I need you to breathe." Val's familiar caring revealed itself once again as he moved toward me, crouching to meet my eyes and speaking directly. "Breathe."

It couldn't have been that long.

"How?" I inhaled deeply, exhaling far too soon and croaking out singular words. "Just…how?" Violet decided to take the reins of explanation, calming me and trading places with Val as my physical caretaker.

"One thing at a time. Wrap your mind around this first. Okay? You're alive. Val's alive. Kara's alive. Time has passed, but you woke up. Damn, her lips are *pale*." She remarked to Val, who was slowly shaking his head.

"She's strong." He returned, not breaking eye contact with me. I was staring at a spot on the black marble tiles, trying to keep my breathing and heartbeat in check. It took all of my physical energy and I was completely unable to bear looking at him in return. "She just needs answers."

"She won't get them if she passes out." Violet mumbled, leaning against the stage and watching me closely.

You're over two hundred years old. Nineteen years is worth a second chance at life. Deep breath. Pull yourself together. It's not that big a deal.

Slowly, I stood on my own, straightening my posture and regaining control of my senses. I pulled the jacket off of one shoulder and wiped my eyes on the short sleeve of the scrub top, exhaling with a gust of wind and closing my eyes for a moment.

"I'm sorry, I-"

"Don't be." Val interrupted, running his thumb and forefinger through a long strip of my hair. "Everything seems different right now. It's gotta be chaotic in there." He ended the gentle stroking with a quick, humorous tap on my temple, prompting a responsive opening of my eyes and a quick chuckle.

"Nineteen years. Jesus…" I marveled. "No wonder the city is so different. Where is everybody? Why does it look-"

"We can do this one of two ways." Violet's voice was direct, but gentle. "We *can* answer questions as you ask them, or we can just tell you a long-ass story. You'll still have questions, but I think Val and I would rather go over everything in order. We've rehearsed once or twice." Val smirked, his cracked lips curling into a smirk behind the thick hair of his beard.

"Then…I guess it's story time. I'm going to need to sit down. I already feel…" I shook my head slowly again, the lightheadedness fading to a mild headache. Val nodded to Violet, who ran behind the bar and grabbed a comfortable-enough looking lawn chair. Dragging it over to the side of her bed, she propped it open and motioned for Val to help me across the room. I shrugged off his offer for help and stood steadily, making my way over to her and taking a grateful seat.

"I want to say I've been through worse, but…" I bit my lip thinking about Kara's death. "This is rough. Sorry for-"

"Stop apologizing. It's gonna get old." Violet chuckled, taking a seat on her bed and crossing her legs. Her calves were perfectly outlined in the long black boots she donned, forcing me to realize she had grown up considerably in the time I was gone. While she was never the naïve teenager the way some people perceived her, the confidence in her voice and posture along with her sense of bodily confidence was enough to contrast sharply from the meek introvert I once knew.

"We wanna start from her view or ours?" Val asked. The question was directed to Violet, who slunk back into her bed and sprawled her arms across a pink fleece blanket.

"Um…hers. Yeah. It'll be a gentler start." She sounded tired, like the speech was something they had prepared at length and had been waiting to tell me.

"You need anything before we start? Food? Water? You're gonna be here a while." I shook my head despite my thirst, praying that my enlightenment was worth forsaking basic needs for the time being. "Alright. Vi and I are going to take different sides of the story. I'll cover what happened with the rest of the world, and she'll explain the stuff regarding the city and your…recovery." He hesitated with the word, fully aware it was an ongoing process. "You can start first." He beckoned. Vi sat up straighter, clasping her hands into her lap and closing her eyes briefly to recall events as they happened.

"So…we're at Val's wedding, the night after Kara got married and shortly after Schillinger was killed, and it's interrupted by one of Schillinger's brainwashed citizens. That prompted Kara and Jalix to go after Kilkovf with Val and Jared. Kilkovf, Val, Jared all die, Amy comes as a surprise, and Kara dies in childbirth. Eric does his thing and we launch a rescue mission, killing Raven in the process. Remember all that?" I nodded, silent. "Alright, that's where the story starts - your rescue mission to get Kara back. Raven had been controlling all the scientists in their endeavor to manipulate the virus to bring back dead cells, a.k.a. Project Catalyst. I don't know what kind of assets they had, but they had enough stem cells, DNA, and samples of virus to bring Val and Kara back to life in whatever freaky, sciencey way they did. Jalix grabbed them both while you were…I can only assume setting the self-destruct?"

"Yeah. In the control room." I confirmed. She nodded, staring at the blanket while she spoke.

"Val was a mess during the rescue and our fearless leaders aren't here right now to vouch for exactly how things happened, but the thermite that all of Schillinger's labs were equipped with went off as expected. Between that and the explosive charges, the building and its sublevels crumbled into melted pieces. You were…presumed dead. As much as no one wanted to believe it, we came to accept it. We had a funeral at your mansion and planned a trip to the lab site to say our goodbyes once and for all. This was a few weeks after everything happened, so they had construction crews and hazard teams clearing the area and cleaning things up. We had Jared's funeral in the meantime." I felt a tug on my heart as I remembered he had died alongside Val, who looked equally as uncomfortable at the mention of his friend's passing.

"So what happened? If I was...dead, I mean. Did their version of the virus get to my body? The one they used to bring back Kara and Val?"

"That's the thing, we don't know whether you ever actually...technically...died. Alice, Jalix, and Kara went to put flowers down over the engineering wing and they froze. Solid. Alice nearly lost her mind when it happened. She started tearing pieces of concrete out of the ground and digging for you. Kara literally could not pull her away. Alice set herself on fire like...six times just to keep everyone away." She chuckled, shaking her head. "After a few hours, Eric had worked his magic and we got Tony's crew to take over the site. We got some heavy equipment, started digging...and we found you. Encased in a six foot thick block of solid ice."

"Holy crap." I chuckled. "After weeks of being unconscious? I'm surprised my abilities even worked for that long without our medicine."

"Yeah, well..." She grimaced, sucking air through her teeth. "You didn't look good. Your body was emaciated. Any little bit of muscle or fat you could imagine was gone. You're right, you didn't have sustenance, and you're lucky the cold kept your metabolism slowed, because you started to decay. That's why I mentioned Alice watching over you for months. You flat-lined a handful of times once we chiseled you out. Your organs were failing. Your brain activity was minimal. When I say you were comatose..." She looked up at me for the first time, her chocolate-brown eyes full of sadness and caring. "You were a corpse on that table. And Alice was fighting hand-to-hand with death itself to keep you alive."

Val decided to chime in, clearing his throat and running his fingers through his beard.

"Yeah, you...looked like shit. She slept in her office for months, getting...two, three hours of sleep a week. She had one of the other doctors monitor her while she dosed herself with cocaine and amphetamines to work faster. Sometimes at the same time."

"Jesus Christ." I blurted, imagining my motherly, nerdy sister ripping a line of coke from a surgical tray. "Why?"

"She was worried she was going to miss something." He shrugged. "All day, she would take samples of your tissues, images, blood tests, you name it. She came up with something to help accelerate your recovery, a medicine that ended up being used in hospitals everywhere. Her eyes were glued to a piece of you for months on end until finally you started to stabilize. You gained a little bit of weight back and showed signs of recovery."

"But as you got better, the world got worse." Violet resumed. "Especially here in the city. Eric was working with Alice to code specialized programs to handle the data from your test results. I don't know the details, but they were running simulations to test what different medicines would do to your body. Once you finally stabilized, he came to see us and told us he was moving to the surface and wouldn't be coming back."

"What? Eric?" I couldn't imagine the pressure he would have had upon him, but knew he wasn't the type to readily give up his lifestyle.

"Yeah. He felt responsible for what happened to you, to Kara, to Val, to Jared…the stress was too much. And it was our fault, I guess. We leaned on him for too long, relying on him to be our sole source of information. He couldn't do it anymore and left. Amicably, I should say. He left on a positive note. At the same time, Sonya was doing the opposite and reconnecting with everyone in the city. She got her confidence back after the rescue mission and decided to stay. Since Alice was busy with you, Jalix took over as second-in-command for the city and Sonya didn't have a specific job. She'd help with a little of everything and overall try to keep people happy. It worked. At least for a little while." She looked at Val pointedly, resuming her relaxed position as he started to pace and tell me another side to the story.

"Alright, so all of that was happening *here*. Within these walls. But shit was happening outside, too. Raven Biopharmaceuticals was a huge company and suddenly people are dying, labs are exploding...suspicion was rampant across the country. Raven's death came out, Schillinger's death came out, and us taking over the cleanup to dig you out at the lab was the final straw. The Department of Homeland Security ordered an investigation, fearing some sort of biohazard attack. In doing so..." He took a deep breath, sighing heavily. "They excavated the rubble from the lab you were buried in. The lab Raven was using to resurrect Kara, and therefore where she was keeping samples of every version of the virus she had ever tampered with. We...knew what and where to avoid when we dug. They didn't."

Oh, no. God, no.

"One of them was the same version they were using for the D.C. attack, back when Schillinger tried to bomb the U.S. One of them was the version they used to bring back Kara and I. And some we couldn't even identify. But they got out. With Alice preoccupied, she didn't catch it until it was too late. I started seeing the news, months later, and watched people get sick. Dying inexplicably. The lucky ones became Vampyres like us. It wasn't as fast as we initially feared, but it was enough to raise alarms. We didn't have another choice. Kara, Sonya, and I met with agents from Homeland Security and explained who we were. What was about to happen. To avoid a genocide, we came out of hiding."

"How did they react?" I asked hurriedly, my heart pounding in my chest to the point of severe discomfort.

"*They* reacted well. Alice couldn't help you anymore at this point and was waiting for you to wake up. Homeland

Security *gave* her Raven Biopharm, their headquarters building, and funding to research a cure for the Vampyre virus. She...left the city with most of our medical staff, hired a few hundred employees, and went to work. The public...they did as well as could be expected, for humans. The media labelled us Virally Modified Persons, or VMPs." He shook his head and rolled his eyes.

"VMPs...Vamps. They kept the Vampyre designation, huh?" I smirked.

"Yeah. A politically correct insult. Didn't affect anything. Alice started living in Boston, still a city of humans by majority, and working almost round-the-clock. But she knew she wouldn't have the answers in time, so she convinced the government to close our borders. Completely. No one in or out of the country. Airports, shipyards, all of it was taken over by the military and guarded with lethal force. This was about eighteen months after we dug you out. The outbreak started, and within a few weeks of the Homeland Security investigation, everything was walled off to the rest of the world."

"Seems harsh, but...I guess I get it. Try and keep it from spreading, right?"

"Exactly." He replied. "It *almost* got out. There was a bad pandemic in Mexico after a few years, and a huge portion of the population was wiped out. Poor healthcare. The global community decided we were on our own and set up blockades at the Canadian border and the Panama Canal. Trapped us in order to protect the rest of the world."

"And at this point-" I nearly jumped out of my chair when Violet started speaking, being so immersed in Val's words that the sound startled me. "-if you care about the little details, I'll backtrack. Amy turned out to be a Vampyre from birth. So she reached adolescence at about five years old. That's around the same time the world governments decided to intervene and guard their *own* borders. Kara and Jalix made amazing parents and I played big sister the whole time. I've never seen anything like the three of them, to be honest. Jalix and Kara would be handling a global catastrophe all day, and then come pick up Amy at night to play with her and raise her. I can't fathom how, but they managed to give her the best possible life while tackling all these issues. And she was growing fast."

"Yeah, she was." Val added. "Crazy smart, too. Must've gotten it from Kara. That little girl was doing algebra at three years old, calculus at four. Keep in mind, that's the human equivalent of twelve years old, but still...she read books constantly. And she's more emotionally mature than anyone I've ever met, to this day. No pun intended, but it's inhuman how well she knows the workings of the mind. By the time she was *biologically* eighteen, around six years old, she was running the city instead of her parents while they were off tackling bigger issues with the U.S. government. And she did a damn good job."

"Bigger issues?" I feared even asking the question, but fourteen years of explanation were still missing, and it unnerved me to my core that the world had the potential to change so much. Val cracked his knuckles and wandered over to the bar, searching for something. My more human urges got the better of me, and I finally asked for a drink. "Can you grab me some water, if you have any?" I called quietly, hoping it wouldn't interrupt his search. He paused, chuckling, and wandered back with three bottles of water, tossing one to Violet and handing one to me. I uncapped the cheap plastic bottle and drained it within seconds.

"Bigger issues. Yeah. Shortly after going public, not just with the government but with the nation too, the virus mutated. Like it always has. Like it always will. After about five years of spreading too slowly, it changed." He sounded exasperated. "Alice and I visited each other frequently to talk about the status of things, and she caught on that it was changing. She called it Phase Two. Remember how Schillinger's original attack using the virus, Project Cerberus, was supposed to kill about ninety percent of people and convert the rest? Well, it finally happened. Something, probably trapping it in our borders for too long, made the damn thing snap and it slaughtered millions."

"Holy shit. How-…what's-" I leapt to my feet and started pacing, staring at the ceiling and wondering what the world on fire looked like from below. "How many people died? And how, how did we not stop this?" Violet saw the precursors for a panic attack and approached me, taking my wrists in her hands and locking her eyes onto my own.

"It's over." She said quietly. "It's already done. This is old news, and things are different now. I understand this is difficult, but you can't change it. Take a deep breath and relax so we can keep talking."

Millions dead. The greatest country in the world shattered. Vampyres exposed to the public. How is any of this okay?

"We need to keep explaining, Krystal, but I can't do that if you're freaking out. Relax." Val suggested, gesturing to the chair. I shook my head, but crossed my arms and stood silently, maintaining control of myself for the time being. He pressed the advantage and continued.

"Those that were converted instead of killed did the right thing, for the most part. Most people wanted to keep the world going strong. Especially after our government fell. It wasn't possible to keep a chain of command with people dying so quickly. No one knew who was in charge. So Alice shifted her focus to keep churning out our medicine, using Raven's old assets to manufacture it and the country let Val govern whatever he could get control over."

That's why Raven's logo was on the IV bag when I woke up.

"Power grids stayed relatively active, but the sharp decline in population meant that the survivors started to consolidate. They left their small towns and kept the bigger cities occupied. Local government became king, mostly on the city level. Only way to keep some kind of order intact. We got a little lucky in that it didn't kill as many as we were expecting. The U.S. population dipped to about fifty million, but it was enough to keep infrastructure intact."

"I can't believe that's considered *lucky*." I mumbled. Violet stopped twirling a lock of her hair to look at me in hesitant confusion. "I mean, it's old news for you guys, but I was just told that three hundred million people died."

"It's not that it's old news." She started, playing with the zipper on her jacket. "It just could have been a lot worse. I think the most awful part was having to deal with the bodies. Cemeteries became prime real estate, so a lot of people's families had to resort to cremation that didn't initially want to. Bodies kept in refrigerated trucks, some opting into mass graves that couldn't afford anything else. It was rough for a long time. People had to bury their friends, their family, and move into a big city. Society depended on the charity of others for a good while."

"Which ones are still populated?" I asked, trying to paint a mental picture of what the world looked like.

"Um...a lot of the urban areas." Val said thoughtfully. "Let's see...Boston is not one of them, just because it's where all this started. I guess people didn't feel comfortable there. I think the nearest would be New York. Philadelphia and Pittsburgh are good. As far as the East Coast goes, I know Miami, Charlotte, Atlanta, Baltimore...where else? Jacksonville. D.C. is fine, but I haven't been there in a while, myself. Not since I worked there. A good amount of them are intact. I know California is doing well, and so is Texas. Chicago is okay. Otherwise, you'll see a lot of ghost towns with not much in between." I nodded slowly, wrapping my mind around the subject.

"That still leaves five years. And what about everyone in the city during that time? People were just living normal lives? What about Alice?" Val looked around the room, giving me a second chance to take in the environment. With the state of things, it didn't look like they had been living in Archangel for altogether too long, and nothing yet had indicated what happened to the city.

"Alice and I hit...a rough patch. She was too occupied with her studies to really contribute to a relationship, and my sole job was to be a liaison to the government. I was the chief diplomat of our species. We didn't get a lot of time together. But we made it work. She hadn't...*hasn't* made a lot of progress on a cure. It's too complex, and after Phase Two, she hit a roadblock.

"So...do I need to worry about a zombie apocalypse above my head right now?" I asked the question somewhat rhetorically, but nothing would have surprised me at that point. Val didn't find it as humorous as I thought he would, shaking his head and answering sincerely.

"No. Just a little more empty space." I took a deep breath, closing my eyes as I leaned against the bar and ran a hand through my hair. It surprised me once again with its length, something I had quickly forgotten in the hailstorm of information.

"And that's all that happened?" I asked slowly. They both looked at each other, shrugging and nodding like I was asking their opinion on a new pair of jeans. "So how far does that take us in the timeline? Like...after you guys figured out what was going on, what did you do?"

"Well..." Violet grunted, pushing herself off the bed and deciding to approach me. She wrapped her arms around my shoulders unexpectedly, giving me a brief hug and smirking. "Aside from missing the hell out of you and waiting for you to wake up, we split up and made sure we could still get supplies to each other. Someone had to stay here in Aerael and watch over you, plus keep your body infused with meds and nutrition. Amy needed a stable place to live, so Jalix,

Kara, myself, and Sonya moved into your mansion with her, and Alice and Tony live at the Raven headquarters working together on cure stuff. We trade places to keep variety every few months. I actually just got back from being with Alice and assisting her with research. Tony was here with Val. Amy and Sonya stopped by a few weeks ago and stayed with us a few days to say hi." She took a step back while Val approached us.

"Maybe I'm asking the wrong question. What are we doing? As in, what's our plan? What are we working on?" They looked at each other oddly for a moment, a brief confusion across their faces.

"Nothing. That's it." Violet said quietly. "We're just living. No mission, no bad guys. We've been playing the waiting game for your recovery and for a cure to be found. We'll make a trip to one of the cities for supplies every now and then, but there's no grand scheme anymore."

"We lost." Val clarified, looking away and starting to exude an inner rage. "Schillinger got exactly what he wanted, minus the ability to control it. The city got attacked by a group of assholes, and everyone left after that. No more war, no more fighting. This is the peace we fought for." His words were heavy, thick with emotion and an inherent anger. Violet said something quietly to him that I missed, softening his face and invoking a nod. "But we're glad to see that you're okay."

"*Okay* is…overstating it. Very much so. I'm alive, though." I sighed, touching Val's arm in a sign of thanks. "Let me…go over this one more time. I need to get all this straight."

"Take your time. We're here all night." Violet cocked her head ironically, smirking.

"Kara and Val got out of the lab alive. I didn't, but I kinda survived and you guys dug me out. Virus broke out, killed slowly, and we exposed ourselves to protect the humans. All the while, life is going normally."

"Right." Vi confirmed. "That's up to about a year and a half after your...incident."

"Okay. You mentioned Amy growing up, but I'm confused about what was happening at the same time." I rubbed my temples, trying to recall the details.

"Not much." Val answered, giving Violet a brief reprieve. "Alice was trying to get the ball rolling with the company she was handed and gather researchers. It's hard to pull in experts from elsewhere in the world when no one can come in or out. Her progress was very, very slow when she first started. The city ran like normal, and the outside world was just scared shitless. Kara and Jalix used a bit of your cash to start a project in Jersey. The Kane-Hudson Charity Teaching Hospital. Place for infected to convert and for doctors to figure out how it all worked. Despite the panic, things were okay for the most part. Like we said, the virus wasn't rampant yet. There were...maybe a few dozen cases a day?" He asked, directed toward Violet. She nodded, shrugging.

"Alright. Fast forward five years of slow progress. Phase Two rolls around and gets lethal. People die left and right, Alice races for the cure, and the world tries to compensate. New Vampyres consolidate into the cities. Did Alice not make *any* progress? My sister is hands-down the most medically intelligent person on the planet." It pained my heart to imagine the agony of millions of people dying while she was in charge of preventing it.

"Not anything significant. Don't forget, a lot of strains must have escaped that lab. It's on par with trying to cure all cancer at once, but imagine if each cancer could adapt itself to resist different treatments. Any solution had to be a perfect one." I could tell Val was trying to be polite, but took offense to the thought of Alice being a failure. "And the outside world was terrified that we would spread it. They started to get...passive-aggressive. NATO stopped helping, the World Health Organization stopped helping. Everyone stopped helping, And then Alice, plus her researchers, were on their own.”

“Alright. Damn. So no progress. For ten years, this thing ravages the country until there’s no one new left to convert or kill. In the meantime, the city is attacked, empties, and you guys spread out to focus on what you needed to do at the time. You wait for a cure. Then I wake up, go through all of this with you, and die of a stress-induced brain aneurysm.” Val took a long draught from his bottle of water, clearing his throat and setting the bottle on the bar.

“Actually, Alice said that was entirely possible. She gave us a long list of ways you could have died within minutes of waking up.”

“Comforting.” I croaked.

“But you didn’t.” Violet’s chocolate-brown eyes sparked with a subtle happiness as she said the words, rocking back and forth in excitement. “And my best friend is back.”

“I know.” I sighed, the rate at which I was being hugged normally something I would have vomited at. As her arms squeezed my torso ever so gently, a subtle surge of blood to my head reminded me of the splitting headache I continued to struggle with.

“Hey, um…” I took a step back and looked around the room, wondering about their state of supplies. “Do you guys have any medicine in here? I need something for this headache. Some caffeine wouldn’t hurt, either. I…I’m still processing everything, but it’s a little hard right now.”

“I got it.” Val said quietly, standing up and whisking away to the front doors of the former nightclub. His steps slowed before he was able to reach for the door handle, swinging around slowly to look at me. His dark eyes studied me for a moment, more intense in gravity than I was used to. His beard helped nothing in the way of appearing friendly, a sudden and mild hostility sweeping over his appearance. Violet and I were both stuck in place, trying to figure out what the issue was before a low rumble came from his throat.

"What kind?" It took me a moment to put his question together, realizing what he was trying to ask.

"Oh. Um…whatever painkillers you guys have that aren't in short supply. Nothing strong. I need a clear head." His head tilted half a degree before he opened the door and left without further questions. "What was that about?" I whispered to Violet, turning back toward her. She shrugged passively, as if she knew the answer, but wasn't comfortable explaining it to me. I decided it was the least of my current worries and began to amble around the room at a painstakingly slow pace.

PHOBIA
KRYSTAL

Every crevice Kara and I had built into the hub of refined sin had been mutilated into a domestic domicile. While comforting to the eye, I felt a mixture of wariness and concern that such a radical change had needed to be made to the city's main source of stress relief and entertainment. While there was plenty of living and breathing room in the more cavernous, social corners of the settlement, it was odd to think that Violet and Valterius had chosen to confine themselves to a comparatively tiny prison.

"How are you holding up? That was... a lot." Violet sighed, taking a decisive seat on the edge of her bed and flipping her hair so it rested behind her shoulder. The streak of purple that normally ran in a thin band from her scalp was gone, replaced by her natural black tone. It was an impeccable replica of Kara's appearance, somehow captured in somebody she had saved so long ago.

"I'm okay. I guess. Everything feels...off. Weird. You know? It's like I'm looking at you and Val through a filter or something. The differences are subtle, but they're there."

"Like what?" She chuckled, furrowing her brow. "I kinda want to hear this from your perspective. Val's beard doesn't count, by the way. That was fairly recent."

"Well...I don't know. I mean, you look more mature. More confident. Just the way you carry yourself, it's more proud than you used to be." She laughed, picking up a paintbrush and slowly pulling out pieces of dried paint from between the bristles.

"Thanks. Kara and I spent a lot of time together and...I don't know. I think some of her personality rubbed off on me. Watching her become a mother to Amy, who was a *complete* handful, by the way. Seeing her come talk to me every day. I don't know. I felt like a big sister to Amy and everyone else started to really gravitate toward me." She wasn't a braggart in her words, but exhibited a sense of honored pride. "I guess my life became a little more social, a little more meaningful. I had a bigger role to play in things. After what happened in Los Angeles and after helping Eric while Jalix was getting involved, I guess I saw the need to adapt to the situation. To fit in a little closer to our family." She beamed at me, an impossibly white smile shedding any sadness I could have had left in my soul. "What about Val?" She asked, turning back to her paintbrush with the presumption that she was being self-centered.

"He's quiet." I replied, almost immediately. "And melancholy. Like...normally, that dude never shuts up. But I swear, if he had my tits and your hair, I'd have called him Kara once he started talking."

"Yeah, he took this whole situation a little hard. I mean, that's a vast understatement, but..." She chuckled, stopping in the middle of her sentence. "Look, we all got hit hard when the humans started dying. Kara was actually the center of positivity for our people. She was always talking about hope and solace and sanctuary. But Val? I guess...I think he believes that everyone he cares about suffered for no reason.

When Jared…" Her smile faded to a smirk of remembrance. "When he died, Val couldn't have known. Obviously. He was dead, too. But when he woke up…came back, whatever? Jesus, I mean, we brought him back to the city and I saw him genuinely mourning. He couldn't handle you and Jared being gone. He didn't drink to hide the pain, he wasn't angry at anyone. He was just devastated. You know? And at first, he thought maybe it was all for a grand purpose, that Jared was the martyr he needed to be. That you finally had peace. When we found out we failed? Your coma, and possible imminent death, Eric leaving, Alice having to go through thinking her husband was dead…it was all for nothing. He's gotten better." She reassured. "But better than desolate isn't a life. It's just all he could do."

"Poignant, Violet."

"Thanks. Like I said, Kara really got my inner Valkyrie going."

"Valkyrie? More like Viking. What's up with the ear piercings? I love them, I just-" I stopped to look up and watch Val walk into the room. His presence lost none of its edge in the few minutes he had been gone, approaching me with the intent to kill. In his hands were a small assortment of pharmacy-sized pill bottles, and likely ones retrieved from the same cabinet I stared at when I had first awoken. He set them gently on the bar next to me, reaching into his pocket and withdrawing a clear plastic bag of our IV medicine, handing it to me and pointing to a small drawer on the other side of the bar.

"Alice said you'd need this every few hours for your cravings. At least for a few days, then you can go back to the shots. Needles and tubing are in that drawer. I grabbed all the pill bottles I could find. I'll let you pick what you want."

Why the sudden hostility?

"Thanks." I said honestly, trying to sound as pleasant as possible. I looked down at the assortment, my hair unexpectedly falling to touch the bar. I watched the blue strands dance lightly for a moment before sweeping it all behind my head in a mass, holding it to the base of my scalp and reaching a finger toward my wrist before I realized I didn't have any hair ties.

"Hey Vi, do y-"

"Yeah, I gotcha." I turned around to wait as she rooted around her dresser, catching Val sitting on the edge of his bed and staring at me with a loathing glare. I avoided moving my eyes in his direction, instead choosing to focus on Violet approaching me with a fabric-covered elastic band for my hair.

"Thanks." I reached out and took it with my free hand, finishing the ponytail and returning to the medicine on the bar. The first bottle I picked up was useless, being some sort of muscle relaxant I wasn't familiar with. The second bottle was smaller, containing small yellow caffeine pills. I opened the lid and pulled out two, setting them on the bar top and closing the lid. I picked up the last two containers and inspected them closely, the writing far smaller and more technical.

After a moment of deciphering, one contained morphine tablets and the other held large white capsules of anti-inflammatory painkiller. After carefully reading the dosage instructions and deciding that my metabolism was likely not what I had become accustomed to, I poured two out and replaced the cap. Luckily, the bottles of water were an arm's length away and sitting on the surface Alice traditionally used to rim salt onto glasses whenever she would take a break from her work and tend the bar.

As I moved a bottle of whiskey aside and reached for one, I felt the soft seismic activity of Val's footsteps, one followed by another until he was alarmingly close to my body. Hesitant, I uncapped the water and took my four chosen pills, draining the rest of the water as a precautionary measure against dehydration.

What the hell is he doing?

I whirled around, a sarcastic remark on the edge of my tongue before I was silenced by the raw and unmatched strength of a rabid grizzly bear. His arm swung to knock aside the bottles before grabbing a fistful of my scrub top, twisting it to create a vice-like grip around my chest and pressing me into the bar. He leaned into me, his eyes alight in a rage of smoldering coal. I lifted up my head enough to breathe properly, looking to Violet for help before I realized she was unmoved and still playing with her paintbrush.

"Val, I-"

"Don't you dare say my name." His breath echoed from deep within his lungs, a shaky hatred filling the slight void between our faces. "Tell me about Kara." I was stunned beyond words, heavy breathing escaping the part in my lips in the absence of proper language.

"What? Val what the hell is-"

"Tell me who she is!" He roared, pressing my body further into the unforgiving surface I laid on.

"Val, you're scaring the shit out of me! Stop it!" I screamed, trying to turn away from him or roll onto my side. My silent tears were a fearful and predominant echo in the large room.

"Krystal…we love you. But please answer him." Violet said quietly.

What is going on? What did I do?

"What? What do you mean? Kara?" I shook my head, trying to understand what he wanted from me. "She's your sister. We just talked about her. You know who she-"

"No." He said quietly. "Who is she to *you*?"

"She's…she's one of my best friends. She trained me. She saved me. I loved her for…as long as I can remember. I died for her." His grip didn't loosen, but I could feel the subtle trembling of his fingers as he decided what to do.

"That's not enough." He decided, looking up at Violet. She sighed, tossing the paintbrush at a perfect angle to land in her artistry tray before approaching the two of us and standing next to Val.

"Why didn't you take the bait, Krystal?" Violet asked quietly. It clearly unnerved her to see me in such a vulnerable position, but her eyes held a purpose I couldn't determine.

"What bait? What are you guys talking about?" I asked in earnest.

"I brought back a bottle of morphine pills and left a bottle of whiskey behind the counter. The Krystal I know wouldn't have let either of those pass her by. Now you're either some kind of experiment Schillinger left behind, or he wiped your memories and-"

"Val, I've been clean for a while now. I mean, *before* I went into a coma. I had one slip-up about a week before I died, but-"

"Bullshit." He barked. "You were high when you took Jalix to kill Schillinger. After Kara broke your ribs."

"No." I shook my head, remembering the pain more clearly than I would have liked. "Whatever Alice gave me while I was in surgery was it. I didn't want anyone to worry about my condition, so I said I was dosed. But I wasn't, I swear. During that whole mission, all I had was whatever stuff Eric kept in his first aid kit. The last time I took *anything* hard was when I was home, alone, and Kara came to see me. It was the last of what I had left in my house and the last dose while I tapered off."

"Wait, so you've been clean for-"

"Almost twenty years if you want to get really technical, Violet." I hissed, finally getting angry at the situation. "Let me the hell up." I groaned at Val, who surprisingly complied. My back screamed in pain from being slammed into the hard surface as I stood tall and looked them both in the eyes. "And you all have proof of it that you don't even know about. Violet, did I or did I not take you back to my mansion after Kara's wedding?"

"You did." She said quietly.

"Was I ever out of your sight?"

"No."

"And did I ever take any pills?"

"Well, your birth contr-"

"Okay, besides that. Did I take anything else?" She was silent, but shook her head.

"And what did you steal for me after Kara died? Do you remember when we were sitting in the bar?"

"A sedative. Because you couldn't stop crying or shaking."

"Right." I mumbled, a lump in my throat from the most painful memory I ever carried. "You're not the scared girl everyone saw before. Not anymore. Use your judgment. Isn't it possible, after everything I went through, everything I promised you, that I finally got clean?" She sighed, taking a step back and letting Val make his own decisions.

"And what about the booze?" He asked quietly.

"What *about* it, Val? Look, everything I knew is gone. Everyone I care about is scattered. The fight we spent centuries on ended in a fireball. I thought I was dead. And I'm just learning about all of it. I'm absolutely terrified. Do I want to drink right now? Yes. Do I want to process everything a little bit first and get some of the gaps filled in? Do I want to go find my sister and my friends? Yeah, *way* more so than my urge to drink." I could see the confused shame on both of their faces, pondering the moral direction of their actions. "But...I know *me*. And I know you guys. I get it. Especially after everything Schillinger was trying to do. I'm still...me. The same hundred and thirty pounds of sarcastic, blue-haired hatred you guys know and love." I promoted a chuckle from Violet and the slightest imitation of a smirk from behind Val's beard. "Here, you know what?" I concluded, turning around and lifting the scrub top along with the back of my jacket to expose my shoulder blades.

"The blue rose." Violet's smile was audible in her words. I lowered the clothing, trying to keep the exposure as minimal as possible, considering I still hadn't found a bra.

"Yeah. Val, you were there the day Kara and I got those tattoos. That was the day I came out to you. So...memory and body are all original. Schillinger could never have duplicated that artwork. Can't kill a cockroach." I smirked and poked at Val's earlier words.

"I'm sorry, Krystal." Val started, taking a heaving sigh. "It's been a paranoia for twenty years, now. I wasn't sure if you'd end up the way Sonya was, or-"

"Well, we've made the conclusion that I'm still intact. So throw all that crazy shit out the window. I've had way more than enough crazy today. And I've been awake for an hour. Let's figure out what to do next."

"Well..." Violet started, picking up an intricately-painted piece of canvas and setting it on the bar. She moved its easel to where my lawn chair sat. "This will work as an I.V. stand for now. We should get that medicine in you. Alice said it would keep you in the recovery process. I guess if you don't get it, you're going to feel a lot worse. And meanwhile, we can answer any more questions you have." Apparently content with how the situation was unfolding, Val went back to his bed and began rifling through a dresser drawer for something.

I nodded to Violet and began to admire the painting sitting in front of me as she went to retrieve the I.V. bag. It was a family portrait of sorts. Alice, myself, and Sonya stood in the back with Val and Violet posed carefree on a couch in front of us. Jared, Eric, and Tony all held a part of a large, dead bird that dangled limply in front of the couch while Jalix stood off to the side with his arms crossed next to a stoic

Kara. It was a perfect representation of our personalities, and something she had clearly spent a great deal of time perfecting.

As I looked closer at the faces, I could see minor details I wouldn't have caught at first glance. Jared had the faintest glow of a white halo suspended inches above his head, nearly transparent without close inspection. My face was slightly more gaunt than I had come to know, a clear sign she had been using my comatose visage as a reference. And Violet's eyes, as they always were in her paintings for some reason, were a forest green instead of their traditional, deep chestnut brown.

"Hey, Vi?" I called over my shoulder as she connected the bag of medicine to her easel and attached a winding piece of surgical tubing.

"Sup?"

"Why are your eyes always green? In your paintings, I mean." She failed to reply for a minute, busied in her work before she beckoned for me to come sit down.

"I don't know. I've always hated my eye color. I'm super jealous of your sister. Or Kara. Or even you. Anyone, really. I just hate mine. I can't really explain it." Val cleared his throat quietly from across the room, his eyes similar enough to Violet's that he took offense. "Oh, don't pout, you big baby. I like *yours*. But they're a different shade of brown. It suits you. I'm supposed to be *pretty*, not intimidating. Feel like I got evil eyes." She mumbled, pulling my wrist up onto the armrest of the chair.

"Vi, I am living proof that you can be both pretty *and* intimidating. So is Kara."

"Exactly." She said, sliding the needle into my arm. "And both of you have beautiful, light-colored eyes. I don't know, it's just a jealousy thing. Amy got Kara's eyes, too. Brighter, maybe. It's crazy how-"

"Holy crap." I sucked in a gust of air, the sudden energy of a thousand jaguars pounding through my chest and legs. "What's in this stuff?" Val spoke up for the first time in a while, his voice projecting from behind me and across the room.

"Alice made it specifically for your recovery. She called it Factor Five. Actually ended up using it to fight those that were dying from the virus, mass produced and used in hospitals everywhere. Something with accelerating cellular regeneration. It's bad for Vampyres in the long-term, but as long as you're not taking it too often, you're fine."

"Fine is…not the word I'd use. Damn, I feel like I could fight a brick wall. And *win*. It's not a euphoria, it's just…an energy." I chuckled, flexing my free hand as it began to grow cold. My abilities obviously still present, it was a good sign that I didn't have any long-term damage.

"Oh, you took those caffeine pills too. So yeah, I'm sure you feel like a cheetah with an adrenaline rush right now." Violet chuckled, shaking her head at my simple amusement with feeling better.

"So…" I started, trying to focus on something other than the overwhelming urge to lift several hundred pounds all at once. "Tell me more about Amy. Sounds like I missed a lot of her growing up."

"Wasn't a lot of growing up to do, honestly. I swear she came out of Kara's womb with a doctorate. Or five. She's…well-spoken. Quiet, for the most part. Hyper-intelligent, even for a Vampyre. When she walks into a room, she just studies everything. Not in an annoying way, she just looks at things you wouldn't normally notice. Listens to how people talk, not just what they're saying. She's absolutely, one *hundred* percent my adopted little sister, by the way. I claimed her, and she is mine."

"Oh, is that how that works?" I chuckled. Val decided to join the conversation and approached us to chime in.

"Kara and Jalix kind of made it that way. Violet helped raise Amy, and as repayment, they had dinners together and whatnot. Violet got adopted out to Kara and Jalix. Or vice versa." He shrugged. "Honestly, it was great. Amy had someone to grow up with and see as a great role model." His quiet compliment forced the faintest tint of blush into Violet's pale cheeks.

"She's super sweet, though. I think she got her outlook on life from her Aunt Sonya. She doesn't rub her intelligence in other people's faces. She would just come by the hospital and help Alice with her work. Alice even gave Amy her blessing to practice medicine, *and* her own wing of the hospital when she was eleven, as birthday presents."

"Seriously?" I was elated to hear that the city's princess was so obviously successful.

"Yep. Alice gave her kind of an honorary psychotherapy license. She worked part-time listening to people…vent, essentially. Give advice on how to actually fix the problem instead of just talking it out. Including when the city was…attacked."

"I was here when that happened. Involved." Val mumbled. "Alice and Tony were at the old Raven headquarters doing their thing. Jalix, Kara, and Sonya were away for some reason, I don't remember what."

"Supply run." Violet added.

"Right. And Amy, Violet, and I were the only ones left from the core group. Amy acted like she had the situation completely under control. Even Kara would have struggled with seeing everything unfold. That girl is as perfect as someone can be. But…seeing as where her genetics come from, it probably just runs in the family." I felt immediately victorious in that moment, realizing he was growing comfortable enough to resort to his old sense of humor and referencing himself instead of Kara.

"Hey, Krys-…dammit." Violet grimaced, beckoning to the I.V. line. "You froze it. Looks like that's all you're getting today." She flicked the nearly-empty bag, only a few drops of the solution left.

"That's alright. I'm feeling so much better. Thanks for everything, guys. I…still can't believe how long I was gone. But I couldn't have asked for too much better under the circumstances. I'm sorry I'm struggling right now."

"Wanna go walk around? Clear your head?" Violet offered, carefully extracting the needle and replacing the protective cover to ensure its safety before throwing it in the garbage can next to her bed. Her leather-bound arm grabbed my own and helped me to my feet, beckoning toward the main hall.

"That sounds great. I mean…the place is a depressing graveyard, but I'd like to see it all again." I looked back at Val to see if he was going to join us.

"Mind if I take my jacket back? I'm going to walk down and see if I can get the generator fired up again. Try to get the lights on, at least."

"Yeah, sorry for stealing it." I shrugged the material off my shoulders and held it out to him.

"Not exactly stealing if I left it for you." He smirked, leaving the room ahead of Violet and I.

He still cares.

"Anything you want to see in particular?"

"Not the infirmary."

"Fine by me." She sauntered to the door, withdrawing the same flashlight she used previously to ignite the way. "Wanna go see Amy's room? We bunked together for a while, so I still have a lot of my stuff there. Saved space when we started taking in more people." She explained.

"Sure. Anywhere is fine right now. I just really need to stretch my legs. Oh, do you have a pair of shoes I can steal? And maybe a bra?" She looked down, grimacing at my bare feet before we took several steps back into the room. She reached under her bed and withdrew a pair of black sneakers.

"I know they're not your style, but they're better than nothing. And as for the bra, you might just need to tough it out. I...don't think I have one that'll fit you."

"Right, sorry. Kara and I were the same size, and I'm just used to stealing Kara's clothes whenever I'd...wow, there were a *lot* of times I have needed to steal a bra from someone. I was seriously doing something wrong in life." I slipped on the sneakers and immediately was immersed in a greater sense of comfort.

"You're fine, I didn't take it as an insult. I don't need your curves to know I look good." She stuck out her tongue and proceeded back toward the door. I followed closely behind, prepared to be guided through the dark hall.

"Question." I said quietly as she began to close the doors behind us. "You both mentioned the city being attacked. But...I mean, I don't have the full picture." The doors fell entirely closed with a dull, echoing thump before we began to trudge toward the end of the city that used to house hundreds of inhabitants.

"Well..." She began, looking down at her feet. She trudged along in the same way as before, the bottom of her boot scuffing the ground before landing several inches in front of the next with a quiet tap. "Not everyone thought life was going to go on. People are selfish. But it went downhill fast. Not exactly sure how...the memories are fuzzy." As she spoke, she shined the light on the ceiling of the cavern, a massive bell curve of concrete arching over the city in a protective layer of dampening echoes. "But it could have been way worse. They weren't trying to massacre anyone. They were just trying to bully us into leaving."

"So what's with the bloodbath, then?" I gestured to a large, browned splash of color next to the decaying cafe.

"Val and some of the others took it personally. It is *our* city, after all. Our home. We pushed them back. They started running once Val bashed a guy's head into the concrete and it exploded like a water balloon. He took a round to the shoulder from some dude with a nine mil. Never even stopped."

"Jesus." I whispered. "Reminds me of some of the times that Kara has snapped."

"It looked like it, too. You can tell they're siblings. He had that same...emptiness in his eyes. Like people didn't exist anymore. Everything's an object at that point." I sighed heavily through my nostrils, trying as hard as I could to think of a more pleasant subject of discussion. We idly walked through the long depth of the hall, passing by the last of the small boutiques that lined the center part of the cavern and stepping down a short, wide set of stairs that led to the former inhabitants' apartments. Row upon row of two-story complexes were marked by interspersed alleys leading to the city's electrical and plumbing junctions.

"So you and Amy moved in together, huh? You can't tell me it was just to save space." Violet considered my prompt while she approached one of the doors and turned the knob, strolling inside without breaking stride.

"Well, no. She needed a place to be on her own, but still have some support. Jalix and Kara didn't want to smother her, but she still needed someone to have her back. I volunteered, since I've had a place of my own for years and years without company. Having her here was...awesome." She clicked the light switch repeatedly, knowing full well it was useless without a central source of power and decided to leave it on before turning right and making her way into the kitchen. The flashlight's cone of white hovered over the refrigerator for a moment, two half-finished grocery lists in different handwriting scrawled across a small whiteboard. "I wasn't kidding when I said I adopted her as my sister. She was…well…" She looked back briefly, starting to say something and deciding against it.

"Your best friend." I tried supportively. "I wasn't here. It's okay to have someone close to you. I'm not hurt or insulted. Except that I didn't get to meet this girl." Violet chuckled, maintaining her slow meandering into the living room.

Two easels each held a canvas, one displaying a well-drawn face in brushed oil paint. Violet was clearly drawn on one, without the trademark of her own style. The piece was made with emphasis on technical skill, focus being brought heavily into realistic shading and subtle reflections in the glossiness of happy brown eyes. The traditional streak of purple was still present in her black hair, marking the timeline of the piece of art's completion. The other was a breathtaking woman, wreathed in a silky cloud of silver hair and dressing a quiet smile across perfectly rose lips. Her eyes were an unmistakable hybrid of Jalix and Kara's, creating a storm-cloud silver with tinges of steely blue. Her ash-colored hair smoothed itself onto slim shoulders and rested in silence across a chest swelled with silent pride.

"Wow. She's beautiful." I remarked, straining to pull my eyes away to look at Violet.

"Yeah, that painting is crap. I couldn't begin to do her justice."

"What?" I reacted confusedly, shaking my head. "What do you mean? There's nothing wrong-"

"There's nothing *wrong* with it, no. It just isn't a good representation. I couldn't…capture everything. You know? Like, I could draw you and never be able to fully articulate your attitude. Kinda the same thing. You'll meet her soon, you'll know what I mean." As she started to move into the bedroom, I asked a question.

"Why is her hair white? Or light grey. The flashlight made it hard to tell." I'm not sure why I was surprised, but it took me a moment to realize we were standing in Violet's dedicated bedroom, and had been occupying separate sleeping spaces.

"*Silver.* Yours is blue, hers is silver. Don't ask me why. Alice could tell you. Probably has something to do with her powers."

"Powers?" My heart fluttered for a moment, an odd combination of excitement and surprise capturing my attention. Violet spun around to look at me, an open-mouthed smile cast in my direction.

"I didn't tell you? I could have sworn I mentioned it." She waved for me to move into the adjacent bedroom with her as we spoke. "Yeah, that's where Alice got the foundation for Factor Five. Amy was the first one in…forever to be born with abilities like you and Kara have. She…*convinces* a person's body to heal. Way more than it would on its own. There's something in her blood that lets her literally heal others. And it's not draining or taxing like what you or Alice would go through when using your abilities. She's able to use the other person's energy and their body to do all the work. It's super cool. It just…didn't work on your head for some reason. I guess repairing a brain is *infinitely* trickier than a body."

"Yeah. As we saw with Sonya and her lost memories." I mumbled, looking around Amy's room. There was a mass of textbooks on her bookshelf, the quantity of texts overwhelming the quality of the wood to the point that the shelves bowed with stress. Topics from software engineering to neurobiology and psychology were arranged in alphabetical order by author and treated with the utmost of respect, each bearing a smooth, straight spine and crisp edges.

"Yeah. She couldn't do anything about that, either. Unfortunately. Still, she saw a lot of broken bones and fixed Val's gunshot to the shoulder. It's a miracle, if you ask me. I'm sorry she couldn't do more for you." I turned slowly, shaking my hair loose from its ponytail as I realized it no longer served a purpose.

"There is no reason for you to say that, Vi. None of you owed me a damn thing. I have a second chance I didn't earn. The only thing I can do now is pray I can make it up to any of you." She contemplated what to say for a moment, her face falling into an odd curiosity.

"What was it like?" She whispered finally, looking up at me.

"What do you mean?"

"Dying." I froze, unwilling to know anything that had transpired after I locked myself in my arctic prison. "What was it like?"

"I, um...I'm not sure. You ever have a dream, and you *know* you had a dream, but you remember none of it when you wake up? It's like that." She nodded, looking around the room in thought.

"I guess it's better not to know. I'm sure it's all you can think about right now."

"No, actually." I realized. "I haven't thought about it much at all." I tried to recall the moments just before I awoke, nothing but an empty void in my memories.

Traitor.

A surge of pain flicked from the base of my spine into my skull, forcing a quiet groan. Violet stepped toward me, placing a palm on my right shoulder.

Coward. You should have let yourself go.

A second wave was overwhelming, rattling my eyesight and staining it with a red shade. I gasped, my chest far too tight for comfort. I felt Violet's other hand reach to my left shoulder to hold me upright, realizing quickly that it would be a losing battle.

The most perfect you've ever been was without a pulse.

The sensation of touch was completely lost, my eyes playing a movie in fast-forward as I fell to the ground.

Go back to your grave, you selfish whore.

The oak rush of a dresser passing my eyes preceded my head snapping sharply backward, void of all physical control.

You've lost love. You've lost friendship. You've lost everything. Go back to the solitude you've always wanted.

The last semblance of fight was ripped from the rest of my throat in the form of a whimpering howl, watching the sight in front of me shudder and shake as my body seized.

Return to the prison you made for yourself.

Violet screamed at me, no language decipherable in a brain filled with static.

Go back to the tomb.

The empty vibration of Violet's voice rammed against my deafened ears as she cried for Val.

Go back to your sorrow.

COLLISION
VIOLET

Swinging the door open carefully so as not to strike it against Krystal's head, I held open a space for Val to place her body into the backseat of his truck. Following my previous advice, he trusted in a mindset of carefulness rather than haste as he laid her silent and shaking physique against the seat. I closed the door slowly, ensuring none of her hair would be caught in the door.

"She'll be okay, Vi." Val imparted quietly, leaving my side of the vehicle to climb into the driver's seat. I followed suit, sitting in the passenger seat and quickly rubbing my hands together. The friction began to drive away the out-of-control freezing temperature that covered Krystal's body.

If she dies after all of this, I'll bring her back to kill her myself.

"I know. I'm fine. I just...freaked out at first. We were fine, having a conversation, and just..." I paused as he started the engine and pulled out of the neglected alley next to the frame shop. "I don't know. I just felt like it would be better to-"

"I know. I'm not against it. Alice is her best bet right now. Let's hope it was just a seizure. Probably a side effect of everything." He said softly, accelerating to a reasonably quick pace along the road. I waited for him to say something else, but he chose to remain silent.

"Still. I know you didn't want to leave the city."

"I don't think we were supposed to be there anyway. Krystal woke up. We had no reason to be there anymore. Things aren't going to go back to the way they were before, and I'm okay with that." He paused "But she was right. We need to do something about our lives, whatever that might be. Otherwise, what's the point of even keeping Krystal alive? Without a reason, she might as well have died on the operating table. We didn't give her anything to come back to."

"Tell me how you really feel." I scoffed, scowling at him.

"You *know* what I mean. Most of us got a second chance. What's the point unless we do something about it?" He scratched his beard briefly. "She was right. We're…letting ourselves waste away. Letting the world waste away,"

"You know we'll rebuild, Val. But this is something that no one has ever seen. And *certainly* wasn't ready for. The cure, the repopulation…it's going to take time."

"Well, it's time we don't have." He concluded, turning onto the ramp that led to the empty highway. "The longer we wait, the longer the world alienates us. We're walled in, cut off, and completely isolated. Guarded borders means no one else wants us. We should-…we *need* to prove that we're capable of being a part of the global community. Before it resents and condemns us. Until then, they're going to see Vampyres the same way they have for so long: as monsters."

"It's not like Canada is gathering with pitchforks and torches, Val." I chuckled, trying to lighten the mood.

"They may as well be. Have you noticed that no one has offered aid in years? No airdropped supplies, no submitted research, not even a military takeover. No interaction whatsoever. They're afraid. Alice and my sister are the only two people in the world convincing the others not to drop napalm on us and call it a day. And once the federal government collapsed and control went to local city leaders, it was like the two of us didn't matter. No one listens anymore, not even the foreign nations' agencies. Not to me, not to Kara…one of these days, the world is going to decide to remove the risk."

"Jesus Christ, I get your point." I snapped. "No one is going to *bomb* us. Okay? I get it, we need to get our shit together. But what else do you want? What can *I* do about it?" He gritted his teeth, a pained expression across his mouth.

"That's not what I'm asking, Vi. I just need someone else to hear it. You're…young. You and Amy, you're the next generation of us. And when we're not around anymore, you two will need to carry us forward. *You* are going to be the one to bring this world back together." I sat in stunned silence, my eyes locked onto the side of his face. I looked away for a brief moment as the rare sight of a car across the median from us, headed in the opposite direction, crossed my peripheral vision.

"What makes you say that now, Val?"

"Nothing in particular. But with Krystal coming back…" He sighed, tapping the steering wheel with his thumb and tilting his head to the side. I could feel the vehicle slow down slightly, as we had nearly reached a hundred miles an hour during his moment of despair. "It's a sign. And not in some spiritual way, but…it has to mean something. It has to." I shivered suddenly, realizing how unbearably cold it was growing in the interior of his truck.

"Can you turn the heat on?" I asked quietly. He shook his head, checking his rear-view mirror before returning his eyes to the road in front of him. "Being comfortable isn't going to kill us." I scoffed. I reached over against his contradiction and touched the screen of his vehicle's climate control before he grabbed my wrist quickly. His grip was light, and more in speed than in strength. Before I could ask why, he nodded to the backseat. I turned my head as he released my arm to see Krystal more limp than before, her breathing slow and steady. Her mouth was open slightly, a soft breeze escaping from between her lips as her body stopped its tremor.

"She's comfortable." He said quietly. "I want to maintain that for now, if at all possible. Sorry for not elaborating. If she's only lightly asleep, I don't want to say anything to get her attention. The cold's her natural habitat, so to speak. She needs to rest."

"You'd think she would have had enough of that already." I smirked.

I wish I had the old Val back. I miss him so much. The laughter. The smile.

Letting my somber thoughts occupy the space in my head was unsettling, changing slightly when I saw him reach for the handheld microphone attached to the modified radio in his truck. Taking his eyes off the road for several seconds at a time, he made changes to settings on the touchscreen before pressing the button on the handset.

"It's me. You there?" His entrance to the conversation was quick, followed by a bitter drop of the handset onto his lap. I could see the discomfort, even after so long, in calling Alice so impersonally. Nevertheless, she answered after a few moments of us speeding down the highway.

"Go ahead." The voice was broken and soft, despite the audio being crystal clear.

"We're headed your way. And we have a short, sarcastic guest." As Val let go of the button to talk, he realized he needed to elaborate before allowing her to respond. "She was awake for an hour or so. Collapsed in a seizure. She's asleep now, I think. Seems okay." He tilted his head to look at Krystal's softly snoring silhouette in the rear-view mirror.

"Wow." A breathy whisper came through the speakers, a sound of awe and gratitude. "Okay. Um...we're at her mansion. Tony and I moved away from the Raven building for now. I'll explain when you get here. I can't talk about it right now." As Val did moments ago, she immediately came back into the conversation after a brief pause. "How was she? When she was awake?" Val handed me the microphone, seeing fit that I answer.

"She's still Krystal. Through and through. She's...different. But in a good way. I don't know if it's shock or if she had a moment of clarity before she went into her coma, but...I think you'll like the result. We needed to bring her. I wasn't sure what to do when she collapsed." Val rotated the wheel, turning our vehicle onto an exit and heading toward the section of highway that led to Krystal's mansion.

"If that's the worst you guys saw from her and she's doing okay now, it's more than I could have ever asked for. I can take care of her when you get here. Just be ready for some changes, Vi. Things are a little...different now. For the time being. I need you guys to be ready for a situation."

"A situation?" Val snapped, snatching the device from my hand and nearly ripping the cable out of his dashboard. He leaned into the gas pedal more, the roar of the truck's engine purring with happiness. "Allison, I hate when you say things like that. What's going on?"

"*Not* right now, Val." Her bitter tone threatened to crack our windshield with its edge. "I will explain when the three of you arrive safely. Just...be careful. And get here fast. I want my sister back."

Before either of us could think of a response, the number that displayed Alice's frequency disappeared from the screen and was replaced with a series of dashes, indicating that she had turned off her radio. The lower portion of his jaw retracted with the hidden clench of his teeth, the handset carefully set in its holster against the air vent of his vehicle. I avoided saying anything, staring through my window and watching an approaching hill grow slowly closer. The trees whirled past, a slight lean to my left enough to see that the speedometer read nearly a hundred and thirty miles an hour. I watched the white hood of his truck shudder for a moment as we began to travel uphill.

"You gonna be okay seeing her again?" I asked, looking over at him. He nodded slowly.

"I want to hope she's doing well." He answered plainly, his lips remaining parted. "But I know she's not." I grimaced and nodded slowly in response, trying to think of a way to carefully continue the discussion.

"If you guys need someone to listen while you talk about things-"

"We don't." Another long silence as we crested the hill.

"I'm not saying it has to be couples' therapy, but-"

"Not necessary." I caught in the distance an uneven group of shapes close to the road, several miles away and dismissed it as it fell out of view while nearing the bottom of our hill.

"Well if you need me, I-"

"I don't need you involved in my-" His deep voice caught me off guard as his volume increased, falling silent unexpectedly. "You don't need to be around other people's problems."

"Oh, is that right?" I scoffed, leaning over to his side and beckoning at the scene around him. "Do you remember when there were *people* on these roads, Val? Remember when humans used to drive through here, like all the goddamn time? Because the fact that they're not here is a pretty big problem!" I had forgotten about Krystal's slumber in the backseat, apparently undisturbed by my outburst. I persisted out of sheer anger. "I'm not a kid anymore, Val! I haven't been for a very long time. When Sonya was hurt, who was on the mission that found Schillinger? When Krystal needed someone to steal drugs and listen to her problems, who was there? I've been in the middle of this goddamn fight for too long for you to treat me like a child. I'm *tired* of being tiptoed around and-"

"I'm sorry that-"

"I am not done, Valterius." I seethed. He closed his mouth, partly in amusement, and listened. "I have been through a lot in the last...almost fifty years. And yeah, I played the part for a while. I stayed quiet, minded my own business. Acted like the kid you all saw me as. But that by no means indicates that I am any less intelligent or capable than any of you."

"It shows." He replied quietly. "Your hands are shaking, but you didn't stutter."

"I don't need your kudos."

"I'm just saying, Vi. You've grown up, but you're still comparatively young. I was a tired old man before you were even born. There's a...point at which your experience is measured differently, and you just haven't reached it yet. Where you see things in a completely different light. Certain facts of life start to matter more than others, and your priorities shift. It doesn't mean you're lesser, we just try to protect you from all of these bad experiences to help shape the kind of person you deserve to grow into." I felt like I was speaking to the father I never had at this point, trying to take in his words while calming my own frustration.

"Bad experiences are clearly unavoidable in our lifestyle. And lifespan. So why bother?"

"Because the day I stop trying to protect you is the day I stop caring about you. You'll always be family, Vi. Always. Okay?" He looked over for a moment, catching my eyes and reaching a hand over to hold my own. It was unexpectedly warm, even in the chilled cabin of the truck. "Maybe I get it from Kara, maybe it's just the classic trait of being an older brother. But I've always loved you, related by blood or not.

Always will. And I'll always protect you. Kara brought you into this family on her own, but we all love you by choice." Hearing the word *love* from his mouth melted my heart in a thousand ways, tightening my throat to the point of pain. "That such a bad thing?"

"No." I whispered hoarsely, holding his hand tighter as I turned my face toward my window.

"I promise...when I need you, I will ask. Until then, I just want you safe and happy. Don't worry about me. Or Alice. When this is all over..." He sighed, shaking his head. "No. It'll always be one thing or another. Fine, no more excuses. I'll talk to her after I know Krystal is okay. Alright?" I nodded, hiding a quiet sniffle and pulling the collar of my white shirt up to wipe my eyes. As the truck crested its next small hill, I could see more clearly the roadside shape I had previously identified. It was a group of armed individuals, standing around two parked SUVs that blocked the road in front of us.

"Val?" I suggested quietly, looking at the concrete median between our side of the highway and that of the opposing direction. Both my tears and residual emotions were quickly suppressed by a minor twinge of fear.

"Can't get over that median without snapping an axle. We'll talk to them. It's fine." His tone was surprisingly calm for nearing a group of nearly twenty people with rifles and whatever else was hidden inside their trucks. He applied the brakes slowly and smoothly, ensuring Krystal wasn't disturbed by the gradual decline of our speed.

"*Talk* to them?" I asked for clarification as we came to a stop, roughly thirty feet from one of the individuals in the front of the group.

"They could have shot us already, in all honesty. They need something. We'll either give it to them or they'll understand our situation. I've got this." There was the briefest hint of his machismo exposing itself before he unlocked the door and stepped out onto the asphalt. I followed suit, immediately crossing the front bumper and standing at his side.

"What can I do for you?" Val asked, gesturing with his hands as both a show of peace and that he wasn't carrying a weapon. The man in front was no one to intimidate us, and approached with his weapon carried passively at his waist.

"Not here to start trouble or anything. The guns are just for our protection. But we do need the truck. We're willing to give you some meds and water for the walk to wherever you're going, but we're in a tough spot. Group's gotten bigger and we need the extra vehicle."

Val scratched his beard thoughtfully, nodding at him. There was no single description that would have distinguished the man as any kind of thief. He was just under six feet tall and an average build with brown hair that stayed just above his ears. I felt more relaxed hearing his tone of voice and the indifference with which he spoke.

"I understand, I do. But we have a girl in the back that's having seizures. She just came out of a coma and we need to get medical attention. Wife's a doctor. Going to see her now and try to get some help. I wish I could do something for you, but we're not much better off."

"Man. Sorry to hear that." Our captor remarked, peering to try and look in the backseat. "You've gotta have *something* we can use, man. We're not exactly keen on taking things by force, but we're really between a rock and a hard place. Anything?" The group behind him was stoic; Unmoving, but not hostile. Even in their stillness, there was a hidden degree of eagerness in their eyes, an uncomfortable way they stared at us like prey. They seemed, above all else, bloodthirsty in their gaze.

"Nothing in the truck bed and just some injections in the center console for the trip. We really can't help. The best I could do is offer to bring supplies back from where we're going, but even that wouldn't be enough to make a difference with a group this size." I could see a diplomatic approach in Val's efforts, but not one that I believed was going to be successful.

"What about the doc? We could follow behind you and pick her up from wherever your group is." He suggested.

"Afraid I can't offer you that one. Trading people isn't in our line of business." Val's innate sense of protection seemed to cut an edge into the conversation, the man taking a single step and closing the space between us by a foot. I watched the delicate movement of the people behind him as he approached, each of them shifting and growing uneasy.

"And what is...your line of business? If you don't mind me asking. Where you headed?"

"That way." Val pointed between their trucks along the highway and gave no further answer. Our renegade laughed genuinely, shaking his head.

"Oh, man. That's funny. Not enough people joke around anymore. Everything's so serious." He paused, the smile fading quickly. "But really, we need some help. Either we can take your truck or follow you out. I don't think you have a choice in the matter. I mean...without any weapons, how would you keep us from staying behind you?" Val took a deep breath, his appearance staying firm.

"By asking nicely. The people I associate with...they're not people you want to make enemies of. And I say that for *your* benefit. If I wanted a fight, I might be able to take a few of you. Same with Vi here." He nudged me for reassurance. "Obviously we wouldn't make it through the fight and our friend would die along with us. All you'd have to show for it is a new truck. That's a shitty trade with bad morals, and your people would probably lose faith in you. I've seen it happen before. If you follow us out, you'll be gunned down and torn to pieces by our own people. And that's not something I want to see happen. If I try to carry the girl all the way to her treatment, she won't make it. So the way I see it, *you* guys can wait for the next car to come along this road. We can't. So *I* will ask nicely, too. Please. Let us pass." While his words were submissive, Val forced a respect I couldn't have hoped to create myself if I had spoken the same.

"Or what, Valterius?" The man asked simply, smirking. Val remained entirely silent, his breathing nearly stopped completely.

"You know who I am." His voice rumbled from somewhere deep in his throat like the workings of an ancient volcano brewing to life. "You're not here by accident. And you're not here for the truck." I started to understand the gravity of the situation in realizing that Krystal's life was at stake. There was no easy solution, no simple way out. I looked behind us, staring at the truck for a moment and trying to think of an alternative that would keep the three of us alive.

"Or...what?" The man repeated slowly.

Startled, I jumped as a flurry of piercing gusts stabbed at my right eardrum, a sudden burst of suppressed gunfire ringing from between the trees at the side of the road. Several of the thieves were pressed backwards by the bullets that found a new home, carving a hole into the center of the group.

"Run." Val's colossal hand met my back with a forceful shove as he turned around, pressing me toward the truck. I hunched as I sprinted, listening to the array of gunfire exchanged between the mysterious attacking force and the group that had stopped us. The moment I found a place in the passenger seat, I slammed the door shut and threw myself over the center console to check on Krystal. Her eyes were open in a semi-drunk state of groggy consciousness.

"Go, Val." I said forcefully without yelling in Krystal's face. Her eyelids fluttered before her body went limp again, crashing into the leather with a quiet thump.

The truck lurched forward and my morbid curiosity forced my eyes to peer through the windshield. We barreled toward the small space between the two blocking vehicles: our only escape to freedom. I could make out a figure emerging from the shoulder of the road with a tan rifle, placing accurate shots around our truck. I stared as long as I was able, the singular second as we passed creating a mental photograph. The attacking figure was smaller than Val, but oddly clothed and unidentifiable. A vest of body armor was conformed around a hooded sweatshirt, obscuring the face and body of the person wearing it. Combined with the navy blue cargo pants they wore, a physical build, gender, or identity was impossible to determine. The hood was withdrawn slightly by their movement, the side of their head shaven and cropped close to the scalp. Prior to further discoveries, we lurched forward as Val's bumper forced the vehicles aside and thrust us into the open road. The dying sound of armed conflict began to fade into the distance behind us. I closed my eyes for a second, breathing deeply and trying to calculate how we weren't shot in the process.

"We're both thinking it, but what the hell was that?" My heart was racing beyond control, an incident nearly fatal to the three of us being far too close for comfort. I stared in the passenger side mirror at one of the last defenders, huddled behind one of their SUVs and being approached rapidly by the lone wolf.

"No idea. Don't wanna know. Just want to get really far away. How's Krystal?" Val questioned. I turned around again, an uneasy slumber snorting and twitching its way across her body.

"Fine, I think. How far away are we?" I knew we were close by the change in surroundings to a more rural environment.

"Five minutes or so at this speed. About ten miles. Did you see who started all that?" He ran a hand through his thick hair, the faint shine of a layer of sweat coating his brow.

"Not who specifically, no. I saw someone...wearing body armor and loose clothing. Looked like a shaved head or buzz cut. I didn't see anyone else." I tried to recall any other figures near the scene, but I failed to recall anyone else.

"Why didn't he shoot at *us*? Why did he target that group?"

"Maybe he's a friend of ours? Or...just someone that hates that little gang. I don't know. But he very intentionally avoided shooting our vehicle."

"Yeah, well...I'm not buying the guy a beer anytime soon. That other group could have shot you, thinking it was *us* that started it." He sighed, clearing his throat and moving past the adrenaline rush.

"They were just as surprised as we were. He had to have been sitting there, waiting for a reason to shoot. No way it was just someone walking by at the right time. That was...too much of a genuine rescue to be considered a coincidence."

"Which begs the question..." He started. "Which was the reason to shoot? Saving us, or killing them?" I shrugged, beyond reason or logic at this point. Out of reflex, I turned around again to stroke Krystal's unfamiliar length of hair.

"That could have turned really nasty."

"Yeah...no way was I giving up my truck." My mouth opened slightly as I began to fume at his statement, but knowing he would have a good reason, I stayed calm.

"Why?" I asked quietly. He stared at the road in front of us, the trees that anticipated their winter slumber dropping the last of their dead leaves under our tires.

"It was an anniversary gift." I took quiet pride for a moment in being right about his reasoning, pushing the feeling outward with a deep breath and letting go of Krystal's hair.

I could feel the truck start to slow as Val touched the brakes, exiting the main road and taking the ramp onto a rarely travelled residential avenue. The occasional house dotted either side of the road for a few miles, the quiet countryside ride a known route after so many adventures with the sleeping woman in the backseat. Out of habit, Val flicked on his turn signal to change course onto Krystal's driveway: a half-mile stretch of gravel carved into a dense assortment of trees that shielded her property from roadside view.

Clearing the privacy barrier, we drove at a shallow angle uphill and stopped in front of the Victorian-style manor and its dozen rooms that overlooked a substantial portion of the surrounding area. Alice's black sedan was parked near the front door, with Tony's van several yards to its left. We pulled in between the two vehicles, stopping before our tires trampled the bright orange extension cable that ran from the back of the van to the house.

"They must have a generator hooked up, but I don't hear it running. Probably for Alice's medical equipment." I suggested as he turned the truck off and opened his door.

"Probably. You want me to carry her?"

"Might be best." I opened the back door, appreciating the remaining light in the sky as I fumbled under the seat to find Val's spare blanket. Somehow, the outside air, while chilled, was warmer than that of the arctic menace that surrounded Krystal's body. My fingers curled around a bundle of coarse fabric, pulling it free and draping the covering over as much of her body as I could. I took a step back and looked at the front doors of the mansion while Val shifted Krystal's weight around before moving her. The ornate brass door handles were closed tightly, likely to keep any heat trapped inside. No one stepped out to greet us by the time Val reached me.

"I'm assuming it's unlocked." He beckoned with his head, his arms keeping her frame still and comfortable while draped across his chest. I swung the door open, allowing him inside before I stepped in. A rush of air washed the frigidity away from my cheekbones and invoked a sense of comfort I hadn't felt in years. The door closing behind me, only minimal light from the drapery-covered windows gave Val enough of a resource to find the couch inside the foyer and lay Krystal's body across it. I rolled my neck, letting the comforting sensation of my second home wash across the rest of my body.

"Dark in here." Val commented, taking a step toward me. "Wonder how long the generator's been out."

"The fireplace isn't going. Couldn't have been off long with how warm it is in here." I wondered, looking toward the grandiose oak staircase as a quiet set of footfalls wandered toward the top. Alice's ruby hair fluttered around her shoulders as she trotted down to us, her eyes sleepy and cast onto the floor.

"Not much use for a fireplace when you *are* one." She hit the last step and took a long stride forward, pulling me into a tight hug. "Hey, sweetie."

"Hey, Alice. It's good to see you." I held her for a moment before letting go, studying her face as she sighed. Her cheeks were more gaunt than they were a few weeks ago, although not to such an extent that her health was in question. They both held onto the rubbed-off black fade of ash that matched the thin layer of soot on her palms. Although the brightness of her beautiful eyes wasn't diminished, they were weary with exhaustion and emotion and endless tasks. The green orbs flicked sideways to look at Val, who stood idly over Krystal. I could see her pupils widen for the briefest moment, even the most buried feelings of love still dormant and ever-clear.

"Hey, Val." She whispered, her stoic expression failing to change.

"Hey. She's, um...I wasn't sure where-"

"Yeah, she's-...that's fine. Wherever she's comfortable." Alice reassured. Val nodded for far too long, eventually making the decision to walk into Krystal's kitchen and leave the two of us by ourselves. Alice slid next to the couch and knelt down, inspecting every inch of Krystal's body before looking back at me.

"She's okay. I was pretty sure this would happen. A lot of repairing still to come. Her body has to do some of it while she's awake, and that's tough on anyone. Even someone as strong as she is." She stroked Krystal's shoulder-length blue hair, the sight of the siblings' close resemblance only ever so obvious in the state they were both in at that exact moment. Their hair matched in both length and characteristic waviness nearly as much as the pale shades of their skin and the darkness that surrounded their eyes.

"I'm glad to hear it." I returned, placing a hand on her back. As unusual as it was, she wasn't wearing a lab coat and had instead decided on a blouse that was half a size too small for her. I could feel a radiant heat from her body, enough to explain the shrinkage in her clothes.

"I'm going to take her upstairs and start her on another bolus of Factor Five. Mind coming with? Bring Val with you, if you would." She gingerly placed a hand under Krystal's neck and I took that as a cue to fetch her husband from the kitchen. Moving around the couch, I crossed the barriers into the next room to find him empty-handed and leaning against the countertop. I waited for a moment, hearing Alice retreat upstairs with her sister before asking him any questions.

"You okay?" He shrugged at my question, his hands lifting off of the black granite countertop by half an inch before settling back down in a defeated position. He hadn't turned on the lights or retrieved a glass, apparently only occupying the room for its solitude.

"Harder than I thought it would be. Seeing her again. Like this." His words were muted, speaking softly so we wouldn't be overheard.

"Yeah. It'll take time. For now, we're needed upstairs. I think Alice wanted to talk to us about that situation from earlier."

"Yeah, and we should tell her about what happened on the highway. I don't want her in trouble if anyone needs to leave for supplies." Inhaling through his nose, he pushed off of the counter and strolled alongside me as we made our way up the steps. "Where is everyone, by the way? It's dead quiet in here. She say anything about Amy or Kara? They're usually the first to see us." I shook my head, assuming that it was the topic of discussion. The stairs opened up to reveal a sort of parlor room on the top floor, branching out into two hallways and a balcony that overlooked the back of the property. The balcony doors were shut for insulation, but the parlor room had been converted into a small, basic laboratory. Barely a tenth of the equipment was present from her workspace in the Raven building, but it was enough to know she had been working diligently on something. Alice flitted between a pair of tables and the hospital bed Krystal was now laid onto, creating a horseshoe shape in the middle of the room.

"As soon as I get this I.V. hooked up, I'll explain all of that." Alice asserted, uncapping the gleaming silver end of a stainless steel needle.

I wonder how much she heard.

"Sorry, I didn't mean to-"

"It's okay. I appreciate you keeping your voice down. Thanks for trying not to distract me." She accepted Val's apology, pressing a series of buttons on a small device attached to Krystal's wrist. Turning to us, she cracked her knuckles and removed the sterile blue gloves from her hands before throwing them in a hidden trash can.

"Sonya should be here any minute. Ran over to the Raven HQ to get some stuff I left behind. Amy and Tony went out for a walk out back. Generator needed to start back up after Tony replaced some parts, but we didn't want the noise to wake Krystal on the way in. So we'll have lights and toilets back up in a little bit."

"Very considerate of you." Val remarked.

"Yeah, well...after all she's been through..." She turned her head to observe her sleeping sibling. "It's the least I could do."

"You've done a lot for her, Alice. More than she has any idea." I offered. She smiled, a thankless life becoming more rewarding for the moment.

"Where's Jalix and Kara? I thought you guys were good on fuel and water for a few weeks, yet." Alice grimaced at the question, locking eyes with Val.

"Promise to keep a cool head, and I'll tell you. But you're not going to like it." We nodded, leaning against the railing that overlooked the bottom floor. "They left." She continued. "Of their own will, but not of their own choice. A group came by here a few days ago. Wanted to see who was living in such a prominent home. Tony and I happened to be here visiting. Jalix had suggested a...family dinner." She chuckled. "God, he's a terrible cook. Anyway...they came, wanted to take the place. Said they had...plans, or something. I could tell they were trouble, Val, I really could. They had zero fear walking into this place, even after Kara and Jalix introduced themselves."

"What?" I said, dazed. "No one wants to be anywhere *near* Kara after what happened with Schillinger and his empire. She's like...universally feared."

"Not by these guys." Alice looked away for a moment. "They said something about being different than the rest.

Having a different kind of leadership, one that actually functioned in this weird world. Kara wanted to keep Amy safe, and Jalix wanted to find out what was going on. They struck a deal. The group doesn't come back and doesn't tell anyone about the rest of us, and Kara would leave with Jalix to be trophies for their new leadership. Obviously they don't plan on being guests for very long, but both parties were willing."

"Look, I don't mean to come across the wrong way, but you just let them leave? With a group of people out of nowhere, going someplace we don't know about to meet an obviously powerful figure we've never seen? Why?" Val maintained his temper, desiring knowledge more than an argument.

"It was *those* two. What was I going to say to change Jalix or Kara's mind? And besides, it was a fair deal. Kara was…submissive. And Jalix was being diplomatic. It worked for the time being. I don't think they're in any danger, but even if they are, they can take care of themselves. We needed to figure out what was going on. They were looking for…something. I have no idea what, but they were *more* than willing to leave with Kara."

"Maybe they think she has the answer to all of this." I suggested quietly. "Who would know more than the original Vampyre Queen?"

"Yeah, well…if it's that easy, I'm going to kill her for not telling me twenty years ago what the answer was. Look, I'm confident they'll check in."

"*Too* confident, Ally." Alice's nickname slipped from Val's tongue quicker than his active thought, taking them both by surprise. He continued, wanting to spare me an awkward moment. "Are you really sure about this?"

"Very. I wouldn't have let them go otherwise. Like I said, it was…weird. They weren't trying to attack us or take what we had. They were barely armed. It was like a scouting party.

Once they found Kara and Jalix, they stopped caring. I mean, they *knew* who we were, despite trying to act like they were ignorant. It wasn't an accident."

"I'm surprised they didn't go after Amy, too." I observed.

"They tried. Asked specifically, actually. She was upstairs in the bathroom when they showed up. Girl was smart enough to listen and stay quiet. Jalix made something up about her leaving to stay with a friend in Virginia. They bought the story. I've been keeping an eye on things ever since, but I haven't seen anyone even come close to the mansion." Val and I exchanged an obvious glance, immediately captured by Alice. "Oh, no."

"I don't know if it was related to all this." Val dismissed. "They knew who I was, though. Not sure why they stopped us or why they tried to play it off like they didn't. Led by a guy about this tall, brown hair?" Val held up a hand near the base of his neck.

"The spokesperson for the other group was a blonde woman, dolled-up makeup. And they didn't look like the type to work well with others. I couldn't say if it's part of the same thing. I haven't heard about anyone acting up all these years. Everyone's integrated. Why now?"

"Well, I don't think they're going to be a problem anyway." Val finished, scratching his jaw.

"Why not?"

"They're dead." I explained, still trying to get over the chaos of our unexpected stop. "I saw something on the way out of there, or at least part of them. Somebody in oversized clothes with body armor and a rifle. One person. Shaved head, but not bald. Dark hair. He moved a little bit like Jalix used to when he was training some of the city residents. All…tactical. When I looked back, he had killed them all. Some kind of ambush set up. Just the lone wolf. Friend of yours, by chance?"

"I don't know, but I'll thank him if I see him. Saved you guys, looks like." She smirked. "And my sister."

"When it rains, it pours." Val mumbled, approaching one of the tables Alice stood in front of. "Any chance it was Jalix?" He continued.

"No, definitely not." Alice answered without reservation. "Not unless you made a broadcast that you were coming here. He would have had to camp out in that exact spot at that exact time. Besides, Kara would have been with him *and* they would have reached out once they were done with…what they're doing."

"This is a damn mess." I sighed, flipping my hair over my shoulder. "I mean, I'm sorry, but…why is it that we can never *just* have good things?"

"Well…" Alice smiled genuinely, giving rise to a dramatic pause. "There was a second reason we agreed that Jalix and Kara could go with them. If there really is a group we don't know about, one that lives outside governance of normal cities…we need to know where they are." She started rocking back and forth on her heels like a giddy teenager.

"Spit it out, come on." I chuckled, waiting.

"I hit a breakthrough. There's no cure ready, but I sequenced a set of genes that lets me access more of the virus's potential. Everything I tried to introduce it to, it adapted out of. But I finally got to the nuts and bolts of what makes this thing tick. I think we're close. Maybe…a year, if I can keep going at this pace. The downside is I have no idea how we're going to disseminate it. So we're going to have to make sure it's ready in the most populated areas and distribute it all at once-"

"You did it?" Val cocked his head, his eyes cool with a calm that hadn't been seen for years.

"I did it." Alice's smile grew, exposing a brilliant set of teeth that worked its magic even into her eyes. "Like I said, there's a lot of work – and setbacks – to come. But this could be our chance to finally get re-integrated to the world."

"Holy shit, Alice." I sighed. "That's a lot to take in. When did this-"

"Literally last night. I would have called, but I've been running sequencers all night just to confirm it. It's not done yet, but I'm confident of the results already. Speaking of, I've asked everyone else far too often…can I steal a blood sample? I only need a tube."

"Sure. Anything I can do to help. This is…amazing. What do you need ours for?" I rolled up my right sleeve and approached Alice's table as she put on another pair of gloves.

"Just to compare results. Everyone's a little bit different, you know? Seeing multiple angles of this thing goes a long way." She reached under the tabletop and pulled out a small plastic package, its contents sealed for sterility.

"I almost miss the days when you'd give long, drawn-out answers I couldn't understand." I reminisced. She chuckled, tilting her head as she watched my vein pour an offering into her small, clear vial.

"I can, if it would make you happy." I could hear she was looking for an excuse to elaborate on her recent endeavors, and much to Val's discontent, I encouraged it.

"It would indeed."

"Well…" She started, discarding the needle and opening a new pack as Val approached. "The virus that causes us to be what we are, is part of a genus called a *Pandoravirus*. They-"

"That is…not real." Val whispered, shaking his head at her while she took his sample. She pursed her lips at him, taking the needle from his arm with a certain degree of swiftness and causing a hurt growl.

"It's very real, and I've spent the last hundred years of my life studying it, thank you very much." She cleared her throat for effect, turning back to me. "More accurately, it's also part of a satellite virus. Kind of exactly how it sounds. Basically, there's a big virion and a little half-virion and-"

"And when they love each other very much, they make babies." Val asserted, nodding once.

"Somehow…" Alice rubbed her forehead, sighing. "You're actually *somewhat* right. God, I hate you sometimes. Yeah, the little half-virus hangs out around the big one because the Pandoravirus can't replicate without help. Ours, anyway. Some strains of Pandoravirus can. I'm getting sidetracked…The satellite itself isn't a whole virus. It's just a little…piece. A helper, basically. It fetches the materials needed for the big one to replicate itself, using proteins from our blood cells. With supplements from our medicine, it's not enough to kill you. The cells just need replaced and replenished once in a while. The Pandoravirus – meanwhile – is a database filled with bajillions-"

"Is that more or less than a jillion? I'm just-…I'm trying to keep track, and I-" Val was interrupted by a set of discarded nitrile gloves slapping his chest and falling to the floor.

"Bajillions of different things that break off and bind to our DNA. Our DNA replicates all the time, every single time we eat or drink or breathe, our cells divide and grow. The DNA from the Pandoravirus breaks off and attaches to our own during the cellular replication. The problem I've been having is that every time that our DNA is changed, the materials needed for the satellite to do its duty changes. Which is why each of us developed as a Vampyre a little bit differently. Not much of a change, but it's kind of like if I have a half-inch hole and every time I pick up a half-inch screw to put in, the hole turns into a different size." I inadvertently stifled a laugh at her analogy of holes, and Alice's enraged eyes immediately shot over to Val for his inevitable comment. His face was set in a deadpan stare, seemingly benign.

"No comment. Good analogy. I'm listening." Taking a moment to clear her thoughts, she paused before continuing.

"Luckily, I boiled it down to a common denominator. Every request this Pandoravirus makes contains a specific set of instructions. I had to look past the *what* and start looking for the *how*."

"So like, it's always making a shopping list for different ingredients, but the paper it's written on is always the same." I turned my head to Val, raising my eyebrows. Alice did the same, surprised at the accuracy.

"Um...yes. That's-...yeah. And I think I found a way to put in a kind of shutdown code into the...paper. The satellite can be changed to fetch the wrong proteins. Once the modified satellite is introduced, it'll bring gibberish back to the host virus and shut both of them down. It won't be able to replicate."

"And it can't adapt to this?" I asked, trying to understand her train of thought.

"No. We'd be starving it. Without nutrients and a way to survive, it won't be able to adapt anymore. Without the virus to change our DNA during cell replication, our normal DNA would take over again. I can get a working trial within a year or so, and after another few months, I think I can artificially supplement our immune systems to survive long enough that we won't die from a common cold." Val and I both stared, failing to understand the statement. "Well, we've been so used to being resistant to disease, our bodies have like...no natural immunity. Some, but...it'll take time to come back to full strength."

"Ah." I said, enlightened. "That was...surprisingly easy to understand. I mean, I'm sure you dumbed it down-"

"A lot."

"A lot, but still. Thanks for the explanation." She smirked, placing our tubes of blood into a small, glass-enclosed rack by her centrifuge. Val took a deep breath.

"So back to this half-inch hole…" I could feel the tension build as Val started down into a spiral of poor taste.

"Valterius, I-"

"What…you gonna…give her your half-inch screw, Val?" A soft, dry voice slid through the air, Krystal apparently awake enough to follow the conversation.

"Krystal!" Alice exclaimed quietly, throwing her body over the hospital bed.

"Hey." Krystal returned quietly, lifting her arms to cover Alice's back. "Long time no see, sis."

"Too long." Alice's voice was muffled and teary, buried in Krystal's shoulder. I couldn't help but to feel emotional, myself. Watching Alice have her moment of victory after so many years of effort and labor was more than gratifying. "I'm so sorry, Kryssi. I tried so hard to fix you faster, but-" I watched Krystal extend her arms, holding Alice's face in front of her own.

"You brought me back to life." She smirked, her pale, cracked lips still recovering from heavy breathing. "You rebuilt me. No one else on Earth could have done that. Don't you *dare* apologize for doing the impossible." Hearing Krystal in her brutal, emotional honesty forced a hoarse choke from Alice's throat, shaking her head violently before leaning in for another hug.

"What do you need?" Alice leapt backward suddenly, shifting gears and becoming borderline manic with paranoia. "Are you hungry? Thirsty? Oh, God, I didn't give you anything for the pain, you must be *suffering* right now."

"I'm good." Krystal chuckled, lifting her head and silently waving at Val and I while she ranted. I waved back, amused at the bliss of the scene.

"-supposed to, but if you wanted a glass of wine, I can-"

"Alice. Sweetie. I'm good. You're a rock star, but calm down. I feel fine, just…groggy. Need to walk off that seizure." She rolled her legs off the bed, letting them dangle a few inches off the ground. "Speaking of, what are the odds of that happening again?"

"Um..." Alice finally became quiet for a moment, inspecting her sister. "Slim. But...possible. Avoid any intense thinking and heavy brain activity for a bit. Let your mind acclimate to all this new info and try to relax."

"Yeah, I'll just hang out with Val. So little brain activity that I might go back into a coma." She chuckled, looking around. "So...out of the city and back home, huh? I thought Val said you and Tony were in the Raven building."

"Long story." I sighed. "But you're home now. We're all here, minus Jalix and Kara. Tony and Amy are outside for a walk. You wanna go walk around your house again? I'm sure it seems like you were just here, but-"

"Yeah. Actually. Somehow, it *does* feel like it's been a lifetime since I've been here. The... whole house isn't like this, is it?" While trying to sound respectful, Krystal had a mild look of disdain for the tables of laboratory equipment.

"Everything is just how you left it. Jalix and Kara have a room up here, and Amy is next door to them in your office. I've been sleeping on the couch and Tony took the garage. Your room is just how you left it, and your kitchen...aside from a little bit of wine, it's actually better stocked than it was before. All you had in your cupboards was-"

"Ramen. Noodles." She smirked, jumping off the bed and somehow landing on relatively steady feet. "And now I know what I'm going to do for the next few minutes. Besides finding some underwear to put on. Kitchen if you need me." She smiled at us before making her way toward the staircase.

"Drink lots of water. Instant ramen is high in sodium and your kidneys-"

"Thanks, babe. I'll stay hydrated!" She called from the bottom of the steps.

"New and improved." Val sighed contentedly. "It's good to have her back. I have a strong feeling that she'll be less of a pain in the ass after everything that happened. She seems to be taking everything with a fresh outlook."

"I could tell." Alice commented, leaving her island of study and standing in front of the balcony doors. "I offered her something for pain and-"

"Apparently she's been clean for a while. Weaned herself off of the morphine and quit entirely. Little known to the rest of us." I remarked.

"I'll be honest, that might have saved her life." She turned her head, her eyes staring down at the floor. "Her ribcage and skull still had a little bit of healing to go when she…went missing. Her body went into a recovery mode to fix the problems, and when she was frozen, it stayed that way. If she had systemic depressants in her system, it could have kept that from happening, and I might not have been able to help her body recover."

"Man, you're smart." Val chuckled. Alice wanted to smile, but the compliment was a tender spot in her heart. The feeling was reflected onto Val, who quickly realized the mistake of his timing.

"I should go check on Krystal. I'm sure she-"

"Wants to be left alone right now, Alice." I said sternly. "But I think two more people need to heal. Before we launch into a rescue mission, which you know we're going to, you guys need to fix this crap."

"Violet, I-"

"She's right." Val mumbled, taking a step toward her and interrupting her chance to protest. "Come on, Ally. How long have we been going like this? There's never going to be a better time. Ever. We need to fix things before it's too late." Alice sighed, crossing her arms and facing the thin panes of glass on the balcony doors.

"What is there to fix? I still love you. 'Til death do us part, right?" Her answer was halfhearted and entirely defeated.

"Yeah, but look at us." He asserted. "I can't even remind you of how smart you are without it being awkward." I took the opportunity to become a wallflower, taking a step back and listening rather than intervening. "How did things get this weird between us?"

"You had your job, and I had mine. It was no one's fault, but we never saw each other. For years, we'd have what, a day or two every month? That's not a marriage." I could see the pain in Val's face as Alice began to describe her sense of distance.

"What about everything we had before? That time more than makes up for it. We were bound to have our bad spots."

"A bad spot?" She scoffed. "Val, the world ended. It took a lot of casualties, and...we were one of them." My heart sunk, realizing she wasn't trying to reconnect. "I will never love anybody the way I love you, but...we stopped being a team. Things ended. It wasn't your choice or mine, but it ended."

"Ended?" Val muttered, his mouth unable to close. The silence between them was endless, a black hole of sound.

"It's not what it was. I...don't know if it can be. I mean, look at the way things are. *Nothing* can fix this." She ran a hand through her hair, shaking her head slowly as her chin trembled.

"News to me, Alice." Val whispered, his terracotta eyes glistening with complete loss. "Because I lost hope in everything. The entire world and everything in it. Except my family. Are you telling me you don't *want* to be a part of that?" She tried to speak, but a heaving sob caught her off-guard, her shoulder blades thumping against the frame of the doors. In every situation, Val had managed to take some form of control over the effects that the world had on him. For the first time, he failed in every regard as a tear made its way down a weary face and disappeared into the blackness of his beard. I took another step back, disappearing into a shadow of the room and slumping to the ground, trying to cry silently as I watched the hell I made.

"I can't anymore, Val." She whimpered, lifting her hand to stare at the titanium wedding band she still wore. "I look at this damn thing...every day. And it just reminds me about the husband I *used* to have."

"You still have me, Alice. I'm not gone. I'm right here."

"And for how long?" She tilted her head, sniffling. "How long until you're gone again? Until you have to go do the right thing? Until the world pulls you away?" He shook his head.

"It doesn't matter, I-"

"How long until I go two years without seeing you again?" She stood straighter, angry at herself and at him. He coughed a hoarse breath, trying to salvage anything from his own mind.

"How long, Val?" She took a step forward, her angry cries lashing out at him with every word.

"I'll always be here, Alice."

"You can't know that!" Gently, but with conviction, she shoved his right shoulder and pushed him away from her.

Why did I do this? How did this happen?

"I'm never going to leave you." He said quietly, reaching to cup her face.

"You died, you bastard!" She pushed harder this time, Val stepping to the side as he stumbled to back up against the wall rather than the railing of the staircase. "I thought I watched you die! Twice! I mourned you twice! I hated you for dying because I loved you so much!" My throat roared with pain as I stifled any noise, shuddering with angry tears. She berated him, driving the sides of her fists into his chest with every sentence. "My sister, my best friend, my husband, they all died! What stupid thing are you going to die for next, Val?" As she swung again, he reached out and grabbed her arm with the coolness of an ironclad bear paw. Leaning away from the wall, he moved his face to within an inch of hers, inciting a complete stillness from both of them.

"I died protecting my family." He breathed, his voice low and rough. "And I'll do it a thousand times again if I know it keeps you safe." Alice exhaled quickly, completely still as he held her arm in place. "Time, distance, and death doesn't do us part. And I'll never let it."

"Why?" She croaked, looking up into his eyes.

"Because through the years, no matter what I said before..." He lowered her arm, intertwining his fingers with hers. "You were always the hot one." She became motionless again, a heavy panting escaping through her gritted teeth.

"You giant goddamn idiot." With a force that could have knocked over the house, she shoved his torso into the wall and slid her arms behind him, squeezing him with all her strength. "I love your stupid face so much. Don't leave me again."

"Even if I have to, I'll always come back, Ally." He stroked her hair silently, resting one hand on her waist as they slowly rocked back and forth. As quietly as I was able, I recovered myself and began to stand up, freezing cold and my face swollen from tears. He looked over and gave me a soft smile, enough to warm my heart more than the heat Alice's body was giving off.

"I can't go through this again, Val. Please. It's been so damn much over the years..." She leaned back to look up at him, as if she was pleading for her own life. He ran the back of his hand against her cheek, wiping away the freshest tears and smiling at her.

"The worst is over, Ally. All we need to do is pick up the pieces of this weird world and put back together what we can. You've done so much to make that happen, and it's something I can never repay you for."

"You don't *have* to repay me, Val. I just want you here to see it." She sighed, placing her hands on his chest. "I want you here for everything, all the time. I can't sleep anymore without you next to me. I can't get through the day without your sense of humor. God, your smile." She closed her eyes and brushed her fingers through his beard.

"Through everything that comes next, I will stand by your side. I promise, Allison. Through centuries-old sickness and in health."

"'Til death do-"

"We tried that already. Didn't work. The factory sent you a new one. Sorry." She giggled in happiness despite the context of his statement. She turned her head to face me, deciding to remember that I was in the room.

"Violet. I'm sorry you had to see all of that."

"Why?" I laughed hoarsely, clearing my throat and wiping my face. "You guys just went through twenty years of trauma in five minutes. I wasn't expecting everything to be fixed that fast."

"Maybe it didn't need fixed." Alice offered quietly with a sniffle. "Just remembered."

Val was right, I can fix things. Maybe there's hope for the rest of the world.

Val leaned in to kiss his wife and was interrupted too soon by Krystal reaching the top of the stairs with a bowl of noodles, some of which dangled from her mouth.

"Oh fit. Muh inferrupfing?" She swallowed heavily, dropping her chopsticks into the bowl and slowly walking backwards down the path she came from.

"No, Krystal. We're good." Alice chuckled, taking a step back and waving for her to come upstairs. "Just sewing shut some old wounds."

"Alright, well…keep your shenanigans away from the medical equipment that holds our entire future. And any of my expensive furniture. It's a little bit tougher to replace nowadays."

"Shenanigans?" Val inquired. "We don't have any shenanigans."

"Doesn't look like shenanigans to me." I shrugged, beckoning to the distance between the two of them. Krystal sighed and took another massive bite of ramen, chewing with one side of her mouth.

"I'm going to punch the next person that says-" She turned her head quickly, moving out of the way as Tony and Amy ran up the stairs, both nearly out of breath. Tony looked around the room in alarm, unsure of who to address in the oddity of the present crowd. His face was faintly streaked with the same dark dirt as Alice's, likely from working on the generator prior to his woodland stroll. Amy stood silently, equally as unnerved but not prepared to address anyone in particular. We locked eyes for a moment, and in the innate bond of our deep friendship I could feel an unsettling anxiety behind the mirror of her perfect grey eyes.

"Val, there's someone here." Tony's voice was rough, clearly a precursor to the adrenaline he was fighting. "In the driveway."

"Is Sonya back? She was supposed to-"

"I think I would recognize her, Val. They're just standing there, staring at the manor. It looks like he's holding a rifle. I don't know if it's another scout from the last group that came through, but-"

"Wait, are they wearing a hood? Body armor?" I asked hesitantly. Tony's head snapped over, wide-eyed.

"Yeah. A friend?" He returned his questions to Val.

"Not sure. But we're going to find out. Stay here." He said to the group. Considering myself separate from the rest of them in terms of experience with the individual, I followed behind Val, nearly knocking Krystal over as I realized she didn't see me approach or start down the stairs. I stopped for a moment, watching her eyes stay completely locked on Amy.

"Hey." I murmured quietly. "You're not going to collapse again, are you?" She jumped as if I startled her, looking at me briefly before shaking her head and continuing to stare. I left my confidence for her health with Alice as I ran down the stairs, sprinting to catch up to Val before he opened the front door.

"Hold on. Krystal has a nine mil somewhere around..." I opened the drawer of the small table next to the entryway, curling my fingers around a black pistol grip and handing the weapon to Val.

"Thanks." He mumbled, pushing the door open and leading me outside. He closed the door behind him as he stared ahead, the same lone figure unaccompanied at the end of the long gravel driveway. The only motion I could discern was a steady breathing, gradually bringing his shoulders up and down along with the rifle he held. He was leaning to the left by only a slight degree, a possible sign of nursing an injury from the fight we witnessed. Val took a rough aim at the silhouette and executed several steps forward, calling out to him.

"Drop the rifle. Now." On command, the figure bent over with the slowness of a turtle and placed the tan rifle on the driveway, slowly raising his gloved hands as he stood once more. "On your knees." Val continued, incrementally edging his way forward. The combination of dying sunlight and drawn hood was still too much to make out any discernible features, and I moved to Val's left to try and get a better angle. "Stay behind me." He mumbled quietly.

"I think if he was a threat, he would have tried something already."

"Yeah, that's called a false sense of security. There could be a dozen people in the trees behind him. Are you alone?" He called again, squaring his shoulders to acquire a perfect shot, should the need arise. The hood moved upward slowly before drawing down, a slow and deliberate nod.

"What's your name?" I called, hoping to hear his voice in reply. He remained still and silent, no hint that I was even heard.

"Who are you?" Val echoed my question, hoping to intimidate him more than I could. We were only a dozen feet away, our slow approach marked by a clarity in details. The body armor sported splotches of blood; the vest was stained a deep wine-red in some spots and untouched in others.

"No one." The voice came unexpectedly, a breathy chill of wind grazing my ears with a robust softness. The voice was husky and dark, but smooth like the musk of smoke and whiskey. It seemed too feminine to be true, but the longer I looked, the more I realized they very well could have been a woman.

"Drop the hood." Val demanded, stopping just outside of arm's reach. Their head fell downward slowly, their hands still intertwined behind the hood and keeping it in place. With no intention of moving, the figure remained still and defied our demands. "I said *drop* it. You're running out of chances to be an ally. And you don't want to be an enemy." A quiet puff of air escaped their nostrils as they apparently found Val's comment to be amusing.

Tired of the theatrics and unease, Val reached over and ripped the hood backwards with one hand, keeping the weapon squarely aimed at their head. A cascade of black hair fell to touch the webbing of her body armor, the side of her head shaven and the rest allowed to grow to quite a length. Her facial features distinctly feminine, I could make out a fragile face and a color of skin the shade of coffee with too much cream. It took me a moment before the realization dawned on me, her ember-infused mahogany eyes heaving a long sigh at Val.

That's not possible. She wasn't a part of the experiments that brought back Kara and Val. Jalix killed her.

Like milky caramel, the outline of her face and neck became clearer as she rolled her head upward to meet Val's eyes. Her head tilted, I could see a grotesque group of scars on the side of her neck that spanned several inches across in a clean diameter.

"Raven?" I whispered, taking a step back. She stared into Val's eyes, statuesque as a willing prisoner. I couldn't pry away my gaze, watching the silent exchange between the two of them. Val's index finger twitched more than once, an obvious battle raging its way through his heart and mind. I said nothing, more than willing to accept his judgment in a situation I was barely grasping. He slowly lowered the barrel of the pistol, his teeth silently clenched in fury. Raven took a breath, her lips parting to speak before the back end of the weapon was rammed against her skull with enough force to instantly crumple her body to the ground.

CAMPAIGN
VALTERIUS

Deliberating my own moral compass, I dropped the limp body onto the same couch I had placed Krystal onto less than an hour ago, using notably less caution.

None of this seems possible.

"Alice?" Violet called, facing the stairs. Krystal, Amy, and Alice were all leaned against the railing, staring down into the foyer like they were watching a theatrical production.

"Is that who I think it is?" Krystal decided to verify Raven's identity while her sister made a hasty jog down the stairs. I beckoned to the body, shrugging in as much agreement as I was capable.

"Looks like it. For the most part." I decided.

"What, does *everybody* get to come back to life?" Krystal mumbled, allowing Amy a head start down the staircase in front of her. "Thought I was a little more special than that." Her grumbling, while pessimistic, contrasted a spark that lit the electric blue of her eyes, watching Amy as she rounded the corner and stood in front of the couch. Crowding around the scene, I watched as Alice carefully removed the thick straps of Raven's body armor, casting it aside and starting to inspect what was underneath.

"Here, Amy. She's wearing a shirt underneath this sweatshirt. Let's get the loose stuff off so you can get closer to her skin."

"Her skin…?" Krystal posed aloud, raising an eyebrow at me. The pair worked diligently, pulling off the hooded sweatshirt and carefully pulling down the waistband of her cargo pants to ensure there was a layer underneath. Sure enough, an insulating pair of athletic pants was enough to warrant undressing further.

"Her healing powers." Tony chimed in quietly, taking a seat on the only available chair. "By the way, hello, Val."

"Sup? Sorry we, uh…"

"Brought a guest?" He finished, shaking his head. "I always thought you had good taste in women until now."

"Let's just say she followed me home."

"Yeah, and why?" Violet turned away while Alice and Amy talked about how to treat the wounds. "Like…we *hate* this bitch. And we were all pretty sure she was dead, unless I missed a memo. Why wouldn't she maintain her cover, and more importantly, why show up and turn herself over to us?" I stared at Raven's face, the cut on her forehead from my strike beginning to close itself and stop bleeding.

"I would just like to say…" Krystal raised her hand meekly, standing at the rear of the group. "I am *really* glad this is a surprise to everyone. I figured I had missed something again."

"Nope. This is new." Alice sighed, taking a step back as Amy placed her hands on the top of Raven's shoulders. Amy's eyes closed, a deep breath was drawn through her nose and exhaled through her mouth. As often as I had seen the process for her patients, the fascination of the practice never ceased to amaze me. She started to speak slowly, furrowing her brow and tilting her head.

"Collarbone...smooth and straight. Strong bones. Underneath...very firm muscle. Some strain, she was exhausted. Working my way toward her back, lungs are good. Again, strong. Spine...tired. Sore. Okay, here. Alice...Rhomboid Major, a one inch deep laceration. Penetrating wound cavity under the shoulder. Bullet must have come in from the side of the body armor. Exit wound an inch and a half shy of her T5. Clean channel, clotted. Shouldn't take more than a few hours to heal. I'm going to work my way downward toward her legs." There was a long pause followed by some quiet mumbling, skipping over any unimportant details of the internal exploration.

"What's she doing?" Krystal's cool breath caught me off-guard as she leaned in, trying not to disturb the scene.

"She can feel the electricity of Raven's nervous system. Every nerve ending in her body, like it's a chess board. If there's pieces moved or missing, she knows about it. Apparently, it helps when she talks through it." I whispered back, forgetting she had never witnessed it before. "But she feels the pain, too. Sometimes it's a bit much."

"Wait, so she just *felt* a gunshot wound? That hurts like a mother."

"Yeah, it does." I smirked proudly, nodding. "She used to take day trips to human hospitals and spend hours at a time acclimating herself to the pain. Healing the patient eventually. She learned how to cope with it and work around it. Her own injuries still hurt like everyone else's, but now the ones from other people are...lesser. More distant."

"That's incredible." Krystal smiled, returning to her fascination. "I never thought I'd see abilities in somebody new, let alone something like this. I feel like she's wasting it on Raven, though. Why not just let her die?"

"Because...she knows something that we don't." Amy interrupted herself to answer Krystal.

"You can read their minds, too?" Krystal asked, dumbfounded.

"No." Amy chuckled, rolling her shoulders. "But why else would she be here? She at least knows how she survived Dad's wrath, and that's something I'd like to find out for myself."

"Fair...point." Krystal fell silent as Amy gently released her hold.

"We should take off the shirt and clean off her back. The clotted blood is going to get in the way of a clean heal. Short of that, she's fine. Not much I can do about her throat. It's already too far healed and scarred. In the meantime, I'm starting to get hunger pangs. I'm gonna go take care of that while you guys talk." She glanced at us for confirmation, edging past the crowd to walk into the kitchen.

"Me too, actually." Krystal said abruptly, crossing her arms. "I'll be right back."

"You just had another dose of Factor Five. That should have taken care of any cravings." Alice returned confusedly. Krystal shrugged, turning toward the kitchen and leaving the room.

"She might just need a moment to take all this in." Tony suggested, leaning forward and resting his elbows on his knees. "I know I do."

"I'll get the fireplace going. Keep her body temperature up. Not letting her die before she gets to explain herself." Alice took several steps over to the marble fireplace and picked up one of the wooden logs, holding it for a moment before it began to smoke and glow faintly around its edges.

"How long until she-" A quiet groan answered my question, Raven's eyes opening quickly and roaming around the room in a rapid frenzy. Alice decided that her fire-tending was taking too long, choosing to drop the log into the fireplace and quickly unleash a controlled torrent of fire to kindle the wood. Her task completed, she moved to my side and placed her hands on her hips.

"You're welcome for keeping you alive." She said firmly, staring at our guest. Raven took a moment to breathe, holding up her hands in compliance and sitting upright. She winced as her injury reminded her of a precarious situation, leaning to one side slightly.

"Yeah. Thanks." Raven whispered, shaking her head. She looked down at the pile of clothes, then up at me in confusion. "Why?" She asked, referring to her undressing.

"Because we fixed you. At least for the most part. Couldn't do anything about the brain damage, though. Or the ugly-ass neck tattoos." I kept an even tone, trying not to grow furious at the thought of hosting her so near my family. She ran a hand through the longer portion of her hair, staying silent for a brief time.

"I can assume the first question is why I'm here?" She looked up at me, the former rage and cockiness I had come to know from her face completely hidden from view. She looked almost hopeful, as if we genuinely had saved her life.

"Why and how." Alice clarified.

"Long story short, I know where Jalix and Kara are, *and* how to get them back." I wasn't fazed by her words, knowing full well it was either a lie or came with strings attached.

"Sure you do. How are you alive?" I pressed.

"Amazing how well you can heal when you're the inheritor of the most advanced medical research company known to any species. Jalix…should have finished the job." She smirked, running a hand over her scar tissue.

"Give me five minutes. I'll fix that." I growled, taken aback when I felt Alice's elbow ever-so-slightly find its way into my side. The most subtle of gestures, I understood she wanted me to yield to patience. Raven, having missed the interaction, bowed her head and tapped her foot against the ground.

"I can only assume that will be the end result. I have no misgivings about that." I could hear Amy walk back into the room with Krystal closely in tow. They stood idly next to each other, quietly finishing a private conversation. "But you *need* the information I have."

"We can find them on our own. We don't need you for that." Alice reassured.

"That's only the tip of the iceberg." Her low voice struggled to maintain a steady tone, the rasp of a half-whisper making its way into her voice. "I can help you put everything back the way it was."

"Exaggerate much?" Krystal chimed. Raven laughed, meeting her eyes.

"Hey, sweet pea. Finally awake, huh? Hope you're caught up on what you missed during your nap. Shit's about to hit the fan. Crazy times we live in."

"Live in? Not for much longer." Krystal echoed my earlier sentiment in both ferocity and meaning, once again silenced by a firm set of eyes from Alice. Deciding to take the reins, Alice took a step forward and knelt down.

"Fixing things is *my* job. The cure is my responsibility. How do you have any hope of fixing this when I'm the one that's been working on it with a twenty-year head start?"

"Well, *doctor*...I hate to break it to you, but you're not alone in your endeavor. My people have been working toward the same end goal." Raven cooed.

"Your people? You really don't know when to quit, do you?" Violet scoffed, running her fingers along the piercings in her right ear.

"What's the angle, Raven? We've been over this too many times over too many years." Tony sighed, clasping his hands together. Raven cleared her throat and stood, the entire group tensing before her eyes widened in fear.

"I'm just warming up. Wanted the fireplace." She reassured, stepping to the left of the couch and kneeling down in front of the flames. "There's no angle. I wanted the glory and riches my father promised, but it was too far out of reach. And out of touch. I don't know what motivated him, but it wasn't the same thing that motivated me. I wanted the power. The luxury. When he…when *I* lost everything, it wasn't worth it to continue. Not with the company, not with Project Catalyst, none of it. I hid like a coward and made a living from what I had left. Then, when the world went to shit, I figured I had just enough resources to do something about it."

"And what resources are you talking about?" I pressed, hoping she would continue to be as open in her speaking.

"People, mostly. A bribe here and there got some of the scientists from my company to come back. Not all of them were prisoners, and not all of them died in the labs. You weren't the only one to be saved by the compartments in those buildings, Valterius." She turned her head and smiled at me, the snakelike fangs of pure malice still finding its way onto her face. "That, combined with a theory my father didn't get around to, and some former inhabitants from Aerael made for good progress. But I was missing something. Something vital."

"Common sense?" Krystal quipped.

"Blood." A breathy whisper, her gentle laugh returned to the fire. "The prodigal daughter's blood." We all turned to look at Amy, who stood with the grace of a lioness. I waited for her reply, no one deciding it was necessary that we speak for her. Finally, she tilted her head and took two steps toward the center of the room, looking down at Raven.

"My powers…weren't an accident, were they?" As if driven by a giant wheel, we all watched for Raven's reaction once again. A long silence lingered, and Raven seemed to enjoy how much control she had within the dialogue.

"When we captured Jalix all those years ago, copying his memories was just a bonus. We already tested that machine on so many others, we knew it worked. But the experimental virus we were working on to infect the humans, the one that made him stronger and faster than even my father...the one that ran through his veins when he conceived you...the same one that kept me alive? It was potent. Volatile. It was the reason that Jalix was strong enough to kill my father. The reason he was able to rip through my security the night he tried to kill me. Why Kilkovf left him alive at the cabin. We knew the child of the oldest and youngest of the Vampyres would make something so superior, it couldn't be anything but raw evolution." She paused, chuckling. "I'm surprised no one ever asked why we even bothered kidnapping Jalix. He was useless, otherwise. Too new to know anything and too young to have any interesting mutations in his virus. But he was fresh. And he was the perfect candidate."

"So you...*knew* it would make Jalix stronger, and you did it anyway?" Alice pondered aloud, trying to find a way it fit into her master plan.

"*I* didn't. Neither did Kilkovf, in fact, but my father did. And there was never any changing of his mind. He was too confident and overstepped his bounds, interfering with Project Catalyst. I knew from the moment I met Jalix that he was no one to be trifled with. I warned him repeatedly. But...my father was the epitome of ambition. And he turned Jalix into the ultimate soldier, alongside the ultimate huntress."

"I think we're getting off track here." I interrupted, putting a hand on Amy's shoulder so she would stop pacing. "Why do you need her blood, and what's the real reason you're looking for a cure? Because it's not out of goodwill."

"If I am going to live forever, it will *not* be as a failure." She reproached me, spinning around and standing up. "My father was a controlling, abusive flaw in our evolutionary step. His work went too far. Mine? Brought others back from death. His work only led to it. That won't be my legacy.

Allison, your work is likely more advanced than mine, but my laboratory and technological processes can expedite your research by a year or more. Now you can all stand here and decay like you have, or you can ally yourselves with me and fix what we've done."

"*We?*" Krystal mumbled. As I looked at her, I could see the unfortunate edges of a rolling frost radiating from her forearms. "I think you mean what *you* have done." She gritted her teeth, trying to keep control of herself. Raven, apparently inexperienced in Krystal's volatility, provoked what could only have been described as a growing storm.

"Oh, look at you." She clicked her tongue at Krystal, her tone beyond condescending. "Still failing to see how much damage your interference has caused over the years. How much Kara, Val, and Sonya have given to see this moment."

"They fought against your father. They opposed this longer than anyone."

"And without them, we wouldn't be here, now would we?" Raven smiled again, an apparent permanency of her exposed fangs an unintended side effect of something from her past.

"You need to shut the hell up, Raven. Before I remove the rest of your throat." I took Krystal's aggression as a queue, grabbing her shoulder before sucking in air through my teeth and releasing my grip. The tips of my fingers burned with the bitter sting of frostbite.

"Be my guest, snow cone. You'll regret trying." Raven strode forward, unimpeded by Amy's attempt to stand in her way.

"Bite me, whore." Krystal flashed her fangs, hers nearly half again the size of Raven's. She managed to weasel her way past my body, the only force between the two of them being Alice's finger in Krystal's face and Tony struggling to restrain Raven.

"Krystal, stop. We can't kill her." Violet protested from across the room. Alice had managed to wrap her hands around Krystal's shoulders, an internal warmth enough to prevent injury.

"Raven, sit *down*." Tony commanded, grunting with effort.

"Let me get to the other half of that neck." Krystal growled, her eyes crazed with manic fury and locked on Raven's face.

"Krystal, sit down." Alice reprimanded, beginning to lose her grip.

"Not this time, sis."

"Krystal!" I moved in front of her body, a precaution against breaking free before Tony's grip on Raven released and I spun around to reinforce him. I wrapped my arms under Raven's, pinning her hands behind her back.

"Stop it!" Alice screamed at her sister, no one else able to touch Krystal's body. Alice tried to reassure her grip, a colossal failure as Krystal broke free. I could see the spark of victory in her deep blue eyes as she twisted to the side, lunging forward as I turned to shield Raven from an impending and violent death.

"*Catherine Elizabeth Vicente!*" Preceding the most deafening lack of noise I had ever heard in my entire life, Alice's absolute power of voice shattered all sense of reality, a concussed sensation of numbness bringing my flesh to a crawl. A long moment passed where I questioned my existence, waiting for any kind of reaction from outside of my huddled stance. I stood gradually, looking up in bewilderment to see Krystal only an arm's length away, mid-stride and mouth agape.

Holy shit. She swore she would never use Krystal's full name.

Though she was paler by nature than everyone but Kara, all semblance of color had escaped her face and left a vacant sheet of pure white in its place. I could see her eyes flitting back and forth against the ground, a state of pure shock working its way through her brain. Her muscles slowly released their adrenaline, a slump overtaking her shoulders as her eyes glistened. Alice approached her from behind, leaning over her shoulder and growling into her ear.

"You will sit your ass down on that couch and not move until I tell you to. Understood?" Her lips trembled in anger, a redness in her face nearly matching the waves of hair that framed it.

"Okay." Krystal whispered, turning to sit on the couch and bringing her knees to her chest silently. Even Raven was eerily motionless in my hands, maintaining her defensive position. The only discernible noise in the room was Alice's heavy breathing, the snorting through her nose hissing into a hostile air. Violet's mouth was hanging open, her lips moving multiple times with no sound to accompany it. Amy simply raised her eyebrows, a bewildered stare locked onto the two sisters. I let go of Raven cautiously, my decision warranted as she continued to move away from the crowd in reserved fear. Alice meditated for a moment, clearing her thoughts and kneeling to meet her sister's eyes.

"I need you…to show some restraint."

"Okay." Krystal repeated, the ocean blue of her irises still flicking back and forth between her feet. "Sorry." She whispered, nodding.

"And you…" Alice continued, placing one foot in front of the other and descending upon Raven. "If you ever raise a hand against my sister-"

"No, ma'am." Raven croaked, shaking her head. "I wasn't *actually* going to-"

"And you will continue to avoid doing so. Am I clear?"

"As glass."

"And you…" She turned to me, anger fading from her voice and subsiding to a lethal brand of affection. She leaned in, her lips a fraction of an inch from my own. "Forgot to kiss me when you came back in." She gently pressed her lips against my own for a moment, returned in a hollow gesture of stunned surprise. She smiled gently, winking at me.

"Everyone's getting a glass of wine." She turned and made her way toward the kitchen, the swagger of her hips outlining an image I had greatly missed. "And then…we're going to talk."

***

I stared at the scarlet liquid in my crystal glass, swirling it gently to avoid the exaggerated silence that ricocheted through the room. It was nearly empty, but the desire to cross our social domain to retrieve more liquor was impalpable and enough to force control over the pace of my consumption. I allowed my eyes to drift upward, intentionally drawing a straight line across the room with my vision to watch Violet continue to sit in her designated spot on the floor. She wore the same look that I did, watching the gentle reflection of the fireplace in the surface of her glass. Amy sat directly next to her, one hand on Violet's knee and the other twirling a peculiarly wavy lock of silver hair. Alice tried once more to delicately broach discussion by clearing her throat, which served only to lead back into silence. Tony shifted his seated stance, instead choosing to stagger his left boot in front of his right and continuing to kneel over his legs as if he were going to become sick.

Our foreign guest nursed her glass slowly, wishing inaudibly with each sip that she had never crossed the threshold into Krystal's territory. I could smell the drying blood from her clothes wafting into my nostrils with each slight shift of temperature from the fireplace, replacing the scent of fermented grapes with that of wet earth. Violet lifted her head briefly, glancing at Krystal's unmoving eyes before breaking her gaze to return the gesture, staring back at Violet in a cry for help.

Someone needs to say something.

As if hearing my thoughts, Alice lowered her glass and tilted her head, staring at me in an unmatched look of pointed suggestion.

I am not that person.

"It's good." Violet suggested quietly, tucking a stray lock of hair behind her piercings.

"Mm." I grunted, nodding and pursing my lips.

"Yep." Raven whispered, slowly finishing her glass and setting the goblet on the floor by her feet. She ran a hand over the scars on her neck as if bringing back the physical pain would be enough to deter the discomfort that wracked her ears. One of the logs snapped quietly, punctuating the conversation and summoning another long period of overwhelming quiet. Amy exhaled, the end of a long train of thought in deciding whether to intrude on the discomfort.

The low rumble of a car's engine approached quickly, reverberating from behind the thicket of trees at the end of the long driveway and falling silent as it stopped at the exterior of the house. Our heads all turned, watching the front door with more anticipation than necessary. The crunchy hiss of plastic bags was muffled by the exterior walls, giving us a sign that Sonya would be bringing something with her as she entered the house.

No one stood to get the door, each of us solidified in our unbreakable unity. Decisively, the door handle to the foyer turned and gave way to Sonya's arm, loaded with plastic grocery bags filled with provisions. Her breathing heavier than the rest of ours, she became the focus of our attention, struggling to enter the foyer fully and close the door behind her. As it fell shut, she turned into the room and started to speak, interrupted by her own boundless surprise.

"Hey, I...what the...hell..." She dropped the bags onto the ground, smoothing the wrinkles in her auburn sleeves with a brisk stroke before cocking her head and staring at Raven.

"We…got you a gift." Tony suggested quietly, affirming that her recognition was correct. Sonya stood in stunned astonishment for several seconds, looking at the rest of us for answers. It didn't seem to help that Krystal was suddenly alive and well, staring at her sneakers in perturbed angst while Violet and I acted as though it wasn't a significant development.

"Raven?" She voiced, her lilting tone stained with uneasiness.

"Sonya." Raven returned, clearly anxious. "Don't think we've met in person."

"We-…it…" Sonya took a few steps further into the room, kneeling by my side and allowing her cheek to rest on my shoulder. "What the hell is going on?" She whispered.

"You know what? I don't even know." I shrugged, answering honestly. "But I am already over it." She placed her hand on my arm for a moment, rubbing it gently in a brief sign of consideration. She turned to face the couch, standing in the center of our circle. "Krystal, I'm *so* happy to see you. Just-…I'm a little confused right now."

"So are we." She croaked, nodding slowly. Before the fear of another interminable silence set in again, Violet decided to send the conversation careening toward the elephant in the room.

"*Catherine?*" She clarified, peering at the mess of blue hair and darting eyes.

"Ohhhhhh shit, I have other stuff outsi-"

"Don't you dare, missy." Alice warned, forcing Sonya to take a seat by my side and put an end to the attempted escape.

"Mom's name. Never knew her. Don't like it." Krystal answered swiftly, hoping to end the topic.

"And you've never told me because…?" Violet posed.

"Never came up." She grimaced. "Not important."

"Yeah, but...you're..." Violet paused for a moment, collecting her thoughts. "But *Cathy*?"

"Look, it was my fault. I shouldn't have used her full name. She doesn't like it. I needed to break through to her and that was all I could say at the time. Let's just...drop it and pretend this never happened." Alice decided to mediate her own mistake, averting further conflict. "Sonya, we just found our... *visitor* about an hour ago. We haven't gotten too many answers yet, so you haven't missed much."

"I missed quite a bit, apparently." Sonya grumbled, borrowing from my characteristic cynicism.

"Krystal is alive and well. Brought back to us by Violet and Val, who were interrupted by Raven on the way back here. She followed them, catching up as Alice brought everyone up to speed on our current situation. So now we're just waiting on answers to bring it all together." Amy summarized bluntly, placing the weight directly on Raven's shoulders. Seizing the opportunity to move things forward, she stood up and started pacing.

"Alright, so...do we want your family or the cure first?" Her question was posed to the room rather than any one of us specifically.

"Both." Amy answered, firm but polite.

"I can't-...they're two different subjects. What first?" She sounded exasperated, but mild-mannered.

"Family first." I said sternly, nudging Sonya lightheartedly.

"Alright." Raven took a deep breath, closing her eyes for a moment. Even Krystal was roused by the anticipation, looking up from her shoes for the first time and staring with curiosity. "They're with a group led by someone in D.C. The group is a bit fanatical. They talk a big game, and they'll probably be well-armed, but now's a good time to try and move in on them. Grabbing Kara and Amy was desperate, and they couldn't even manage to get both of their targets."

Raven shook her head and knelt down, reaching for her body armor before grunting quietly in pain. Continuing, she dug through its surface, combing over half a dozen ammunition pouches before withdrawing her cell phone. She played with the display for a moment before handing it to Alice.

"That picture is a map of the area and where some of their guard posts should be located. Text it to your number, and to anyone else that you think needs it." Raven took a step back, scratching the shaven part of her head and rotating her injured shoulder slowly. Alice held up the phone hesitantly.

"Thanks. This goes a long way."

"Yeah. Not all the way, though." I asserted, draping one arm over my knee. "What's all this about a cure? Alice seems to have it covered." Raven's brow furrowed for a moment, looking over at my wife.

"How far?"

"Sequenced. PCR for site-directed mutagenesis on the satellite virion is running now. Trial and error, I say six months to a year."

"Functional samples for testing?"

"Live bodies. Volunteers. I'm not pushing anything out en masse until I'm comfortable with it."

"Dispersion mechanism?"

"Direct injection therapy. Established centers for treatment all over the country." Raven clicked her tongue, shaking her head at the response.

"Won't work." We all stared at her in stunned silence, hardly believing the arrogance against Alice's expertise.

"I'm sorry?" Alice asked, attempting to remain calm.

"It won't work. If you miss a single person, a single child, anyone, it's going to spread worldwide when the gates open. I'm assuming we don't want that, yes?"

"Obviously, Raven. But everyone wants-"

"It's not about what everyone wants. You cannot guarantee to anyone in this room that a hundred percent of the people outside want to go back to being humans. Right? So if one person decides not to show up to your medical pow-wow, then every containment measure put into place so far was a waste. You can't take a chance on people volunteering to line up. You need a forced, widespread mechanism."

"It sounds like you already have one." I interjected.

"Plant pollen." She confirmed. "Tree pollen, actually. Effective across the country and will spread over the borders."

"Yes, that's a great idea. I was going to ask all the leprechauns to do it, but they're busy. Do you have any idea how nonsensical that is? It's literally-…it doesn't even make sense. In *any* regard." Alice's bitter tone was markedly sour.

"It's possible, despite how it sounds. And I'm not going to lie, I don't know all of the science behind making it work. But I have someone who does, and they've worked with me directly for years. You go meet them, and I *guarantee* you won't have any doubts that this could work. Combine his technique and your progress with my lab suites and you can have your cure in weeks. Not a year."

"They're *lying* to you." Alice emphatically insisted. "Or they're deluded. What you're saying is *im-poss-i-ble*." She enunciated.

"Just who is this magical medical expert?" Tony posed.

"Not a medical expert. Someone you need to meet in person. I'm not giving out any more information. For my own sake." I stood slowly, taking a step toward her as she avoided a direct answer.

"We need answers, or we're doing it our way. It's that simple." I demanded. She hesitated, glancing at Alice.

"If you want to fail, Valterius, then be my guest. I'm not disclosing anyone's identity. Especially not someone so close to my line of work." Raven defended.

"Val." Alice mumbled as I grew too close for her comfort. I paused, staring down into Raven's eyes with a fire that rivaled Alice's. "We need her."

"That's to be determined."

"Val." She said sternly, more firm this time. "Don't touch her."

"Why are you so protective of her?" I spun around, clueless as to the source of her empathy. "I see you stick up for her around every turn."

"Because it's not our job to decide who lives and who dies. Not anymore." She paused, looking at Raven. "You're right. We need to start rebuilding, not tearing ourselves down. But my generosity only lasts as long as you're forthcoming with us. One wrong move, and I'll let them handle you however they want." Whether from guilt or shame, Raven combed her fingers through the long, black hair that fell down one side of her body. The delicate structure of her face was set in a somber stare, echoing from her inner thoughts.

"I'm well aware. But if I couldn't find Kara...you were the only ones that could get this all done. It's the only reason I'm here."

"Alright, so let's sum this up." Violet said suddenly, standing and briskly making her way over to Krystal. With no regard for personal space, she sat squarely in Krystal's lap and leaned backward, as if the woman had become her personal sofa. Krystal, finding it humorous, wrapped her arms around Violet and held her as a playful prisoner. "Raven, you're still a bitch. But if you have a way to fix all this, we can be bitches together. That being said, this sounds like the good old days. Half goes with Raven to her secret hideout, and the other half goes to saving mom and dad. Sound cool?" She looked around the room for approval, gaining only a few disapproving glances. Amy chuckled at the joking reference to her own parents as Violet's.

"Vi-" Sonya started.

"She's right." Amy nodded, finishing a braid in her silver hair that no one had noticed she started. "If we're going to make this work, we need to move now. This…" She spread her hands, beckoning to the room. "Family is the best shot the world has. I've heard the stories about you guys and what you've accomplished before my time. Sometimes the same story from different people. And if it doesn't work…at least we tried. It's better than living out a future we could have changed." She put her hands on her hips and looked at Violet. "And yeah, I'd like to save my parents. As much as they can probably help themselves, it's going to be nice for them to have backup."

"Speaking of…" Tony started. "We don't have much in the way of armament. I mean, we can cowboy it like we always have, but I'd like to have an advantage besides surprise. A handful of people taking on a town isn't a good idea. Even for us. What's the deal with D.C.?"

"No idea." Raven shrugged. "The intel I get is what I can scrounge. You guys will have to figure that out on your own."

"Aw come on, Tony. We're badasses, remember?" I joked.

"Yeah, I think my membership card expired a few years ago. Not to mention, we don't have the same level of front-line aggression. Krystal is recovering, Kara and Jalix aren't here, and we have to exercise caution to keep everyone alive. It's not the same old suicide mission."

"Tony's right." Alice warned, exhaling abruptly. "It's not going to be as sexy as it's been in the past. Amy's never been in these situations. Nor has Violet. And I don't want Krystal exposed to gunfire just yet." Krystal shrugged, a slight nod of compliance enough of a sign that she was in agreement.

"Then we have my lab group." Raven quipped, shrugging. We all paused at the realization, seeing the honesty in her statement. "Alice, I'll need you, too. But the four of you plus myself are going to be a good combination for handling the more complex side of things. No offense." She looked over at me, fearing I would retaliate for the mild insult.

"None taken. She's the doc."

"Yeah, and so is Amy. Krystal needs to be kept in good health, so I get the two of them being near her, but why wouldn't I be suitable to the rescue? I can handle it." Violet started griping, very obviously taken aback at the limited options presented to her.

"Because *you're* part of my good health, too." Krystal mumbled, tucking her chin in the crook of Violet's neck. Vi smiled gently, returning the sign of affection with a gentle kiss on the forehead.

"Fine. I'm super important, I guess. Can you three handle the rescue?" She looked at Sonya, waiting for a response.

"Yeah, definitely. Val and Tony are good partners. Once we get to Jalix and Kara, it'll be an even fight. Besides, it might be better to go in with a smaller crew. Less intimidating. We might even be able to talk our way in and work from the inside out. What do you think?" Sonya looked over at me, nudging my knee. I nodded approvingly, matching Tony's reaction.

"We're still short on guns. Armor. Food. Water. Medicine. We won't know how long it's going to take. Could be separated for a while." Tony mumbled, groaning and leaning back in deep thought.

"I can cook up another batch of medicine as long as-" Alice was interrupted by Sonya, who pointed outside.

"It's in the car. I grabbed everything from the old Raven building that you asked for."

"Cool. So yeah, I can make us enough injections to last two, three weeks apiece. If we're still separated by then, you might have to hit up a nearby town and buy more. I can't help with the rest of our supplies. I'm a doctor, not a factory."

"I...might be able to help with the rest of it." I looked up to see Krystal staring at me and gently pushing Violet off her lap. "Val, remember our shooting matches?"

That feels like it was a lifetime ago. Actually, it was. For both of us.

"You still have everything?" I asked in bewilderment.

"Most of the freeze-dried food is going to be expired, but we might be able to salvage the rest. At least the guns and ammo. Maybe some extra goodies." She smirked, looking over at her confused sister. "Alice, you remember when I'd go on rotations with Val? So he could help keep an eye on my mental health?" I could see the gears of thought turning behind her eyes.

"Yep. Distinctly."

"They were more like...vacations. Sometimes." I added.

"Actually, it's better if we just show you." Krystal sighed, pushing off of the couch and making her way past the set of stairs leading to the second floor. I followed out of excitement, curious as to what was left of the good times we had. I could hear the room follow me, a chorus of footsteps echoing as we made our way into the garage.

Krystal opened the door to reveal a meticulously maintained workshop with several immaculate cars showcased across its floor. Although it could have fit a half-dozen vehicles, only four took up the space with a roomy distance between each of them. The aggressive geometry and streamlined designs of two vehicles were partially covered by tight-fitting beige dust covers, leaving two highly customized sky-blue machines in excess of a thousand horsepower exposed in perfect condition.

"Krystal. Have you been keeping secrets from me?" Violet warned sternly. Krystal stopped at one of her workbenches, gripping the edge and sliding it several feet across the floor.

After a few moments of loud screeching from the metal legs of the table, she dropped it and drew a breath.

"Yep. You'll forgive me." She grunted, stopping as a white trapdoor was exposed, seamlessly pressed into the polished epoxy floor. She grasped the handle and pulled, revealing a clean and faintly-lit passageway at the bottom of a short set of stairs.

She led the way for the rest of the group, Alice beginning to grow nearer as I kept close behind our host. The hallway, shorter than I had remembered, stretched about ten feet from the bottom of the stairs and ended in a vault-style metal barrier.

"No comment?" Krystal asked, turning to face her sister.

"The supervillain shit? This is…very much like you. I'm not even a little surprised." Alice shrugged, smirking.

"Oh…wait for it." Krystal replied, winking at me and pushing open the heavy metal door. Krystal stepped to the side, beckoning to allow Amy, Violet, Raven, and Tony inside before the rest of us. Amy's feet stopped quickly after the first step, only moving as Violet nudged her further in order to look around. Alice glanced at me inquisitively before following them inside, stopping in the same way the rest of them had.

"Oh."

"Jesus Christ, Krystal-"

"My."

"How and why do you have-"

"God."

"-could have warned us, at least-"

"Why."

"And I thought I had psychological issues-"

Krystal and I stood outside for a moment, exchanging satisfied smiles before wandering into the vault unapologetically. Each of our friends stared at a different wall, the anodized black of forged steel rods outlining the recessed lighting that illuminated the rest of the room. Each cage held its own system of hangers and fixtures, carefully allowing firearms to rest peacefully against their chosen walls. Without remorse, the large room echoed a sense of peace, filling the space with diplomatic aggression and the gentle smell of charcoal and phosphorous. For the sake of memory, I looked to the immediate left of the door, basking in the sight of my old rifle: still perfectly oiled and free of any imperfection.

"I'm a collector." Krystal quipped quietly, looking around at her collection. "Val and I used to shoot competitively during our rotations. Target practice, and something to pass the time. Every country we visited, I brought home souvenirs."

"You brought enough home to outfit an army." Alice remarked.

"Two. And part of a navy." Tony mumbled, curling his fingers around the wire of a cage. Violet stood, transfixed by a pair of smaller machine guns before whirling around.

"And you kept this from me? We could have had so much fun." She whispered.

"Still can." Krystal smirked. "It looks more impressive than it really is. Some of these are obviously just for show-"

"Yeah, is that one-"

"Gold-plated. Twenty-four karat. Friend of a friend brought it back from an infamous Iraqi palace." Krystal interrupted Raven's somewhat rhetorical question.

"I am...*so* turned on right now." Sonya whispered, leaning against one of the cages with her eyes closed. Krystal laughed, sliding past her and throwing open the door.

"Help yourselves. Ammo should be in the boxes on the floor. I don't have anything tactical to carry it all in, so we'll have to improvise."

"You're okay with arming *her*?" Amy asked gently, looking at me directly in spite of the question regarding Raven.

Everyone stopped moving long enough for silence to overtake the room, Amy's eyes flaming with convicted intent as they looked into my own.

"We're gonna have to be." I said quietly. Raven tilted her head, looking at Violet.

"I've never tried to kill any of you. Nor have I sent anyone to do so. I was a scavenger in collecting the Valencia siblings' remains. I didn't pull the trigger."

"Because Kilkovf beat you to it, on *your* orders." Violet seethed, moving to stand next to Amy. "Is this really a good idea? I don't want desperation to lead to bad decisions."

"She's right though, Violet." Alice defended. "She's not innocent. But Schillinger was the real monster. So was Kilkovf. And they're both long dead. We'd make a lot of mistakes judging people by who their fathers are. We need to let it go, or we're going to be fighting in two directions." She looked at me again, clearly trying to get her message across. I opened the cage containing my prized trophy, gently pulling back the bolt to peer into the chamber of the rifle.

"I'll leave it in the past, but I'm keeping my eyes open for the foreseeable future." I concluded, relaxing my shoulders and approaching Raven. "Which is a big deal considering the kind of people I'll be trusting you with."

"I know. They'll be in good hands." She conceded.

"If not, we'll rip her to pieces and feed her to her own kind." Violet said cheerily, holding a large duffel bag and disappearing through the way we came. Raven unexpectedly decided to follow her, taking nothing from the room and hastily walking away. I could faintly hear the rasp of her voice say something to Violet as she caught up, fading as they made their way back into the main parts of the house.

"Maybe I'm not experienced enough to judge the situation properly…" Amy started. "But I feel like you still have a lot of hate in that head of yours. And you're looking for the people to blame. The problem is…they might all be dead,

Val." The impossibly blue silver of her eyes sparkled in the lighting of the room, glimmering with a truth I didn't want to hear. With little regard to personal choice, she plucked a smaller handgun from one of the shelves and made her way out of the room, leaving behind a flawless aura of her mother in her cold and logical truth.

"Okay, and now that the kids are gone..." Sonya remarked, sighing and gesturing to Tony. "Am I required to say something, too?" Tony studied me for a moment.

"Eh. He's had enough for today. We'll have plenty of time on the road trip." They both nodded to one another and left the room with a shared bag of armament.

"Am I a bad guy here, Ally?" I asked in desperation, hoping for an answer that wasn't filled with sentiment or cryptic messages.

"No, Val. And don't change anything." Her statement came across as a warning, her eyes darting toward the door to ensure we were truly alone.

"Sorry, what?"

"She doesn't deserve judgment for someone else's crimes, but that doesn't mean I trust her." Alice kept her voice low, enough that I knew that I was the only one she wanted hearing her sentiments. "I'll be keeping an eye on her, too. I trust her to do her job, I'll say that much. But I'm not sure what's going to happen once this is all fulfilled. Until something changes...we need to show her the same respect we need from each other. So no more death threats. Okay?"

"I can do that." I shrugged, her hands lifting from my shoulders as she rested them on me in a light hug. She touched her forehead to mine, breathing deeply for a moment.

"I missed us so much, Val. Don't think otherwise for a second."

"I know." I wrapped my fingers around her hips, rocking slowly. "I did, too. I'd trade anything to get the last twenty years of our lives back, Ally."

"Then trade the next little while. For us. For peace."

"That's a tall order." I mumbled, kissing her perfect lips in sign of a silent promise.

"Wait, Krys-" We pulled away from each other, staring at the door as a faint voice rattled down the stairs and into the hall. "Alice!" It became apparent that the voice was Sonya's, now calling for help. I let Alice take the lead as she sprinted back into the main part of the house, whirling around each corner until we had returned to the foyer. Krystal's body was pressed into the side of the couch by Raven and Sonya's combined efforts, maintaining a steady posture as she shook violently and whimpered loudly. I gritted my teeth, understanding that there was nothing I could do but wait. Alice knelt down, taking over for Sonya by maintaining her sister's shoulders and neck.

"She's okay." Alice grunted, locking her elbows in place to prevent Krystal's neck from tossing around. "Hopefully this is the last one. Amy, anything you can do?" Amy stepped forward at the request, lifting Krystal's shirt enough to slide her hands underneath. With her palms resting lightly on Krystal's stomach, she closed her eyes and sighed, rolling her head and shuddering briefly.

"Never...grabbed someone...with a seizure before." She coughed, shaking her head and struggling to maintain control. Krystal's spine attempted to arch again, lesser in severity than the previous movement before relaxing and falling still. Amy and Krystal breathed synchronously for a minute before Amy stood up and opened her eyes.

"Eh, she'll be asleep for a little bit. But she's as comfortable as she can get for now. I can't fully stop the seizures, but I can suppress her nervous system for a bit so they calm down. Nothing I can do about healing a brain."

"Thank you, Amy." Alice's appreciation was noted as she nodded to Raven, helping lift Krystal onto the couch to rest quietly.

"No need. She deserves whatever comfort we can bring right now. I can't imagine what she's going through. To be that strong, that...resilient? I wish I had a tenth of the strength that she has. There's...something special in her. Unique. I can't quite place it." I agreed quietly, grunting an affirmative hum before placing a hand on Amy's back.

"You guys will get a chance to bond. I think you'll like each other. Especially now that she's more stable. Emotionally."

"I don't know if I'd go that far." Amy cautioned, sitting next to Krystal and running a hand over her leg. "I could feel...stress. Something emotionally significant, anyway. There's a lot going on in there. And she's hiding most of it. She's going to need a lot of support, physically and otherwise. I'll see what I can do when she's awake. I'll try and stick by her side, do what I can medically."

"Speaking of..." Alice started, looking at Raven to garner her attention. "Is this lab really as good as you say it is?"

"Yes. And I'll make sure she gets priority everything."

"Then we need to go." My wife affirmed, hugging me tightly again. "The longer we wait, the more time we waste. The sooner I can get her to a stable facility, the better."

"You don't think we're rushing things a bit?" Sonya asked.

"Not much of a point in waiting." Tony sided with Alice on the argument. "We're as screwed as we're going to get. I don't think we're getting any luckier than we already have. Raven's right, we need to push while we have our bearings."

"It's settled, then. We'll move as soon as she wakes up. You guys are taking Val's truck, I'm assuming?" Violet asked, picking up her duffel bag from the floor.

"We might as well. She's got a couple bullet holes now, but there's only three of us-"

"Shotgun." Sonya interrupted.

"-so you guys may as well take what you can. Tony's van is a safe bet. Plenty of space in there for the generator and the research instruments. Plus it'll draw less attention than taking one of Krystal's Italian pieces of garbage." I got several confused looks, inciting an explanation. "I am an American-made man. I don't do imports."

"You're holding a gun made in Germany." Tony retorted.

"I...did not ask for your opinion." I concluded, displaying the measure in which I cared via the length of my middle finger.

"So...Tony, Val, and Sonya in the truck. Alice can drive Tony's van along with..." Amy started to clarify the arrangement before it dawned on all of us that someone would be in a confined space with Raven. She sighed loudly, much like Violet would have many years ago, and sulkily picked up her body armor.

"I'm driving." Alice stated plainly.

"Does the back of the van have seats?" Raven asked, hoping for some semblance of comfort.

"No, you'll ride in the front with me. I'll need directions, and if I'm trusting you enough to take us to a secret super-villain lab, I might as well trust you enough not to kill me on the way there." Alice's skepticism was apparent, although the minor symbol of trust was enough to incite a gratified nod from Raven herself. "Alright, kids. Looks like you're in the back." Alice looked at the youngest two, hardly children by anyone's standards.

"Great. Just what everyone wants. An hours-long road trip in the back of a van with a nerd and an unconscious woman." Violet smirked at Amy, the two of them chuckling as they started to gather their belongings. "I won't have *any* good conversations."

"You...have fun dealing with that." I hugged Alice again, moving to pull away before I realized she was holding onto me.

"I love you." She whispered. "Don't do anything stupid."

"Come on, it's *me* we're talking about." I reassured.

"You're right. Limit the stupidity to ten items or less. I'm going to have Sonya count them." I looked over to see Amy combing over Krystal's body for injuries, despite having inspected her only moments prior. She was talking about something quietly to Violet while the rest of the crew were gathering their belongings.

"Your sister will be in good hands, Ally. Amy already seems to have taken a shine to her. I know she's going to heal up in no time."

"Yeah. I agree." She pulled away, looking behind her. "I'm looking forward to reconnecting. It'll be like getting to know her all over again. Minus the...stuff we went through with Sonya. We really lucked out, Val."

"Then let's make sure she has a world to go back to." I smiled, kissing her on the forehead and approaching Tony and Sonya's conversation. They continued to chatter about something minor before pausing and allowing me to impose a question. "What do you guys need before we head out?" They paused, looking at me and requesting the same thing.

"Snacks."

"Food."

"Whatever is in Krystal's kitchen is all we're going to get. So...go grab some ramen and beef jerky." I chuckled, pointing toward the kitchen. As they left, Violet turned away from Krystal and approached me rapidly, wrapping her arms around me.

"Stay safe. Alright? And call my phone whenever you get them out of there. Alice might be occupied."

"Will do." I smirked.

"And…be careful. Jalix and Kara are essentially my parents at this point. If anything happens to them-"

"I know. It's my sister and my brother-in-law. They have the best of the best going in to help. I promise I'll be back in no time. With everyone intact."

"Yeah. Because intact…" She glanced over at Krystal. "Is getting harder to come by."

"Hey." I put a hand under her chin, which she held with her own fingers. "We can do this. Last push. Take a deep breath and get through it, just like you always have." In a show of faith, she closed her eyes, a volume of air leaving her lungs in a sigh before she nodded and turned away, trotting into another room with Amy.

"Come on, let's go pack." Sonya suggested to Alice and Tony, the three of them following the youngest guests out of the room. Raven was staring at Krystal's slow breathing and uneasy facial expression, a subtle nightmare within her uneasy sleep. She was only an arm's length away, and I could feel a nervous heat radiating from her body.

"I'll get them there as quickly as I can. And after we-" She started explaining something, lost in a drowned sea of white noise that rung in my ears. I looked toward the guest rooms, listening to how far away the rest of the family was. Deciding that I had adequate privacy, I threw the entirety of my body weight into my left shoulder, cupping Raven's neck with an open palm and lifting her gracefully off the ground. It was a form of art to watch the pain and fear in her eyes as her legs kicked, her hands clawing at my own to fight my hold on her throat. I tightened my grip, making no effort to ease the pain or force behind my gesture.

"I will *kill* you, Raven. Do you understand that?" She couldn't acknowledge me, the fight against my strength taking her full attention. "And I don't mean a bullet through your skull. I'll tear open your stomach and leave you to stray animals. I'll cut every square inch of skin off your body and cauterize it with a car battery. I don't care about you…your life…your goals." Her face blossomed into a caramel-infused plum color, her effort to fight me fading into a messy thrashing. "You tried to kill me. My sister. My friends. Tried to use my niece as an experiment. I'm done with you. I'm sick of knowing that you're alive. So trust me…you step one foot out of line, you do anything other than kiss the ground my family walks on, and I will rip every bone from your body while you're conscious." I didn't ask for confirmation, dropping her suddenly onto the ground and letting her cough for a few moments.

"Everything okay?" Alice called.

"Raven needs to lay off the smoking. Her throat's a mess." My lighthearted tone threw Alice off the scent.

"Ah." She replied distantly, understanding that I was referencing the old damage to her neck. Raven's legs were curled into her body as she laid on her side, her teeth gritted as her watery eyes stared up at me in fear.

"Why?" She whispered, clearing her throat and coughing again.

"Because I hate you." I knelt down, taking great satisfaction in watching her recoil and slide backward several feet. "I hate everything about you. Where you came from, who you are…everything."

"You don't really know who I am. Where I came from." She shook her head, her teeth bared at me in anger. "If you had *any* idea-"

"I know everything I need to."

"No…you don't, Valterius." She whispered, something strange driving the anger away from her gaze. "I promise you, you have no idea."

What is she talking about? What else is she hiding?

I heard footsteps approaching the foyer, prompting a quick hoist of Raven's body into an upright stance for the sake of appearance.

"Val, aren't you packing?" Sonya asked, dropping a duffel bag next to the couch.

"All my stuff was in the city. Just needed my old rifle. I'm good to go whenever you guys are."

"Well, that's right now." Tony added, strolling into the room with a bag settled between his shoulder blades. "Let's go get our family back. And meet whoever had the balls to kidnap them."

ENCOUNTER

SONYA

I could see Val squirming uncomfortably out of the corner of my eye, shifting positions to get a better look out the window and avoid the discomfort of our impending situation. I felt much the same way, my abdomen a mixture of sensations and ready to escape into oblivion at the slightest disturbance. Val wiped his forehead, a bead of cold sweat dripping down his brow as we accelerated down the highway at an increasing pace to arrive as quickly as we could. I could hear his breathing, once steady and quiet, escalate to a discomforted, shallow pace. Tony leaned forward, ready to say something before retreating to his normal posture in the backseat in a far more comfortable situation than Val and I.

"I'm sorry, but-" Val started.

"No, I understand. Trust me. We have to."

"We just can't keep pushing this off." He returned, anxious but grateful.

"I know, Val. I'm stopping." We both sighed heavily as I started on the brakes, giving reassurance to the sedan in front of us that we weren't intending to catch him. I continued to apply gradual pressure to the brake pedal, finally turning the wheel slightly and dropping the car onto the shoulder of the road near a patch of evergreen forest, the border of which faded from the highway into a small mountain. The moment the car stopped, Val leapt out of the car and began to walk hastily toward the tree line, retreating just far enough that we couldn't see him any longer.

"He gonna be okay?" Tony inquired.

"Yeah, we both will. As long as he's fast." I unbuckled my seatbelt, ready to run in the same direction. Unpleasant seconds passed which developed into two or three agonizing minutes before I saw his face emerge between two large ferns. I jumped out of the car, waiting for his direction.

"About thirty feet that way." He pointed to his right, back into the tree line and hopefully toward the small clearing he promised to search for.

I slammed the door shut, nodding to Tony and withdrawing my pistol from the holster that sat near my appendix. Half-jogging, I managed to push through enough firs and pines until I spotted the clearing, roughly six feet in diameter and adjacent to a shallow ditch. A log, recently shifted by Val, was placed parallel to the ditch and marked by a path of scuffed dirt from where he dragged it. Sighing with happiness, I placed my pistol and its holster, as well as a pack of tissues, on the log before unzipping my jeans and lowering myself to the ground as close as I was able. Six hours' worth of energy drinks, water, and electrolyte supplements were hastily forced away from the agonizing discomfort in my lower abdomen, inciting yet another and much more pronounced sigh of true relief. My bladder thanked me silently as I finished my task and replaced the holster and its charge into my belt once again. Val could see me emerge from the forest boundary as he looked over his shoulder while leaning against the side of his truck.

"You good?" He called quietly.

"Oh, yeah. If I have to do that again-"

"That's what you guys *get* for chugging energy drinks!" Tony called out his window.

"My bladder...cannot take that kind of assault again." Val whispered, chuckling as I approached.

"Trust me, dude. Same way. Wish more gas stations were open on this stretch." I looked over my shoulder as I spoke, watching several more cars than would normally be on roads back in Boston travel down the highway toward the general vicinity of our destination.

"Back on the road?" His tone was positive despite us heading toward what was likely a fight.

"Yep. Only a few minutes left if Raven gave us the right information." He scoffed, rolling his eyes and climbing back into the passenger seat. I moved from his side and slid behind the wheel.

"Fat chance she's trying to work with us." He continued.

"I know what you're saying, but...how and why would she lie to us? She saved you and Violet-"

"She kept us alive. That doesn't mean she *saved* us. And that's not a point of pride, but who the hell knows what she wants to do with us? Any of us. I know you're still fuzzy on your history-"

"Hey." I snapped, upset at him for thinking I was less than what I was. "I've read and heard everything. The full story. And probably some details that you don't even remember or know about. Don't talk to me like-"

"I'm *not*, Sonya, I'm just saying-"

"You're just saying I'm not going to be as biased as the rest of you. You're *just saying* that I don't harbor the same hatred toward her. And you're right. But I dislike her and I know what she's about. Don't presume that my lack of memory means a lack of understanding."

"That's not what he meant, Sonya." Tony said reluctantly, choosing to insert himself into the dispute.

"It is, whether he regrets it or not. May have been a poor choice of words, but those words meant exactly what he was trying to say." Val licked his lips, biting the lower one for a moment and running his hand through his beard.

"Sorry. I'm…I feel like there're two of you and I'm trying to get over that. Your personality is…well, you're awesome. Always have been. You're one of my closest friends, and outside of this…conflict, I don't see you any differently. But those experiences…they change things, and sometimes I have to see you differently than before. Not even in a bad way, but-"

"Then treat me like Jalix." He stopped, completely confounded by the simplicity of my statement. "Treat me like I'm new to the war, but proven. Which is basically the case, right? And you trust Jalix like he's your second wife."

"Okay, that's-" We both paused as a short laugh escaped from Tony's mouth, quickly suppressed and replaced by a tight-lipped grin. Val decided to continue, laughing. "Whatever. You guys suck."

"Do we? So between you and Jalix, which one does the sucking in the relationship?" Tony quipped again, justifying my massive grin and the firm slap of a high-five.

"Tony, why do you *only* seem to have a personality when Sonya's around?"

"She's fun."

"Yeah, dude. Having tits just brings life to the party. Ask Krystal."

"Yeah, she's been a blast the past few years. Really did a great job at Halloween as a corpse." The car got silent immediately, much to the discomfort of its passengers at how quickly the fun became sour. There was a long pause, a silence excepting the sound of the engine and small bumps in the road.

"We all got hit hard, Val." I softened my tone, returning from buddy-mode to supportive friend.

"I know. Sorry. I just-...I watched over her for so long..." His voice was low and somber, all three of us remembering the near-dead stasis she remained in for months before reviving to a normal, comatose state. "My wife was thinning away to nothing, slaving over her. Kara was a mess, believing it was her fault. And I just-....I got stuck in the middle. Me and Vi." I let him get out his emotions without interrupting, Tony aware enough to do the same. "And we made it. She came out like she was a new person. Ruined immediately by my own paranoia." Not knowing what he meant, I decided to offer some semblance of comfort.

"You've done more in your lifetime than almost anyone alive right now. I was out of play and had a hard reset just like her. Well, not exactly, but you know what I mean. Alice got trapped in her work, Violet shut down, and the rest of us just...waited. You, your sister, and Jalix kept us all alive. You kept a society, a nation, together. Hell, *you* were the one we picked to be a politician and liaison to the U.S. government. You saved us from extinction. Take some pride in that and let it make up for the same missteps we all take in our lives."

"Val..." Tony drew a deep breath, drawing on both my tone and my passion for our friend. "I've got your back. Always have. But you do have to stop berating yourself for shit you can't change."

"This has officially become an intervention, apparently." Val chuckled, looking over at me. "I'm fine, alright? I just...I have to fix this."

"Nope. *We* have to fix this, Val. You absolutely, positively, cannot fix anything on this scale single-handedly. Neither can your wife, or Kara, or anyone else."

"Damn, I miss Jared. You guys remind me so much of his advice." Again, there was a silent groan exchanged between Tony and I as Val subverted the positivity once more. "Why, of all the times we've brought people back to life somehow, including *Raven*, couldn't we have done something for him? Why did he have to be the one to go?"

"We lost a lot of people over the years. We can't forget that. The family murdered when Kilkovf took them hostage. The people hurt when Aerael was evacuated. And everyone wiped out by the virus. Look, we-..." I chose my words carefully, trying to focus on the road as we neared the mark of being two miles away. "We've all lost people. Tony knows, he knew Jared almost as well as *you* did, and Jalix, even for a short time, lost Kara."

"No, we *all* lost Kara." He stated firmly, avoiding anger. "We all lost her, Sonya. And with her, our hope. The same as what happened with you."

"And with you, we put our hope in to continue on. Even once she was back. My only point, if I have one, is to please see that. And let it...guide you." He exhaled quickly, looking over at me in some form of disbelief. "What?" I asked, almost offended.

"No, it-...Jared prayed for us. In the city, before Kara left for Afghanistan. And he said something I can't remember, but it was about guidance. About letting your faith fall into those you care about instead of yourself. It just...what you said reminded me of that. I think about it all the time, and-"

"Find it hard to stick?" Tony asked, his voice increasing in strength. "My brother *left* us because he put his faith in himself too heavily. He gave up on us because of the shit we put him through and he took it on his own shoulders. You can't live like that, man. It breaks people. Lean on us. We can handle it, alright? Take the-...damn advice you gave your sister all those years ago. Before you become what she almost was." Tony rubbed a hand across his forehead, his mouth tensed in controlled emotion.

"Yeah. I'll do my best. Thanks." Val put his hand on mine briefly, a silent gesture of thanks before returning to a relaxed posture in his seat. The sarcasm dripping into every motion, Tony slowly moved his hand from the back seat onto the center console, clearing his throat loudly and nudging Val.

"Man's gotta get some affection too. Hold my hand, come on." The three of us laughed harder than we should have, the tears in my eyes making the road in front of me a blurred set of white and yellow lines. I wiped them away, grinning and starting to say something before our truck lurched, a grinding noise from the front-left side preceding a repetitive thump.

"We get a flat?" Val asked, peering to look out my window.

"Yeah, but there was nothing on the road that-" A second pop, more pronounced, took out the right-side tire as I struggled to slow the truck and keep it moving in a somewhat straight line.

"Someone's shooting out our tires." Val confirmed, looking ahead as we rounded a turn and saw a blockade of concrete barriers and orange traffic cones blocking the way into a region of downtown D.C. Still fighting the steering wheel, I caught a glimpse of the roadblock, a sentry tower set up on either side using small construction lifts and manned by two individuals with sleek, long-barreled rifles coated in a matte black protective coating.

"These guys are pros. Play it straight and don't bullshit anyone." Val almost sounded intimidated, which was nothing like his earlier sentiment of the scenario being a strong possibility upon our arrival.

"Val, what-"

"They're reminiscent of the original Pyrates. Once they started modernizing. Look at the military-style structure. Scouts, snipers, lookouts, entry control points. We have an old enemy coming back to haunt us." He spoke with conviction and metered hatred, keeping control over his feelings enough to instill a sense of discipline and courage.

I slowed the truck to a stop without altering course, ensuring the outlaws knew that we were as compliant as possible. Before the vehicle was immobile, there was already a team securing a perimeter around the front bumper, ensuring our escape on foot would be rendered an impossible feat. A woman approached us, matching the description Alice gave of the individual that had ventured to Krystal's mansion. Her hair was scattered slightly in the wind, a bleached platinum blonde indicating she held standard of appearance in high regard. I rolled down the window, stretching my fingers across the steering wheel to indicate a lack of hostility.

"Where are you coming from?" She demanded, confused as to the absence of any expected fear.

"Virginia. Fuel run up to Boston. Wanted to stop in D.C. on the way for food and medical supplies. Why'd you shoot out my tires?" My answer was short and direct.

"Boston? Why not New York? They have resources from the northern oil lines." Her retort implied an ardent hostility, and her refusal to answer my question led to a brief and uneasy silence.

"We have friends here. And it was time we paid them a visit." I implied heavily that we were here purposefully, hope in my heart that we would be taken directly to Jalix and Kara. The woman studied me carefully, looking at Val and Tony briefly while paying them little attention in the end. I knew Val well enough that he was making calculations based on the guards at our front. His look was similar to what I had seen in Kara previously when engaging in deep, contemplative thought. Tony's eyes were similar in movement, instead looking at the urban landscape that stretched into complex roadways and buildings a distance in front of us.

"We've been waiting for you three. Our leader said to expect you. Never thought you'd all be stupid enough to use the front door. Where's the child?"

"Child?" I responded in question. "We don't have any children in our group."

"Amelia. The prodigal daughter. Empress to Vampyres and humans alike." The woman spoke as if she were a thirteenth-century throne-keeper rather than a person like the rest of us.

"She's not a child by any means. She may be *Kara's* child, but she's an adult. And she's not here."

"We'll figure out where she is." The woman smirked, snapping her fingers and allowing the guards to quickly descend on our vehicle. A rush of shouted commands sent the air into a flurry as some of them opened the doors while others maintained their positions in aiming their weapons directly at us. Rough hands grabbed me and removed me from the vehicle, aided by my own willingness before I was shoved to the ground and searched thoroughly. I could feel my holster and handgun removed from my belt, a pocketknife also confiscated as they apparently left the small case of syringes in my pocket in knowing they were medicine.

"You guys good?" I could hear Val's voice, muffled by his face being pressed into asphalt, casually call out to us.

"Yeah. Weather's holding out." My arms were dragged behind my back, three sets of cold steel handcuffs locked onto my wrists. "Don't have to pee again, thankfully. Tony?"

"I'm fine. Just...hanging out, I guess." We were all on opposite sides of the truck, our voices an unamusing conversation to our captors. I was pulled to my feet, realizing that over the leather of my boots, I couldn't feel that shackles had been clasped onto my ankles. Walked to the front of our disabled truck, Tony was bound the same way while Val had an additional set of handcuffs and zip-ties securing the entire length of his arms.

"Get out of *that* one, strongman." I nodded in his direction.

"Guess they think I'm tough. It's cute. Nice compliment."

"Shut up!" One of the guards lost his temper and pulled down his face mask. He reproached me and stood inches in front of my face. "Do you have any idea who we are? Who our leader is? How powerful we are?" His eyes moved frantically, as if he was fueled by primal rage and too much caffeine.

Please don't let anyone be dragged back into life. We've had enough resurrections for a century.

"No, I don't." I replied curtly. "Enlighten us." Val grunted quietly as I watched the veins in his arms swell and bulge, a brief set of popping noises preceding every piece of equipment that bound his arms and hands falling to the ground. He immediately put his hands up and smirked.

"All I was trying to prove is that there's no point in restraining us. We're gonna break out. But if you want to take us someplace, we'll go. We want information as much as you do, and I guarantee we can work out a trade." He spoke with intense confidence, hardly bothered that Tony and I were no longer under the guard of multiple weapons or that there were a dozen potential bullets that could have ripped through him at a moment's notice. The woman, previously speaking with someone at the makeshift gate, turned around and appeared at that point to finally notice the chaos. She sauntered over, standing uncomfortably close to Val.

"Will you behave?" She asked tauntingly.

"No. But I won't hurt anyone. I'm a pacifist, you know." Val shrugged, maintaining the most sarcastic form of innocence he could imagine.

"Those two stay cuffed. You can walk freely, Mr. Ambassador."

Are you seriously flirting with him right now?

I gently rotated my hands in a circle, letting my fingers caress over every inch of steel and chain that made out the detail of my bindings. I imagined the metal as glass, fragile to the touch and ready to shatter if handled improperly. And with a single thought of a thousand broken pieces of steel, Tony's handcuffs fell into fractured metallic fragments and crumbled to the ground.

"Val isn't the only one strong enough to break free." I offered in retort, simultaneously hinting to Tony that my abilities should be kept a secret. Val understood that I was offering myself as the weakling, and the bait was taken by our captors' confident leader.

"And what about yourself, darling? I think you forgot about your own situation." I let my face relax, pretending to fall into angst as I gently pretended to struggle against the cuffs. Val caught onto the act, taking half a step toward me and cementing the thought in their minds that I needed help. He was obviously stopped at half a dozen shouting men, but the woman made the decision to buy into my deception.

"Good. I'll take *you* directly to him."

I swear to God, if Schillinger or Kilkovf are alive somehow, I'm gonna lose my shit.

"Sonya!" While Val was staring down a guard, Tony was watching for my well-being and called out far too late to act. I was unfortunately too preoccupied with the conversation to hear the quiet step of a guard move behind me and insert the full length of a needle directly into the back of my neck.

***

While I couldn't remember the specifics of recovering from anesthesia during my near-fatal injury, a vaguely familiar feeling saturated my limbs and mouth as I started to gain consciousness. It felt like my whole body was still asleep, each endeavor to move one of my limbs a great effort and an unknown result as I could hardly feel them shift against a hard floor.

"Propofol." An enticingly low voice struck out against my ears, helping to sharpen my senses enough to clarify the mystifying blur of shapes my eyes were making out. "It's an anesthetic. Normally takes about two minutes to kick in. Vampyre biology lets it work faster at the cost of a shorter half-life. But that's good. I wanted you awake." I slapped my hands against what felt like marble, shaking my head and realizing that it was, in fact, a smooth white tile made of stone.

"Come now, Sonya...I don't have all day." The voice urged again. Despite the sense of coercion in his words, he sounded subdued enough to warrant no immediate threat of danger.

The drugs started to wear off more quickly, my senses returning smoothly like the last few seconds of a sunrise. I was able to stand on my own and look around, images now clear enough to make out. A rich set of walls were supported by chiseled, cream-colored framing and delicately gripped a set of paintings from presidents long dead. As I became less disoriented, I started to realize there were no corners in the room, and a man sat at the most iconic desk the world had known. My assumed captor was mostly bald, suiting a round but masculine face with more than a few subtle signs of graceful age. His eyes pierced my own as he stared, tilting his head slightly in an obvious interest.

"Welcome to the White House." He stated simply, void of any dramatic indication or body language.

"Mmm." I tested my vocal cords more than trying to speak, believing I was capable of doing so.

"I'm sure you have questions-"

"Yep." I mumbled, nodding to the best of my ability. "Lots. Who're you?" I gestured roughly at his position. He smirked, looking behind me at what I realized were several bodyguards. They closely resembled what I had seen years ago in Val's Secret Service attaché, wearing sharp suits and carrying only a handgun at their waists.

"I am the Legacy." I turned my head back at him, a puzzled and somewhat disdainful look on my face.

"Alright...got a normal name? Like...Fred? Or something?" I had most of my body's awareness in my possession finally, feeling as close to normal as I could hope for.

"Nothing so pedestrian." He smirked. "Only a purpose. You and I are here to fulfill that purpose."

"*Alright...*" I started again, the theatrics of an obvious enemy starting to present themselves in the most generic of ways. "What do you need me to do?" He laughed abruptly, shaking his head and standing to silhouette himself against the draped windows behind him.

"To be quite frank, I need you to find somebody. Or more accurately, I need you retrieve them. I'd rather not make threats, so if you could provide some assistance without them, it would be more civil for all of us."

"And you're looking for who, exactly?"

"Amelia." He said her name and closed his mouth, saying nothing further for a moment. "And before you ask, I need her *here* and *alive*. My associates have been unable to locate her successfully and I've grown quite tired of waiting." He spoke formally and quickly, getting to the point of his demands without any suspense.

"I'm gonna regret asking, but...for what, exactly?"

"To continue." He raised his eyebrows, positive tone echoing through the chamber. "To continue the way Vampyres should have. Far long ago. I *need* her here as a leader. An icon. As a cure and as an ally to our species."

"Cure." I sighed. "I'm assuming you're familiar with Schillinger and Raven."

"Yes. I am. Both…great losses to the world. But required ones. They had the wrong perspective. I'm here to provide a fresh one."

He doesn't know Raven is alive. They can't be working together.

"How do you know she can produce a cure?" I asked, hiding the fact that I had known the information already.

"She can't. She was *born* a cure. She was made a cure by my predecessor."

"Predecessor?" The conversation instantly became more interesting. "So you worked with Schillinger."

"The Vampyre patriarch you knew as Robert Schillinger made me, yes. I was implanted with his memories, his knowledge, but blended with my own and without his personality. Although in a past life I was a…trusted ally. One of his few confidants. So I had been chosen to resume his legacy after his well-anticipated death."

Raven's effort at a consciousness-implant technology makes a lot more sense now. But you seriously think nothing from his personality seeped in? You're monologuing.

"Well, no, just to clear that up." I started carefully, taking a step forward in the office to lean against an expensive chair. "I have no idea why I would help you with that, even if you're telling the truth. If you want a cure, we have it handled. If you need leadership, provide it. Not really a problem at this point." He exhaled through his nose, a slight laugh behind closed lips.

"It's more com-"

"Yeah, more complicated than I know. Sure. Heard it before. I'm sure Schillinger loved that line, too. Just…*try* and explain it for me. I promise I'm smart." I was already exhausted at being in the room, a failed imitation of our last generation's chief problem becoming a broken record before my eyes.

"We don't need the cure given out quite yet. We need to create and preserve it for when the borders open."

"Ah. Kill the humans outside of the country, make more Vampyres, new world order. Right? Am I close?" I asked in earnest, at least hoping to cut out the parts of the conversation I knew would be inevitable. He rolled his eyes, smirking at me patronizingly.

"Yes. But I have a much more efficient plan for killing the humans. One that merits full control over what remains of this...scorched planet. I, unlike my forerunner, have little patience for plans and machinations. I want them dead. And I will do so once I have the cure in my hand."

"And since that's not happening...?" I asked slowly, giving him a mockingly apologetic look.

"Hmm." His smirk remained, and I could tell that he was somehow entirely removed from the fact that he wasn't getting what he wanted. "Geoffrey." He called for someone, his voice maintaining its exact pitch and tenor while increasing ever so slightly in volume. I looked behind me to see one of his attachés step into the room while cradling a soft-sided bag of some sort.

"*That* is not a laptop bag, Sonya. That's what the government used to refer to as the Presidential Emergency Satchel, or the *nuclear football*. Previously inactive after the Outbreak due to security measures and superseded by newer algorithms. Thankfully, the chain of succession for government eventually led to me and I was allowed access. I've held onto this device for nearly fifteen years. Would you like to see me use it?" He cocked his head, waiting for an answer.

There's no way this is possible.

"It-...there's not *any* way that-"

"Not a problem. It only takes a few moments, actually. My people are well-prepared for the process." He cleared his throat and moved from behind the desk, taking a step toward his employee. I lunged forward to grab his shoulder, stopped promptly as the suited minions drew their handguns in the flash of a split second and levelled them at my head. Their reflexes and movement clearly indicated a high level of training and discipline superior to even some of Aerael's best soldiers.

I'm no use to anyone dead.

I stopped in my tracks, slowly standing upright and resuming my stance where I had previously stood.

"I won't lie to you, this would be a terrible bluff." He chuckled, taking the bag and holding it in his hands for a moment as if it were a trophy. "What would I stand to gain by exposing my hand unless I truly had the power to destroy any city in the world? Any nation? The answer is nothing, by the way. The same item you hold in advantage to your situation." He pursed his lips and handed the bag back to the man he referred to as Geoffrey, allowing him to step out of the room again and close the door that blended into the rounded walls. "I want to see this world turned to glass. Returned to a primordial state and allowed to decay until evolution takes its grip on those strong enough to survive the nuclear fire. This *will* happen, and there is no doubt in my mind of that. The question simply becomes how many you choose to save."

"How? What am I supposed to do?"

This is impossible. We would have found out about this, learned of it somehow.

"Deliver her to me. Promptly. And unharmed. In exchange, I will give seven days of notice prior to detonation for the cities I level. Your people survive and I get my cure." His voice was dark and insidious in the same way Schillinger's was, but his words were more blunt and decidedly less eloquent.

"What? *Inside* the country? Why? To destroy some buildings? And even if we evacuate, there's nothing left to kill!"

"I'm not here to kill. I'm here to cleanse. The United States had roughly three thousand, six hundred and fifty active nuclear warheads before the Outbreak. Not all were armed and attached to a projectile, but I have ensured that task complete. It's enough to destroy what's left of the outside world, as well as the major cities inside of the country. With our own major cities destroyed, there are no hard targets for the rest of the world to hit in retaliation. The survivors within our borders will take back to the small towns, the…ghost towns. Breathe life where there is none and stay free from a ruling authority. Self-sufficiency and survival of the fittest. Vampyres survive. Humans don't. Your previous opponent was a sword, and I have no reluctance in stating my role as a sledgehammer." He leaned against the desk, a heavy breath heaving through his chest as if he internally struggled with the weight of his role. "But the work will be done. A smarter, hardier, *better* species…renewed and refreshed periodically by the cure. True order at long last."

I have no way out of this without complying. How are we supposed to stop something this massive? Even if I lie, what happens when he finds out?

"Where are my friends? Including the two you kidnapped, not just the ones I brought with me."

"They're safe." He stated firmly. "But caged, I'm afraid. We wouldn't risk an escape with the type of power that Karalynn holds. I'll take you to them, and you may leave with your party unscathed. But I'm afraid that comes with a trade." I sighed, beginning to seriously stress over the logistics of trying to kill him before I left the room.

You could knock the goons back with your powers, then close in on him while they're down.

"What's the trade?" I asked, curious as to his answer while stalling to formulate a proper strategy.

Even though he's a Vampyre, I should be able to take him if I get the first move in our game. I'll have to push in both directions to knock his thugs down and make him stumble. Then I can close the distance and get behind him. If I get my arms around his neck, it's over. My abilities should be able to get me there.

"You will have two weeks to retrieve Amelia and bring her to me. Alone. I believe she's far too old now to need a guardian, but I'll allow a chaperone to witness that she's uninjured in the transfer."

"You're right. She's an adult. Makes her own decisions, has her own wants and needs…Can't guarantee *she* won't try to kill you, either."

"I have more than enough security-…*either?*" His confused response coincided with a split-second decision for my actions. I smirked, blinking hard to throw out my arms in either direction, smashing his contingent of guards against the wall and turning to charge at my target. My heart settled into a rhythmic fluttering of raw fear as I recognized the sensation of immobility. Confirming my incapacitation, Legacy stood in front of me unmoved and staring at me in morbid curiosity.

Oh, no. Please, no. Don't let anything happen to my family if I've messed up and get killed.

"Sonya…" He sounded genuinely disappointed. "I thought better of you. I expected you to understand my…position here. I wasn't chosen at random and I certainly wasn't handed a mixed bag of information from some villain's evil mind. I was crafted. Perfected. Even given his abilities at the cost of…everything else he had."

Even Schillinger could never do this. Kara said we were…immune to each other.

"It's not possible. It doesn't work that way." I whispered, my throat closing tighter the longer I was held in place. "Our powers don't work on each other. Schillinger, Kara, me-"

"They do now. The experiments took a toll on his being, which is why Jalix and his ragtag band of infiltrators were able to so easily dispatch Schillinger nearly two decades ago. He was weakened to give *me* the strength he could never possess. Control over Kara and over *you*. The two he could never overpower on his own." I heard his guards stand and brace themselves against the wall, drawing their weapons again at a slower pace. "Please, gentlemen." He continued, looking over my shoulder and beckoning at me with one of his hands. "I think I have this handled."

"If you're going to kill me, do it now. I'm not waiting around to listen to you tout your power."

"I'm not going to kill you. I need you to deliver-" He looked over my shoulder again, shrugging. "It's like she's not even listening to me." He sighed before continuing. "I have a job that you need to do. You have incentive, I have motive. Why on Earth would I keep you from doing that?"

Okay, he's officially a psychopath. How do I stop this?

"Then take me to my family. I'll bring her back, and you can take blood samples. Then she's leaving with us." I remained firm in my position, allowing him full awareness that I would never surrender her. He sniffed once, nodding.

"I wish it could be so easy. But our new order isn't depending on me to run things. It's time for the proper lineage to take the throne." I was stunned for a moment, trying to comprehend some sort of meaning from his words.

"So you have *no* interest in being in charge?" I asked hesitantly.

"Correct. It's not my place. In fact, no other course was ever intended in spite of what my predecessor may have said aloud. Either Kara or her child were designed to take the reigns on a new society. A position with absolute power and no recourse for emotion or passion. No theological interjection over quibbling belief systems. A purely sovereign and logical life for those lives reigning eternal. The only way it should be, wouldn't you think?" The question seemed genuine enough, his eyebrows raised against a passive demeanor within his eyes.

"I'm not having this discussion with you. If you plan on installing Amy as a leader and stepping down, she'll do the right thing. So would Kara. They're not like you. And speaking of, you're stalling. Take me to the rest of them."

"Absolutely. Procrastination…Quite a fault of mine, I must admit. I enjoy slowing down and…taking in the finer things of life. Speaking of, we'll be within walking distance and I would very much like to keep you unbound so you might take in the full beauty of what we've made here in our country's new capital. I'm assuming you don't need a blindfold and gag for some ungodly reason? We try to maintain the same civility now that we expect to see in the future."

"Yeah, I think I'll be okay." I scoffed as he motioned to the cadre of security and allowed them to open the door leading out of the room.

"You should be grateful, Sonya. You're the first to see what we've been building. To see the center of world peace." He motioned for me to go through the door, my footsteps keeping a quick pace as his security led me through a maze of hallways that seemed to circle into nowhere. I could hardly take in the history or the prestige of the environment I had been forced into, instead focusing on escaping to fresh air and the likelihood that I would at least lay eyes on my family again. Offices and workspaces passed by as my heartbeat deliberately pushed its way into my neck, each room scattering a bevy of professionals tending to some form of hushed work. I was led by the front and rear, Legacy's guards maintaining a spacing too close for natural comfort. Despite not being physically restrained, I felt like a shackled prisoner being escorted to their grave, watched by eyes that didn't care enough to look up from their paperwork.

"World peace takes a significant amount of labor." My captor remarked as he noticed my head moving slightly to look at the workers. "We've been addressing various nations monthly through the country's government-secured telecommunications systems. Quite admirable work, I have to say. And from aspiring politicians, at that." He chuckled quietly, as if mocking the democratic process of our nation was amusing.

Wait a minute.

My footsteps nearly faltered as a piece of the grand puzzle fell into place, so neatly and easily discarded by the entity in charge of it all. We entered the foyer of the building, starting to make our way outside while I pressed my luck.

"Those briefings...those monthly addresses. You've been feeding other countries bad information, haven't you? To keep them from aiding us, to make us seem dangerous."

"Not as much dangerous as unwilling." He retorted coolly. "But yes, a subtle mixture of both. Between some tactful passive-aggression and an outright denial of continuing alliances, the distance between the United States and its former allies has grown astronomically. No one is willing to tread on the proverbial snake, and we get the peace required to finish out our endeavors. I have even gone so far as to discredit your...former advisors. Kara's counsel will not be regarded by foreign nations until Amelia clears their names. Everyone else has been branded a traitor, an accomplice to the Outbreak and the country's genocide." My blood started to boil at the mere thought of his audacity, but I was more shocked that his plans worked so efficiently. I tried to calm myself, retaining the temporary sanity I held onto for dear life in the hopes that Jalix, Kara, Val, and Tony would have some semblance of a plan. As we strolled out into the daylight, the relief I felt at the chance to break free was swiftly interrupted by a group of three, slightly less-armed guards than the ones escorting me. Legacy moved past me to greet them, shaking the lead man's hand firmly and welcoming him with a warm voice.

"Yuri. Very glad you're here, I have a special guest that needs taken to the Hall to see her friends. They're going to be running an errand for me, so do see that they're all carefully attended out of the city?"

"Yes, sir." The man's voice was firm, influenced by a Ukrainian accent and directed toward his superior with absolute confidence. Both he and the two guards at his side were dressed differently than the others; each wore gray and black combat apparel without encumbering themselves with unnecessary tactical pageantry. Yuri turned his head to look at me, a slim face and firm jaw accompanying a thin but muscular build. His posture and composure matched what I had seen in expertly trained soldiers, and the sense of awareness that filled his eyes and stance could only be attributed to the best of what any military had to offer. While I wasn't afraid, I knew my intimidation stemmed from a truer sense of real danger. As I stood on the south lawn of the White House and took in a vast mixture of feelings, the two of them dipped into a brief conversation.

"She is still stable, by the way. Her husband gave us some trouble at first, but we believe he'll remain calm for her sake. The others only recently woke up. We'll take precautions." Yuri's accent was heavier than expected from his first words, but the resounding clarity in the meaning of his words diminished my hopes of outrunning the group.

"Excellent. I truly appreciate your help. We'll talk more later. For now, please see Miss Sonya taken to her family."

"Consider it done." Yuri took a step back and glanced at me briefly before looking back at his men, clearly believing that I was not a threat. Legacy began his walk back into the White House and paused at my shoulder briefly. I could feel a change in the air around me as his presence became close, both chilling and unnerving me. I maintained my composure and inhaled sharply, snapping my head to look into his eyes.

"Listen to me closely, Sonya. Do as I say, and you will get what your family wants. If you step out of line...I will not consider myself responsible for the retaliation. I do not want a war. I want this fight concluded." He spoke whatever truth was in his mind, as corrupted as it may have been by the memories of his predecessor.

I haven't truly hated anything this much since Schillinger, and I know that without remembering it. Now our enemy is all the more despicable.

"You're telling me not to start a war, but you're holding a gun to my head. What the hell do you expect?" I hissed, leaning in closer to his face. He stood his ground, but every Vampyre with a gun slowly began to unholster their firearms. I kept my hands at my sides and leaned in, nearly grazing my nose against his. "You want to call yourself a legacy, but you're a shadow. A bastard child of hatred and greed. You can't avoid war when you're bred to start it." I took a deep breath, my powers manifesting as a result of my hatred and filling my chest with a familiar feeling of unchained destruction. "If you want to pull your atomic trigger, then I'll die happily knowing that one of my family will end this. Permanently. We're not just going to come for *you*. I promise that." His eyebrow cocked in confusion as I gritted my teeth. "We're going to come for everyone."

"I expect nothing less." He smiled gently, tilting his head and nodding once. "Yuri." He called, snapping his fingers and walking back through the grandiose doors. My new escort approached me quickly, ushering me to walk forward without coming into physical contact. His entourage of two followed suit, standing directly behind the two of us as we walked side by side. It was only quiet for a moment before he spoke, seemingly leaning toward me to convey his words in a more subtle manner.

"Your family is being held at the Daughters of the American Revolution Hall. They needed as much security as they could on Jalix, and they have Kara sedated for our safety." I nodded slowly, looking around as I started to realize that the White House was not the only building teeming with armed security. The grounds that lay ahead of us were crawling with paramilitary soldiers; each and every monument, building, or structure was kept under watch by teams of armed guards, and patrols paced in the spaces between them. The greenery and natural history of my surroundings were illuminated under a lightly clouded sky and bathed the scene with an image of aggressive occupation. Large crates of unidentified material scattered the landscape, some containers open and heaped with sandbags while others were sealed with plastic banding.

"Why tell me? Isn't your type in the habit of keeping secrets?" I mumbled, matching his low volume in case he had a good reason.

"Not me. Or not *us*, I should say." He looked over his shoulder at the two standing behind us, nodding briefly as his grip on my shoulder loosened to a light touch. "Do you know who we are?"

"Well, my friend back there mentioned your name was Yuri. Not sure who the goons behind me are. But I'm guessing all three of you are bad news."

"Vona ne pam'yataye." The guy to the left side of our group said something in a language I didn't translate, but the second was understood rather quickly.

"Eye travma realni."

Her injuries are real.

"Ya takze govoryu pau-russky, mudak." I responded in kind.

I also speak Russian, asshole.

"My znaem." Yuri said, the lightest smirk infringing on the corner of his mouth.

We know.

"What injuries, and what's with the language barriers here? You don't seem to mind giving me information, so how about a little more?" I pressed, eager to uncover the answers of my enigmatic chaperones.

"Your injuries affected your memory. We've worked together in the past. But I can't say any more. Not here. Not safe." Yuri mumbled, intentionally picking up his pace along the concrete we strode on. "Jalix and Kara should be able to explain."

There's no way to tell if he's lying...but I swear I know him. Images of...sand. Dirt. Teamwork...

"I'm starting to get the feeling you're not exactly playing on a level field. Whose side are you on?" I finally had to ask, the seemingly diminishing hostility lending credence to the possibility that he was an ally.

"They can explain more." He repeated, his head turning to meet my eyes with an intense gaze and becoming the only sign he could convey among the thirty troopers that stood watch outside of our destination. They moved to the side, allowing him access to the recessed front doors of the building while we made our way up the white concrete steps. I watched the soldiers carefully, studying as many aspects as I could in the most finite level of detail.

Mostly men, but no clear sign of racial or sex-based discrimination on who serves in the ranks. Issued military gear, some even sub-par to what's available on the civilian market. Body armor, magazine and accessory pouches, cargo pants, combat shirts or tactical jackets. Rifles match, military serial numbers and standard features. They raided this equipment from a military base. They seem...twitchy. Eager. Pacing and gripping their weapons tightly as if they really are expecting a fight at any time. Every set of eyes is darting, roaming. Breathing is slightly heavier, faster than normal.

We crossed the barrier from outdoors to the interior of the building, immediately confronted by another mass of soldiers standing directly inside. There were at least a dozen, sprawled across the lobby and performing in the same manner as their counterparts on the exterior of the building. Several of them wore gear that was significantly heavier than the others, carrying bulky machine guns or rifles with various attachments on the undersides of the barrels.

They smell musky. Unbathed. They've been on duty for days, no showers or hygiene. Posture and gait varies between them. A few are preferring one leg over another, one arm instead of the other. They're hiding injuries.

As if one of them heard my internal thoughts, she swiveled her body to face me and stare me down like an animal of prey as we walked by. Her face was mostly covered by a woven cloth of some sort, nothing but a small tuft of auburn hair and set of piercing, hate-filled blue eyes visible from the neck up. Her pupils constricted when she looked at me, a deep breath and audible swallow from her throat indicating that she was a caged beast awaiting her next fight. I could see the silhouette of her back and shoulders shift slightly to match the aggressive step she took back with her dominant leg. Yuri and his friends remained closer than I would have expected, but it was enough to be a comforting sign of protection. They seemed to ignore the activity, but the subtle increase in heart rate I felt through the beat in Yuri's palm led me to believe that they were equally as unnerved below the surface.

"Left." He said quietly, turning my shoulder to face an open doorway that led to a set of stairs. I complied readily, willing to show submission for the audience that watched us. We disappeared through the door, marching silently down a set of stairs that led a short distance to the next lower floor. Once we reached the hallway of the basement, he released his grip entirely and allowed us to walk unimpeded through an unguarded corridor lined with aged office doors.

"Listen to me carefully." He whispered, looking behind him as one of his allies closed the door at the entrance of the hall. "There are cameras in these hallways. Don't do anything for the time being. The...animals upstairs will react rather harshly. The room you're going into holds Jalix. Kara is in the next room to the left, and your other two friends are across the hall from your door. Remember this."

"Got it." I said quietly, knowing the importance of staying oriented to my surroundings.

"At the end of the hall, there is a door that leads to the back of the building. It's more heavily guarded than what you've seen so far, but that is your way out. It'll be taken care of for you by the time you get there. Once you get out, you're going to be on Eighteenth Street. Look to your right, and there will be a group of vehicles waiting for you." He stopped in front of a door as one of his compatriots reached into a cargo pocket to grab a set of keys. He looked at me and gritted his teeth, a menacing warning echoing through his accent. "Get in the first vehicle you see. And do not look back. Do not wait for your friends. If one of you gets out alive, we have succeeded. You may not make it as a group."

"I don't understand." I shook my head, taking in his information as a flood of concerns overwhelmed my immediate reaction to start planning. "Legacy said we were free to go. Why the prison break?"

And what the actual hell is going on? Who is taking care of the guards? Are there more like him on our side?

"I can't answer many questions right now. Time is very limited. The next patrol is on its way for this hall." His ally opened the door, the inside of the room not visible from my vantage point against the wall. "But know this." The unoccupied one of his group took out a cell phone and dialed a number, walking briskly back the way we came. "We were not sent to deliver you here. We were sent to execute everyone but Kara and yourself." I paused, baffled at nearly every aspect of my circumstance.

"Why?" I asked finally.

"To make you see the consequences of what standing against him looks like." He motioned at the room, nodding to indicate that it was time for us to part ways. "But fortunately, that's exactly what we plan to do." I stopped, the darkness of the room hiding a seated figure against the wall on the far end.

"When will I know that it's time?" He smirked at my question, closing the door and sealing a barrier between us.

"It will be loud." He said simply, turning to walk away and disappearing from view. I stared for a second as he disappeared, having no idea what to do with the information he provided. After a moment, I spun around, realizing I was within arm's reach of Jalix. He was slunk against the back wall of the small room, seated with his head bowed.

"Hey. I'm glad you're okay. How's Kara?" I approached his figure, beginning to question why he had been sitting in the dark.

"She's seen better days." He remarked, his voice low and rough. "We both have."

"Are you okay?" I put a hand on his back, immediately feeling the crunch of dried blood on the shirt he was wearing. I withdrew it and finally inhaled through my nose, taking note of the overwhelming scent of copper and iron. "You're hurt."

"Mostly emotionally. Pretty offended you didn't come after us sooner, to be honest." He chuckled, his voice tainted with pain. I retreated to the entrance of the room and flicked on the light switch, bathing what was apparently an office space with fluorescent light. He cringed slightly, the light shocking against his eyes. I combed over his body with my vision, trying to count the open wounds, cuts, and bruises that covered his body. The clothing he wore was assumedly scraps he was given, a pair of weathered cargo pants and worn t-shirt both stained deeply with crimson and torn or cut open in spots.

"Oh, no…Jalix…" I breathed, rushing to his side and crouching down to comfort him.

"Stop that. I'm fine, I've…been through worse." He rolled his head away from me, obviously trying to diminish his state of weakness.

"What the hell is this? Been through worse? I can't imagine you getting put through a woodchipper like this before."

"They're just a bunch of assholes." He groaned, leaning heavily into his knees to stand. "As if I was going to give up my daughter over a few rounds of unfair fights." He chuckled, flexing his hand and gazing at his knuckles. "You should see the other guys."

"I bet." I returned the gentle laughter, feeling terrible for his situation. "But you didn't answer me. How's Kara? And *why* have you two not broken out yet? It would be rough with the guards, but-"

"Kara is…incapacitated. For the time being." He groaned, reaching down to touch his toes and stretch his body. "They wouldn't touch her. Wanted her alive, but they're keeping her knocked out with drugs to act as bait for everyone else to show up. Especially Amy. They're not even taking the risk of having Kara's powers be…accessible."

"Damn. Did you see Val and T-"

"Yep. Across the hall. They're fine, we've been yelling to each other through the doors to talk. You've only been up there for a few hours, if your sense of time is off from the meds they gave you. Probably the same shit they're giving Kara. And as for breaking out…" He took a deep breath and seemed to cast his own pain to the side, his posture becoming more rigid and natural.

"I stayed here to get information. Yuri is an old friend of mine. Long story short, we ran some ops together in Iraq. He was…like me, had his own version of an elite combat unit. Ended up working next to Kilkovf and decided to join that life for a bit. Didn't last long." He leaned against the door, peering through the slit of a window to check on Tony and Val's room. "Decided he liked being a Vampyre and hated being an asshole. So he spied on them for a long time, gathering information and not knowing who to give it to. When Kilkovf bit the dust due to my badass of a wife, Yuri moved up the ranks of what was left and ended up where he is now. In this…administration."

"Yeah, what the hell is with that? Have you met this Legacy guy?" I was glad to see he had more information than I did and was capable enough to pass it on.

"Yeah…Sonya, this guy is no joke. Okay? Forget Schillinger. Schillinger had a contorted mind and some chess game of a plan, but that's not what's happening anymore. This…Legacy asshole is serious. He has no punches to pull and no reason to hold back."

"How did this even happen? I mean, we wiped out-"

"We didn't wipe out the ideology. The concept. We killed the people involved and made them martyrs to everyone else that saw what they were trying to do." His voice was heavy with emotion, clearly angry at his own actions. "But it might work to our advantage this time."

"Wait, how?" I grew quiet as a patrol of four guards made their way past our door, a heavily armed silhouette of troops creeping past our window.

"Because each of *them*…" He watched them walk by, staring with a burning and flagrant hatred. "Are hollowed-out puppets. Legacy is controlling them, keeping them in check. Whatever was left of the Pyrates started pulling people off the street a while ago and breaking their minds. Torturing random civilians. Survivors of the virus, the new

Vampyres. Then he would dose them with Factor Five and do it again. He could break their legs and watch them heal in minutes. Cut into them over and over again and see the flesh close itself. He kept them in torture until they would break and become addicted to the healing. Obsessed with the sensation of being invincible. He showed them immortality by cutting off their limbs and sewing them back on while they watched in a mirror. So they're junkies, motivated by their next dose and brainwashed into thinking they're a part of the right plan. The immortal race, the perfect people. Seduced through torture and repeated highs."

"Jesus Christ…" I wanted to throw up, imagining the poor souls that had been subjected to the brutality of their methods.

That explains why most of them looked like they were hiding injuries. Wait…

"Is that…did they do that to you?" I realized, taking a step toward him. He recoiled a bit, grimacing at me and continuing to watch the hallway. His breath was steady and peaceful, but a resolute silence gripped his throat for a long minute.

"They tried. Yeah. But I wasn't going to break. Not when my wife and daughter…my family and friends, not when they're on the line." His face hardened into an expression I had only ever seen in Kara, and from events I knew were traumatic beyond human comprehension.

"Jalix, you've been gone for two weeks. How long did they…how much did you have to endure?" I was afraid of the answer, but needed to know the extent of trauma so I could try to help.

"Ten days." My heart dropped while he continued. "Twenty-four hours a day…they would cycle in new drones to keep working me over. Former doctors, sadists, people that wanted revenge for the Pyrates we killed. No sleep. No pauses. No offer of stopping."

Oh, my God…that had to have been a living nightmare. And we didn't save him from it.

"Jalix, I'm so sorry. I-I…can't even imagine how-"

"No. You can't. And don't try, there's no point in taking on those experiences. It's not going to help me by having someone else burdened with-"

"Jalix, it's not a burden." I protested, closing the distance between us. "I want to help you." He released his hand suddenly from the frame of the door and faced me, trying to keep himself in check as he unleashed his memories. His pupils constricted quickly, then dilated as if he was reliving the physical pain of those events as he spoke.

"You *can't* help me, Sonya! I had my stomach cut open and my ribs broken while I watched through a video monitor! I had-…I had organs removed and put back, I had pounds of muscle cut off my body and put back! I was a jigsaw puzzle to them!" He was yelling in shock and fear, tears glistening in his eyes as he shouted at me, trying to cope with his pain. "I had to *shit* on the medical table where I laid because they wouldn't unstrap me! You can't understand, Sonya. I love you, and you're my family, but you can't *possibly* understand what it's like to go through two hundred and forty hours of being beaten by pipes, being blinded, having my eardrums repeatedly ruptured from the barrel of the same gun that was firing bullets into my leg…but I…they can't break me." He growled, pounding his fist against the door and denting the metal. "Because I'm still in one piece, and my daughter needs me to come back." I was openly crying, a silent river of tears flowing across my cheekbones and dripping into a mouth that tried to form words.

"I'm sorry." I whispered, looking up into his eyes. "I didn't move fast enough, I didn't know you were in danger and-" He shook his head violently and put a strong hand on the side of my neck.

"Don't you *dare* blame yourself for what they did. Don't you dare, Sonya. Those…animals don't deserve your guilt." I sniffed, nodding and trying to believe his words. "No one knew. No one knew a lot of things, things I haven't even told you yet. But now we do. Do you understand?" I continued nodding, my chest heaving as I tried to contain myself. "Hey!" He barked unexpectedly, cupping my face with his other hand. "I need you right now, Sonya. This is why I said it's *my* burden. I need you to take a deep breath. There are still a lot of things I need to-" A sharp crack through the air outside and the vibration of the wall we stood near forced a brief retreat into the far side of the room as chaos broke out a short distance from us. After a moment, we both ran to press our noses against the door's slim window, seeing nothing in the hall but Val and Tony looking for the same signs we did. Immediately following the explosion, there was a roar of gunfire, a massive barrage from opposing sides along with a bout of muffled, distant shouting and the screaming of orders.

"Kill 'em, Yuri." Jalix mumbled.

"What's with this plan? I didn't get a lot of details. I need to know what's going on." I gushed, desperately needing to plan for what was to come.

"You got details?" He asked, surprised. "He just told me some cryptic shit about biding my time."

"You're kidding me." I groaned, taking a step back as an echo of footsteps lumbered down the hall toward our respective doors. Separate groups of guards divided themselves up, quickly surrounding our only exit and shouting at us. Their weapons varied, but each was pointed directly into the window in a show of force.

"Get back! Get the hell back!"

"Hands up!"

"Back against the wall, now!" Jalix and I both immediately responded, levelling our open hands with the tops of our heads and slowly walking backward to the far wall. Despite our compliance, the noise was nonstop. Gunfire intensified outside of our building and smaller explosions rumbled through vibrations in the floor. The security in the hall continued to scream at us, leaning into the door and nearly fighting over control of what we were supposed to do.

"On the ground! On the ground now-"

"Get on your knees, hands above your head!"

"Move and you're dead! You understand me?"

The chorus of roaring demands drowned out my ability to think, a raw obedience and unusual fear creeping through my chest. I stared uncontrollably, watching their eyes get wider with hunger and the desire for combat grow as they started to beat against the door, rationality losing its hold over their minds. One of them lashed out, a rabid scream contributing to the chaos as he beat against the metal frame with the intent of breaking in. His eyes were bloodshot, a crazed glare seething raw fury at the two of us. Without warning, a much closer enfilade of shots pierced the air and the animals clawing their way into our cage each snapped suddenly to the side, jerking unnaturally and falling to the ground with fatal wounds. The soldiers outside Val's door fell in the same way, an unseen cadre of death attacking from the near end of the hall. While the combat continued outside, the immediate area was deadly quiet for several moments, no one making their way down the hall as saviors.

"Stay here." Jalix mumbled, dropping his hands and approaching the small window.

"Jalix, we-"

"Enemy of my enemy is my friend, right? Well, they just killed a shit-ton of my enemies." His head turned to either side several times before he spoke. He stared down both sides of the hall, scrutinizing its details in confusion. "No one's there. I can see the doorway you came from. It's empty. Had to be Yuri's men."

"They *had* to have come from that direction, whoever they were."

"Well...they left. Time we did the same." Jalix assumed, taking a large step back from the door and readying himself for a hefty kick.

"Wait!" I called, reaching out and using my telekinetic abilities to keep him in place momentarily. "Don't break your leg. You've been through enough. Let me take care of it."

"Right. Your abilities. Sorry." I dropped his leg and strode forward, double-checking the hall as if Jalix was wrong in what he saw. Confirming his assessment, I gripped the handle on the inside of the door and slowly crawled my way through its contents.

Handle, lock cavity where the key goes...tumblers...one, rotate...another...tiny metal pins pushed upward into their respective places. Turn.

I turned the handle and pushed the door open, the metal slab stopping its motion after roughly six inches. I shoved the panel, realizing the dead bodies blocked our path to escape. After enough room for my torso to squeeze through, I pulled myself into the hallway and stepped over one of the bodies. I made my way to the left of our room, pushing out with my mind and sending the pile of corpses tumbling toward the door at the near end of the hall.

A loud pop erupted from the wall next to me and a shower of concrete and metal pattered against my hip as one of Val's muscular legs pushed through the latch of his own door. He and Tony scrambled out quickly, confronting Jalix and I.

"Does anyone know what the hell is going on?" Val asked with exasperation, trying to catch his breath from the experience of nearly being shot to death.

"I do." I said confidently, moving to Kara's door. Without as much intricate thought as the last handle, I broke the mechanism's interior enough to contort the handle and allow

Jalix and I to walk into her room. "Stay there." I warned Val and Tony, who were also eager to see Kara.

"She's my sister." Val demanded, taking a step forward. Jalix flicked on the lights in the room behind me and was moving quickly while my back was turned to him.

"Watch the hallway. She won't be your sister for long if none of us make it outside. Go grab some of the weapons those guards had. We might need them to get out. I'll help Jalix with Kara." Val nodded once, allowing me to take control in an emotional situation. I spun around, watching Jalix inspect an intricate medical setup surrounding Kara's body. She laid flat on a medical bed, her head resting on a soft pillow while her hair dangled from the side in a web of onyx strands.

"Help me out. Is she safe to disconnect and drag out of here without all this crap?" He asked, looking at one of the monitors.

"Don't worry about the electronics. Look at anything that actually goes *into* her. Needles, ports, whatever." I grasped her right arm, following one line of medical tubing to an IV bag filled with saline. I gently removed the needle and pressed down on the mark on her skin, allowing her vein to heal and the puncture to close itself.

"This one goes to a bag." Jalix said quietly, holding up a line and pointing to a hanging container of solution. "It's not labeled."

"Just disconnect everything. We need to get her out of here." A reminder of the war around us rang out as another explosion rocked the room and forced the displays and monitors to stutter. I could hear Val and Tony's footsteps return, the quiet clink of metal being an assumption that they gathered weapons for us. As Jalix disconnected the last of Kara's restraints, he swooped one arm under her leg and crouched, sliding her whole body onto his shoulders.

"I can't fight." He admitted as he stood, holding her body solidly against his back. "I can't carry her *and* a gun. I'll need you guys to give me cover."

"We've got your back." Tony said confidently. He passed me a rifle and discarded the third that he held, knowing that moving with a sense of urgency was more crucial than having additional firepower.

"You sure?" Jalix asked, much to our surprise. "I can stay behind with her while she wakes up." He shifted his glance to Val, realizing he wasn't talking only to Tony. "You guys don't owe us anything, and we can make a break for it once she's up and running."

"Jalix…I think we're only going to get one shot at this." I acknowledged reluctantly, realizing the weight of my words. "Something big just kicked off and we don't have time to try to figure out what. But we do need to get out of here if we want to have a chance outside of these walls."

"We're here to the end, brother." Val nodded, glancing at his unconscious sister. "For both of you." I double-checked my rifle, loading a fresh magazine and taking another from the lightweight vest Tony had donned.

"Let's get you some payback, Jalix." I touched his shoulder as I moved past him, a fresh sense of adrenaline readying my senses to join the combat storming outside. I took notice of it more than I remembered, the experience having been dormant for more than a few years.

Heartbeat nice and slow, saving its energy for the moments it's needed. Eyesight sharpening the outlines and silhouettes of objects. Colors more vibrant. I smell…dust, dust from stone and masonry. Gunpowder and smoke. Blood from the hallway and sweat from all four of us. I can hear noise in three concentrated areas outside, one close, two more distant. At least a few dozen feet from the building. Guns, small arms. A few larger machine guns. A strong draft from the end of the hall; the door must be ajar.

I could hear Val grunt quietly as he started readying himself in the same way. His abilities likely forced an urge to tear things in half, but there was no outlet for the level of rage he fought to contain. Tony's footsteps were solid and consistent, his years of marksmanship and gunsmithing enough of a confidence to hold his own against whatever force we would confront.

The corner of the hallway approached rapidly as we walked, the mix of smells becoming significantly stronger while my suspicions of the door being open were confirmed by small rays of light trickling across the floor.

These aren't people anymore. They're monsters, deprived and removed from sanity. Killing them is a mercy...and I won't let them touch my family.

There was a moment of hesitance as I was confronted by the door that led to the warzone outside, some small semblance of thought that begged me to turn and run the other way. Familiar with fear and knowing full well that our only option for escape was to carve a path along the predetermined route that awaited us, I raised my rifle and used the weight of my body to push the door open, allowing the full scope of our task to fill my eyes. A short set of stairs waited in front of me and remained the only barrier keeping us out of sight of the two factions that were fully and wholly engaged in apocalyptic battle. Rounds cracked over my head from weapons employed across the street, aiming at everything except our group and breaking off pieces from the stone masonry of our building.

Eighteenth Street. We need to go right.

I looked behind me for a moment, watching the group's waiting eyes as they understood that I was the only one with a sense of direction in our predicament. I crouched and slid up the first two steps, peering my eyes over the pavement and collecting a sense of awareness for the directions of both our enemies and our allies. They immediately became distinguishable, Legacy's army firing from protected positions with no regard to their own safety while their targets desperately fought to achieve a few reasonable shots from behind cover.

Their behaviors were polar opposites, with one group attempting to stay alive and suppress while the other sent an uninhibited barrage of firepower in the opposite direction. I could see undisciplined but consistent efforts on the enemy's side to maintain some sort of order, a soldier stepping into the light from within a building as soon as one of their comrades fell to the efforts of our rescuers. It was a no man's land, the only way to the set of massive, armored vehicles to my right being a nearly unprotected zone of smoke and screaming lead. I ducked back down, issuing directions as fast as I was able.

"Bad guys to the left, good guys to the right. It's going to be a sprint to get to the nearest vehicle. Move from cover to cover, whatever you can find. Looks like we'll have to skirt the building or hide behind the concrete barriers on the road to have a chance at getting there."

"That bad?" Jalix responded quickly, realizing there was no exaggeration in my voice. As if to answer his question, there was a deafening roar from the side of our allies, followed by a brief hiss and a massive explosion at the far end of the street. We all ducked down, huddling together as we were smacked by a shockwave and several pounds of debris. Waves of dust and smoke rolled down the stairs, smothering us in a protective cloud. I nodded to Jalix, lightly pushing him back while Val and Tony moved their way forward.

"Tony, you and I are going to give Val some cover. Val, go about fifty feet along the building and grab the nearest crevice you can. That'll get you halfway there and we'll send Jalix to catch up to you while we stay back. We'll give you about fifteen seconds to get secure and look for our ride before we make our way down. As soon as we break cover here, take off and get Jalix to the nearest functioning vehicle. If we're more than ten seconds behind you, tell them to go. We'll catch the next ride out of here. It's just leapfrog, but with bullets. Got it?" They both nodded grimly, the time for arguing quickly becoming a luxury we didn't have. I took a last, deep breath and jumped up the stairs alongside Tony, diving behind a cement inlet along the side of the building. Without waiting for Tony, I slid as little of my body as possible along the edge and looked down the sights of my rifle at the loudest noise I could focus on. A fixed-position machine gun was chugging away at our side's troops and keeping their heads down. I fired two shots, crippling their ability to run the weapon continuously.

Sand. Heat. Gunpowder. Watch your head.

As I rounded back into cover, Tony was already crouched and taking over for me while Val made his way up the steps and ran with all his speed down the street. I watched him for a few seconds, thankful that the settling cloud of dust still afforded him the opportunity to maintain a low profile. Tony tapped my calf, signaling another switch. Val tucked himself against the building, out of my line of sight before I swung around again and took a more deliberate assessment of their side.

Large hole blown through one of the pillars near their barricade. Must have been one of our guys' rockets and the noise we heard earlier. Reinforcements are pouring in with increasing strength from behind the barricade. We don't have much time.

"Jalix, go!" I called over my shoulder, nudging Tony with my foot to suggest we both start firing. I was able to pinpoint a few of their gunmen, ensuring my rounds were only spent on shots that would immediately confirm a kill.

Cold winter night. Snow. Buried in snow. Red stars. Gold scythes. One pull of the trigger.

I took a risk and let my arm reach out from behind our barrier, ripping away the rest of the damaged pillar with my abilities and sending the remaining stone tumbling across a small patch of their barricade. Several of their soldiers were aware of the impending collapse, choosing to remain focused on their last few shots instead of saving their own lives. A few became distracted and looked for a source, realizing there was no explosion to indicate what had happened. I turned around, locking eyes with Val as he peered out to check on my status.

"Tony, go!" I roared, sprinting to replace Val and Jalix as Kara's slumped frame bounced against her husband's shoulders in the last seconds of our hurried struggle.

The outline of a man against stone. Fragile. Wounded. Vulnerable.

Being a highlighted target against the street, I felt several shots pierce the air far too close to my body and dove to my left behind the first vehicle on the road. Its massive tires and steel frame were more than enough to provide a temporary relief as I looked for my next path, although it had clearly been disabled early in the fight and wouldn't have been where my friends ended their escape. Several men were already occupying my position, one of them severely wounded while the rest took turns firing around the opposite side to the best of their ability. Fortunately, there was a straight line forward from my position in cover to the vehicle that my friends were entering, all blocked from direct fire by the blockade I hid behind. I nearly stood up, freezing for a split second as a sliver of thought hindered my effort.

Why isn't Tony here?

I looked to my right, praying that he was huddled in the crevice that Val and Jalix had utilized, and found it empty. Panic flooded my veins before the rationale set in that he may not have moved when I did, or that he found another reprieve from the gunfire somewhere else along the street. Staying as low to the ground as I could, I tilted one eye out from behind one of the tires and scanned the street for any sign of where he would have gone.

Our previous hiding place was vacant, and no other clear indicators of cover were present where I could identify a body that hadn't been torn to pieces. I continued to look, the thin slice of my face that was exposed almost certainly unnoticed by the enemy's increasing strength. I glanced quickly at their force, the blockade of trucks and sandbags meant to inhibit the flow of traffic becoming a floodgate of soldiers leaping through and making their way onto the street.

Focus. Retrace your own steps.

I drew a straight line with my eyes from the stairs to the road, combing over the details of each body in case the worst had occurred. Corpses littered the pavement, their faces smeared with blood or smashed into the surface. One exception began to accentuate itself, a head lifting its eyes from the pavement slowly and shakily looking in my direction. A deep gash occupied nearly half of his face, a matching red to the shade that was spreading from the holes in his back.

"Shit!" I pounded my fist into the concrete, Tony's eyes burning a hole in my vision even after I looked away.

He's family.

I struggled to keep tears away, letting anger do most of my work as I came to a crouch and approached one of the few soldiers still firing to my left.

"Hey!" I yelled, grabbing the shoulder of one man who had taken a short break to catch his breath before engaging again.

"Is anyone alive in here?" I roared, pointing to the dead vehicle.

"No!" He shouted as his teammates both began firing again. "All dead!" I reached over and grabbed the arms of the other two troops, the fourth from their group having apparently succumbed to their injuries.

"Run! Now!" I locked eyes with one of them, pointing to the intact escape vehicle before pressing my hands against the armored hull. They complied immediately, leaving me alone to do what I did best.

Several tons of steel, hollow interior to make room for the crew and equipment. Heavy tires reinforced with Kevlar for durability. Engine the size of a refrigerator, also heavily reinforced with plating.

I attempted to wrap my mind around the weight of the object, realizing that it was far heavier than anything I remembered lifting. I forced out the impending feeling of despair, knowing that my ability's nearly paralleled Kara's and her exploits would never have allowed such a weakness to stop her from doing her job. I reached out again, encompassing the vehicle in a field of complete control and digging my heels into the ground. The tug of resistance against my body's will was taxing, a palpable sensation of fatigue quickly overtaking my mind. I fought against it and conjured up my last ounces of strength to push outward and trade gravity's embrace for a moment of control.

With a satisfying release, the forest-green vehicle lurched sideways and was flung down the road several dozen feet before clipping the ground again, rolling and plowing through Legacy's resistance. Like a bullet through a sheet of paper, it crushed everything in its path and punched a clean hole through the left side of the blockade. While lightheaded and dizzy, I wasted no time in sprinting through the dwindling gunfire toward Tony's body. His head was lain against the road, a ragged and shallow breathing occasionally warping one side of his torso. I ignored the possibility of causing more damage and grabbed the back of his vest, lifting his body as much as I was able and dragging him toward the direction I came from.

"I got him." Val called, apparently having approached after seeing my goal. "Dammit, he looks bad."

"We're…all going to look like that if we don't get out of here." I was gasping for air, speaking in quick sentences as we were both able to resume a fast pace back to Jalix's waiting arms. He laid Kara in a seat several feet behind him, taking hold of Tony's shoulders and bringing him up the ramp to the inside of the vehicle.

"Drive!" Val yelled to the cockpit, pressing and holding a silver switch next to the opening at the rear of the vehicle to slowly raise the ramp as we lurched forward. Jalix laid Tony down on the floor, swiftly tearing away the outer vest and underlying shirt. I let Jalix assume custody of Tony, turning my head to see who else had made it to the end. Only one of the soldiers I had run into was present, along with a still-unconscious Kara and somewhat familiar face.

"Yuri?" I asked, confirming his presence. He looked up from his phone, nodding at me briefly and making a quick comment on our situation.

"You made it. All of you."

"Yeah, that's not going to last long without help. I need a first aid kit, and I'm not talking about one with some gauze and a tourniquet. He needs surgery. Now." Jalix's voice was steady and calm, but firm and determined in purpose. I looked down at Tony's body, his back seeping blood onto the floor of the vehicle. "Looks like a punctured lung and who knows what else. Heartbeat isn't good. He needs help." He elaborated.

"Mikhail." Yuri called to the cockpit. "Medical bag." At the end of his request, the vehicle bucked as we assumedly jumped across a curb or some other rough surface.

"Are we safe? I mean, are we getting back into a fight anytime soon?" I asked him, hoping to glean a few more answers amidst the chaos.

"The path out of the city is cleared. Although I can assume we…likely took many more casualties in the process." He responded, locking and placing his phone in his pocket.

"Was it worth it? All of this? He was going to let us go-"

"You know what you were told." He interrupted sternly. "You don't know the reality." He sighed, reaching over to grab a large bag being handed back from the cockpit. "But once we fix your friend…you'll be closer to the truth."

"We don't have time for-" I was interrupted by another jolt, followed by a quick radio transmission from the cockpit of the vehicle.

"Eight-six, still with us?" One of Yuri's men asked, pressing a black button on the side of his vehicle's speaker.

"Yeah…yeah, we're here." The responding voice sounded out of breath, and the conversation became the focus of choice while Jalix began to extract surgical tools from the bag he was handed. "We lost three teams and had casualties from some others, but the rest of us are split as discussed. We'll meet you at the rally point."

"More than expected." Yuri commented, still standing with his hand on the grip of the vehicle's roof. "Less than what we hoped."

"There's more of you?" Val asked, briefly looking up as he started applying clotting agents to the most urgent of Tony's wounds.

"Many more. We had eight teams, not including this group. Each was supposed to sabotage something and make their escape with some of the enemy's armored vehicles. Sounds like the theft was successful." There was a quick bump before our vehicle settled into a steady pace along what I assumed was the highway out of the city. The gunfire had stopped, no chaotic sounds echoing in my eardrums as they had moments ago. Yuri turned to the driver for a moment, staring in silence before addressing Tony's condition. "Do you have a place for him to get treatment?"

"No. We have to do it here. I'll call Alice." Val responded confidently before pulling out his cell phone. Jalix was all but frantic, connecting an IV as swiftly as possible before touching Tony's head.

"Come on, man. Hang in there." He mumbled, shaking his head at the substantial cut that stretched across the length of his face.

"Alice." Val announced excitedly, placing his phone on the floor and turning up the volume. Even with my hearing, I struggled to make out her response on the other end of the line.

"Val! Is every-"

"Tony's hurt, bad. Everyone else is alive and we're on our way out of the city, but he needs surgery in the next two minutes or he's dead." Val's blunt language struck a nervous chord in my heart, but I understood his need for being candid.

"Shit...okay, just...start describing his injuries. I have to pull over." Her last statement was made to her passengers, inciting a brief chorus of comments in the background. Alice ignored them and remained silent as Jalix answered.

"Three gunshot wounds to his back, exit wounds for two of them. Left lung collapsed from the third. Facial laceration, low priority. I don't feel any spinal injuries, but he's unconscious."

"Alright, answer yes or no and be *quick*. Is his airway obstructed? Can he breathe?"

"Breathing." Jalix responded, following her instructions.

"Is any bleeding uncontrolled?"

"No. Clotting agents applied." He clarified quickly so she would have more information.

"Aside from his face, does he have any bruising or cuts on his head?" Jalix examined Tony's head for a moment, parting his hair several times to be sure.

"No."

"What equipment do you have?" I heard Alice exit her vehicle as she spoke, likely pacing as she contemplated the situation.

"Field-grade surgical kit. Scalpel, iodine, bandages, clotting agent, NCD, IV dextrose and saline, morphine, diazepam, chlorhexidine scrubs, forceps, stapler...let me see...sutures, hemostats. I don't even know what some of this stuff is..." I heard Jalix's nerves set in as he pulled out several unfamiliar tools. Val spoke up, leaning toward the phone.

"Alice, we have a Kelly Clamp, a ten through fifteen blade set, and a Weitlaner Retractor, along with some other meds. No ultrasound and no CT capability, so we have to do this unguided. Plus...we're in a moving vehicle." Jalix looked at him in confusion, Val's face dedicated to the phone.

"Val, how...you can't-"

"Alice, I've watched your surgeries from the observation room a hundred times. I've learned from the best. Guide me through it." He rooted through the bag again, grabbing a bottle of hand sanitizer and dousing his hands and forearms with it before donning a pair of gloves.

"Alright...okay. Scrub up and get your things laid out. Jalix, I need you to *very delicately* feel his back. Can you feel the bullet anywhere close to the skin?"

"I'll check, you hold him." I said quietly, allowing Jalix to continue supporting Tony's frame to avoid further injury. I slid my hands under Tony's back and felt around, gingerly avoiding the open wounds. Finally, my fingers brushed against a small object embedded under the skin.

"Yes! Alice. I can feel it. It's between the bottom of his shoulder blades on his left side, just under the dermis. Should be easy to dig out." Alice breathed a sigh of relief, audible through the phone's speaker.

"Alright. I need the three of you to do *exactly* what I say."

EXCURSION

KRYSTAL

I chuckled at Violet's lame joke, shaking my head and running a hand through my unbelievable length of hair. There were no windows in the back of the van, but a set of supplies and a battery-powered lamp made for a comfortable-enough seating arrangement for the three of us. Amy's reaction mirrored my own, adding a light slap to Violet's arm.

"Seriously, *dad* jokes? You're better than using *puns*. It was a low blow, even under the circumstances." She remarked, her glossy, silver eyes looking into Violet's with sheer happiness.

"I was stuck with Val, what did you expect from my jokes at this point? But seriously, this guy was *so* desperate. I got another text from him a week ago asking when I'd be back in Charlotte. I don't think he got the hint."

"Or maybe you're bad at hinting." I returned, blissfully happy about hearing from her adventures throughout recent years.

"Nope. I was pretty direct. I think coughing each of the three times he tried to kiss me should have been a sign that I was allergic to his bullshit. Besides, I don't need a guy in my life. I'll just follow in Sonya's footsteps." Amy looked at her briefly, a confused eyebrow raised.

"What's that mean?" She asked, looking at me quickly.

"Sonya's an Ace." I shrugged, keeping the details of her sexual life to a brief minimum.

"Ace...?" Amy continued hesitantly.

"Asexual. She's just not into relationships or intimacy. Wasn't interested before her accident, and hasn't been afterward." Violet elaborated. "Just who she is, who she's always been."

"Oh. I had no idea. She just seems so...outgoing. I feel like whoever she'd pair up with would be super lucky. I respect it, I just think she has plenty of personality to share with someone."

"She does...and I think that's why she is the way she is. When Kara and Val were adventuring with her all those years, they just had each other. I don't think any of them planned on being in relationships. But Val met Alice, love at first sight. Your parents met, love at first sight. But the city and its people have always been Sonya's true love."

"It's true." I added to Violet's ample summary. "Sonya loves our people more than she ever could a single person. And I think it suits her perfectly."

"And I have you two!" Violet concluded, drawing Amy's neck into her shoulder for a visibly uncomfortable embrace.

"Get off me." She pushed Violet away lightly and chuckled, the two of them wobbling as we took a slight turn on the highway. We sat in peace for a moment, the end of the topic drawing out as we mentally searched for another.

"How are you feeling?" Amy looked into my eyes, a blazingly bright stare into my soul before I looked at my feet and shrugged.

"Doing pretty well, all things considered. Thanks for asking." I tried to keep my tone polite, avoiding the unidentifiable tension that persisted between the two of us.

"You sure?" She clarified. "You seem…avoidant."

"Sorry." I cleared my throat and returned her eye contact. "I'm good. Just trying to figure things out…settle into a new world." Violet nodded as she listened, letting Amy and I continue the discussion uninterrupted.

"That has to be intimidating. What sticks out to you the most? What's the biggest change between now and then?"

There's so much of her parents in her, but with Alice's influence, too. She's…so unique.

"I don't know…the lack of people, I guess. Knowing that our other people are so far away from us. From each other. How many died and how empty the country is. It's all weird to think about." I gazed off to the side again, her watchful stare becoming too analytical for my comfort.

"Hmm." She punctuated, failing to say anything for a moment. "From what I heard, and I don't mean any offense, but you were pretty antisocial before you went into your coma. Why do you think that other people are what matter most to you right now?" I shook my head, a smirk gracing my lips.

"I'm okay. I don't need a therapist. But thank you."

"People that need help, people that have something to run from, they're the ones that refuse it the most. It means you're working through something on your own and you think adding another person into the mix would complicate it. But I promise I'm not here to complicate things. I just want to talk to you." I felt uneasy at her words, as if there were an aura of truth that I wasn't going to be able to avoid.

"I wasn't antisocial." I started, thinking back. "My *behavior* was, sure. But I liked being around people. I just had to be the one to control the interaction. It was when I lost that control that I'd hide from it until I could re-enter on my own terms. Once I lost that control for good…I think that need went away. Once your mom, well…while she was gone, I think things became simpler. Not easier. But simpler. And I think I saw my priorities change once and for all."

"In what way?"

"Our…cause became a bit clearer. Less personal. Even though I should have been fixated on a vendetta, I just wanted things back to the way they were."

"It was your home. And I think you finally realized it." Amy leaned forward, putting a hand on my own.

The warm rush of tropical air washed over the bare skin of my stomach, a light kiss from the ocean's mist spraying a layer of salt and cooler temperatures over my skin. I closed my eyes, the smell of heated sand and summer days lifting my spirits into a place of pure paradise. I felt no sense of urgency to move from my position on the beach, an overwhelming calm nearly forcing tears to my eyes as I fought the will to make a decision of eternal serenity. There were no echoing voices of playful children, no idle conversation to draw me away from the moment. I was alone and surrounded in a blanket of tranquil sleep.

I turned, rolling onto my side as the grey silk sheets wicked away the heat from my body and refreshed the air between my body and the lush mattress. I opened my eyes, watching a set of white linen curtains flap in the breeze from a gentle hillside wind. The smell of pine and moss lilted through the bedroom in a slow melody of isolation. If I was waking up, I had no grogginess from a night of restless sleep, and instead felt the gentle energy of a day without purpose coursing through the gentle beat of my heart.

I sat up, tilting my head back to let the tips of my hair dangle in the bubbling water that penetrated the black earth around it. Allowing myself to submerge further, I could only dream of staying forever in the warmth of the hot spring that cradled my body. Dark, snowcapped mountains in the distance complemented a silver-lined cloudy sky and crisp morning air, seemingly crafted by something higher for my own use as a safe haven from the rest of the world. I felt protected by the air itself, a sensation of security overtaking any need for the outside world. I was alone...I was safe...I was at peace...

"Whoa, hey!" My eyes shot open as Amy's voice cut through the indescribable hallucination, both of us recoiling to opposite sides of the vehicle.

"What happened?" Violet leaned toward me as my eyes darted, trying frantically to realign my thoughts. "Another seizure?"

"No." I mumbled, realizing my heavy breaths. "I have no idea what that was."

"Me neither." Amy said quietly, a mixed look of confusion and sickness smeared across her face. She took Violet's hand to reposition herself, moving her braid of silver hair to the opposite shoulder. "That was intense. Are you okay?" Amy asked me with concern.

"I'm fine, just...what was that?" I almost wanted to forget the entire experience, the images of a perfect world presented so quickly and ripped away from my grasp.

"Like I *said*, I don't know. I went through something similar after your last seizure. I could feel your stress, your anxiety. Your traumas. But the moment I tried to touch them, something strange happened."

"Did you see what I saw?" I asked quickly, trying to make sense of the experience.

"See? I didn't *see* anything. I just *felt*. I felt..." She looked away, trying to describe raw and unfiltered emotion with rational words. "Anguish. And elation. Addiction and healing. Self-loathing and pride. And a lot of rage. Opposites, even. Like you were fighting yourself over something."

"That ever happen before? Feeling someone's emotions?" Violet chimed in, watching me rub my temples to alleviate a growing headache as she pressed Amy for more information.

"No. I've healed a lot of people. That has *never* happened before. I...felt moments of her thoughts, almost. Like I got a tiny piece of her memory without being able to see it too clearly."

"You touched…my hand. How the hell did that happen without you trying to use your abilities?"

"I don't *know*." She articulated, beginning to show signs of frustration. "It was terrifying." She sighed, bowing her head and allowing Violet to lean in with a sisterly kiss to the top of Amy's head.

"I'm sorry, I-" She interrupted my apology, her tone dying down to a mild frustration.

"It wasn't you." She returned quickly. "I know that much. I felt a *lot* of myself reaching out for some reason, outside of my control. Maybe it…it has to do something with your recovery, your healing. Maybe you're working through a lot and I subconsciously tried to heal some of the trauma. I don't know, but I'd really like to avoid doing that again anytime soon. I…it wasn't pleasant."

"Yeah, I…sorry. I'll try and keep my distance." Alice's phone rang, apparently answered after the first few seconds. We all turned our heads, able to clearly make out both ends of the phone as she put it on speaker.

"Val! Is every-"

"Tony's hurt, bad." Val's voice struck all of us with fear as he began to explain his situation. "Everyone else is alive and we're on our way out of the city, but he needs surgery in the next two minutes or he's dead."

"Oh, Jesus…" Violet covered her mouth as Alice answered, voicing the dread we all shared. Raven remained solemnly silent in the passenger seat, likely to avoid making the situation worse by shocking Jalix and Kara with the information that she was alive.

If Sonya hasn't told them already.

"Shit…okay, start describing his injuries. I have to pull over." I could feel Alice applying the brakes, turning toward the right side of the road we were on. The van vibrated obnoxiously for a moment as we crossed into the shoulder.

"I knew I should have gone with them." Violet hissed, her left hand curling into a fist at her side.

"There was nothing you could have done, Vi." I tried quietly. "The more people that were on that mission, the higher of a risk they ran in casualties. I'm just wondering who the hell attacked them."

"Raven said they'd be armed." Amy quipped.

"Yeah but this *group* has to have a name, a structure. Something." I griped as the van came to a stop, my hand guiding the rear door open to expose fresh air. "Hopefully they'll have some information for us when they get back."

"Well, they're going to need directions." Amy returned, stepping out to stand alongside me. She kept a noticeable distance, avoiding any contact between us. "We're in the middle of nowhere for the time being."

"Yeah, and Raven isn't being very forthcoming with the destination." Violet's tone was angry, shooting a glance at Alice and her associate at the front of the vehicle. Alice was deeply engaged in the conversation, pacing at the front of the vehicle and issuing instructions about a medical procedure. "I just hope Tony's going to make it. I can't listen to that right now." She finished with a deep sigh, stepping out to briefly touch my shoulder. We stared at the nearly empty highway, a few cars scuttling along the same route we were taking. We were on the waterfront somewhere in New Jersey, but most of the traffic seemed to be heading to New York. Only a few buildings in our immediate vicinity were occupied, most citizens likely having left for the comfort and accessibility of the city.

"I'm sure the rest of the family's okay. And they'll take care of him. Stay here. I'm going to find out what's going on." I made my way to the preoccupied pair, situated a dozen feet from the front bumper. Alice's voice was firm, but notably anxious as she gave directions to the combat crew.

"Okay, Sonya...suture the wound on his back and apply the plastic. Jalix, can you reinflate the lung?"

"Yeah." Jalix said breathily, making a quiet comment to Val. "Yeah, I can do that. Needle goes between the second and third rib, right?"

"Second intercostal space. Should be in a straight line above his left nipple. Give it a good push, wait for a few seconds, and pull the plunger out while leaving the catheter in. It might spray fluid, so lean back as you pull it out."

"Okay." Jalix grunted, fumbling with a wrapper. I listened closely, exchanging a surprisingly concerned look from Raven as she watched and listened in silence. "I got it. He's...his breathing is even on both sides. Some minor fluid leakage, but he's-" Jalix's voice cut to silence for a moment, giving Val a quick instruction. It was quiet for far too long before a resounding sense of panic resonated through the speaker. "His heart stopped. We're-...yeah, move him down! Get the board, we need to have him off the metal floor! Alice, we have a defibrillator, we're going to try that. Compressions in the meantime. Val, get the epinephrine." My heart sank as I realized how desperate the situation became. Alice nodded silently, tears openly streaming down her face as she failed to continue her confident grasp of his circumstances. Her arm trembled while holding the phone and I moved to support her by wrapping one of my arms around her waist in comfort. She sniffled, inciting tears from my own eyes as I silently prayed that this would work.

"Charged. Clear! Sonya, move your hands! Clear!" A single electronic beep was distorted by the weak cell reception, but wasn't followed by a series of repeated heartbeats.

"You son of a bitch!" Val roared, the sound of a dull thud resounding in my ears. He beat on Tony's chest twice, calmed by Jalix's command. I could hear the rage and sadness in his breaking and cracking voice while he bellowed at his broken friend, desperately not wanting to believe how close death truly was.

"Val, move! We're trying again. Clear!" Another beep preceded a long bout of silence before Val spoke again.

"I'm doing compressions. Jalix, give him a dose of our meds. Sonya, get something under his feet." Val and Jalix traded positions of command, each working with the other as a flawless team in the agonizing moments of wait we experienced. I turned my head to look at Raven again, her lower lip trembling while she took a step back. I rubbed Alice's shoulder, whispering in her ear.

"He'll make it, hon. He can do it." I kissed her on the cheek, the wetness of her tears clinging to my cold lips. Val's quiet grunting was muffled by the sound of their vehicle, their medical care apparently being performed on the road. "He can do it." I whispered again, more to myself than anyone else.

I can't lose anyone. I can't lose another family member. Not after what I've been through.

"I'm not going to be the only one that comes back to life, you asshole!" Val screamed, pounding on Tony's chest again as the audible crunch of bones forced me to wince in empathetic pain. "Come on! Clear!" Val roared again, the last beep of a long struggle punctuating the pain we all shared. Almost immediately, there was a second beep, followed by a third. They were inconsistent, and not of the same timing.

"He's in v-tach, we have to shock him again." Jalix said confidently. "He can take it."

"Shocking. Clear." Val affirmed, knowing that, either way, this would be the last chance they'd have to revive him. There was a pause over the phone, a known and familiar hang in the air as the miles between us became a place for combined agony. No one dared to breathe, waiting for the machine to give us a sign that he wasn't gone. With a shared gasp of air, my sister and I folded into each other's arms as a long, steady pattern of intermittent beeps represented a functioning heartbeat.

"Yes! Hell, yes!" Val's screams of victory incited further shaking from Alice as she recovered from nearly losing, yet again, one of her friends.

"He's okay." I stroked her hair, snuggling as close as I could. "He's okay."

"Alice, he's…he's in normal rhythm. We got him back. I'm giving him a second dose of our meds." Sonya breathed confidently, a loud slap indicating that she exchanged a high-five with Jalix.

"Oh, God…" Alice whimpered tearfully, wiping her eyes and trying to gain enough composure to approach the conversation again. I looked over my shoulder, giving a thumbs-up to Violet and Amy, who had both crept slightly closer during the chaos. Amy smiled, her shining silver eyes darting back to Violet and giving her a nod of affirmation. I motioned for them both to give us space, to which they complied willingly by moving to the back of the van and waiting out of sight. As I looked back, Raven had placed the most delicate presence of her fingertips on Alice's shoulder in a hesitant show of companionship. "What the hell happened?" Alice finally asked, breaking the white noise of movement and recovery on the other end of the phone.

"We walked into a goddamned warzone is what happened." Sonya commented abruptly, beginning to sound as though she was recovering from exertion as well.

"A warzone is the only way to describe it." Jalix remarked. "We…have a lot to fill you in on. Myself and some friends, I should say."

"Friends?" I asked hopefully. "How'd everyone else-"

"*Krystal?*" Jalix's voice was elated, and I realized that he hadn't heard anything regarding my condition from Sonya, Val or Tony. "Holy shit. You're…awake?"

"Sorry. Didn't have time to mention it." Sonya quipped, apologizing to Jalix.

"It's...it's great to hear your voice, Krystal. I missed you." A lump formed in my throat as I realized he had chosen to say *I* rather than *we*. "Kara's with me, sleeping off some sedatives from the bad guys, and Val and Sonya aren't too banged up. We'll all be coming back safe and sound, but the drive back to the mansion-"

"You won't be going to the mansion." Raven articulated, her voice drifting through the air like the gentle smoke of a fireplace.

"Jalix, that's another thing I forgot to mention..." Sonya started as another silence broke out. It lasted for only a brief time, Jalix still outside the scope of understanding who had spoken.

"Who is that? Is someone else with you guys?" He asked, still partially occupied with fixing or moving something on his end.

"Jalix, Raven is...alive. She was the one who found out that you guys were taken to Washington. It's a long story-" Alice started to explain, but a violent eruption of Jalix's voice made its way through the distorted speaker at high volume.

"Raven? Wha-...get the hell away from my family!" He roared, smashing something in the background. "Alice, get her away from my daughter!" He screamed, clearly upset beyond words.

"Jalix, calm down." A man said in the background, a faint Eastern European accent coloring his words. Raven raised an eyebrow at the voice, leaning in closer to the phone Alice held.

"Yuri? Is that you?" She asked. Alice and I looked at Raven inquisitively as both sides of the conversation fell catastrophically quiet. The man took a deep breath, sighing and mentally preparing for the remainder of the conversation.

"Yes, ma'am. Reporting majority success to the mission. Most teams are leaving intact. Two convoys are on the way to you, and I have the data you requested."

"Wait, what mission?" I turned, realizing there was more to Raven's presence than she was letting on.

"You're *with* her?" Jalix growled, another crash indicating that his rage was still uncontained. Val said something quietly as Alice turned on Raven, taking a step back and shrugging away the hand that rested on her shoulder.

"Sonya. Call me back in an hour. We both have things to resolve." Alice growled, hanging up the phone and separating our groups once more. The three of us stood in the open air, a chilly wind ripping its way through the remnants of the forest's leaves as my sister and I stared and tried to determine whether we had an adversary. Raven's hair lifted and blew in the breeze, the shaved side of her head exposing itself and accenting the scars on her neck.

"Go ahead. Ask." She said quietly, looking directly at Alice.

"Ask? No." Alice took a step toward Raven, who decided to stand her ground. Whether her previous fear of Alice's anger was a charade or legitimate, it appeared that her confidence in the situation she held with our family was now within more of her control. "You're going to tell me."

"Tell you what? That I knew all along who kidnapped Jalix and Kara? That I planned a rescue mission that hinged on having some of your other family members there? That before I came to you, I rescued Valterius and the girl from the same faction occupying D.C.? Or do you want to hear that I'm my father reincarnated and have *grandiose* plans for you all?" The last part of her statement transcended into sarcasm, a faint smirk an indication that she was bored of her father's theatricality.

"I want to know why you sent them...my husband...my friends...I want to know why you either want them dead by failing or alive by succeeding. What do you want from them?" Alice snarled.

"I want them *alive*, first of all. So stop this whole *Raven is the bad guy* dogma. I'm sick of it." Raven scoffed. Alice took another step forward, creating a space of only inches between their bodies and backing Raven against the guardrail that protected cars from a steep fall. "I need this world to fix itself. And I know how to make that happen. But I can't do it alone, and I *do* have a plan. One that involves all of you." She continued.

"You...have a plan." Alice stated quietly, repeating and somewhat mocking Raven's words.

"I do...at least, most of one. And it involves details that you're not aware that I know. Things my father told me before he died." She stared at Alice with intent, whose eyes became dark and withdrawn faster than I had ever seen. "Things about Kara. Her past. And her-" Raven's sentence was cut short, unpredictably slashed by a hand cupping her throat and slamming her into the mix of concrete dust and dirt that lay beneath her. I was shocked that Raven wasn't knocked out by the impact, let alone capable of struggling to escape her captor's grasp.

"Alice, what-" I started to protest, taking a step forward before the blaze of a rabid wildfire erupted between us.

She's out of control. I remember being like this...feeling that rage...there's no turning it off. No way out. Not without help.

I pressed my hands forward, smothering the bonfire in snow and hail as I strode through the barrier, pulling my sister off of her victim.

"Alice, please-"

"Don't, Krystal." She warned, turning toward me as Raven gurgled and coughed on the ground. "You have no idea. Okay?" Her breathing was heavy, eyes wide with some realization I wasn't aware of. "Raven is dangerous." She whispered, her hands beginning to spark and flicker with the outline of candle flames. "We can't trust her. She knows…she knows too much."

"What could she possibly know?" I asked, gesturing with my hand. "Whatever Schillinger knew died with him. And if she's the only semblance of that heritage, we filter the things she says and does. We regulate her, keep her captive. But killing…it's not you, hon." I pressed my cool palms against her cheeks, letting the tears freeze against my skin. "Don't bow to her level. It makes you no better than her."

Crouching in front of the hotel bed, I press my head against hers, letting the false sense of security lull her into relaxation. Such a strong, sharp chin. So much pretty hair on the back of her head. I twist, her neck snaps, and the body hits the floor.

I shook my head, trying to push away the reminder that Kara and I faced the same conversation a short while ago in my world.

"Krystal…" Her green eyes were inflamed, more than enough tears having run through them in the past few minutes. "The things she's saying she knows…it puts people in danger."

"She *already* put people in danger." I looked over at Raven and glared, watching her recover as she clutched her throat and knelt on one knee. "And I'd like to know why."

"To save…your family." She whispered, an already damaged throat having taken one too many beatings. "I need them to fix things. I knew they'd be in danger…but I sent my own people to look after them. To make sure they got out alive…" A coughing fit disrupted her monologue for a brief moment before she resumed. "If you *really* want to know, then I need to tell all of you. Yuri is doing the same thing with your other half, I can only assume. Let me tell Amy and-"

"Why would I let you anywhere near them?" Alice rebuked, a less forceful stance as she stepped forward again.

"Because you know it's the right thing to do." Raven's voice was unusually clear for a split second as she made her brief but impassioned argument to Alice. As if they spoke a secret language to one another, Alice nodded, her jaw clenched tightly in anger.

"They have *us*." I reassured, wrapping an arm around Alice's waist to try and calm her down. "And they have each other. Raven isn't capable of threatening the four of us. We're family. And she knows that if one of us gets hurt, the rest of us are ready to avenge that pain." I made the statement to Raven as she stood and nodded, crouching at an apparent and overall body pain.

"I have no wish to harm any of you. While sometimes I…will take the more desperate, more hazardous path, it's for a good reason. For the right reasons. They all lived. And our mission, the thing that we accomplished secondary to their rescue, was also a success. But there are things in motion we can't avoid. And risks…catastrophic, apocalyptic consequences if we take a wrong step. But I will tell you everything, if given the chance." My own sense of defensiveness began to subside, my calves and thighs less tense in the anticipation of either killing her or rescuing her from my sister. Alice maintained her level of anxiety, trembling quietly with red, shadowy eyes.

"Fine." Alice whispered, turning to me. "I'm done protecting her, though. If you want to take responsibility of her actions, then feel free." Her teeth were clenched, growling into the dirt as she stared at the ground and pointed a finger downward. "But I'm *done*. It ends *here* and *now*. I'm not responsible for people's lives anymore." She shook her head and stared into my eyes. "I watched you…took care of you. Took care of Kara….and Val…. Took care of all of you. And it wasn't-" A short sob interposed her speech. "It wasn't enough. And I'm done with failing. So from now on…" She sniffled, looking at Raven. "Your lives are in your own hands."

My heart dropped, realizing how much pressure had suddenly and pervasively disrupted her personality. Of everything she had experienced over her lifetime, the idea that violence and bloodshed and the sacrifice of family and friends was over had been so quickly whisked away in a flurry of events outside any imaginable control she could have held. Years of believing that the worst was over had unveiled itself as a lie.

I couldn't blame her as she turned to walk back to the van, her face and clothes smudged with dirt and debris from the road. I couldn't feel pity or disappointment for her as she took one step after another, walking away from being our family's mother figure. And I could least of all blame her for finally understanding and accepting how much she had been through over the years, decades, and few short centuries of her life. As her ruby-red hair whipped through the air behind her, I watched, allowing my soul to bleed for her, and allowing the desolation she felt to be shared as it resonated through my bones.

***

Alice's eyes had borne an indescribable sense of distance from the conversation, an emptiness only seen before in the death of her husband and inflicting a remorse unmatched by spoken language. Raven took a deep breath, leaning against the frame of the van as the rest of us sat inside and made our best attempt at comfort within the unease of it all.

"We're heading to the Kane-Hudson Charity Teaching Hospital in Jersey. Just south of here. No point in hiding that one from you all at this point. And I'm…sorry if the secretive nature of things is wearing down on the faith you've placed in me."

"Not much to wear down." Violet remarked, pulling the leather of her jacket closer to her body. Raven grimaced, nodding once in a confirmation of fairness before continuing.

"Yeah. I get that. There are some things that are just easier to explain once we get there, but the essence of my being here is that I represent another...well, you." She gestured to the group instead of an individual. "I worked in secret to build my own version of your city. I used an abandoned project of my father's. The same design, but for a different purpose, and ensured that people we both trusted could help operate everything." She paused, letting us interject as needed.

"Using...a hospital. That my father helped fund and build for studying new strains of the Vampyre virus and treating those in desperate need while the Outbreak raged on. Where the Outbreak might have started. You do realize how distorted that is?" Amy's question was blunt, but fair.

"That was the whole point. We needed someplace where cure research would be easy. So we started planting our own people within the staff-"

"*Planting.* Not the best choice of words if you're trying to convey a sense of goodwill." Violet added again.

"Look, I'm doing my best here." Raven's words sounded truthful enough, an exasperation mixed with desperation in the raspy half-whisper of her voice. "We didn't hinder any of your peoples' research. We just sent the results to our own projects underground."

"Wait, so this is literally a version of Aerael, under a hospital?" I asked in bewilderment.

"Yeah. Not quite as large, from the reports we received on Aerael, but large enough to do what we needed. We never had a complete vision of your project in Salem, as much as we tried. No one we interrogated over the years would cooperate and our-...my *father's* attempt at planting his brainwashed people ended up turning violent."

"Those infiltrators, back when Jalix first came to the city. That's what they were there for? Surveillance?" Alice finally spoke up, remembering the event clearly.

"I remember that. Tony had some guns go missing, and it turned out to be two of our citizens brainwashed by his...machine. Kara stopped them before they could attack us." Violet recalled.

"Yeah, the whole thing was my idea, minus the violence. I said we needed to map out the city. Get an exact copy of the environment, use it to make plans for...just in case. He decided otherwise." Raven paused, looking at Alice. "I never meant any harm, I just-"

"Just wanted to spy on us so you could attack later." Amy stood her ground, not falling for innocence in the context of her prior activities. "We're not stupid. If you made a mistake, own it, but don't pretend that it was something benign." Raven shook her head, acknowledging the truth in her silence.

"We're getting off-topic. My point is, we're heading to another version of your city. It has some...recognizable faces. Ones you can trust, ones you've met before."

"Oh, ones that you've brainwashed?" Violet's attitude became more aggressive the longer the conversation persisted, and I tried to appeal to cooler behavior by placing my hand on top of her own.

"No!" Raven defended firmly. "*Every* single person is there of their own free will, capable of leaving at any point and living *minutes* away in New York. In fact, we've had to force people to do so because it became too crowded. We had to fund relocation for families. This is a free place. It wouldn't work, otherwise. This is a good place. Former researchers that were freed from my company's slavery were offered generous compensation and ample living conditions to continue working toward a cure. Some of your citizens, ones that lost their faith Kara's Counsel were offered a second chance. One to keep serving your purpose, but from a distance."

"Lost faith?" I asked, keeping my tone respectful. I was genuinely curious, not hearing that side of things from my initial introduction to the world. Violet looked over at me, gently removing my hand from her own and wincing in guilt.

"The raid that emptied the city…it wasn't outsiders. It was a protest of our own people." She whispered, clearly ashamed.

"What?" I asked in astonishment, looking at Alice. She responded immediately, denying involvement.

"Ask these two. I was miles away. Didn't find out until after." She rebuked, keeping herself away from the situation. Amy answered in Alice's stead.

"Half of the city saw failure and decided to mourn. The other half became angry, knowing that Kara kept them away from our impending doom when they could have been out there helping. They felt…betrayed. Used. They felt like children, unable to act on the same level of authority as their parents. Despite our intelligence and despite our emotional stability over humans…things got heated. Val…" Amy clenched her teeth, shaking her head to keep the flushed color away from her cheeks. "Val took it personally. Someone got in his face, mentioned Jared, and he lost control. Like my mother did to you. And it started a revolt. I had to be the one to settle the situation and encourage everyone to leave peacefully." I winced as I remembered again the pain Kara had inflicted upon me in a moment of rage. Once again I found myself bewildered by my perception of Kara, seeing her in a different light than the childlike wonder and teenage heartache I once held for her.

Everything else feels so recent, but Kara…Kara feels miles away. Like I've understood my mistake for a lifetime. Although it has been resolved for twenty years, I suppose. Maybe…that's what happened in my coma-

I shook my head violently and changed the topic, not wanting to relive whatever thoughts regarding my death continued to encourage my seizures.

"I'm going to deal with that later, although I will tell you both right now I don't like that I was lied to."

"Hey, I wasn't there when you woke up." Amy argued, clearly offended. "I have no idea what they told you. But I'll *always* tell you the truth. You deserve it after everything you've been through." Her eyes met my own, more vivid and more reflective than even her mother's as an unseen light illuminated the inconceivably ashen color of her eyes. There was an intrinsic sense of poise, maturity, and intelligence in her presence, providing the false, but convincing, impression that she was older than I was. Above all, there was a sense of understanding between us, as if she understood the fantasies of pain I suffered through in my decades of comatose dreams.

"I didn't-…I didn't mean to start a feud. We should move on." Raven interjected. "We, along with the two convoys from your other group, are headed there. We're meeting up with some people and we'll talk about the details of the cure."

"Yeah, you're skipping everything we're curious about. What was with the other group? What the hell happened to them?" I pressed.

"Right. Sorry. I *do* need to explain that one in detail. Be prepared." She warned, drawing in a breath. "The group that stopped Val and yourself on the road after Krystal woke up…" She gestured to Violet. "Is the same group that showed up at the mansion, and is also the same group that attacked your people in Washington. I'm sorry to say that there's a new wave of an old problem. Possibly worse, even. Wait, just hear me out." She held up a finger, seeing that I was about to ask a question. "There's a man. He doesn't have a name, but he was a scientific project of my father's. I never knew much about its existence, and I don't think Kilkovf did, either. I think this is what he said repeatedly about not being able to understand his plans so far into the future. I think he...*somehow*... intended for all of this to happen. But this man is called the Legacy. He has a...diminished form of my father's powers and memories, but not his personality. He's a different person, keep in mind. This isn't a clone of my father, this is a new monster."

"Please tell me you're kidding." Alice whispered.

"I wish I was. He's the reason that the world shut you out. That things have been hostile from other governments. He acts, speaks on your behalf and tells them that you're part of some secret machination that caused all of this on purpose. He replaced Val as the diplomatic head of the country when you had agreed to abandon a centralized government. It was a shadow coup. No one had any idea. His own form of government is planted in the White House with access to a military base full of equipment and the key to the country's nuclear arsenal, along with all those lines of direct communication with other countries' leaders. The man we heard earlier on the phone was Yuri. He's been an inside agent of mine and a...close friend... for many years. He has the rest of the details."

"What's his goal? What are we stopping this time?" I could hear a tired, echoed voice in my head as I asked, realizing that the cycle of destruction was starting once more.

"Same as always, it seems like. Larger scale. But he wants to vaporize any chance of resistance *within* the country using his nuclear arsenal before he attacks the rest of the world. And he's building an army of Factor-Five-fueled super-Vampyres as his security force. Hundreds of them now, soon to be thousands. Yuri's mission in Washington was to accomplish three things: gain Legacy's trust to gather as much information as possible, facilitate the inevitable rescue of your friends, and get everyone out alive with as many resources as possible. Particularly his fleet of armored vehicles."

"Why was their capture *inevitable*? Why couldn't you have come sooner? Warned us? How long have you known about this?" Violet was irate, standing up and leaving the inside of the van to scream in Raven's face. It was eerie how similar their silhouettes looked. They both held themselves with confidence, seething at the other with opposing moralities.

"I needed them to see it for themselves." Raven growled. "If I came to you at any other point in time, I'd have been killed on sight. I had to *wait*... for *years*...until Krystal woke up, until things were in the *precise* conditions to make this work. If there was even the slightest variation in how things happened, none of us would be standing here. Legacy would have hunted us down and killed us in cold blood. Including me." She swallowed hard, speaking in a nearly pleading voice to Violet. "I am the only other person on this Earth that knows what my father was like. What he did. What his old plans consisted of. I am the Legacy's number one enemy, and he has no idea I'm even alive. So believe me when I say that I am risking everything for you." She bowed her head, tilting it slightly in my direction. "All of you."

"Why did you wait for me?" I asked, wondering how I was so important to her machinations.

"Because you were always a key part of your family. The cold one. The abrasive one. The reminder of what it was like to be human. I've met with enough people that were...close to Kara's Counsel. I've learned a lot about you, Krystal. Don't you ever wonder why Kara kept you around?" My heart pounded in my chest, trying to decipher what was truth and what was intimidation to gain my trust. "You were the most human out of all of them." She finished softly. My heart sank, desperately trying to comprehend how she understood my role in our family, and even more, how it could have possibly been the truth. "Alice tried to be an angel of mercy. Kara and Valterius tried to be the invincible warriors. *You* tried to be the pinnacle of innocence." She made the statement directly to Violet, making it a fact without an insult. She turned back to look at me, huddled on a crate inside of the van and listening to my own heartbeat. "And you were the model of what they were all defending. Emotion. Passion. Willpower. Everything that Vampyres embrace. So yeah...I waited until you woke up. You're a part of this."

"Don't you dare try and show compassion for her, Raven." Alice mumbled, her seated stance similar to that of Jared's whenever he had been uneasy. "You-"

"I did what, Alice? Tell me!" Raven screamed, leaning into the van. Her voice was despairing, a strained emotion making its way to our ears without a physical reaction from any of us. She didn't want to threaten us, but she was certainly angry. "Tell me what *I* did to any of you. I dare you. I ran the Catalyst project. Not Cerberus. It was because of *me* that Valterius is alive. That I personally rescued *both* of them, and not just Kara. It's because of *me* that their memories were copied by the Catalyst technology. That they had the ability to regain their personalities. Those siblings...they are alive because of *my* project. But they were dead because of my father and his brute. Kilkovf brought death and my father wrought destruction. Tell me *one thing* I did to your family." There was a long pause, a sense of hesitant understanding exchanged through passing glances.

"I want to believe that there is a good side to you, Raven. But I don't." Violet shook her head gently. "I'll work with you. I think we all will. But we won't trust you."

"My father was a controlling monster and my mother never wanted me. I'm not a product of-" Raven's protest was interrupted by a quick reproach by Alice.

"Don't go there, Raven. Pity won't get you anywhere. We have nothing left of it. You want to prove yourself, finish your story and get us on the road." Alice decided to leave the back of the van, standing by the driver's door and waiting patiently.

"There's not much left to say." Raven remarked. "Yuri acts as the head of my forces. They're not an army. Just a group of people willing to put themselves in harm's way for the greater good. He's bringing them back to Kane-Hudson and we're going to act on the intel he brings back."

"So we're now caught up? As in, everything from this moment forward is no longer planned." Amy summarized. "You were right." She stood up, leaning into Raven's face with a cool expression. "You *will* need us. Because if what you're saying is true, you're going to need an army."

"What intel is this Yuri bringing back?" I asked, stretching my legs and preparing for the next leg of our road trip. We weren't far by my mental calculation of how long we had been driving, with only a few minutes before we would arrive.

"Legacy's forces – numbers of them – at least. Any important locations he holds close. A map of Washington and his security layout for the White House. And most importantly, the nuclear capability." She paused. "Casualty predictions, locations, and potential targets for any of the missiles. That's his leverage. We take that away, all he has left is some crazed assholes that follow him. I haven't heard about anyone, aside from his politicians that work for money and future power, that are devout to his cause. If we take out Legacy and his army, we're done. We get the cure out and the world…gets repaired."

"So that's our job?" Violet raised an eyebrow. "We just have to take this guy out?" She looked at Amy, her array of ear piercings glinting in the overcast sunlight as she turned her head. "We've done this before."

"Not that it won't be a challenge, but it's doable. As long as we can amass more people. I can assume we'll have...*some* kind of authority or influence over your group?" Amy asked Raven, tucking a stray lock of silver hair behind her ear.

"No, you'll have absolute control. I'll be stepping away from the bigger leadership role. I'll keep things running, but that's it. I planned on Jalix and Kara taking over to make things work the way they always have." Raven sounded implausibly submissive.

"They'll run the city?" Alice asked, crossing her arms and furrowing her brow.

"Yeah. They deserve a second chance at being the leaders they were born to be. We need to win. We...*need* to win this." She shook her head, meeting my eyes with a remorseful sense of motivation.

She means that. She wants to right the ship.

"Good, I have friends in New York. Let's get on the road, bitches." Violet remarked, slapping Amy on the rear and climbing into the van with a great deal of energy. Alice nodded slowly, taking a long moment before opening the driver's door. She still looked ill, as if she was bearing some great burden that none of us could see.

"Thank you." Raven whispered. My head snapped to look at her, her coffee-brown eyes buried in the image of her shoes before looking up at me. "Let's get back. We're almost there." She sighed, affirming our goals and beginning to ease the tension that pulled the five of us toward conflict.

A faint whooshing sound caught my attention, and I turned toward the road to watch the assortment of cars that made their way down the highway at a reasonable speed. The sound persisted, a continuous echo behind each car that passed. I tilted my head and looked around, trying to discern the cause.

"Kryssi. Time to go." Alice reached out of her window and slapped the side of the van to get my attention, assuming I was daydreaming or unfocused.

"Hold on." I protested, the sound becoming clearer. I started to wonder whether it was damage to my ears from a lack of use before my senses guided my head upward to see an airplane making its way through the cloud cover in the same direction as our destination. It was high, miles above our heads, but stood out from the standard air traffic that sparsely populated the sky. Alice decided to use her mirror to see where I was gazing, turning her attention toward the same object.

"It's a plane." She remarked, shrugging one shoulder. "You good?" I continued to stare, letting my vision slowly focus on the object and allow its details to become clear over the vast distance between us. The clouds hid some features, but the outline became more recognizable.

"Alice, isn't that a bit small to be a passenger plane? It's moving way too fast." We watched as it took only a few seconds to pass over our heads, leaving a trail of distorted cloud remnants in its wake. "It looks like a…fighter jet."

"We don't have the capability or a reason to fly one. At least not through anyone we know of." She argued with the details, but agreed with my original point that it was incredibly questionable in the moment. "Raven. This one of yours? It's heading where we're going." At Alice's question, Raven reluctantly climbed out of the vehicle and stared as the craft maintained a straight path north.

"No. We don't have anything like that in our-" She stopped speaking, the concern of the situation spreading through the three of us. Amy and Violet climbed out together, watching the horizon as it sped toward its destination. "Yuri." She had dialed the phone and decided to address the situation with him quickly. "We have a…combat aircraft, some kind of jet heading northeast. Do you know anything about it? Yeah, we're in Union City in Jersey, on the waterfront. We can see it moving along the Long Island Sound. We-...hold on, our specialist is calling." She hung up the call and answered another, holding the phone out and putting it on speaker. "I'm with company and you're on speaker. What's going on?" A distorted beep echoed from her speaker before a modified voice began speaking. It was warped, intentionally pitched down to hide the identity of the person speaking.

"Turn on your screen-sharing." The voice demanded. Raven did as instructed, the five of us huddled around her phone to see a white circle spin for several moments as content loaded on the screen.

"-tack on the government of our recovering country. This terrorism is unacceptable, and will be met with the might of the United States' capability." A man spoke directly into a camera, the video an apparent live address given from the White House lawn. His face was firm, but calm, and had the demeanor of someone whose authority was entirely final. "Although we deeply regret that we must retaliate on our own soil, we have to strike at the heart of potential recruitment for terrorism and the current location of the enemy's activities, according to our intelligence. In doing so, we undesirably damage our country's infrastructure and its people, but we do this to prevent the risk of our country's failure as a whole. For whatever it can be worth, my prayers are with those innocents caught in the atrocities of today's events." He paused, running a hand briefly over his balding head in weariness before regaining his composure and looking directly into the camera. "But to those who oppose our new order, and to those who dare disrupt the coming age of peace and prosperity, you will be hunted and destroyed. This strike will be the first of many unless your compliance is full and complete."

"Strike...?" Violet whispered, looking up at the horizon.

"And Bryant Park, as well as the surrounding areas of Manhattan…will never be forgotten."

No…

"God bless America."

Raven's phone screen distorted into another brief loading image before showing a symbol representing a disconnect of her cellular data.

We each looked at each other for the briefest moment, caught in raw terror before the paralyzing flash of a purely destructive light infested our eyes with unimaginable pain, forcing each of us to recoil in shock and horror at the seared image we were now branded with. The shadow of the horizon of the city was blackened against the light, matched in luminosity with an unchecked sun while it tortured my clenched-shut eyes. I looked back too soon, fully accepting that the brightness had not yet fully faded and watched a column of ash, soot, and vaporized debris heave itself above the skyline of proud buildings and force its way into the atmosphere with no regard to anything that stood in its way.

A translucent sphere carved its way through the horizon, distorting the vision of New York's magnificence and replacing its image with an omen of pure death as the shockwave struck the area around it and covered my entire field of view in carnage. The sound hit me after many seconds, too many seconds, of watching the hostile cloud ascend to godhood. It was a sharp rumble, like the striking of a massive drum only inches from my ear.

The explosion was centered on the island, but its annihilative effects spread across the land mass into the waters and caused, hidden to our eyes, the instantaneous deaths of tens of thousands of people living or working in Manhattan. We couldn't witness the violent massacre caused by the shockwave or the deaths from the sphere of fire and radiation that ravaged the city, but we each knew the consequences of such an apocalyptic act and we grieved in its shadow.

Violet sobbed loudly, doubled over in emotional pain while her eyes remained glued to the intermittent set of falling buildings that followed like dominoes. Some structures stood strong, held in place and broken without being defeated. Others collapsed into dust, as if meaningless to the grand scheme of the city's devastation. Nothing was free from the nuclear explosion's effects, instantly devastating the country's history and ripping an incomprehensible hole through the population in a matter of seconds.

There were no audible screams heard from the distance at which we stood, with the exception of my sister's singular and unfathomably grieved howl at the horizon. The only thing that remained was a reminder of what had occurred. We stared at a scar, watching the lifeblood of our country seep unchecked into the ground. I tried to move, wanting to comfort Amy, who had collapsed into Violet to create an embracing bundle of tragedy and trauma, but I could only stare at the cloud of death and allow the soft salt of tears to enter my open mouth.

No words were spoken between us, entire minutes passing as the reckoning settled in each of our minds as a piece of gruesome history. History that we had no power, no option, and no hope of changing. I decided to sit on the ground, watching the waters of the sound wash continuously against any surface it met. Nature, it seemed, was the only thing uninterrupted by the wretched genocide that befell us. I sat, decidedly, and allowed myself to succumb to simpler thoughts, bringing the cool air of autumn and the habitual swaying of water into my soul to wash away the horrors I would remember for the rest of my long life.

REPRISAL

JALIX

I looked away from Yuri for a brief moment, shaking my head in disbelief. Sonya beat me to the punch on chastising him and berating his sense of secrecy during our nearly lethal escapade. I didn't listen to her words, but I watched her angry expression as she pointed to Tony's fragile and stitched-up body, as well as Yuri's despondent face. It was clear that he felt he had little choice in keeping his secrets, but it enraged the three of us nonetheless. I took a second to think, allowing the breadth of long-held plans to make sense in my own mind.

"I was your friend, Yuri." I interrupted quietly. Sonya stopped in the middle of a sentence and grimaced, holding back more words until she could think her way through the discussion properly. "I fought alongside you. Why keep all of this from us? I was a captive long enough that you could have slipped me a note or-"

"There was no way to tell you without altering our plans. If you knew, things would have played out much different. And we could only afford one shot at this." He explained calmly. "I know it's frustrating. I know it seems like I put you in danger."

"You pissed me off is what you did." I interjected. "Raven? How could you work with her, Yuri? She's the enemy. How the hell is she even alive?"

"Her project Catalyst gave her the tools to partially repair her throat. She was killed in the very place that studied bringing back the dead. With some transfusions and surgery, it wasn't a fatal injury. Her corporation was all she needed. Then it came down to secrecy. She knew you'd kill her if you knew she was alive."

"Damn right. She tried to kill my wife. She *did* kill my wife."

"No. *Kilkovf* killed your wife. Schillinger killed your wife. Raven had nothing to do with any of this. But it's not important right now, she can explain all of that to you later."

"Yeah, you mentioned we had to hurry back." Sonya's tone was significantly calmer than in previous moments. "I'm assuming you have some kind of base."

"I have intelligence to deliver. Straight from the Legacy, things that should cripple his defenses if we act on it appropriately. But yes, we have an area of operations. Raven built a small location under the Kane-Hudson hospital in New Jersey near Manhattan. We're going there." He summarized, pulling a small portable hard drive from his combat vest pocket and holding it up. "And we're planning."

"What was worth risking our lives over?" Val growled, pointing to Tony. "What would have been worth his life?"

"The Legacy's military operations. His defenses, his hardware, his perimeters and personnel records. And where he gets his supplies and trains his men. It's his keystone."

"Which is?" I pressed.

"MCB Quantico." Yuri paused, waiting for my reaction.

"Quantico. He has…Quantico?" I chuckled in disbelief. "Val worked with the remaining military to decommission-"

"Schillinger had indoctrinated people working for him during that time. It's how he acquired the missile launcher for his attack on D.C. during Project Cerberus. Before the federal military disbanded, Legacy took over the men under Schillinger's command and used what he needed. A handful of fighters, helicopters-"

"Yeah, I know what's *at* Quantico, Yuri. Right before the Outbreak, they consolidated with Air Combat Command. They had Security Forces, Explosive Ordnance Disposal, everything. Plus pilots. *Tons* of pilots." I rolled my eyes, the brief memory of trying to get past a line of freshly-minted lieutenants at a bar one of many old memories I had of the military base. "So that's how he's getting all those soldiers equipped, I assume? Just taking from the stockpiles there?"

"Yes. And he has a limited number of those pilots at his side. A small handful of helicopter pilots and one or two for fighters. I'm not sure where they're located."

"Jesus Christ." Val chuckled. "This is *great*. At least Schillinger had the courtesy of being subtle. Now we can expect nuclear attacks, air strikes, ground assaults, and who knows what else? Just tell me he doesn't have a Navy."

"He does not have a Navy." Yuri affirmed.

"Jalix, prepare to swim, because that's the only way to beat this guy."

"Val, not right now. Not a good time for sarcasm." I tried to be gentle, but his tone was irritating and careless in a moment that required focus.

"Sarcasm? No, I'm serious. Because unless we take away the military base he has control of, we're outmanned, outgunned, and *shit* out of luck." Val growled, waving a dismissing hand at me. I was settled on one of the few seats in the back of the vehicle, pensively considering an option before looking back up at Yuri.

"Stop the truck." I called, loud enough for the driver to hear. The driver looked over his shoulder, acknowledging the command only after Yuri gave him a quiet nod. Without windows, I couldn't see where we were, but I could feel the slight dip on my side of the vehicle as we settled onto the shoulder of the road. "Val, open the back hatch. I need some air." Val reluctantly complied, Sonya staring at me with an intense curiosity. I looked at her through the corner of my eyes, conveying that I did indeed want to discuss things with her, but only once we were away from the truck. Somehow, she understood my language and strolled out of the back hatch with me while Yuri and Val began a polite debate over an aspect of Tony's care.

"Jalix, you need to take a rest." She sighed, looking down at my tattered and bloody clothes. "You have been through *hell* and back. You're probably worse off than Tony, because at least he's asleep for all of this." I sighed, nodding and inhaling a gust of comforting fumes from the exhaust of the vehicle. The smell of diesel exhaust reminded me of one too many convoys during my days in the military.

"But I'm in a position to act. Not recover. That's the difference between us. And that's why we need to split up." The next vehicle in our convoy pulled up behind us, coming to a stop more than a dozen feet in front of me and allowing a gunner to start watching the road for Legacy's followers. Pedestrian cars whizzed by, clearly trying to get away from whatever threat they perceived in our group. "You need to get Kara and Tony back to safety." I looked at my still-unconscious wife, whose breathing was as slow and steady as when I first pulled her from Legacy's enslaving machinery. "Whatever they gave Kara is going to keep her unsteady for a while, and she's going to know what to do with the intel that Yuri has when she wakes up. Combine that with Tony's need for a stable environment, and we have a reason to get them someplace that isn't a battlefield. To get them back to Alice."

"No one can be on a battlefield right now." She protested, pressing lightly against my shoulder.

"Val and I can. With Yuri and his men, we might have a shot at taking that base. At the very least, we can do some recon and see what we'll be up against later. But we can't wait. You saw those…animals. You shoot one and another steps out from behind the body. This is what Schillinger imprinted onto the Legacy. The Pyrates were *practice*, Sonya. They were…a trial run. These…Factor-Five-addicted monsters are what the Pyrates were meant to be. An army of disposable drones willing to charge in and die for the cause. We need to be ready for that fight when it comes." She groaned, her eyes widening in frustration.

"Then let me come with you." She pleaded. It was interesting that she didn't make demands, and instead tried to negotiate with me.

She knows I'm right. At the very least, she knows she can be an asset to Kara and Tony, plus keep an eye on Raven.

"I need someone I trust. This is my wife. My friend. My *daughter* that needs protecting. I need someone who loves them like I do." Sonya looked over at Kara, being tended to and carefully examined by Val. "Someone to keep an eye on Raven and make sure that Violet and Amy have some stability in all this madness. I need you, Sonya. Please. I know you're a warrior, but just this once, I need you to be a guardian."

"Alright. I get your point." She agreed quickly, understanding that time was a factor and that there was no logical argument she could make. "Take Val and Yuri in this truck and lead this convoy down to Quantico in Virginia. I'll wait in the vehicle behind us with our two patients until the second convoy catches up, and we'll break off to go to Kane-Hudson with Alice."

"Works for me." I nodded, a mutual understanding enough to compel our next steps. "Val!" I called, raising my voice slightly over the noise of the engines of the two vehicles that sandwiched me along the road. Sonya stepped up the ramp and into the vehicle, patting Val's back as he stepped down to talk to me.

"Sup?" He asked, eyebrows raised.

"Sonya's going to take over and get the sick ones back to your wife. You, me, and Yuri are going to steal this convoy and go take over a Marine Corps-FBI base and its airfield." I recapped.

"Huh. Alright. Well…" He scratched his beard, nodding to Yuri. "Can we actually trust him?"

"Yeah." I verified. "I'm going to be hard on him for what he did by withholding information, but I know him. He wouldn't let us down. He had a reason, however shitty it might have been."

"I didn't think we hit the suicide-mission part of the conflict yet. Us against what, a few hundred of those maniacs? They're not Pyrates, man. They're…hell, I don't know what to call them, but they're freaks. And we don't have the manpower to take them on-" I started to interject, but he held up a finger to stop me. "*And*, on top of all that, they control the base and have access to the equipment necessary to annihilate us."

"Isengard." I quipped, trying to get a word in while I could. Val paused, staring at me for a moment as his face shifted from confusion to reluctant understanding.

"There's no way." He was opposed to the idea entirely, his arms crossed on his chest and stance leaning away from me. "Not a chance in hell."

"But it's a chance." I argued, trying to bait him into the idea.

"What's a chance?" Sonya asked jovially. "I like chances." She had approached us just enough to hear the tail end of our conversation.

"Isengard." I repeated.

"Bless you." Her nose wrinkled in confusion and contempt.

"You've never read The Lord of the Rings?" I asked in disbelief, knowing Sonya was well educated, even after her memory loss.

"Oh, god. I had *so many* books to read after I lost my memory, forgive me if I skipped a few."

"Two seemingly insignificant characters incited a huge force of neutral characters to help them take over the bad guy's castle." Val summed in the most crude of ways.

"Technically they persuaded an army of trees to help out, but the point is valid." I turned to Sonya to elaborate on the idea. "We can't do anything on our own, but if we can convince Yuri to lend us his security force, we might be able to pull a shock-and-awe assault and catch them off-guard. They'd never expect us to take them head-on, not in a million years. They might be stockpiling weapons and vehicles there, but it's not the focus of their defense."

"The closer we are to *danger*..."

"The farther we are from *harm*." I finished Val's reference, knowing full well that he only knew about this subject because of Eric and his fascination with the movies so many years ago.

"Anyone who's spent the last few years building up a usable army is going to be reluctant to send them on a one-way trip. It's going to be a trade. People for equipment, for geography. You do know that, right? Anyone that isn't a professional soldier is going to be massacred." She looked at the two of us, but directed the final question to me.

"Yeah." I paused. "I know. Such is all war. But we don't have much choice. We need the aircraft and munitions to have a chance against Legacy's power. It's not like we can afford to fight this conventionally." I looked at Val. "What about you, man? You've been in enough fights, seen enough wars. You *know* how this goes. People die to take a hill that ends up not mattering in the long run. But in that short time, it provides a critical advantage. Do you think this is worth it?"

"Well, if Yuri's telling the truth and only has a hundred guys or so, we could end up needing to train and recruit a whole new army to take on Legacy. It's…it's a tough call. Not one I'm going to make. What would Kara do?" Sonya grimaced as the three of us looked at her still-sleeping body. Yuri watched her closely, studying her for signs of movement while she slept and dreamt of a world far outside the reality she would awake to.

"Kara…would let Yuri decide." I sighed. "I think at one point, she would have said that this was worth sacrificing people for…but now, she'd want that decision to be on the person that leads them." Sonya nodded, beckoning as the three of us made our way back into the rear cabin of the armor-clad wheeled vehicle.

"Yuri." I started, gesturing to Tony's body. "We need to prevent more of this from happening. And we need your people for it."

"Then you will have them." He affirmed, putting a hand on my shoulder. "It's what they signed up for. Too many of them have wanted a fight for a long time."

"We want to take down Quantico, Yuri. That's…not going to be an easy ask. And a lot of them-"

"Will die. Happily, for our cause. When Raven and I recruited them, we followed in the footsteps of your city's mantra: only those in dire need. So we did the same. We found those that needed to fight back. That had loved ones taken and indoctrinated by Legacy's torture. Every one of my men, well-…men and women…are strong and well-trained. They'll fight and win your battle." He drew his phone from his pocket and tapped the driver's shoulder. "You and I will point at what we want taken, and they will take it." He smiled, holding the phone to his ear and speaking with someone on the other end. I took the opportunity to begin planning, starting with the most immediate of issues.

"Sonya, take Kara to the truck behind us. Val, take Tony. Get them settled in for the drive and have the crew contact the rest of the convoy so they know the plan."

"Come on, dude. Let's get you back." Val grunted, lifting Tony's body like a lightweight pane of glass, gingerly supporting every piece of his body so as not to break anything further. Sonya swept behind me as she moved toward Kara, stopping at my hand on her arm.

"Hey. When Kara gets there, have her go through a couple of thorough physical exams with Alice and Amy. She...shouldn't be out this long."

"Yeah." She agreed, tilting her head. "She should have woken up by now, drugged or not. But...she's okay, I'm sure of it. I can feel it, she's alright." She paused, a smirk crossing her lips. "Maybe it's fate. If she was awake, she'd be going with you to fight. But since she's going back to this new city...maybe she'll have a chance to be a leader again. The way she was all along." I smiled, remembering Kara's golden days, the first years following her phoenix-esque resurrection.

"Yeah, maybe. If that's the case, let me know when you get there. Okay? I don't know how long it'll be until we're all back together. Alice and Kara are going to need you."

"I think the women know how to manage without you guys." She winked, lifting Kara's body and cradling it to her chest. She kissed me on the cheek as she walked by, turning her head slightly to say a few short words. "But I know. And I will." I watched the flutter of her blonde hair disappear behind the other vehicle, saying a silent prayer that I'd see them both again and turning to listen in on the remainder of Yuri's conversation.

"Da. Yes…I'll send-…yes, thank you. Mhmm. My edem na voynu." His closing statement sounded familiar and was certainly Russian in nature, but my language skills had degraded to the point that I ignored it entirely and focused on his open facial expression as he turned to me.

"Our specialist is going to coordinate the rest of my people's movement to us. Once Valterius gets back, we can go over some of the details."

"Speaking of details, I'm assuming you've followed the plan so far based on…" I gestured to the missing bodies in the back of the truck.

"Sonya will be returning Kara and your other friend to the rest of your family while Valterius and yourself work with me and my forces to lay siege. Sound right?" He smirked. "I know how you work, remember?"

"It's been a minute, Yuri…how did you end up in all of this? I figured your standing with Kilkovf-"

"Led to some interesting employment opportunities." He nodded. "I stayed within the ranks of those demons for the sake of appearance, and to keep myself alive. Schillinger wasn't fond of letting people walk away, and I wasn't sure what his daughter would have done. Until Raven was made public by Schillinger and revealed to the world, she was…a mystery to many. Schillinger's…princess, locked in her proverbial tower and guarded closely. An unknown variable. But she contacted me shortly after her alleged death and requested that I stay under her employment. She explained nothing. Only made a polite request and assured that I could act freely as long as I stayed close to those that still followed her father's ideals. It led to a highly beneficial partnership. The intelligence I provided her stalled Legacy's efforts for many years." He looked up as Val started making his way toward us. "I trust her with my life. And the two of us, along with our specialist, have been the only ones to recognize the threat that's been growing under our noses. But we needed all of you to finish what we started."

"Seems like you've gotten as capable as anyone could expect. Why would you need us?" Val rebuffed, leaning against the inside of the vehicle and scratching his beard. He barely fit in the cramped space, a heavy lean the only way to remain upright.

"You're their target. Doesn't matter how much we strike at them. If they know you're out there, they're going to keep coming. The Legacy is single-minded. He wants Kara or her daughter to be at the head of this country once he eradicates his share of humans. Until then, a slave...but afterward, a cure and queen. Luckily, he won't strike at the humans until everything is in place. So we've stalled their efforts, kept them away from you-"

"Wait, you *what?* Kept away? How many times have they gone after us?" My phone rang, ignored as the conversation became of further importance.

"I've lost count." Yuri clenched his jaw. "It's recent, mind you. I think their political setup took a long time. Add the recruiting and brainwashing of the soldiers and it led to the takeover of Quantico just over a month ago. The military occupation of D.C. a few weeks ago. They didn't start coming after you until their plans were in place."

"Speaking of, what about our people in D.C? I only saw the fighters, did he kill the civilians?"

"No, you just weren't near the makeshift residential areas. He pushed back a perimeter, created a demilitarized zone around the White House and relocated any civilians further away. Which is good news for us." He looked at Val. "Civilian casualties will be low or zero, as long as we keep the combat within that zone. Keep it from spreading out."

"Insane that we're talking combat when things were fine just a short while ago." Val remarked as my phone rang again, vibrating against my thigh.

"It wasn't fine, Valterius. It was chaos. We just helped keep your family away from it all." Yuri's remark wasn't made to discourage or insult us by implying that we were cowards, but was attempting to express the sense that he was willing to do what was necessary to help. As I pulled my phone out of my pocket, I realized Val and Yuri were doing the same, each of us receiving a call.

"It's Amy." I said, looking over at Val.

"Alice." He held up his phone briefly.

"Raven." Yuri sighed discontentedly. I had a sense of dread, being fully aware that there was no reason for them all to call at once unless something was very wrong. I answered the call, rushing out of the vehicle to stand off the road and away from louder noises.

"Amy-"

"Dad?" She whispered tearfully. There was a long pause, and I could hear her breaths become more uneven as she tried to hold back heaving tears. "I love you. I'm so glad you're okay. Mom didn't pick up the phone and-"

"Of course I'm okay..." I tried to comfort her, not having heard despair in her voice since she was a small child. "I'm right here. And your mom is on her way back, she's just...sedated. I'm sending her with Sonya. What's wrong? We-"

"Dad..." She interrupted, still struggling to speak. "They bombed us. They...Manhattan is *gone*." She sniffled hard several times, trying to maintain her composure. "We saw the flash and-...he killed them all." Her voice cracked at the end of her sentence and I could hear her muffled cries as her hand stifled her mouth.

"Wait, slow down, baby. Are you all okay? Violet and everyone else, are they-"

"We're fine, dad. We were...far enough away. They sent a fighter jet and it-...the size of the blast. It was nuclear. He wanted them dead. Everyone in New York, just…the buildings and-"

"You're okay, Amy. It's alright, I-…" My heart sank, the horror of Legacy's act pounding through my chest in panic and anguish. It was a familiar feeling, as the old scars of terrorism opened once again a gash in my heart. "Your mom's on her way back to you. Do you guys still have someplace safe to go? Is the hospital okay?" I tried to plan ahead, making sure that, above all, they could get to safety and be shielded from further risk.

So many people dead in the blink of an eye. All because of one deranged lunatic's agenda. Thousands of people, slaughtered. My family at risk of it happening again.

"Yeah. Did Yuri tell you about their city? The one Raven is in charge of, under-"

"Under the hospital. Yeah, I know."

"Okay. Raven said it was definitely outside the blast radius, a few miles away. We have to drive *around* the city, but we'll be there soon. Just tell…wait-…" Amy's voice faded away from the speaker, talking to someone else in the background. There was a second or two of shuffling, followed by a brief voice.

"Jalix? Can I-…you mind?" The hazy smolder of Raven's voice was distinct now in my mind, having burned it into my memory after the prior conversation.

"What, Raven?" I prompted, knowing it had to be important if she was willing to speak with me directly.

"We're in Jersey, just outside of Manhattan. We're taking a path around the city as much as we can to stay away from the radiation and the rubble. Cell signal is weak here, and if we get into the radiation, it'll be gone. You won't hear from us until we're in the city and settled. I'm texting you and Val the directions in case Yuri gets separated from you." She paused. "I'll keep them safe. Okay? I…" She struggled with her words, a mix of anxiety and fear evident in her respectful tone. "You had every right to kill me. Still do. But if you want to finish the job, wait until this is all over. Please." My chest heaved in an odd mixture of solemn necessity and regretful trust, my emotions still in turmoil after hearing about the destruction wrought on the remains of our country. I looked over at Val, leaning heavily into the truck and holding back tears as he spoke to Alice. I could hear his reassurances and comforting words as he tried to relay them to someone who witnessed an incomprehensible trauma.

Amy and Violet…my wife….Alice and Krystal and everyone I'm sending back. Their lives in her hands. Under the dominion of Schillinger's progeny. I'll never forgive myself…

"Okay." I whispered, angry tears starting to form in my bloodshot eyes. "Okay. Get them…get them safe, Raven. At *any* cost, do you understand?" I pleaded. "If anything happens to them-"

"I'll do whatever it takes." She whispered, becoming emotional, herself. "I don't care if you trust me or believe me. But it's the truth. And you *know* that."

"You get one shot at my trust." I growled, shaking my head. "*One*…chance, I will give you. Val and I…and Yuri, we have to do something that's going to delay us for a while."

"Our specialist let me know after Yuri called him. I relayed the plan to everyone here. That's why I offered to take them all to safety instead of waiting for you." She waited for a moment, looking for the right words. "I hope you're successful. It's not going to be easy. But Yuri's a good man. A good soldier. You're lucky to have him." Her voice softened when she spoke about him, arousing a suspicion that they were more than friends.

"Let me talk to Amy again. I'll hear from you soon."

"Yeah." She finished quietly, handing the phone back to my silver-haired daughter.

"Hey. I'm sorry, I'm trying to keep myself together right now." Amy sighed, taking in a long, deliberate breath of air. "I know I'm usually the level-headed one." She chuckled, a thin veil of pretense that she was okay.

"There's no such thing in a moment like that. I've...I've been in your shoes. Seen terrorism happen, seen what it does to people. People close to me. New York, when I was exactly your age. I lost people in that attack. History repeats itself and you ended up being a victim of it."

"I've always been very much your daughter." Her remark came from a place of soft humor, but was lost in the realization that I had to ensure she handled the situation better than I did at her age. "I'm okay. I'll *be* okay. Krystal is taking it harder than the rest of us. I want to spend some time with her and...try to connect. She seems like she'd make a good friend."

"She's a good person, and I trust her completely. I hope you guys get to bond a little bit while I'm gone. Keep Violet and Alice close, okay? They need you. They're going to listen to your judgement, especially when it comes to Raven and handling things in a new environment. Just...be the badass you've always been. Your mom will be back in no time to help. Alright?"

"'Kay, dad. I love you. Stay safe, alright?" I was warmed by her affection, allowing it to steel me.

"I love you, too. Call you when I can."

I won't make any promises unless I know I can keep them.

I ended the call, swiftly walking over to Val to provide whatever support he and Alice may have needed. He had apparently just hung up, our conversations each taking roughly the same amount of time. His tired eyes held a shade of red that I didn't recognize on his face; it was something that didn't match him in any way. It was a mixture of anger and of sadness, but it most prominently implicated suffering.

He looked hopeless, as if his previous fervor for our cause was torn down and burned in front of his eyes.

"Is she okay?" I asked, making direct eye contact to draw his focus. He didn't hesitate, his lips moving to create a single word.

"No." I let the silence afterward linger, trying to avoid listening as Sonya stumbled down the ramp of her vehicle and crumpled onto the gravel in agonizing howls of defeated anger and grief.

"*Is* she okay?" I asked firmly, gripping his shoulder and leaning in closer. Through something that could only be described as brotherhood, my own emotions broke through to him, a grit hidden behind his beard accompanying an animalistic snarl.

"Yeah..." He shook his head, finally returning my gaze. "They're alright. I'm...I'm not, though, man." He sighed deeply, tilting his head back to avoid damaging his masculinity with tears. As he slid down the side of the vehicle and sat upright against the massive tires, I knelt down and continued pressing.

"Val, I need you to realize something." I sighed, looking away for a moment and letting the lump in my throat dissipate. "I don't know how bad you had it when Kara and Sonya were first infected. But that instinct? The time when only their being alive mattered? That's where we are. Except they're not helpless anymore." He looked up at me, exhaling strongly again. I extended my hand, standing up and opening my palm. "And they're not alone, man. Not as long as we're there for them." He nodded, grabbing my arm and pulling himself back onto his feet. He failed to let go, instead pulling me into a rough bear hug and clapping my back.

"I've been through...too much *shit* for this to happen again, Jalix." He mumbled, his thoughts finally coalescing into reasonable words. "We all have. But Kara...Sonya...they had time to reset, they had things that helped them forget the past." He backed up a few inches, still holding my arm and keeping me close. "But I can't forget. I can't move on. All the things they've done to us. Even to you, tearing...tearing you apart like they did. How can you keep walking?" He asked honestly. "You know *exactly* what I'm talking about. That shit that weighs on you, that you never forget. How do you function with it? How do you handle yourself and still have enough left over to keep people close...and help them with their own suffering?" Yuri caught the corner of my eye, reaching out to hand me a backpack-sized protective case and motioning to Sonya.

"It's the hard drive I stole from Legacy. Have Sonya take it back with her. We need to go." He said it with remorse, understanding that we were all coping with tragedy. I took the case from his hand, putting a fist on Val's chest as I stepped away.

"By turning it all into a lie, Val. When you defeat the shit keeping you down, it turns into a lie. All those *maybe* situations, all the risks, all the potential catastrophe, it's all a lie until it actually happens. The enemy isn't an enemy. The trauma isn't a trauma. It all turns into memories...lies that life told you. And then you make new memories. Better ones, ones that hold the truth about your life and what's important. Don't believe the lie. Our family's alive, and we're going to get rid of anything that endangers that. For now, that's our truth." I could see a shift in the light behind his eyes, his shoulders setting back into their proper place as his posture recovered to a proud soldier. Turning away finally, I approached Sonya and watched her stand to greet me.

"No lectures, Jalix." She started, wiping away tears. "This sucks to hell and back, but I'm alright. My priority is getting back to the rest of them."

"I know." I smirked, handing her the briefcase and watching her set it in the cabin of the vehicle. "You're the one that gave me the same advice I just gave Val. I wanted to say thanks before we parted ways." She tilted her head, smiling at me through her red eyes. I took a step forward and let her wrap her hands around my shoulders.

"No more goodbyes. Go be a soldier. Come back in one piece." I nodded, saying nothing in return. She kissed the top of my head in spite of my matted hair and took a step back, retracting the vehicle's ramp and closing the hatch. I waved briefly, watching my sleeping wife slowly disappear and become one of the two people I couldn't say goodbye to. I stepped away, trotting back to the inside of my vehicle as Val closed our hatch, as well.

"My people are already mobilizing. They're…adequately driven to perform in the manner needed for our upcoming events. This is their home, too." Yuri said confidently, retrieving a backpack-sized case from under a seat and opening it.

"When you say upcoming events, you do mean to tell me that they understand what we're asking of them?" I verified with Yuri.

I can't send people to their deaths unaware. Or worse, unwilling.

"Jalix, these are people. Not slaves, not soldiers. They're the same as the citizens that lived in your own city. In fact, some of them *are*. Perhaps you'll see some familiar faces." Val remained silent, staring at the floor as Yuri pulled a laptop from the case and turned it on. "There's a small party that will meet with Raven and get everyone to safety. A security contingent. They should be there within the hour, maybe two."

"You good with this?" I asked quietly, nudging Val's foot. "We're about to head into a combat zone. It's been a while…for both of us. You ready?" His head rose slowly, turning to lock his eyes with my own and growl his response.

"Just point me in the right direction."

DELIVERANCE
ALICE

There wasn't a sensation to describe the blitz of scents or sounds or other distractions that permeated the air as I exerted my legs to their upper limits to sprint across the piles of still-shifting debris. The air was acrid, stinging my eyes every second with a fresh layer of dirt that ended up streaked on the side of my face in a mixture of sweat and cleansing tears. I stumbled more than once, my thoughts and senses focused on my next goal rather than whatever laid beneath my feet. I slid on my knees, skidding down a small pile of pulverized concrete and throwing the bag off my shoulder. The body in front of me was quivering, a mass of red skin half-hidden behind a veil of blackened burns and melted polyester clothing.

They're dead.

I craned my head, watching a pair of stark white eyes dart its pupils back and forth nearly faster than I could track. The stench of their burning flesh reached my nose with a whiff of sulfur, iron, and sour milk, and I did my best to ignore it as I reached into the bag, hastily withdrawing one of the last bands of red fabric before tying it loosely around the only visible place it would stay: the victim's neck. I debated whether the pair of eyes had attempted to look in my direction, the briefest flicker either the last act of a doomed soul or an electrical impulse along desensitized nerve endings.

They're dead.

My feet fell flat against the surface as I stood again, pushing myself off the summit of the small mountain before a hand and set of exerted lungs stopped me.

"Alice…" Amy breathed quickly. "Please. There's nothing you can do."

"No, I just need to find them." I shook my arm in an attempt to force away her grip and was surprised at her tenacity. She held on, standing behind me and anchoring her feet in the rubble of the building I walked on.

"There's nothing you can do. We don't have the supplies to deal with this, and we're going to get sick if we stay here too much longer. Our virus can't handle much more radiation damage, even with my abilities." She pled with me, pulling me away into a safer area of the rubble.

"That's why I need to find them quickly. Anyone that's left, I *have* to find them." I argued, glancing into my bag. The white strips I had torn from an old tank top were all present, but the red strips that I was using to distinguish victims fated for death were entirely depleted.

"We can come back." Amy continued. I paused, weighing her words. "Anyone this close to ground zero is dead, and anyone further away either died instantly from collapses or will live long enough for Raven's reinforcements to find them. Let the search teams handle it. But please, we need to go."

"Alice!" Krystal called, finally catching up to us. Amy took the bag from my hand, weak and trembling with indecision. "Come on, we need to get back to the van and get out of this air. Please."

They're dead.

Around me, a swirl of brown and gray dust on the wind picked up a hail of indistinguishable sound from across the city as life slowed to a forlorn crawl. I nodded, grimacing and starting a slow and careful jog across the mountains of unstable building material. Glass was reduced to dust in the ashy remains of once-proud structures, the majority of our ground consisting of concrete and sheared metal beams. I hesitated, stopping to look into a large gap between two massive columns of supportive stone before realizing the chasm was too quiet to hold any form of life that was still capable of drawing breath.

"Alice, come on." My sister reassured, standing still for a moment to allow Amy and I to catch up. "We have time, we just need to get further away for now. If you want to help, we can comb the highway on the route around the city. We might find people there that need help, people that are fleeing."

They're dead.

"Yeah…yeah, good idea. Back onto the highway. Back across the bridge." I tried not to take large breaths in the threat of radiation and searing dust, but calmed myself with focused bursts of oxygen as we neared Raven and the van once more. Her long, black hair was caught in the breeze, making the scars on her neck more obvious as she pulled on the door to let us in.

"My people split up. There's a small group that's dealing with survivors just north of here, and the rest are going straight to Yuri. We can help those refugees on the way." Raven reassured, trying to placate me with a sense of inspiration. "Sonya and the rest aren't far. They'll catch up with us in less than an hour."

"Don't treat me like a child, Raven. I'm five times your age. I don't need patronized." I snarled, closing the door after Krystal and Amy were both safely inside with Violet.

She argued while sliding behind the wheel, not bothering to maintain eye contact with me as I made my way to my seat.

"I'm not, Alice. I understand that you want to help these people, and so do I."

"I want to *help* them, not recruit them." I countered pointedly as the vehicle lurched forward. She gritted her teeth and sighed.

"This shit again…I'm not playing this game, Alice. This was our home, *my* home. Don't-…" Her words were halted with another short sigh. Her eyes flitted over to me, for a moment appearing to roll in irritation. "You worry about your family, I'll worry about mine. We can part ways when this is over. It's not my job to appease you. Bigger shit to worry about." I wanted to reply, but even if I had tried, couldn't have possibly cared less about what she thought of me. I stared through the window and remained busy within my own thoughts, trapped in an endless cycle of stress between a vast multitude of problems in varying complexity.

"I watched this place grow." I said quietly, a rough and jarring dip in the road a quick obstacle before we were on the highway once more. I looked forward, still able to see plenty of towering buildings that were intact, less the dignity of shattered windows and ashen walls. The majority of the city was completely untouched, but it was a reality I had yet to deal with. Despite the blast being relatively isolated, the horror and abruptness of the attack increased its scale in my mind.

"New York?" Raven asked quietly. I sat for a moment and listened to the idle chatter in the back, Krystal and Violet talking about something while Amy listened, as per her usual self.

"Yeah. It was always meant for greatness, if you ask me. Not all places are. But there's a certain…spirit that surrounds some things. A charm, an allure. It started out of necessity and blossomed into a vision of something greater."

In a quick glimpse out at the water, I saw the green majesty of the Statue of Liberty, intact and proud.

"You're not just talking about New York, I can tell." She lowered her voice, scanning ahead on the bridge despite a void so far in traffic and passers-by. We finally crossed the river, continuing along the road as we escaped the dusty air. "I'm sorry for-"

"Don't be." I interrupted, leaning my head against the glass. "Aerael would have become a crypt for my family, a memorial for our race, or a mausoleum for my sister. We...evolved out of it the moment we were known to the public. We didn't need to live underground anymore."

"Still, that doesn't take the sting away any less of leaving your home. I'll never understand it the way you do, but I know the feeling of being without a place to call home. With this new city...only in the last few years have I truly felt that it was my own. And I know I couldn't imagine losing it. You may not want it, but you have my sympathy." Her voice sounded sincere, a jarring sense of amicability between us only serving to make the message awkward in spite of its words.

"If you really feel that way, just help us win and rebuild. That's all I'm asking from you." I imagined what Val would do in my place, and ignoring his likelihood of ripping her head from her spine, I decided to implement his sense of diplomacy.

"With any luck, the rebuilding will come easy. It's the winning that's hard." Her words rang true, but were kept short as her attention was diverted to a small group of military vehicles headed our way. They were in the opposite lane, a short convoy of Humvees and transport trucks crawling down the road.

"We should speed up-" I took a moment to redirect my thoughts as the first two vehicles turned to the side and stopped, blocking the road a few hundred feet ahead of us.

"Shit." I whispered, knowing full well they weren't Raven's people. "This is similar to what happened to Val and Violet."

"I was there, remember? I killed them all." Raven remarked, bringing the vehicle to a lower speed and continuing to crawl forward. "But I agree. I don't like this. My people are still a few minutes out in that direction, and I pray they didn't run into this on the way. Hopefully not more Factor Five junkies. More Tortured." She was genuinely concerned, alarmed at the fact that her people were at risk.

I still can't believe they're using my own medicine to fuel an army. This, it…part of it is my own fault…

"What's going on?" Krystal asked, leaning into the small space between the back of the van and the driver's portion. "Shit." She finished, seeing what was ahead of us. The younger two peered out from behind Krystal's head, observing the same thing.

"What's the deal with me getting mugged today?" Violet chimed, retreating to the back of the van as it slowed to a stop. My eyes were locked on the lead vehicle of the four, a woman jumping out and assertively shouting commands at us.

"Out. Now. Weapons stay in the vehicle." She demanded, deciding not to brandish the pistol that was holstered at her side. Several men climbed out of the vehicles as a protective measure, but less than a dozen was far fewer than I had expected in total. I heard the rear door open slowly as Raven and I opened our own doors and climbed out, closing them behind us. We left the van running, which was a detail that was either overlooked or ignored by the woman in charge. She looked familiar, but my scrutiny was distracted by Amy's voice. She was the first one to catch up to us, taking her place by my side and taking the verbal reins.

"I'm going to be short: we have nothing of value and little to no use to you. But we mean a great deal to some rather pissed-off people, so it's ill-advised to shoot us. Let us leave and you'll never see us again." Amy's words were a mixture of aggression and confidence, but didn't prove enough of a challenge. The woman chuckled briefly and looked at Violet as she silently appeared behind Raven.

"Good effort. You're exactly what we're here for, though. Told to keep an eye out for you guys quite a while back. Quite a catch. This can't be your whole group. This all of you from the van?" Krystal had apparently failed to make her debut, hiding out of sight.

Smart girl. Good job, sis.

"We're all here." I nodded. I didn't need to make any obvious gestures or eye contact to the others to convey a sense of secrecy.

"Good. Turn the van into Swiss cheese." Our captor said over her shoulder.

"Wait!" Amy's voice stopped them as they raised their weapons. Krystal was smart enough to understand what was going on and practically fell out of the van, scrambling to her feet as I turned my head to look. She stared at me in the near-death shock of close-calls that we were unfortunately so used to and shook her head.

"I tried. Sorry." She whispered.

"It's okay. Glad you're safe." I mumbled, looking back at the woman. "Kind of safe, anyway."

"Safe for now…" The woman mumbled, taking several large steps forward to look at Krystal closely. Krystal stared back confusedly for a moment before her eyes widened and her mouth parted to expose the tiny white tips of barely-exposed fangs. "Krystal?" The woman breathed, her reaction almost joyous.

"I…Alice, I'm hallucinating again, I think." Krystal mumbled, refusing to look away.

"Nope. I think you're seeing me right in the flesh." The woman seemed to be taunting my sister, hanging a weird combination of sardonic and disbelieving tones on her voice. She put her hands on her hips and leaned in as if taking in Krystal's smell.

Pupils widening, cheeks flushed, jaw clenched. What is this girl getting out of this?

"I am." Krystal said quietly, licking her lips. "With the rest of the world gone, I thought you were-"

"Dead?" The woman scoffed. "You'd have liked that, wouldn't you, *mi belleza?* You always did want me out of the picture."

"Rach, I wasn't myself last time we talked. I truly am sorry." Krystal meant what she said, but it didn't make a difference in Rachel's gradually more vengeful eyes.

"Wait. Your ex?" Violet clarified. "This is…The country gets ravaged by a virus, then taken over by a homicidal science experiment, New York is vaporized through nuclear fire, and now we're held at gunpoint by your ex-girlfriend-…am I making sense with these words?" She asked Amy. Amy shrugged, her brow deeply furrowed as she tried to think her way out of our predicament. "So what do you want? You work for Legacy now, I assume?" Violet asked.

"Si, until about five seconds ago." Rachel chuckled and took a few steps away, turning her back to us. "I'm not here by accident. When I heard Krystal was awake…I took *personal* interest."

"Oh." Violet continued. "Great. Then…we can go?"

"Vi…" Krystal's head bowed slightly, a look of significant concern across her face. Despite saying nothing to me, she nodded slightly and was fixated on something with her eyes, as if telling me about something on Rachel's body. I scanned over as much as I could and found what she was referencing after a brief moment. A cluster of track marks on Rachel's arm highlighted a barely-visible IV line; a clear line ran from her arm to a small satchel on her back.

Factor Five. This just got a lot worse.

Rachel seemed to be relishing the moment, nearly giddy as she skipped several yards back to her starting position and bounced on her heels briefly. It was apparent that she was originally from Mexico; her accent was Latin and distinguishable from Southern American variants.

"You cannot go, my friend. Because as of right now, I work for myself. I went through hell when Legacy recruited me. In fact, *most* of us in D.C. went through hell because our *great saviors* were off dicking around in god-knows-where and pretending to be politicians. I promised myself that I'd work hard and get something nice out of the new world. Legacy offered things we wanted in exchange for loyalty…and there was nothing I wanted more than to find my busty, blue-haired little slut."

"That's *our* busty, blue-haired little slut. She already broke up with you." Violet defended.

"Jesus, Vi." Krystal breathed. "Could have left *some* of those words out of that sentence."

"We're not the people you want to challenge, Rachel." I spoke up finally, igniting my fingertips as I began realizing the futility of our position. "You're going to get a lot more than you bargained for." Her personal army pointed their guns again, deterred at a click of her tongue.

"No guns, güey. Let's be civil about this." She cooed. Several of them chuckled, throwing their weapons into whichever vehicle was closest to them. "And who are *you?*" The new girl? Did she finally get a new flame for that cold heart of hers?"

"I'm her *sister.*" I enunciated, starting to panic as the mass of restless fighters settled into a state of eagerness.

"*Órale!*" Rachel squeaked, tilting her head and approaching Krystal at an uncomfortable pace. "That's your *sister?*" She stopped only a foot away from Krystal, leaning in while her eyes were studying me from head to toe. I could see

Krystal's fist emanate swirls of cold mist that rolled down her leg.

Don't, Krystal. Be patient.

Rachel looked back at Krystal, taking in a deep breath.

Stay calm. We don't need to escalate this into a fight. We still have a chance to talk our way out.

"What a missed opportunity." Rachel whispered, turning her head back to Krystal and standing to match her aggression. Her lips curled into a smirk and uttered a single sentence. "I should have slept with the hot one."

Oh, shit.

Krystal wasted no time, making the smarter of several moves and driving the first blow, a quick right jab, into Rachel's stomach. Her left hand moved at the same time to strike the back of her head, anticipating Rachel's movement as she doubled over. Krystal's body spun to one side, opening some space between them as her fist went in for the killing blow on Rachel's skull. I was fixed on the two of them, the fractional moment taking Rachel's militants by surprise as they stood entirely still.

As the flames that licked my fingertips spread up my arms in a comforting embrace, preparing me for the first fight in a long time, all sense of heat left my body with wisps of disappearing fire and numbing shock. Rachel's arm, moving much faster than the time it took for Krystal to throw a singular punch, withdrew a long combat knife from her calf and twisted, plunging it into Krystal's right shoulder. Her aim was meant for the heart, but Krystal's last-second jerk of shock allowed for a new home for the blackened blade in the joint of her arm. The force of the thrust was so strong that it knocked Krystal off her feet, stumbling backwards onto the hood of the van where she slumped to the ground and stared at the wound in her chest. Her left hand shuddered violently as it moved, caressing the handle of the knife in disbelief and disorientation.

No, not Krystal. Not my baby sister. Not again.

My internal pain wanted to lash out of my vocal cords, scream at our attacker, and let out my anguish. My adrenaline begged me to become a scorching wrath, wreathed in flame as I descended upon the woman who would take away my family. My heart poured out for the poor, maimed girl, having been through so much and confronting anguish at every turn through her brief time awake in our horrible new world. My body didn't get a chance to react to any of my desires, instead being interrupted by another scene of brutality as Violet's athletic figure became a blur of merciless movement.

She disappeared briefly behind Raven's body as she pushed our mutual acquaintance out of the path of harm. Her distance to Rachel was too close for anyone to interfere, and too short for her to react in time to defend herself. As Rachel recovered from the lunge, Violet's lithe stature devastated the few feet between them with an open mouth, meeting Rachel's neck in the span of less than a second and knocking her to the ground. Violet shook her head hastily, using her teeth to tear a small opening without killing her instantly. Despite the drugs coursing through Rachel's veins, a mix of shock and terror defied the odds and allowed Violet to maintain dominance and drain Rachel's blood into her mouth as a satisfying form of revenge.

The entire ordeal spanned a matter of moments in a flurry of hatred and ferocity, taking everyone else involved by complete surprise. Amy's reaction was stalled by a moment, but she leapt forward at the same time as Rachel's guards and landed between the small militia and Violet's body, placing one hand on her adopted sister's forehead and the other in a halting sign to the approaching attackers. Violet's head slumped forward, her body becoming entirely limp as the crowd came to an armed standstill. After a brief count, I saw a total of eight, all men, staring at the scene that Amelia had taken charge of. She looked down at Violet briefly, her face in a growing pool of someone else's blood.

"Stop!" Amy shouted, beckoning briefly to Violet and her gasping, croaking opponent. "I suppressed her central nervous system. She'll be out for a few minutes. And I can heal your friend, but I'm not doing *anything* unless I have a promise that we'll get out alive. You let us go, I save her life. You have a few seconds to decide, and I'm not the one counting." Amy barked, nodding to Rachel's neck. The decision was made quickly, one man in the front snorting and growling an order.

"Fine. Fix her." He didn't seem to be their leader, but none of them carried a posture that suggested they assumed responsibility for the group.

What the hell is happening?

I shook away the paralyzing fear of our circumstances and dashed over to Krystal, who had started breathing rapidly as she stared at the enormous blade in her chest. I slid on my knees as I approached her, taking a quick look at Amy as she placed her hands gently on either side of Rachel's neck. In a moment of self-awareness, I looked back at the New York skyline, realizing the impossibility of my circumstances. The devastated horizon stood in partially shattered remains as if a massive hole had been torn through its center. On the other side of us, the remnants of an old civilization remained untouched. Empty storefronts lined the other side of the street as if waiting for customers that would never arrive. Krystal whimpered quietly, grabbing my attention again as the first tears of many began crawling down her cheeks.

"Alice-" She wept, invoking a warp in my own vision as tears formed. I sniffled, looking back at her in an attempt to show strength.

"I know, baby sis. It's okay. You're going to be okay. You're breathing, you're not bleeding too much, you'll be okay. We'll get it out-"

"It hurts...so much, Alice." Her face was contorted in pain, alternating between biting her lip and sobbing with an open mouth, sucking in air during random moments of control.

"That's your bad shoulder." I realized, slinking back. She nodded, emitting another coughing sob. "I need to get it out. Amy can stop the bleeding. But we need to get it out so you can use that arm. Okay?"

"No. No, please." Krystal's concern grew exponentially, becoming desperation in a matter of moments. "Alice, please! Please, don't!" She begged with me, her cries developing into a prime signal for Amy's shift toward me. She let Rachel's head rest on the concrete, a shallow but steady breathing indicative that her wounds were not yet fatal. Amy's silver hair fluttered around her shoulders as she knelt next to me and gazed into Krystal's darting eyes.

"Hey." She said quietly, placing a hand on Krystal's arm. While a shirt sleeve covered Krystal's skin, she acted as if the touch was shocking and immediately calmed down to a reasonable level of anguish. "You're going to be okay. A few seconds of pain, and it'll all be over. I promise." Amy's voice was reassuring, inciting an immediate and trusting nod from Krystal as she gritted her teeth. I looked over my shoulder, seeing Raven crouched protectively next to Violet's unconscious body to guard against any of the group's potential threats.

Satisfied for the moment with the state of affairs, I trained my attention to the wound and decided that the best course of action would, unfortunately, be the fastest one within the scope of battlefield medicine. Unnoticed by Krystal, I nudged Amy's boot with my own foot twice. She nodded just enough for me to see that she understood my message and gently pressed on the fabric on either side of the wound. Krystal shuddered and gasped in pain for a moment, taking in quick breaths.

"I know it hurts, but I'm applying some pressure so I can slide my fingers over as soon as Alice pulls it out. Are you ready?" Amy offered. Krystal shook her head violently, afraid of any further pain.

"No, I'm not. I'm not! I-..." She shivered, crying for a few seconds before reverting her attention to us. "Do it." She whispered quickly. "Do it. Just do it."

"I'm going to count to three." I glanced at Amy, who nodded again as a sign of understanding toward my earlier message. I wrapped my fingers around the grip of the knife without moving it, being extremely careful so as not to inflict more damage. I positioned my shoulder so I would remove the blade at the exact angle it entered. "Okay." I breathed, more for myself than for anyone else. "One...two-" Before the word had fully left my mouth, I pulled with all my strength and let the knife fly through my fingers toward the side of the road as it left my hand and was discarded. Amy's fingers were already pressed across the wound, the weight of her whole body leaning into Krystal as she screamed quickly, turning it into a pained growl as Amy worked her magic. Krystal relaxed quickly as Amy's hold over her pain receptors became more and more effective.

Amy twitched without warning, a quick whimper from her throat preceding a pained expression and a rigid posture in her shoulders. It was unusual to see such a severe reaction, as her training over the years had eased the effects of pain on her psyche. Her breathing slowed, gradually becoming synchronized with Krystal before her hand fell away from the wound. While it hadn't been fully healed, Amy appeared to be incapable of aiding any further. Her eyes fluttered and were only half-open as she fell next to Krystal in a semi-seated position against the bumper of the van. Despite the apparent toll, she was breathing normally, and a rapid pulse was faintly visible against her neck.

What the hell was that? Why did she pass out?

Realizing she wasn't the only one unconscious, I turned back toward the crowd and quickly approached Raven and Violet. The men were standing over them only a few feet away, gazing down as if we were a meal waiting to finish cooking.

"She's okay." Raven whispered. "Just asleep." She had rolled Violet on her side into a hasty recovery position, the blood on her face smeared across her cheeks and eyes like Viking war paint. "Please, if we can go free, then leave. I *beg* you. Leave us alone. Take Rachel and go. You don't need us." Raven's head bowed after a moment of staring at them, presumably coming to the same conclusion I had.

We should have let her die and taken our chances in a fight.

"How fast can your fire melt bullets?" One of them asked me, withdrawing a pistol from the small of his back. "Can you melt them before they hit you?" He didn't disengage the safety on the weapon, providing reason that he had more incentive to threaten us than to kill us.

"What do you want?" I asked, standing up alongside Raven. They looked at each other for a moment, smirking to one another and communicating through subtle body language and shrugs.

"Six girls, all alone, some even asleep. Eight guys, in need of some company…what else *could* we want? Rachel wouldn't give it up to us. Kept her legs crossed tighter than a Catholic nun. Killed the last guy that tried, actually. Maybe it's time we take what we deserve. We can start with the sleeping ones…maybe move to the live ones once we get some practice in." He chuckled as my blood ran frigid and locked by body in place.

It's time to fight them. Kill every single one of them.

My right foot lifted less than an inch off the ground before the safety clicked off the weapon and forced me to stand completely still.

"I like 'em feisty, but come on. I can't have you killing us. There's six beautiful bodies here to…devour. If I have to kill you, we still have five. Or four. Or three. We'll take whoever gives us the least amount of trouble. So don't be trouble." He winked at me, a gag rolling through my throat as I started to grasp how vile the situation could quickly become.

"Okay. I'll give you *anything*-" He fired a shot into the asphalt next to Violet's head, intentionally missing by a fraction of an inch. Raven's eyes shot open as I closed my mouth, staring at how easily Violet's life could have ended.

This can't happen. This isn't happening. Not to them. Not to me. Please…

"Shut. Up. The next one goes in her skull. Doesn't bother me. They're still good as long as they're warm. Right, boys?" He shrugged.

I need Val here with me. And Kara, and Sonya…they wouldn't let this happen.

Two of them stepped forward to pick up Violet's body, holding it between them and shuffling toward the side of the road. Another plucked his rifle from the bed of the truck he arrived in and ushered Raven in the same direction.

"Chronic Factor Five use drives up all our primal needs, you see. Short term, you don't notice it. But you use it for a while…" He explained, stepping toward me and pointing toward the rest of the group. They shifted behind me to pick up Krystal, who was also unconscious at this point, and supported a delirious and recovering Amy. "Food, blood, sex, and even those fun needs in the back of your mind to just…beat the shit out of things. Know what I mean? Just that…urge to rip shit in half. We all have it. In fact…" I tried to repress my abilities, a faint trail of smoke disappearing into the air from my fingertips. "*You* have it right now." I finally looked into his eyes, a hazel mixture of crazed arousal matching a kinetic energy in his dilated pupils. "Let's go take care of those urges. I'll let *you* get them out, too, don't worry. I like 'em when they fight back. This isn't exactly my first time."

I would be much better off dead, but I can't let the rest of them be vulnerable. I have to find a way to save them. I don't care what happens to me, but I will not let those girls be hurt.

I walked in the direction he pointed me, trying to use Kara's method of threat evaluation. I could see each of the men holding us, but the risk of my doing anything to interfere put one of us, or more, at grave risk of becoming a casualty. With each step I took, a discouraging thought echoed in my head and instigated my growing nausea.

They're faster than me. They're stronger than me. Even my powers mean nothing when they'll shoot as soon as I try to use them.

The soldier at the front of the group wasn't attached to one of us and used his freedom to smash the front glass door of an empty massage parlor and create a passage inside.

"Look at that." He chimed. "We're gonna get massages like last time. What are the odds?" My own captor chuckled at the remark, unnerving me further that this was apparently routine for them. I was next to Raven by that point, walking up a small hill to the storefront before a faint purr caught my attention. The rumble of a car's engine grew close enough to take a risk and I whirled around, seeing a minivan of people slow to a stop near the convoy's blockade.

"Scout vehicle. My people." Raven whispered excitedly. I went against all rationality and shook my shoulder free, taking several steps away as fast as I could and shrieking to the vehicle's occupants.

"Help! Please, anyone. Help us! Help us, *please!*" I screeched, my vocal cords threatening to tear. I felt the muzzle of a pistol rest against the base of my skull and fall still as I closed my eyes and prayed for a quick death, should it have come in that moment. I heard shouting from the rescue vehicle and the opening of its doors, several tactical commands echoing through the air.

"Come on." Raven hissed, hoping that the effort would be enough.

"Waste 'em." My handler commented passively, lifting his own gun and taking a few shots that pierced the air far too close to my ear. I opened my eyes to see each shot bore into the skin of one of the occupants. A pile of body armor and bloody faces quickly amassed on the near side of the vehicle, and a few seconds passed before the scene fell silent. The soldier-captors that carried rifles apparently had ammunition that was capable of ripping through the vehicle and obliterating those who cowered in fear on the far side. Raven's people were shuttered in a matter of seconds, leaving us to the same situation we had been in only moments before.

"No…" Raven whimpered, true and resolute fear gripping her throat.

"Not even good enough for target practice!" One of them commented, inciting the group to begin moving us again. I was shoved toward the opening, a metal frame covered in glass being the only visible entry or exit to the forsaken parlor.

Not here. Not like this. Anything but this.

I finally succumbed to the circumstances and its horror and doubled over, vomiting on the floor just inside the door. The stresses and disgust that I felt were rejected even by my trained mind and quickly became too much for my body to handle.

"Get it all out." The man nearest to me commented, gripping the hair on the back of my head and shaking me. "Be a good little girl and get it out now, before we get started." I spit violently onto the floor, trying briefly to shake free from his grip. I failed, and he punished my effort by shoving me several feet backward. I hit the wall on the far side of the parlor near the corner of a hallway that led to several private massage rooms. His strength was surprising even for a Vampyre, and I knew he was stronger than both Raven and I combined.

I could see the rest of the women in front of me, Krystal and Violet being thrown hastily onto the lobby's massage tables meant for quick sessions and student lessons. Raven was pushed into the opposite corner of the room, along with Amy. Amy was struggling to stand upright, still heavily impacted by the work done on Krystal.

She's never like this. Her powers don't make her fatigued like mine or Krystal's do.

"She needs medical attention." I spat quickly, trying to find a way to postpone what seemed like the inevitable. They all looked at me for a moment, then at Amy before leaving the talking to the man that had been in charge of most of my movements.

"I think you're a doctor. Ever play nurse?" He asked, leaning closer to my body.

"She could die. She's not supposed to be like this, and-" He rolled his eyes, pointing the firearm in Amy's direction before looking back at me.

"You know what we do to sick animals? We put them down. That what you want?"

"No, I-"

"Then *shut*...that pretty little mouth up, Red." His breath was nauseating, every gust of wind only inches from my face. I looked around him to see Rachel, the last of the women, be dumped on the third and final chair in the lobby. "So where do we start? I'll let you pick." He smirked, turning to the side so I could see the three unconscious women. They were equally defenseless, the men behind them nearly salivating at the thought of their horrific crimes. I gagged again, turning to the side as my head spun in dizziness.

This can't be real. We aren't supposed to be here. This isn't supposed to happen.

"*You* can pick…or I can." He articulated menacingly, tracing the muzzle of the pistol along my face. I couldn't say anything, frozen in fear at the sight in front of me. "You said the blue-haired one is your sister, right?"

No, please…not Krystal…not my baby sister…after so much…

He approached her quickly, grabbing the waistband of her jeans and tearing them open, pulling strips of denim off of her thighs in violent tugs.

"Stop!" I screamed, taking a step forward as my body started to flicker and spark in arcs of flashing heat and light. I restrained myself as much as I could, knowing that Krystal's life was a single twitch away from ending. I covered my arm as a torrent of fire erupted from my fingertips and spread to my elbow. Taking a deep breath, I cooled myself down and looked at my sister. Her brow was furrowed in a pained sleep, her legs parted to expose pale skin and blue underwear.

"Not her. Take me." I struggled to get the words out, but hoped I could at least kill a few of them in the process. "I'll go first."

"You know this isn't, like…a stalling process, correct? None of you are strong enough to take us on. You're just putting yourself at the front of the line at this point." He chuckled. I realized that they were distracted by the drama, staring at me and paying no mind to the other women in the room. I locked eyes with Raven for a moment, seeing her face set into absolute disbelief and dread while reality set in for her.

She has no powers, but she wants to help me. She'll die before I do, if she tries something.

"The sooner you're done, the sooner we can go. We obviously can't do anything in retaliation, so there's no point in killing us before we can leave." I argued, at least hoping to get us out with our lives intact.

"You're going to tell others-"

"What, and get them killed, too? You *have* to let us go. Or we'll die right here, and we'll take you with us." I said firmly, trying to avoid the thoughts of what the next minutes or hours of my life would consist of. He smirked again, taking his left hand and running it through my hair. I closed my eyes, trying not to squirm as the smell of his sour body odor violated my senses yet again.

"So…you'll consent and give me a good time, and my boys get to share the rest of the girls-"

"No. They don't get touched." I whimpered, trying to sound strong as my emotional strength waned.

You're committing yourself to something worse than death. Don't do this.

"Just me." I finished. "*Only* me." He smiled, pointing at me and looking to his friends. I cringed and nearly doubled over, a physical pain wracking my abdomen at the thought of his words.

"Hear that, boys? We have a party, here. Little Red wants to get us *all* off." He turned quickly and shoved me hard enough that I stumbled, nearly knocking Krystal off her chair. One of the others picked up her body and tossed it to the ground without care, her skull bouncing off the floor with just enough luck not to cause severe injury. The same man pushed me into the chair and continued to push, pinning my shoulders to the cheap, pink leather of the piece of equipment.

Please let something save me. Anything.

"Stop!" Raven cried, trying to pull away from her captor. "Not her! Take me!" Her offer went unheeded as two more men took their place by my feet, pulling off my boots after briefly untying the laces and starting to tug on my jeans. Out of the corner of my eye, I could see her throw a heavy punch at one of the two men at her side, starting a brawl that ended with her being quickly overwhelmed.

Go to your happy place.

My boots came off with an unfortunate amount of ease, followed by the white socks they hastily discarded to the floor. Raven wailed several grunts of exerted effort, appearing to be overcome by the strength of her assailants.

You're back home with Val after a long day at the clinic.

One of them grabbed my foot, pressing it to his lips before running his hands over my leg and digging his nails into my skin.

You're leaning into his shoulder. The smell of his cologne, the feel of his strong chest. His heartbeat against your skin. Your protector, guide and mentor. The smile on his face as he tells a joke that only we understand.

The man who had berated me and battered me up to this point was arrogant enough to look me in the eyes as he slid his thumbs between my hips and my underwear, sliding them past my legs and dropping them to the ground.

Paris…that's where he said it the first time. A rotation in Europe at Kara's request, he told me. Breakfast outside the Louvre, a walk down Champs-Élysées. I can't believe I berated him so much for ignoring whatever mission we were supposed to be on. I never got to enjoy the day. Not until sunset…standing on the Eiffel Tower and listening to him apologize for how unoriginal he was in his efforts. And then he told me he loved me. The most perfect moment of my life, the most perfect anything had ever been. It's…so far away. It's a memory. Memories…they won't save me now.

I finally tilted my head back and screamed at the top of my lungs, unleashing several hundred years of aggression and agony into the dimly-lit, squalid excuse for a massage parlor. My thoughts couldn't successfully transport me to a place of my own, and I instead was tortured at my own peril by exposure of myself to the worst breed of species ever to have transgressed the planet. I emptied my lungs into the sky, hoping that whichever deity, whichever god would hear me, would believe that I could sacrifice anything to be saved from the impending cruelty I knew I didn't deserve. I swore to the world with the echoes of my agony that I would surrender anything to be free of the demons that would take me, that would rob me of sacred rights and decency. With every ounce of oxygen that left my body, I begged that by raping me, the rest of my family would be free from ever experiencing anything like this.

I coughed, lightheaded as I ran out of air and struggled to stay conscious. I breathed heavily, sweat pouring across my face as I started to panic, keeping my eyes clenched shut as much as possible. I breathed, each inhale becoming slower and slower as I realized the room was silent and no movement shook the chair I was pressed into. In fact, the pressure on my shoulders had lightened, giving me enough room to lift my head and open my eyes to see what horrific things were being performed or contemplated. I shuddered as the face in front of me slowly began to turn colors, his mouth agape and head tilted back as he shuddered violently. I looked down, letting waves of relief wash over me as I realized his belt was still buckled and my vanity was intact.

What's happening? What's going on? They stopped, they…they stopped.

I looked to my left, seeing one of the men drop my leg to clutch his eyes, which poured blood from around each socket. He groaned in pain, crumpling to the ground and clutching his face. He screamed, catching me by surprise as his fingers, trying to claw away the pain, snapped and bent in unnatural directions across every digit. The process repeated, his screams becoming louder as the bones in his body audibly cracked, split, and broke, one by one as the process made its way down his body. I could only stare in grotesque disbelief as the pain finally became too much for his brain and his eyes fluttered with the threat of unconsciousness. Finally, his lips parted for a final cry before his skull split evenly in two, ripping both the bone and the matter underneath in half all the way down to his jaw, which fell in two pieces on the ground below him. The man holding my other leg suffered a similar, quicker fate while his nose crumpled backward into his face and caved his entire head in as the rest of his facial bones followed suit.

I pulled my bare legs to my chest and huddled quietly, not wanting to be detected by whatever force was saving me. I stared straight ahead as their screams followed one by one in a circle around me, each of them lasting for nearly a minute before succumbing to pain and disfigurement. The process repeated for each man, seven sets of agonizing bellows filling the air around me and saving the man to my front in a state of suspension. His face was nearly purple, but he could gasp quick breaths of air to maintain life. I closed my eyes, breathing quietly and waiting for his death to follow suit. I dared not look at the other women, in fear that something would happen to them, as well.

I whimpered, jerking violently as a hand, cool and firm, yet impossibly soft, rested itself on my knee.

Please don't hurt me.

"Alice...Allison."

Please don't hurt me.

"Hon...it's me...it's okay. You're okay, love."

It's not real. Don't believe it. It's not real.

"Alice, it's okay. I need you to look at me. Okay? Please, I need you to look at me."

Don't do it. It's a trap. The voice is going to hurt you, just like it hurt them.

Knowing that almost nothing could be worse than what I had already been through, I slowly lowered my knees, keeping my eyes clenched shut as hard as I possibly could. Sweat stung them regardless, drops having beaded in the corners of my tear ducts and infiltrating them with its pricking bite. They were indistinguishable from tears at this point, and I made that fact clear by sobbing quietly.

Open your eyes.

My vision was blurred from the salty mixture that stung my retinas, but I quickly made out a face that triggered a handful of thoughts. I knew the face was loving and caring. I trusted the face with my life, knowing that those bright green eyes nearly matched my own and were so filled with life and with love. I realized that I was looking at two faces, the second nearly blending in with the shadows behind her. They were distinct, one having bright yellow hair the color of straw and the other having hair the color of night with eyes to match its stars.

Kara. Sonya.

My senses returned to me in moments, flooding my body with an array of sights and sounds, finally catching up to the reality of the situation. People had swarmed the room around me, picking up the other women with great care and carrying them quickly outside. Commands were uttered quietly, with the authoritative presence of someone who respected the people they influenced.

Tony.

I shook my head for a moment and let the last of my tears fall, freeing me from a prison of constricting emotion and protective shock.

"I love you." It was all I could utter to Kara and Sonya, and was enough for them to understand that I was as mentally present as I could have been. "I love you." I repeated as both of them fell across my body in a shared, protective embrace. "*God*, I love you both."

"We love *you*, Alice. You're safe. You're protected." Kara sniffed, failing to hold back tears of her own.

"I love you."

"We love you, too." Sonya cried with me, understanding that the situation was beyond words I could ever relay. "Nothing else is going to happen to you." I sat up quickly, looking at the one man that still stood, teetering on the edge of life and death. His expression hadn't changed, an intangible suspension keeping him immobile and agonized. Kara gripped my wrist tightly, looking at me directly as my head snapped over to her.

"I want you to be able to live without the nightmares that they're still out in the world. Without the fear of this happening to other women. Without this haunting you. I...will let you decide. This *one* time, his life is under your complete control. Whatever happens to him next...it's your choice. I can't fix this. But I can at least give you back the power of choice." Kara's words resounded loudly and repeated themselves over and over in my ears.

Kill him kill him kill him kill him kill him kill him kill him...

"He *has* to die." I whispered, looking Kara in the eyes. "And he has to die slowly. In pain. As much pain...as you can inflict." I snarled, looking up into the man's eyes. His expression went from being terrified to being helpless in mere moments, realizing the futility of his fate. "And I'm going to help." I whispered, standing up and attempting to ignore my lack of clothing from the waist down. I was too filled with rage to bother with protecting my modesty, especially since the others had cleared out and the four of us were alone. Neither of them protested with my request, instead lifting their hands and slowly beginning to manipulate their fingers. The man grunted in pain as I started to hear various pops and cracks from his body.

Kill him kill him kill him kill him kill him kill him kill him...

"His skin. Tear his skin open. Start with his back." I whispered, standing as close to him as I could and gazing into his eyes. His growls quickly turned to agonized whimpers as I heard the leathery tear of skin snap and crack as it worked its way up to his skull. I reached around him, igniting my hand and running my fingers along every nerve I was familiar with. His closed mouth emitted howls of pain to its utmost extent, his eyes rolled back in absolute agony.

This is the reckoning of justice. And no one knows it better than Kara. But I…I know the human and Vampyre bodies. I know how to heal, and I took an oath to do no harm. But harm has been done, and I will repay blood with blood.

I pulled his lower jaw open, exposing his throat to the world and letting his screams increase in volume. I pinched two fingers together on his left canine, twisting and pulling downward to rip one of his fangs out entirely. It left a gaping, bloody hole in the top of his mouth and was quickly matched by a second as I performed the same work on the other side. His mouth gushed blood, but was stopped when I closed his jaw and let Kara and Sonya resume keeping it shut with their telekinetic abilities.

The Factor Five will keep him alive longer than a normal Vampyre.

I could hear him choke and cough on his own blood, some spraying from his nose as the only route of escape as the breaking of bones reached his legs. He buckled as his shins snapped, the only thing keeping him upright being the unseen forces of my friends' supernatural abilities.

"Stop." I whispered. "Put him on the ground. Gently." I somehow ignored the grimy floor as I knelt down, letting the black layer of dust and dirt cover my knees as I crawled my way toward him, giving him the perfect sight of his executioner. They kept him still, a mass of bent limbs and macabre features representing the most tortured of beings. I sidled up to his face, leaning in closely to see his darting eyes, unable to focus on any one point.

He's breaking. This is worse than what Legacy did to him…and he deserves it.

"You know what we do to sick animals?" I growled through clenched teeth. His brutalized figure quivered, shaking in immense amounts of suffering and misery. "We put them down." I reminded him, sliding my palm across the broken ribs of his chest, leaning my head against the fractured bits of his skull, and resting my fingers on the skin above his heart. "Is that what you want?" I breathed, letting the pure rage of his presence bring my fingers, palm, and wrist to a temperature I had never achieved before. His broken jaw fell open crookedly as a smoking, violent chasm of flames tore through his chest, a gurgle finally corrupting the remains of his throat with the sounds of death before the unfortunate mass of flesh fell perfectly and silently still. The imprint of my hand was burned into his chest, scarcely visible amongst the blisters and bruising around it.

My next few breaths came in short bursts, heaving gusts of air into my body as I fought off the sense of despair and disgust that had haunted the last few minutes of my life. I breathed through my nose first, giving up and heaving oxygen in through my mouth as it became harder and harder to grasp reality again.

"We're here. You're safe. You're loved and protected." Sonya said quietly.

"No one else will hurt you. And we are *right here* to support you for as long as you need. Take your time. Take deep breaths. Remember we're here." Kara reassured, going unnoticed as the ringing in my ears came and went repeatedly.

That shouldn't have happened. I shouldn't be here.

"I'm okay." I whispered, shaking my head.

I shouldn't be here. I don't want to be here. I don't deserve this. I didn't do anything.

"I'm okay!" I croaked, punching the ground and pushing off of the tile to stand uneasily. They both stood quickly, supporting me with their hands on either side of my body.

They ripped off your clothes and threatened your family. They're animals. They're the enemy.

"I'm okay…" I sobbed, staring at the dead body and shuddering with the thoughts of more violence.

They did this to you. It can never be taken back. They tried to steal a piece of you. A part of your soul.

"I-…" My voice caught in my throat as I leaned forward, lashing out at the body while Sonya and Kara lightly restrained me. "I'm still here!" I screamed at the corpse, staring at its disfigured face. "I'm still *here*! I'm better than you!" I screeched, wailing at the cause of my worst memories as Kara and Sonya tried to hold me back from further mutilating the corpse. "I fucking *killed you*!" I pushed my friends aside and let the built-up craving of my abilities unleash in the form of a controlled cloud of pure energy. It set the body ablaze instantly and began to melt the skin from his muscles.

I watched the layers of flesh slowly disappear, turning to smoke and ash and a vile smell that I relished in the moment of revenge. I stared as the plastic melted on the walls behind him while his bones exposed themselves and turned stark white in the searing heat of the flame. I stared at nothing but a skeleton, broken into pieces like a shattered pane of glass as the last of my energy was poured out into the world. The heat slowed, the light dimmed, and my thoughts diminished to match the intense drain of energy that finally took a toll on my failing body.

"I'm alive…you piece of shit." I mumbled, leaning into Sonya as the edges of a black sleep rolled into my vision.

Go to sleep. You deserve it.

"You are safe. We have you, Alice. We're going home." Kara's comforting voice reassured my fate as I let myself slumber, daring to dream again of falling into Val's arms.

STRANGLEHOLD

JALIX

I started to rub my temples in a futile attempt to take away the sense of annoyance that stemmed from our vain attempt at planning.

"No, no…" Val sighed, pointing to another spot on the map. "We'd get *crushed* from right here. Jalix is right, we need to stick with the southwest side and push in as far as possible."

"And Jalix is not in charge of the two hundred lives I pulled from their homes." Yuri argued, the tension swelling between the three of us. "While his tactical advice-"

"It's not *tactical* advice, Yuri, it's common sense. Your people are going to get slaughtered-"

"Don't pretend that this boils down to common sense." Yuri interrupted me. "I respect you, but we're starting a war. And I know how my forces work."

"You don't *have* forces; you have a bunch of people with weapons. That's what I'm trying to tell you." I kept trying to prove my point, pushing the subject with him.

"Jalix specialized in unconventional warfare, if I recall correctly. Your operators were door-kickers. There's a distinct separation between raid forces and asymmetric warfare, and *this* is the time to let that settle in." Val took my side in the situation as I took a step back and leaned on a small pile of closed plastic crates, taking in the smell of the woods as I collected my thoughts. Our encampment was concealed well, and the people occupying it remained appropriately quiet as they removed brush and other small obstacles by hand to set up equipment or personal areas. The hiss and snap of moving foliage stretched across the diameter of the camp and blended well with the natural noise of the forest. Our vehicles were parked in a small circle a few dozen feet from the main road, giving the center of the formation a clearing for the three of us to deliberate courses of action. I turned back to the argument, placing my hands lightly on the cheap, plastic table we used for laying out our documents. While my body felt more recovered after a change into a clean combat uniform that resembled my old one, falling back into familiar habits seemed too sour with the stakes we faced.

"-weapons anyway. We have no stealth capabilities, no equipment for crowd control. It's old-school, but we can make it work." Val was finishing up as he presented his side of some detail. I lifted my hands briefly to interject, doing my best to calm the mood.

"Yuri…if you had every option available, how would you do this?" I wanted to hear his position, eager to stop arguing and begin the real planning. "You have a hundred trained soldiers and a hundred pissed-off civilians with rifles. All Vampyres, all dedicated to winning the fight. How do you wipe out Quantico and its five hundred guards?"

"With a lot of bullets." He sighed, running a hand through his thick black hair. Like most of us, he was still sporting a coat of dirt and grime from our previous fight and was unwilling to take the time to change that fact. "The only thing we can do is surprise them with force and get them caught in a solid crossfire. We mix the civilians and the soldiers fifty-fifty, split them into two groups, and have them go in with a shock-and awe. And you're right. If we can take the operations center on the southwest side, that would effectively give us control. Master keys, electronic vault combinations, it should all be there. Including the information I need to get us to the next step of our counterattack on D.C. From my understanding, the fighter jets are also dispatched from the top floor of that same building, so they won't have time to ready their air support if we take it quickly enough."

"At least there's that." Val muttered. "We should send a small detachment to watch those jets. Make sure the pilots don't try an emergency takeoff anyway. After Air Combat Command merged with Quantico, there's always a minimum of two combat aircraft ready to fly with armament."

"To protect the White House and for rapid response, yeah. You're right on that part." I mumbled, starting to piece together a more solid plan. "*We* should be the ones to provide overwatch on the aircraft." I pointed again, taking out a marker and placing a small red dot along the airfield. "It's just north of the operations center. If Val and I sit *here* with rifles, we can hit any pilots or stragglers on the north end. We're both marksmen, it makes sense. Then your forces hit from the west in a combined assault. Once we get the bulk of them rushing to respond, break off half your forces and go south to push upward. So basically-" I picked up a pencil and drew some light lines. "We have a force attacking from the west, from the south, and from the north. They can only move east. Which is fine, because we can do a sweep of the base from west to east and catch anyone else once the ops center is ours."

"It's right inside the main gate and gives us a chance to regroup and recover. We'd have access to the security cameras at that point, as well." Yuri agreed. "That makes it a lot easier to sweep the rest of the base."

"So that's our plan." Val confirmed, bumping his fist into the table lightly and nodding. "We need to arm up."

"Those crates behind you are ours. The rest already have their equipment. I'm going to assign leadership roles and establish the two major attack teams so they can set up our munitions and vehicle-mounted weapons. Meet me back here in an hour." Yuri stepped off immediately, disappearing behind the other side of the armored vehicles. Val grabbed the other side of a crate as we started unstacking the boxes to open them up.

"This is insane." I mumbled, shaking my head. "I…we have a plan, but this is stupid." I tinkered with the handle of my combat knife, sheathed and strapped below my left shoulder.

"Stupid is all we've got, my friend." Val popped open one of the boxes to expose a set of handguns and spare magazines, along with their holsters and some ammunition. "Stupid and bullets. We'll see which one of those gets us to victory."

"I'm going to take a guess and say the bullets are the important part." I sat down and started loading magazines, mentally calculating how many I could fit in my vest's pouches. We sat in silence for a moment, the memories of loading magazines in the desert more than twenty years ago giving me a strong sense of nostalgia. The sulfurous, metallic smell of ammunition leaked into the air and shrouded Val and I as we tried to verbalize our apprehension. Val sat up quickly, pulling his phone out and staring at the screen for a moment.

"It's Sonya." He said, his tone even and assured. "Kara and Tony are awake and doing well. They're just outside of New York, on the Jersey border. They don't have much signal."

"Sure the radiation is playing hell with cell service." I thought aloud, thinking about Kara and her wellness. "Why didn't she text me?" I asked him, opening a new crate to expose rifles and the same matching paraphernalia as the other crate. I pulled out a sling and some magazines, continuing to load them with rounds.

"She knew I'd pass along the info. I wouldn't take it personally-"

"No, I meant Kara." I cut in, shaking my head. "I figured she would have called me. Or something."

"She just woke up from a very long sleep, dude. She's...I'm sure she's essentially drunk at the moment. Her coordination and thinking are going to be off until the drugs are out of her system, and they hit her *hard* with that shit." He reassured, wiping away any concern I had. "She'll be fine, man."

"I know. Glad Tony is up and around, too. That whole thing was-"

"Don't." He said quietly, dropping the magazine in his hands. "Not yet. Too soon." I turned to him, my brow furrowed.

"He made it. He's fine, what's-"

"Jalix, drop it, man. Please. Okay?" He grumbled, sitting still for a long minute. "I felt his heart in my hands. Through his chest, when I was doing compressions. I could feel it. It was like anything else in your body. Just a squishy...nothing. Not moving, not even trying. His body tried to give up on him. And after Jared..." I let him consider his words, courteously allowing him to vent what he was thinking. My own heart panged, thinking about our fallen friend. "I just want to kill Legacy. And the...Tortured. All of them, I just want them dead and I want us to move on."

"It sounds like you haven't moved on." I countered, beginning to piece together a modern rifle from one of the kits at my feet. "And I dealt with the Tortured a lot longer than you did."

"I know, I just-..." He stood up, kicking one of the boxes and turning to face me as I resumed building. "I should have been the one to stay dead." He said firmly. "Jared should have lived. If he was here instead of me-"

"Don't play that game, Val. No one wins. I fought that feeling for *years* and the guilt is just going to bring you down. You don't want to go there."

"I'm already there, Jalix. This isn't something I'm getting into, this is something that bothered me for the last twenty years. This...shit is just stirring it all back up. He died for *nothing*." He spoke passionately, his hands moving with his words with frustrated mannerisms. "And I know there's nothing I can do about it, but shit like Tony getting hurt just brings it all back. Thinking about losing one of you guys, *again*." He looked off into the woods, watching a group of people move a pile of sandbags into a truck.

"You both died." I reminded him quietly. "Unfair and square. You both got ambushed. Shot. Killed. And-"

"And I don't *remember* it, Jalix. My memories were copied before that, so I have a nice empty length of time where some of the most important shit of my life happened. I don't remember my sister dying, I don't remember my niece being born, I don't remember my own *goddamn wedding*!" He threw an empty magazine into the dirt, watching it thud against the ground and smack into the tire of a vehicle before stopping. "And I don't...remember my last moments with Jared."

"And that was the sacrifice you had to make to get a second chance. To live long enough to enjoy the results of it all. To watch Amy grow into a beautiful young woman, to-"

"Yeah, and he can't. He can't do any of that. He's dead. The world, the entire *world* knows who we are. We were famous. Well, you were already famous-" He added dismissively. "But the rest of us were seen as the ones who stopped the bad guys, the ones who defeated the villain that the world never knew existed. And Jared? He was in a grave. And the world never knew his story. They never knew about the man that turned against his friends when they started trafficking women. The man who got shot and nearly killed for following his moral compass. The proud black man who crawled from living in poverty with nothing to his name to being a guiding hand to dozens of kids in an advanced society. The story of the man who married my wife and I. And no one gets to know his story. No one gets to know his name. No one knows his face. It's not right, man. It's not right that I get to live and someone *that* strong, someone *that* selfless gets slaughtered without the chance to defend himself. In the back of a car filled with bullets, the *same goddamn thing* that landed him as a Vampyre in the first place. Assassinated by a bunch of thugs. But no one gets to know that story. They know about *me*. The *politician*. The one who - "

"Val, stop. I mean it. Listen to me." I let him get everything out as he paced, increasing in volume over time. "You know his story. And so do I. And when we win this, *when* we win this...we'll dedicate buildings in his name, we'll build statues, we'll mount plaques, we'll make sure the world knows about him. But *this*...this isn't a world that appreciates him. Not yet. We need to give him a home for *his* legacy. He's only dead if you forget him. And if you're thinking about him this much, he's still alive in this world."

The same advice Kara gave to me about my old team. God rest their souls...

He sighed heavily, huffing through his nostrils as he struggled to combat the anger and sadness that equally pervaded him. I watched his fist curl several times as I took a step closer to him, watching his body language roll through the thoughts in his head.

"I know. Sorry. Lot of things going on and I'm trying to wrap my head around it all." He sat back down, resuming his tasks. "Glad my sister is okay. Glad everyone is okay, honestly. Especially Alice. She's been through a lot. I can't wait to see her after all this. Really reconnect and spend time together the way we used to."

"Then let's get through this next part. We capture Quantico, we take some of the power away from Legacy and add it to our own. Then we can start thinking about our counterattack."

"Who's to say he doesn't drop another nuclear missile on this place? He did it already in New York, why wouldn't he crush our military advantage?" He started affixing pouches to his vest, spreading it out on the ground for better access.

"If his plan is to decimate the U.S. cities, he needs to do it all at once. One bomb was enough to freak out the rest of the world and I'm sure he's handling that nightmare right now. It's going to be tough to convince other countries that we're not a threat. But if he does it again, he's going to become a target for drone strikes and whatever else the rest of the world decides on. He's not going to risk it. And I'm sure he believes that his army in D.C. can fight us on foot anyway, even after we snag Quantico. He'll plan a ground-based counterattack, but not more missiles."

"He's not wrong." Val returned, looking into the woods again. "That he could take it back. We're going to lose half the people we have in this attack. Maybe more. We're gonna get a lot of cool toys and no one to use them. No one to carry on the fight back to the Tortured or Legacy in D.C. We're going to need luck on our side, or at least one hell of a miracle just to last long enough to come up with a plan."

"Eh. Luck will come. But luck favors those with the most ammunition." I smirked, tossing him another box of rifle rounds. He chuckled, shaking his head.

"You never grew out of being a soldier, did you? Carried it with you even when you left."

"Yeah, it's for life." I nodded. "Specialist Kane, Sergeant Kane, Lieutenant Kane, Captain Kane. Still hear *sir* more in my head than my own first name. But you put your life on the line for your country, for your friends, for your family…it carves something in your heart that you don't get rid of. People trust you with their lives, even other soldiers. Men and women willing to die all the same and taking your word as their absolute truth. A commander, a leader. *You're* no different. We're no different from one another in that regard." He looked at me with profound realization and a matching gratitude for the words of kindness. An unspoken thanks, he donned his vest and began strapping a holster to his leg. My own phone buzzed finally, a sign from the others that they were alive and kicking. A text from Amy stretched across the screen as I unlocked it.

Kara and Sonya here with Tony. All together now. Ran into danger, we handled it. Shaken, but unbroken. Pressing on to the city. I love you both. See you soon.

"Shaken but unbroken." I whispered, both concerned about the event she mentioned and proud of her resilience.

"Sounds bad, but they got through it. Whatever it was. Probably more Tortured assholes on the road. No doubt they're on orders to look for us." Val remarked as I placed the device in my pocket again.

"Especially if Legacy finds out he missed his target." I agreed, finishing the assembly of my weapon and appreciating the quality of my optic.

"Missed? He took out a chunk of downtown New York."

"Yeah, but his announcement was that he was eradicating any sign of rebellion." I returned. "He knew Raven's city was *near* New York, but not exactly where. Someone either gave him bad info, or he was hoping to catch Raven's city in the blast as a cover-all." I turned my head as Yuri spoke up from behind me, apparently returning early.

Maybe Yuri was the source of Legacy's bad intel. He did say he was working our angle for a long time.

"We move *now*." Yuri said quietly, throwing a duffel bag into the back of a troop carrier as a driver climbed into the front.

"What the hell?"

"We can't yet." Val and I spoke at the same time.

"My scouts called." Yuri said, his jaw clenched. "They know we're here. Satellites, drones, something. But they know we're here. We're getting pictures of the situation now, but the entire base is mobilizing for defense. They're setting up and digging in for a fight."

"And we'll give it to 'em." Val growled, loading a magazine into his weapon.

"Get us radios." I told Yuri, starting to heave whatever crates I could into the back of the nearest truck. "Val and I will circle north in this truck, then get closer on foot. We'll stay hidden as much as possible and stay in touch. Just stay away from the zone between the airfield and the ops building; we'll be dug in."

"Don't want to catch any friendly fire." Val warned, tossing his personal backpack into the backseat of the pickup truck. "Set up the armored vehicles on the west side by the gate; make them think it's our only angle of attack."

"We'll have you covered." Yuri agreed, handing the two of us short-wave radios. I clipped it to the chestpiece of my vest and reached into the driver's seat of the truck, starting the engine and watching through the windshield as the camp descended into chaos. They stayed reasonably quiet, no one shouting or barking orders, but supplies and equipment were quickly left behind as the remaining weapons were picked up in the haste of evacuation. "Just stay alive, Jalix." Yuri gripped my body armor, shaking me aggressively. "Kill what you can. Fight hard. But if this fails, you two need to defend the city. And let Raven know-" He stopped, deliberating his words. "Let her know we did our best." I shoved him away and slammed the door, rolling down the window.

"Those are the words of a dead soldier's eulogy. Not the words of a commanding victor. Take your army and wipe the Tortured out of Quantico. I don't want anything left alive by the time we catch up to you." He took the words of encouragement to heart and nodded, pushing away from the truck and jogging to catch up with his subordinate leaders.

"Any words for me, Captain Kane?" Val smirked, understanding that my commands were to motivate and inspire rather than genuinely instruct Yuri.

"Yeah, watch my back. And don't be a douchebag." I shifted into reverse and slid out onto the road, spinning the wheel to gun the engine away from the camp.

"Pick one. You can't have both." He replied, chuckling and looking at the road ahead. "Sir."

***

"Kinda thought that two hundred guns would be louder." Val remarked, watching a mass of Vampyres slowly inch toward the southwest gate of the military base. I listened, able to hear every shot in the distance that reverberated like deadly popcorn.

"They're saving their ammo. Taking kill shots and trying not to waste it on suppressive fire. Our enemy doesn't care about suppression. Or dying. It's a smart move." I responded, peering through my optic once more at the runway of the airfield.

I had an excellent view from my spot on top of the empty administrative building, apparently only used by the Tortured during times of necessity. Val occupied one side of a roof-mounted air conditioning unit and I was on the other to keep a low and matching profile with the rest of the environment. I took another thankful breath that we had yet to enter the fight itself and maintained my watch.

"I know. Just doesn't sound like enough." It was another complaint, albeit one that was warranted out of the fear that this battle would turn out to be futile.

I don't blame him. Two hundred against five hundred, and they're stronger than us...faster than us...

"It's enough." I said confidently, knowing that our will to live made a vast difference in the grand scheme of things. "We went through the same thing in Iraq about thirty years ago. Suicide bombers took a toll on our military, and that question was brought up more than once...how we fight a force that doesn't care if its soldiers die. Tactics go out the window, things shift. It turns into attrition." I stared at the battlefield, watching our armored vehicles creep slowly toward the gate at a shallow angle, using their broad sides to shield the fighters behind it. "But we can do the same here, today. We take the ops center, establish it as a rally point, and hole up. Let them come to us, let them make stupid mistakes."

"No explosions either." His comment seemed to sidetrack from the previous thoughts, taking note of the type of warfare being conducted.

"Aside from the aircraft munitions, the Tortured probably didn't have many explosives. Maybe some flashbangs for crowd control, but I wouldn't expect much more than that. It'll be guns against guns. And it looks like we're making a dent. See how they're moving?" I pointed to an area behind the gate, watching a horde of fifty Tortured sprint to the other side of fencing and barricades. "They're losing the gate. Our guys are getting inside soon."

"Wish we had a better angle."

"Sacrifice a good view of the gate for a good view of the airfield. It's the best we could do." I snapped into a firing position as a few soldiers ran into the open aircraft hangar, huddling around a workbench and quickly discussing something. "Just saw a few run inside, don't look like pilots." I quipped.

"Hold off, then. We'll keep quiet as long as possible. Unless they're taking a jet, I don't want to shoot." His temper remained calm, a fact I was grateful for as I relaxed and kept a close eye on the group. "Holy shit." He remarked quickly.

"Hmm?"

"Look at the ops building. On our side." He pointed, leaning in extremely close to my face so I could follow the outline of his finger. I failed to see anything significant, despite his hand slowly moving up and down to indicate something.

"What, dude? The garden in front, the small building next to it? What are you pointing at?"

"How close it is. If we can get into a back door, or better yet, get onto the roof-"

"Absolutely not." I denied his aspirations immediately. "We *need* to keep an eye on the airfield."

"Okay, but hear me out. Nothing and nobody on or near the runway, and the hangar is being used as cover, basically. They had time to prep, they had time to anticipate us, and they *have* advanced aircraft. If they were going to use the air, they would have. Legacy's pilots must be in D.C. We can end this fight and save more lives by pushing into the ops center early and getting a foothold."

"*No.*" I enunciated, continuing to watch the hangar. "We have a job to do, and that's right here. We have our roles, and each one depends on the other."

"Yeah, in a perfect world, Jalix. Yuri was right to an extent, your tactical advice is based on a perfect situation. These aren't regular soldiers. They're not going to think or act the same. They want a *fight*, not a win. Legacy wants a win, and he's not here."

He's got a point.

I sighed, much to Val's satisfaction as he rolled over and folded up the bipod of his rifle.

"I didn't say yes." I stalled.

"You could have said no again." He patted me on the back and crouched, ensuring that we still weren't seen. The group in the hangar was obviously occupied with scrounging for supplies and I used the opening to nod to Val, letting him roll his legs off the edge of the building and fall several feet to the ground. The building was small, and a single story barely had any effect on my legs as I followed him to the ground. We huddled for a moment, looking around at the ominously flat airfield that stretched between us and the embattled complex.

"Yuri's men are getting hit. Hard." I gritted my teeth, seeing bodies sprinkled across the low-sloping hill a few hundred feet from the main gate. "There's gotta be sixty bodies there. That's just what I can see."

"Then we need to hurry." Val said, nodding to the fence on the far side of the runway. A dumpster sat on the other side, the only piece of cover for another hundred feet.

"You first. I'll cover you. Go." I lifted my rifle, pressing it into the side of the building for stability and watching the widest angle possible to safeguard his passage to the other side of the field.

For his size, he was unexpectedly fast, and managed to cross the turf and paved airstrip with an impressive agility. Hopping over the tall fence without letting his feet scrape the barbed wire, he rolled behind the dumpster and used his momentum to fall into a prone position. As I watched the outline of his body settle into a watchful posture, I gripped my rifle with both hands and crouched, fleeing along the same path he did.

I leaned forward, trying to cross in as little time as possible and sacrificing an observant eye for the sake of speed. Before I could reach the fence, I was slammed with the unforgiving wall of an adrenaline haze as the ground behind my feet erupted in angrily spitting chunks of concrete and dirt. In front of me, a rapid collection of gunshots affirmed that Val was returning fire at someone that finally caught wind of us.

I forgot they have cameras all around the base. They would obviously have someone in the ops center watching the airfield. How did we miss this?

I barely had time to blame myself for the failure of planning, launching myself high above the fenceposts and crashing into the steel wall of a dumpster.

"Shit!" I hissed, scrambling to scurry to cover as the shots followed my every move. Val was inching backward from his position next to the dumpster, finally caving to the pressure of increasing and rapid spurts of flying dirt that kicked up only inches in front of the barrel of his rifle. Leaning in as he pulled back to cover, he reloaded while I inhaled and tried to collect my thoughts.

"They knew." He said hoarsely, his eyes wide as he looked over at me. "They knew." He swallowed hard, his face and beard smothered with dirt.

"Who? What?" I couldn't follow his train of thought, the disrupting sound of rifle rounds loudly pinging off the metal behind us acting as a distractor.

"In the hangar. They were waiting to give a signal. Jalix, they're pouring out from behind the hangar. They have to have another hundred back there as reinforcements. At least."

"The scouts didn't account for the other side of the base." I realized, understanding how our forces managed to gain traction so quickly.

"Yeah, we need to go. Now." He beckoned toward the next empty building, the only thing standing between us and the large botanical garden of the base's operations building.

There's a door on the face of the building closest to us, giving us an opportunity for cover inside if we can survive the distance.

"Yuri!" I screamed into my radio. "More Tortured at the hangar! We're pinned!" I could barely hear myself over the noise, damage to my ears being repaired as fast as my body could allow and failing to keep up. Not only were the echoing sounds of gunshots increasing in ferocity as they grew closer, but the clanging of metal as the rounds crashed into our only cover gave no opportunity to quiet moments. I pressed the speaker of the radio to my ear, listening to Yuri's reply. Val did the same, leaning closer to me.

"Where are you? We need your location." Yuri's reply was thankfully short.

"A dumpster! Next to the fence on the airstrip!" I peeked around the corner after my reply, wishing I hadn't, and saw a horde of Tortured moving toward us at a rapid pace. They were only a short distance away, having made fast progress from the hangar to our position. It was roughly as many as Val had assumed and absolutely more than we could handle.

We've got thirty seconds before they're on top of us. Maybe less.

"Stand by." I rammed my fist into the dirt at the curt reply over the radio, leaning my rifle out from cover and taking blind shots at the crowd.

It was a futile move, and one that likely yielded no results, but gave me hope that I was at least providing a sign that we were fighting back. Val started to do the same, emptying magazine after magazine without exposing more than a few inches of his body. I flinched while reloading for the third time, a grey, metallic canister landing squarely between my legs at a high velocity and rolling to a stop against my thigh. A thin white trail indicated that it had been launched or fired from the side of our allies. In shock, my eyes read the white print on the decal as my hands moved to shove it away from us.

M-823 Medium-Range Smoke Support Munition, Gray High Volume.

"Yes!" I roared, quickly pushing it away from my body as it violently erupted and spewed thick, foggy smoke into the air around us.

Another canister flew through the air at an incredible speed, landing in the dumpster and only missing Val's head by a few feet. Others began to impact the ground between us and the operations center, flooding the air with a chalky-smelling, thick haze of concealment. I grabbed Val's ankle as he tried to take off in a run, tripping as I pulled him toward me and back into cover. "Wait!" I grunted, pointing as wisps of smoke darted through the air next to the dumpster, a sign that their gunshots were landing where we would have been, had we started running immediately.

They thought we'd take off right away. They're anticipating our movement.

Val nodded once in thanks, continuing to stare into the smoke until the hissing trails slowed, then shifted to more random, sporadic bursts. Val tapped me once, shifting his weight to begin an all-out sprint to the next building. I could hear the voices of the Tortured as they yelled in excitement, screaming orders and shouting at one another in the heat of battle. They sounded hungry, like rabid dogs willing to fight and die for another meal.

We can't let them catch us.

We followed in each other's footsteps, a determined and unyielding strength in our legs and bodies as we pounded through the smoke and left only footprints and panic in our wake. We couldn't see the door, but both of us were able to follow the direction of its last sighting and arrived too quickly, slamming into the stone masonry of the wall and scrambling to find the door's handle. Val gripped it tightly, turning it several times before crouching down and looking at me.

"Locked. I'm going to have to break it." He said quickly, turning his head to listen to the shouting.

They know we went this way.

"Then break it!" I hissed, beckoning with both hands. "You deadlift mountains for fun, what the hell's the-"

"We have to keep moving. This door won't lock again. If we get trapped in here, we're dead."

Val breaks the lock and we get inside. We shore up the door the best we can and hide. Tortured break in, kill us through sheer volume. If we keep moving, they waste time searching the building. Maybe get away somewhere long enough to-

"Break the lock. Make 'em think we went inside. We'll go around and find a place to hole up near the ops center." Val was already following my brief train of thought, raising his fist and swiftly snapping off the metal handle of the door.

With another two heavily weighted punches, the lock mechanism was bent enough for Val to grip the door and pull it open, leaving it exposed so we could rush to the back side of the building. I kept my rifle up as we moved, the main gate of the base nearer to us than ever before. In front of us was the operations building, an ornate yet militaristic structure of glass, concrete, and steel that represented the spirit of the station. We were partially hidden by a short garden wall between us and the building, and we kept low along its edge while moving as fast as possible.

Our magazines, mostly empty, rattled slightly as we huddled together and walked toward the ongoing engagement. I could see the upper edges of the signs and barriers as we crossed into the threshold of the complex, but Val grabbed my shoulder and pulled me down before I could observe further. His finger was already pointed to our previous hiding spot, and the flood of Tortured that was reinforcing the rear of the base now angrily charged toward the main road to reinforce their allies. Assumedly, they had realized that we escaped.

"They're going to get overrun." Val said quietly, leaning into a hedge and attempting to conceal our location. "That's another hundred soldiers that Yuri didn't account for, and he's already stretched too thin. It *has* to be us." Val added solemnly, understanding that it would essentially be a suicide mission to take the complex with anything less than a small army.

"Yuri, are you through the gate?" I rasped into my radio, whispering as loudly as I could so he could hear me without giving us away.

"No!" Yuri's reply was instant, the background noise of his transmission consisting of the same gunfire we could hear only a few hundred feet away. "We're still stopped! More than half of us are dead or wounded." He paused, deciding his next words. "We don't have enough left to flank them. I don't know what to do." My heart dropped hearing those words, knowing he was facing imminent death for him and his people. "We were fighting the last hundred, and a hundred more just arrived. We can't keep this up."

"Let's go. We have to reinforce them." Val said confidently, loading a fresh magazine into his rifle and performing a quick check of his remaining ammo. His shoulders slumped when he looked back at me, understanding that he was expended of all spare ammunition. I exhaled through my nose, pulling every magazine from the pouches on my chestplate and dropping them at his feet. Only two still contained rounds.

"Here." I pulled the pistol from my holster, knowing I still had some protection at my side. He handed me the magazine from his own pistol, effectively trading so we were more or less prepared for another round of battle. "Yuri." I turned back to my radio. "Val's on his way. In the next thirty seconds, hit them with everything you have and *take that damn gate* at all costs. This is where we draw the line." I released the button for a moment, drawing in a short breath. "If they keep this place, we're dead anyway, Yuri. You, me, and everyone we care about. Show these animals what we're made of and give us a chance to kill Legacy. We take Quantico today, no matter the price." Val looked at me proudly, his brow caked in dirt and sweat and the stinging tears of being fired on relentlessly. Regardless of the layers of toil that laid on his face, his eyes were set on mine as his mouth drew into a tight snarl.

"Alright." He growled, breathing heavily. "We'll hit 'em, Jalix. I'm with you." His eyes darted away from mine for a singular instant, and in the distance of his gaze I could see his love for Alice, his friendship with Krystal, his kinship with Kara, and most importantly, his unyielding need to see them again. His fingers mercilessly strangled the synthetic grip of his rifle, a panicky edge taking away from the fighter we both knew he was.

He knows the sacrifices we have to make.

I looked back at him in gratitude and friendship, placing my left palm on his shoulder while my right hand held onto my pistol.

And he'd make those sacrifices if he had to.

I lashed out with my right hand, striking the metal of my pistol against the bridge of his nose and watching as he crumpled to the ground, unconscious, while a steady trickle of blood left his nostrils.

"Not this time, old friend." I sighed, pulling his limp body further into the bushes until he was completely concealed. I left the rifle in the center of his chest, moving away from the scene and checking to ensure that he was fully hidden. The gardens of the complex were full of chaotic color, dying slowly in the cycle of autumn, and teeming with foliage thick enough to conceal his veiled body.

I'm not going to let him die for my decisions. My planning. My failures.

I looked up at the building, close enough that a quick sprint would have me at the front door. No guards outside were posted, likely because they left to reinforce the gate and had withheld plenty more inside.

I won't let Kara live without her brother. I won't let Amy live without her uncle.

The gunfire at the gate increased, bringing a heightened sense of urgency to my actions. Yuri's forces reacted significantly to his orders, nearly doubling the rate of fire and bringing into the fight the heavier, vehicle-mounted weapons. I listened for several seconds, hearing an unfortunate cycle of the larger guns ceasing their fire for a few moments, then resuming as another living soldier was able to take its place.

I won't let these deaths be in vain. I won't keep Yuri from returning to his people.

The gardens passed quickly as I approached the front of the building, ignoring the security cameras that I knew saw my presence. I rounded the corner inside the front doors, the sights of my pistol tracing a clean line at shoulder height from one side of the room to the other. I fired three shots and watched as many bodies fall to the ground before I moved through the now-empty space.

I won't let Legacy kill everything we've worked for. I won't let his army take my family.

New guards scrambled down the steps, moving with ease around the staircase in the corner of the room and nearly landing every shot they took. I managed to slide behind a stone pillar, crouching as I swiveled to take aim at the new targets.

I won't let this country be a failure to the world. I won't let down the people that trusted me.

Stepping over the last of the bodies in the lobby, I treaded each step of the stairway in extreme caution, angling my arms upward to keep protection around every corner. It proved useful, my reaction time taking two more Tortured by surprise as they moved to defend their comrades and ultimately failed.

I won't-…I-…this is my last shot.

I stopped, ejecting my magazine and confirming that my last round was loaded into the chamber. As if my teeth weren't already ground into dust, my fangs crept downward another fraction in reaction to my instinct to kill regardless of the cost.

This is for everything they did to me. Everything they'd do to my family.

I unclipped the latch of the sheath on my shoulder, withdrawing my knife and holding the pistol steadily in front of me. I had reached the top of the stairs, where one of the Tortured I killed lay with a bloody hole through their skull. The open door led to a wide space of some sort, seemingly used for office work and the administrative functions of the base. I couldn't get a good look, staying next to the door to remain out of sight. I looked down at the body again, weighing my options.

You could use his rifle.

I dropped the pistol onto the floor and reached down with my free hand to pick up the available weapon when a searing, ripping pain tore through my forearm and hand, forcing me to recoil quickly against the doorframe. I rolled to the side as a barrage of shots shattered the wall next to me, opening my eyes wider to watch the two holes – one in my arm and one through my palm – gush blood onto the floor.

Shit. Sixteen shots total, close and from the nearest two corners inside. That…hurt.

I took another deep breath, replacing the knife into its sheath and sweeping my body across the opening, deftly grabbing the rifle and pulling it close as my shoulder blades hit the wall on the opposite side of the door. More gunshots missed me narrowly, striking the floor and the dead body, but one was lucky enough to impact the body armor on my back, thumping my spine with a great deal of force and forcing a quick cough in reaction.

One on the left side, two more on the right. Medium-caliber rifles, thirty-five shots fired in total.

My right arm would be useless until the bleeding stopped, so I took the rifle's grip in my left hand and pinned the stock against my shoulder to prepare for the next room. I stepped away from the frame, letting slivers of the next space expose themselves to my watching eye while I rounded the corner.

Protruding corner on the left next to the desks; easiest hiding spot with the best view of the door. Looks like a weaker interior wall. The shot that hit my back felt low. They're crouched.

I fired three shots in a small triangle, watching a body roll to the ground with a satisfactory silence.

Don't let the other two react. Swivel hard and take the inside corner of the room. They'll stand their ground at the cost of being standing targets.

I let my right shoulder touch the doorframe, keeping my body turned to the side and giving them as small a target as possible. I had let loose several shots before I was fully inside, knowing and rightly guessing the position of the first soldier. I didn't watch the fall of his body, but knew from the initial jerk that the shots had landed squarely in his neck. The second target was lined up with me and quickly became a competition of reflexes and muscle memory. She made my third and fourth trigger squeezes my last by way of impeccable aim and impossible reaction time.

Goddamn Factor Five.

I dropped the rifle, crumpling against the wall and coughing up specks of blood while I gasped for air. My left side roared in pain; both of her final bullets, thankfully the last ones of her life, had taken up residence somewhere in my ribcage and within my left lung after narrowly missing the protection of my armor plates. The room was free of further activity, a fact I was grateful for while making long, crawling strides toward the last soldier's corpse.

The last impulses of neurological activity created a jerking, shaking obstacle when I arrived at her body. The weapon she was using was the same as the one I now carried and would be useless without one side of my physique functional enough to support it. I scoured over her equipment to locate anything useful and decided to open her medical waistpack, which revealed several IV-starting kits with needles, tubing, and tape, and a bottle of unmarked, miscellaneous pills.

"Aw, Alice...I could really use your expertise right now. Or your sister's." I whispered, picking up the bottle as I leaned on my side and realized I was better off throwing them to the side rather than ingesting unknown drugs. I looked for a sidearm or anything else of use for a moment before stumbling across the pouch that held her Factor Five IV bag.

I debated the risks of taking it, deciding that my experience with the solution was enough to warrant one last use. I was rolled onto my side, trying to calm myself so each breath I took would be adequately used by my non-collapsed lung. I quickly disconnected the line from her arm, attaching the tubing to a fresh needle and letting it drip long enough to purge any air bubbles. I still held the needle for a moment, glancing at the obvious veins in my arm and reflecting again on the consequences of returning to the same sensations I had under my previous torture.

You won't become one of them.

I slid the needle into my most prominent vein, letting the faint pop of skin provide friction long enough to pin down the plastic port behind it. I withdrew the slender piece of metal, leaving behind a thin plastic tube and taping it quickly to my arm while taking several deep breaths. I pulled the IV bag out of its place and relocated it to an empty pouch on my upper back.

You have a wife to get back to…and the family you made with her. Get up.

Blood covered my right arm in a sticky red coating, but the crimson tide that flowed from its two wounds slowed down enough that I no longer feared losing use of the limb. I continued to struggle breathing, but started to feel my left side tighten significantly. I planted a foot on the ground and made an effort to stand, listening to the activity from the rooms on the other side of the building's second floor. Their delay in responding was likely due to the anticipation that their allies would have won the fight. I coughed loudly, my left lung constricting painfully and adding to the agitation in my chest. With each contraction of my diaphragm, I felt the sharp stab of an object move and shift, growing higher in my chest.

I gagged, suffocating on something deep in my throat before finally leaning against a desk and hoarsely choking it out of my body. With every inch it moved, a slicing pain thrashed at my neck until finally a small, coppery object hit the desk with a splash of cherry-red blood and a quiet rattle. The bullet that had ended up in my chest was deformed after hitting my rib, a sharp edge cutting as it made its way out of my body since the lung expelling it was now partially healed. It was no sooner that I caught my breath than another party of Tortured poured through the doorway on the opposite side of the room.

I dropped to the underside of the desk, using my left arm to grab the fallen soldier's rifle much the same way I had before and letting loose the rest of the magazine. I squeezed the trigger as fast as I was able, hitting most of them as they funneled through the entryway. One had escaped, dashing to the far corner and hiding somewhere out of my line of sight. I stood again, dropping the empty weapon and unsheathing the knife once more from its holster. I started to back away, moving toward the way I entered without turning my back to the location of the remaining figure. A pair of eyes peered out from around a computer monitor, inspecting me briefly before finding me both unarmed – minus my knife – and unusually interesting.

"Jalix Kane? Damn, it really *is* you. In the flesh." He both asked a question and answered it while strolling out of his cover and making his way toward me. He held a pistol in his right hand: a massive cannon that was only ever practical as a showpiece instead of a genuine firearm. I raised my hands slowly, continuing to back up as he advanced.

"Look-" I opened my mouth and got a single word out before he lifted the gun and fired off three shots in rapid succession, striking me squarely in the chest. My ceramic armor plates absorbed the rounds, but the shock and impact stole my breath once more and buckled me to a kneeling stance.

"Well hot damn, I get to be the one to take you out. Know who I am?" He quipped, seeming to want a casual conversation more than a fight. I stared at him, fighting the pain that rolled through the entirety of my body and watching his relaxed movements fluidly wave his gun around as he spoke. "Legacy calls me X. Just X. Know why? Because like him, I don't need a name or a title. I just have a purpose. I'm his personal assassin. I kill things." He took another shot as I began to stand, stressing the breaking point of the body armor and my ribcage underneath.

Who the hell is this guy?

"I'm very good at what I do. So good, in fact, that he told me that I'd probably be the last thing anyone would ever see if they tried to take this building. So…" He lunged across the distance between us, placing the hot barrel of the firearm under my jaw and lifting my chin to meet his eyes. "At least the famous Jalix Kane, the Ultimate Soldier, Schillinger's cold-blooded killer, gets to die by *my* hand. The Ultimate Assassin, and an even better soldier than-" I conjured up the remaining strength on my left side, twisting my body away from the gun and bringing my left hand down with enough force to crush the roof of a small car. My knife landed squarely between two of the vertebrae in his neck, effectively killing him before he could pull the trigger. I waited for a moment, jerking the knife and feeling my fangs strain against my gums as I watched his body slide off the blade and onto the floor.

"You…*suck*…at your job." I spit the last of the blood out of my mouth, shaking my head and walking in the direction he came from. "Asshole." A wave of relief from the Factor Five washed over my chest, whisking away the biological response that caused inflammation and starting to care for the bruising against my ribs and sternum.

I tuned my senses to listen in excruciating detail, hearing nothing else in the immediate area and focusing on the battle still raging outside. The larger-caliber guns affixed to the armored vehicles rattled off consistently, a stark contrast from their previous irregularity. I moved toward one of the large glass walls in the hallway I entered, watching the fight rage below for the main gate. The vehicles were firmly seated against the barriers, holding a definitive line as roughly ten of Yuri's soldiers smartly and expertly maneuvered around them.

That can't be all that's left.

"Yuri." I croaked into the radio, gagging again as my vocal cords rasped against the damage in my throat. "Shit, starting to sound like Raven. Can you hear me? I'm in the ops center." The first statement was made to myself, but I expected a response from the second. None came, and I turned around to climb the ornate metal staircase that led to the open top floor. As I had expected from previous experience in military complexes, it opened to a large room that held a small corner for security operations regarding the base itself. Finding it empty, I limply jogged over to the hub, looking at the various camera angles on the dozen high-resolution monitors that decorated the space. Most seemed like pictures; only still landscapes and calm scenes appeared on the screen. On a few of them, an intense war raged on between the soldiers moving through the main gate and the remaining Tortured that defended it. "Yuri!" I yelled into the radio, hoping a more intense tone would be heard over the sounds of battle. A scratching sound came first, followed by several taps and scrapes. It hissed and crackled, but appeared to follow a pattern.

Morse Code. Old school.

"Yuri, say again." I said softly, understanding that he had some reason for remaining quiet. I listened for a second time, following each tap and scrape as he sent his coded message in the briefest of ways.

Close. Flank. Help.

My eyes hastened to find his forces on the screen, seeing nothing but the obvious until a small, auspicious movement caught my eye. Yuri was waving directly at one of the streetlight security cameras, hoping that I could see him. He was positioned at a perfect angle for ambushing the remaining forces, on the corner of the main street and a side road, but was likely unaware of the fact since his vision was blocked by a building between his unit and the enemy's. He was right outside of the remaining mass of Tortured, and certainly close enough that talking on the radio would give away his position.

"Yuri, listen to me closely…" I looked at the small, black dots next to him and was elated to realize that nearly thirty of his men were hiding in the foliage and at his side. "Send ten of your men up through that building and have them look about fifteen degrees to the right of your current position. They can provide overwatch from the windows while you move to the right of the building in front of you. You'll end up directly behind them with barriers on the street for cover. We can still win, but you need to move *now.*" I emphasized, turning away from the monitors and looking around.

Nearly the entire room's walls were glass, held by an occasional metal strut, but otherwise allowed for a full view of most of the surrounding areas. Two large cracks marred the clarity of the surface, apparently caused by stray bullets, but there was plenty of space for me to press my face against and watch the operation unfold below. I wanted to hold my breath, seeing a dozen of Yuri's soldiers already visible in the windows of the building and getting into a position to start taking shots at the enemy's exposed side. The dozen soldiers that manned the front gate, accompanied by the massive weapons that helped improve the perceived size of the invading force, were an adequate distraction for the remaining platoon of Tortured.

The flanking maneuver worked.

Yuri and his personal cadre were still unnoticed and began to swivel to the side of the building, jumping behind the cover previously used by the rear forces of the Tortured in their initial defense. Sandbags and concrete barriers were enough of a confidence for Yuri to lift his arm, pulling down a fist and giving the signal for the rest of his fighters to open fire. It was a massacre, the initial wave of shots decimating the defending force before they had a chance to turn around and realize what was happening. Yuri leaned into his radio, calling to the vehicles for a cease-fire so there would be no accidents with stray rounds. The large-caliber weapons stopped, a few lighter shots coming from the front gate as the last of the Tortured fell. I sprinted back to the security monitors, quickly looking at each one as my ears descended into a screaming ring of silence.

We won.

In disbelief, I looked at the monitors again, one after another, waiting for any sign or signal that there was yet another auxiliary force or backup death squad waiting for us in hiding. None came and I started shaking, the adrenaline quickly leaving my system and flushing my body with weakness.

We won.

I reached behind me, pinching the small satchel of Factor Five that had apparently been depleted and absorbed into my body over the past few minutes. Being aware that I would quickly succumb to the massive physical toll on my body without additional help, I turned around to head to the lower floor and find either another soldier's IV pack or a quiet place to lay down and nap until medical aid could arrive to help us. I flinched, a heart-stopping panic lurching through my gut before my eyes could recognize that the figure standing near the exit to the room was none other than Val. He smirked, tilting his head and taking a step toward me.

"We did it." I laughed quietly, extending a hand as he fell within arm's reach. He grabbed my arm with one hand, withdrawing his pistol from the other and firing a shot directly into the center of my armor plating. The close distance between the shot and its impact relayed nearly all of its force into my already suffering torso.

"If you *ever...*" He started, grabbing my neck as I doubled over. He lifted me up just enough that I was standing on the tips of my toes to struggle for air. I didn't fight back with any true strength, knowing that he wouldn't truly want to kill me and had shot my body armor on purpose. "Do something like that again..." He continued, pushing forward and throwing my body across a table hard enough that I slid onto the floor behind it. I felt a slithering crunch at my side as another rib broke from the impact. He moved toward me again, throwing the table across the room like it was made of cardboard. "I will hurt you enough that your days with Legacy will feel like a vacation." He crouched down, staring at me as I groaned in pain and did my absolute best to stay conscious.

Man, he's pissed.

"You're...welcome." I coughed, glaring back at him. He extended his arm, which I gratefully took as he lifted me to a standing position like a child's doll.

"Suicide missions have better odds with more people." Val warned. "You had *no right* to do this yourself."

"And you had no right to put yourself in this position." I fired back, not accepting his reasoning.

"Why not? Why can't I-"

"Because you don't want to live badly enough." I snapped quickly, bending over to lean on my knees. "You're okay with sacrificing yourself. Not gonna let that happen."

"What, you don't think I can handle myself through this shit? You don't think I've taken on enough Pyrates back in the day?"

"Pyrates were practice. Trust me..." I held out my right arm, the gaping wounds still working on the healing process. "These guys have better aim."

"It's harder to aim at two things at once, Jalix. This was stupid. And reckless. You had no good reason to knock my ass out and bury me in a bush somewhere while *you* came through like a goddamn *hurricane!*" He was still angry, but trying to understand my point of view.

"You've suffered enough...Val." I said quietly, watching his reaction lose its spiteful edge. "I am *not* about to let you go through whatever I've been through. If they had won, we wouldn't have been killed. They would have tried to convert us. They would have tortured us the same way they were. The same way I was. They would have used our captivity to ransom with our families. They could have executed us, broadcast live on the internet, with Alice and Kara watching. You don't want that."

"You weren't saving my life, you were trying to save my sanity." Val mumbled, starting to understand.

"And that of our families'. What they put me through…you don't want that, man. It's the worst thing that you can't imagine. It's that bad. The healing is…it really is addictive. Not just addictive, it feels like the only important thing in the world. The only thing *left* in the world. Experiencing that kind of pain is the only reason I had the endurance to make it up here after being shot up the way I am. I'm not saying you wouldn't have survived, but you would have come out a different person."

"And you didn't?" He sneered, looking over my wounds. "You just put yourself in a warzone with no one to help."

"War is my *home*, Val." I replied too quickly, hearing the words come out of my mouth. A flood of memories with Kara stormed my brain, the concept of her comforting arms wrapped around me enough to force more than a few tears to my eyes in apologetic memory after I told her the same words so many years ago. "I didn't mean that." I shook my head.

"I know. That's the problem." He pulled over a plush office chair, giving me a blissful opportunity to sit, leaning back against the leather and the cushioning. "You just said, *and did*, a lot of things you'd sworn off. You and Kara both promised-"

"I know what I promised!" I roared, regretting the increase in vocal strain. "I know what I said to my own daughter!" I paused. "But we're…we're not in that world anymore. We'll have to break a lot of promises to keep them safe." He took a step back, staring at me for a long moment.

"Is that you speaking...or is that Sorrow?" He shoved another table, letting it flip on its side and screech across the floor. "Don't you *dare*-"

"Relax, Val." I interrupted, hearing the footsteps of our allies start to make their way up the stairs of the building. "You and I both brought Kara back from being Sorrow. I know just as well as you how damaging it can be. Sorrow is dead. And I'm not taking up her mantle." We both fell silent, a sense of understanding between us solidified as Yuri fell into view.

He came through the wide doorway covered in sweat and grime. Some of his team were behind him, looking equally as battered. Without saying anything, he handed me a small, black nylon case with a zipper wrapped around its edge.

"Vampyre medicine. Spare from the supplies we brought. You need it." He raised his eyebrows, shocked at the amount of blood that saturated the various fabrics around my body. "You need evac?" He gestured, his accent coming through once again.

"I'm good." I unzipped the case and injected one of the vials, immediately feeling the effects on my sense of consciousness. I felt less dizzy and was able to think more clearly within a matter of moments. I followed suit with the second dose, knowing it would be put to good use. "Just a scratch."

"Just a scratch? Your arm's off." Val quipped with an English accent, referencing an old movie we used to enjoy watching with Eric and Tony.

"I've had worse. Just a flesh wound." I chuckled, continuing the joke and thoroughly alarming Yuri's men at my sense of humor in the midst of grievous injury.

"We'll let you rest." Yuri concluded, his men starting to move across the room and search through the various desks and filing cabinets. "We'll work on finding the information we need and bringing reinforcements from the city. I already called Raven." He added. "They know everyone left is safe and we took the base. Reinforcements are on the way. Our specialist was extremely surprised that we defied his odds."

"Never tell me the odds." I groaned, pulling myself to my feet again and watching the soldiers scrounge for documents. Yuri walked past Val on his way to the front of the room, peering into one of the private offices in the far corner. Val stayed behind with me and moved at a slower pace to catch up.

"You sure you're alright? We can send you in one of the trucks-"

"No." I interrupted. "I'll be alright. Long enough to finish this, anyway. Once we get our reinforcements and I know this place is secure, I'll head back with...you." I turned my head to follow one of the men, having spent a long moment at a filing cabinet before scurrying to Yuri's side and whispering in his ear. Had that not been enough evidence of a development, Yuri's eyes darted over to see if Val and I were watching, then looked away as if to pretend it didn't happen. Val caught onto the same issue and followed me to approach him.

"What's up?" I asked, looking at the two of them. The unknown man handed Yuri the folder he was holding, looking up at me briefly. Yuri held up a finger, flipping through the thick contents of the folder before stopping on one of the pages and scrunching his brow. I raised my eyebrows, tilting my head to try and garner his attention, but was wholly ignored as he continued reading with fervor. "I swear, if there's some other sneaky shit that you and Raven cooked up-"

"There is." He breathed, a smile creeping across his face as the documents in his hands slid out from in front of the folder and scattered across the floor. The only thing he was still holding was a stack of pages that were stapled together. There were few markings on it, the Marine Corps logo on the cover sheet and a faded print of small text on the pages behind it.

"Here. Disable everything, unlock everything, shut it all down." He handed the stack of papers to his colleague, who looked as genuinely eager as Yuri. With a renewed vigor, Yuri dashed to the door of the room and disappeared behind its wall, leaving Val and I deeply confused.

"What the-"

"Just follow him." I decided, doing my best to keep up with the flight as we followed him outside and across the courtyard in a near-sprint.

I looked around as I crossed the threshold outside, taking in the smell of phosphorus, sulfur, and a swarm of other bodily smells from the deceased that lay in lumped masses where they fell. The remainder of Yuri's men were huddled around the vehicles at the gate, some of them visibly elated that we took the prized location by a narrow victory, and others visibly mourning those they lost. Many were wounded and holding empty needles from repeated injections of our medicine.

It was a massacre on both sides. We lost more than a hundred and fifty people.

I pushed my legs with the last of my energy, jogging well past the hangar and clearly heading to somewhere a great distance from the operations center. The munitions that previously provided Val and I with cover now trickled the last of their smoke, sending a slow haze across the landscape. We ran across street after street, building after building, my lungs practically catching fire as I swallowed oxygen and kept my right arm tucked protectively against my chest. Yuri was a hundred yards ahead of us with Val intentionally keeping a slower pace to stay between us. I didn't have the breath to ask more questions, and kept moving one foot in front of the other to keep up.

They had families. They had friends and loved ones. They left, and they will never go home.

Yuri slowed his pace, approaching a crisp, white concrete walkway paved across the lawn of a massive building set in reddish-brown brick against the landscape. It was apart from some of the other structures, standing as a great hall of some kind. The front doors were open, a massive crowd of people piling out into the front lawn and spilling along the side of the building. Half of them looked around in amazement while the other half stared at our approach. Val and I had caught up, watching more and more people pour from the mouth of the building and rush outside.

"Yuri, who are these people?" I asked as his smile grew, staring as the population swelled. A few of them cautiously began walking up to us, a young woman with her hair in a tight bun presenting herself to me with an outstretched hand.

"I assume you're the ones to thank?" She asked, gripping my hand tightly and shaking it. "I can't imagine why else you'd look so surprised." She chuckled, a confident voice giving me the indication that she was typically well-spoken and intelligent.

She's military. Too young to be senior enlisted. Likely a company-grade officer.

"First Lieutenant Andrea Scott, United States Marines. At least, back when we *had* Marines. Those assholes have had us under lock and key for weeks. I don't know how you got us out or what kind of army you did it with, but...*thank* you."

"What assholes? The Tortured? What do you mean lock and key, I don't-" Yuri's beaming smile spread to Val as he put together the same pieces I did. "They were going to convert you guys." I breathed, looking out at the thankful crowd.

"They did. Got through a few hundred of us. Some of us have been here for two or three months from the original team at Quantico, others just got shipped in from D.C."

"We found their factory. This isn't just their arms and munitions-" I started.

"This was their breeding ground." Yuri said quietly. "A controlled location for the Tortured to gather their recruits and convert them in a tightly-secured environment. Then train them *here*, on a military base, to fight in their army."

We just cut the head off the snake. This is their crown jewel.

"Are you all okay?" Val asked, stepping into the conversation. "Anyone seriously injured or in need of help?"

"No, strangely enough." She replied, looking back at the mass. "They kept us in good shape until they picked a new batch to take with them. Like cattle." She said it with disgust, reminding me that although she was happy to be free, she had still been a prisoner to them. "Hey, you're..." She looked at me for a moment, tilting her head in realization. "You're Jalix. And you're-" She turned to Val. "You're Valterius. The Homeland Defense Attaché for VMPs. We didn't know that you were still alive. Any of you." She spoke in a sense of shock, as if she were meeting legendary figures.

"How many of you are there?" Val asked, seeing the crowd inch forward to make room for those still making their way out of the building. "The crowd keeps coming."

"The barracks complex is two attached buildings, hold about a thousand altogether when it's at max capacity. And some of us were three to a room instead of two...definitely above capacity. I'd say twelve hundred, maybe more." She remarked, pointing to a colleague of hers and beckoning the woman toward us. "Sorry." She commented, starting to choke with tears. "Haven't seen some of my friends in a while." She turned to hug the woman that approached her, swaying slowly for a moment as they rejoiced. Andrea looked at us again, wiping away tears and gesturing to her comrade. "This is First Lieutenant Goss. Layla Goss. We went through school together. The two of us tried to work with the rest of the people here to break out, make plans for escape. Then you guys arrived."

"Val, do you know what this means?" I started to ignore her comments in light of the massive victory within our grasp. He nodded and looked at the crowd, many of them seeing us covered in dirt and blood and realizing that we had freed them. A cheer started in the back, crawling our way toward us.

"This is our army." He said softly, raising a fist to encourage and animate the mass of free Vampyres. I laughed, recognizing the rewards of our efforts as infinitely greater than we could have imagined. "This is how we're going to beat Legacy." Val continued, contentedly accepting the audible praise resounding through the air.

"Wait, you said school. School here?" I snapped back to Andrea, raising my voice to talk over the crowd. She nodded, looking at her friend and pulling her close.

"Yeah, we went through flight school together, selected for special assignment. Right after Air Combat Command stood up at the new hangar, on the other side of the base. There's a bunch of us here somewhere. Layla and I were in the first graduating class."

"First graduating class. Of pilots." I finished, my gawking mouth turning to Val slowly. "We have pilots."

LUMINESCENCE

KARA

I breathed a sigh of relief as I watched the first white bus roll down the street and take a slow turn into the hospital parking lot. Even after seeing it so many times over many years, I felt my chest swell with pride as it meandered past the sign that bore my husband's name. I felt the cool sweep of wind against my shoulder, taking notice of the pattern of footfalls behind me and determining that Raven had decided to help me welcome the newcomers by my side.

"Kara." She acknowledged quietly, recognizing me without the formality or custom I had received so far from the new city's residents.

"Raven." I turned, the smile still on my face as I felt the sunrise bask me in a warm glow of morning energy. "How is everyone?" She paused, turning her head and averting her eyes from making direct contact.

"They're well. Alice is...well. The rest should be awake soon. She seems to be handling things well."

"Sounds like things are *well*." I quipped, poking fun at her awkwardness. "Relax. You're...stiff around me. I'm not going to hurt you." I sighed quietly at the words, turning back to watch the bus crawl to a stop in the parking lot and vacate its passengers. Most of them started to unload their belongings from the storage space on the vehicle, spreading out luggage and duffel bags to allow their owners to retrieve them. "My hate for you ended a long time ago." I finished, nodding. "If you're helping the family, you have my word that I'll keep you safe."

"Thanks." She mumbled, taking a small step back and unfolding her arms. "I'll have to show you around Vanaheim. If you're…going to be in charge. You'll need to know what's what, and-"

"It's a replica of Aerael, correct? Wouldn't I know more than most in that regard?" I didn't mean to interrupt her, but reacted to the strange statement.

"There are definitely changes. Things may be laid out in a similar way, but they're much different than what you're used to. It's worth a quick walk around." She added, starting to speak more like a normal person. I couldn't help but to take note of her voice again, the sandpaper's rough edge of a stony, coarse layer atop the harmonious timbre I was previously accustomed to hearing.

"Everyone else is probably settled in, already." I sighed, having been separated from the rest of my family for too long. "A day's wait is a lot to make up for."

"I'm sorry, Kara, I-"

"Don't be." I shut down her chance at an apology, as it wasn't needed. "I understand your logic. Your people, and they are *your* people, need a warning before I suddenly show up and take over. I can't have them believing that you're under duress or coercion. The last thing I need is a lack of faith from the people supporting our entire future." Raven contemplated my words for a moment, seemingly confused at the respect I was giving her.

"I appreciate that. We did the best to make you comfortable here in the hospital aboveground, but it doesn't compare to the comfort down in the city. At least everyone else got a solid night's rest and some medical care. Speaking of, we can head down. I'm sure you're eager." She added.

"Then let's walk. I'll assume you have other people that can greet our new residents?" I asked. She nodded, taking out her phone and sending a brief message.

"Yeah, they're on their way. A couple people are going to wait here for the next few buses." I could tell she was interested in giving me the details as we turned, facing away from the glass front doors of the hospital and observing the ornate lobby. A large, round service desk sat in its center, its white finish bathed in a gentle silver light from the chandelier above it. "Jalix said he was sending roughly half of the people he rescued from Quantico. Has that changed?"

Her tone is too respectful, too fearful. Might be an act to garner my favor, but she has no reason to put on a submissive act. She wouldn't have given us the winning hand if she was on the wrong side. So why the change in behavior? Personal growth, maybe. Change in her environment now that her father is out of the picture?

"No, no change." I returned, letting my thoughts amble their way through a line of reasoning. "He and Yuri seemed to have it figured out pretty well."

"Indeed. We can handle that many, but not much more. At our peak, we had five hundred. We have the room for…a *lot* more, just haven't had the resources. Population's going to surge when the New York refugees get here." She paused as we went through the lobby, crossing to the far side and turning into a corner with a clearly labeled staircase next to an elevator. "Elevator works, but I'll show you the scenic route." We stepped into the landing of the stairs and descended several floors, passing one door to the sublevel of the hospital before the environment changed.

The further down we went, the makeup of the railing, the floor, and even the walls seemed to be hastily finished, separate from the initial construction. Finally, we reached the bottom and turned into a hallway lined with the doors of clinical offices. "This is where we did some of the work for the cure. Halfway point between the city and the hospital. Will Jalix and Valterius still be on the last bus?" She decided to continue our previous conversation.

"They'll be returning on one of the vehicles. Not sure which one." I decided to spare details I was intimately familiar with in light of my own doubts. "I'm excited to see them." I confessed, watching a genuine, gentle smile move across her mouth as her head turned.

"I'm glad, Kara. After everything Legacy put you guys through, you all deserve to be together again. As a family." Her tone wasn't necessarily bitter, but nearly sounded jealous at the mention of our reunion. "So the hallway we turned into was B2. So to get to the entrance, we go through the front doors, through the lobby and turn into hallway B2 after either the stairs or the elevator. Then we go through here…" She paused again, opening a set of double doors. Unconventionally, the doors were automatic and wider than one would expect within the inside of a building. The room was cleared out from floor to ceiling to create a large, empty chamber with another colossal door on its opposite end. "And that's the entrance." She finished, approaching the door and stopping on her heels. "*Slightly* more accessible than Aerael's.

"And much less storied." I added. "It's a smart design though. Entrances are large enough to bring down large pieces of machinery, building materials-"

"Forklifts." She quipped. "Brought down pieces, assembled down here. *Huge* help."

"I would imagine." I agreed, letting her open the doors and reveal a flat walkway into a cavernous, grand hall reminiscent of my longtime home. "Wow." I whispered unintentionally, striding through the doors and walking along the path into the open cavern. It was identical to Aerael with minor exceptions that gave the city its own unique sense of culture. There were few rounded corners, as most of the concrete work for the walls and ceiling bore crisp, geometric corners suggestive of machine-made structures.

As I fully entered the main hall, I stood in its center and basked in the light of the cavernous ceiling; an artificial sunlight from carefully placed lamps and lights along the apex of the hall smothered the city's view in peace and tranquility. The arboretum in front of me, dividing the hallway into two halves as its predecessor did, was filled with trees and ferns that brought a natural glow to the environment. I stepped to the right, seeing the corridor to the family's private quarters closest to the city's entrance: a perfect replica of Aerael's layout. Ahead of that hallway, what was previously a set of rustic and chic shops and restaurants was now a neon haven, pulsating quietly with the reverberations of mellow music. I could appreciate that each space along the hallway was clearly crafted and inherited by its residents rather than its creators.

Raven watched me carefully, her eyes wide to watch my reaction to each crevice of my new city. I shifted again, moving to the left of the gardens and quickly becoming elated at sights I hadn't seen in more than a decade. The training room to my immediate left was empty, but was proudly bearing the iconic throne of a caged-in boxing ring supported with supplementary steel struts coated in black paint. Past the training room was an impeccable recreation of the infirmary, the hospital walls consisting of a floor-to-ceiling glass barrier with a large, translucent red cross halfway along its height. I began to walk down the left alley, the sparse number of citizens looking at me with a sense of unease and apprehension as they passed.

"The doors are shut, but there *is* a nightclub. Never been used, so some of the stuff needs set up, still. Same with the chapel on the other side, although that at least has a basic setup. Probably can't see it past the neon. We-" She caught herself, realizing that she was referring to her and her father. "*I* wasn't focused on the personal details when this project was started. So a lot of it was up to the residents to finish."

"Then it's more like Aerael than you know." I remarked, observing the closed metal entrance to the nightclub. It didn't have the same spirit as Archangel's huge oak doors, but I knew it would have potential with the help of my family. "Most of Aerael was accomplished by the inhabitants. The citizens did what they desired to make their living the best they could. People built what they wanted and needed. Added to it over time and expanded..." My words caught in my throat as I reached the short, wide set of stairs that led to the residential area of the city.

I stopped, looking through the hall at the overwhelming number of apartments and people that packed the hall from one side to the other. While the center was bare aside from seating areas and decorative fountains, the people in it created a crowd of steeped and deeply-rooted culture unique in its own right. The number of apartments was at least doubled from Aerael's, spanning in two-story increments so far that I had trouble seeing the last of them.

Each one was decorated in its own style, with some having homey entrances adorned with simple wreaths and natural wood while others were smothered in trinkets of personalization and individuality. All of them were simple; standard doors were pressed into the concrete wall with the actual living spaces being dug out and finished behind the wall of the cavern. Light from neon-style decorations and adornments created the impression of a large metropolitan city at nighttime, glowing with opportunity and begging for exploration.

"It's like...New York or Tokyo. So much more modern than Aerael, but...still spirited." I marveled quietly.

"Vanaheim." She whispered proudly. "Named after a city of Viking deities. Their home for the gods of foresight, wisdom, and…fertility. That one's not quite as-"

"This is incredible." I breathed, listening to the horde of people living out their own lives. "You… did this?" I asked, turning my head to face Raven. "Alone?"

"Not alone." She admitted. "I had help from Yuri, and from a few close friends. But we…knew about Kane-Hudson when it started its remodeling from the previous hospital. We got on board immediately to start on building a space underneath, a space where we could work on cure research separately. And… the concept just grew and became this." She paused, staring at the people below her. "We've had sixteen years to evolve this place. We've used them well."

"Apparently." I retorted, pulling myself away from the sight of the city's residents. "Not a lot of familiar faces, though."

"There are some, scattered." She pondered. "A few that we managed to track down and invite. But most are new, within the last ten years. And they came for hope at a better life." We turned around, heading toward the infirmary.

"Speaking of hope, what's all this about a cure?" I asked, interested in hearing the differences in methodologies from Alice's own work.

"Let's take care of that after Alice is settled. I…want to make sure I explain things correctly. And that I'm right." She added, shrugging. "We have our own roadblocks, just like she does. But we're close. With Alice's help, we can finish this. I know it."

"And what'll you do when the world is full of humans? What will you do when your life has an expiration date?" I asked as we walked through the opening to the hospital.

"This place isn't Aerael." She paused, shaking her head. "Never will be. I'm…not a leader. I'm an agent, an operative, and I do my job well. But planning for their future, looking ahead to the coming years…that's *your* job. The people know that. *I* know that. It's why you're here." She emphasized, beckoning to the space around us. "As for me personally, I'll deal with being mortal when I get there. Cure initially. Aftermath later." She mumbled, leading me into the atrium of the infirmary. I could hear familiar voices echoing through the hall in front of us. "Family first." She concluded, beckoning for me to enter the hallway on the right.

A length in front of me held rooms of every sort, but one exam room immediately on the left held a wondrous sight for my weary eyes. A blur of blue, red, and black sped toward me out of their chairs and tackled me against the wall on the opposite side of the short hall. Their embrace was tight and comforting, a warming sensation spreading through my chest.

This place is home. My family is here.

I did my best to hug them back, one arm pinned to my side by Violet.

"Jesus, we missed you." Alice remarked, chuckling through tears. Violet wasn't in a condition to speak, nuzzling her head into my neck as she sobbed. Krystal released her grip early, being at the rear of the group and sporting a sling on her right arm, and took a step back to look at me.

My god, she actually made it. I can't believe she survived what she did. Fought death with her bare hands and won her life back only to be stabbed, beaten, and tormented.

Her hair was longer than I was accustomed to, which complemented a notably darker set of brilliant blue eyes that watched me with excited confusion. I imagined my expression was similar, gazing at her evolved, matured facial features and studied as a woman – no longer a girl – looked back at me.

"I missed you." She whispered, a broad smile across her face while tears streamed down her cheeks. "I'm so glad you're okay." Her words were different than I was used to. The way she smiled and spoke was as if I was a treasured friend rather than a shiny object to be held with pride. It swelled my heart with happiness to hear her words sound more genuine than ever before, and with no trace of the drug use she had suffered before her coma. Alice and Violet finally let me go, chuckling, as Raven took a step back to let us have some space of our own.

"I missed you, too, Krystal." I stepped toward her, giving her a hug of her own.

She's okay. She's alive and well. I missed her so much.

Rather than having one arm around my ribs and another on my waist, her free arm hooked upward to hold my shoulder blades, our heartbeats pounding against one another. I breathed a quivering sigh, elated at the simple fact of her survival and consciousness. She released her grip before I did, pulling back to wipe away her tears.

I thought she would be more...aggressive. More possessive. More affectionate. Maybe her coma changed some of her personality. Or whatever happened to her after I died. Going through death...of course it would change a person. And she's accepted a life on her own path. One without an obsession to the idea of who I was.

I let my own tears fall freely, not bothering to wipe them away.

"I'm so happy to see you all." I laughed through my crying. Sonya had apparently waited patiently in the room they all came from, knowing that the two of us already had our reunion after I awoke from my drugged sleep. She approached the rear of the group with an immaculate smile across her glowing face. I moved to the side as a doctor from further down the hall trotted through our group to hurriedly exit the hospital.

Right...work continues here.

"Where's Amy?" I asked, looking around. "She wasn't doing too well when we found you all. Is she okay?"

"She's fine." Alice quickly allayed my concerns. "She wanted to spend some time alone, but Tony insisted on staying with her as company. She's in one of the rooms just down the hall. They can probably hear us from here. Her…recovery hit hard. Something happened-" Alice put her hands up as my eyes widened. "Nothing physically harmful, at least that I can tell. Her abilities have been…*on the fritz*, I guess is the best way of putting it." As a nurse and another staff member pushed through our group in an irritated manner, we shifted a few dozen feet to the lobby and stood in a circle.

"What does that mean?" I asked quickly, knowing that Alice wouldn't use vague terminology unless she was either hiding something or was genuinely unsure of Amy's status.

"She, um…has an odd reaction with Krystal. Probably because of everything Krystal's been through. Her healing abilities go haywire. From what I can tell, it's almost…empathic? Her powers try to reach into Krystal a lot further than it does with the rest of us, dive into Krystal's emotions and thoughts. Takes a toll on both of them, but unfortunately, it's been necessary with the surplus of injuries we've experienced."

"Yeah, I don't mean to hurt her or anything-" Krystal grew defensive, but with a despondent undertone.

"It's not your fault." Alice comforted. "Our abilities are something we can't always control fully. And we'll never understand fully." Krystal smiled gently, extending her fingers to hold Alice's hand.

She's…at such peace right now. Showing so much appreciation and passion for life. Maybe she went through the same type of transformation I did…maybe we can understand each other better now.

"What about the other girl?" I asked quietly, looking at Violet.

"Rachel? She's…" Violet looked at Alice for guidance.

"Being kept sedated." Alice elaborated. "I'll explain later. She's not going to be woken up for a long time. Not a concern at the moment." She avoided any further conversation, briefly looking away as her eyes glistened with tears. I could tell that she was still struggling with the events she was rescued from, and her current motivations stemmed from escaping those memories.

"Speaking of the immediate moment…" Raven interjected, looking at her phone. "Our specialist wants to meet with all of you. We remember where the big conference room is, right?" She asked with a dry humor. "I've heard that you've all spent a lot of time there over the years."

"Just like old times." Krystal chuckled as we left the hospital and turned into the main hall toward the entrance. A flicker of remorse and pain wracked my chest as I glanced to my right as we walked, remembering the reaction I had to my confrontation with Krystal so many years ago. The sling on her arm did little to keep any distance from the memory. I could almost see the cracks and chunks of concrete marred against the wall from where I threw her in my fit of unjustified rage.

It ended up saving her life…but the ends didn't justify the means.

I looked at the back of her head as she walked in front of me and happily discussed something with Violet and Sonya. As if she were a zombie, I could imagine the chunk of her skull that was smashed out of place in an outburst of my own wrath.

You're not that person anymore. Sorrow is dead.

I breathed a gentle sigh, letting the emotions and memories wash over me and disappear in the way Jalix and I had practiced for so many months. In a stroke of coincidence, memories of his unwavering support coincided with a text message that filled my heart with overwhelming amounts of joy.

We're almost there, my love. I'll be with you again shortly. Val can't wait to see you and I can't wait to hold my wife again.

I shuddered, gritting my teeth and exhaling to avoid the further shedding of tears. Sonya touched my shoulder, leaning close as we walked.

"Everything okay?" She whispered.

"Jalix and Val are on their way." I hissed excitedly. "They're almost here. I just want him back. After Legacy-"

"He's okay." Sonya reassured. "And he's still your loving husband. He's still Jalix Kane, he's still yours. Just a few scrapes and bruises. I promise. And he missed you *so much*, Kara." I cleared my throat, clutching my phone to my chest. I could hear a slight discordance in Raven's steps as she faltered near the conference room door, allowing Alice to pass and place her hand on the door handle. Alice opened the doors to the conference room, immediately squealing in joy and running to embrace her husband that waited inside.

They're already here. Finally, a pleasant surprise.

"Val!" I squeaked, rushing toward him and falling into the arm he left open for me. He enclosed me in a massive huddle with Alice, his broad shoulders pulling me close.

"Hey, sis. I'm glad you're okay." He kissed the top of my head, starting to push me away after only a brief moment. I opened my eyes, looking at his face as he smirked and stared pointedly into the near corner of the room. I followed his gaze, still leaning into his shoulder and watching the corner next to the entrance. Slowly but surely, a face crept out from behind the door.

A handsome jawline, darkened with scruff from long days without comfort. Strong cheekbones and steely blue-grey eyes that pierce right through to my soul. The man of my dreams. The unparalleled soldier and perfect husband. Father and caretaker. The man I fell in love with, and the man I love most deeply in this world.

I didn't bother keeping control of my powers as they shoved the conference table aside and forced my body across the room in the briefest flash of a moment, letting my lips fall onto his without a second thought. He held me tightly, swaying with his hands on my hips and his face finally against mine.

"Oh, I've been worried about you." I exhaled happily, pulling back. "I was terrified, Jalix...that you wouldn't make it back. That something would happen-"

"Kara." He breathed, holding my face in his hands. "We're all here. We're all safe."

"I woke up without you..." I stammered, placing my hands on top of his. "Amy and Violet, Alice, all of them were in danger. I don't want that to happen again." I stood there and let him take me into his arms while I basked in the scent of his chest. I could feel his subtle movements as he nodded to the rest of them, greeting him in their own ways. "Sorry." I backed away, chuckling awkwardly in self-awareness. "I don't mean to steal you."

"Yeah, move." Violet mumbled, brushing past me coolly and falling onto Jalix. "Missed you." I could hear her muffled comment, holding back tears as she wanted to say more.

Although incomplete, it felt warm to look around the room and see my family together, teary-eyed this time from reunion and the making of new memories instead of the tragedies we had all suffered over the past few days. Jalix said something quietly to Violet, forcing out a chuckle while Alice and Val spoke quietly about some topic that put their faces in a solemn calm. Raven stood quietly, but Sonya remained by her side so she wouldn't be alone.

She gave me a knowing smile, her bright green eyes telling me that she would remain supportive of my decision to keep Raven within arm's reach. As if Jalix could hear what I was thinking, he stepped away from Violet and moved toward Raven as the room fell silent. We all watched his approach, one foot carefully in front of the other at shoulder's width, and with enough vigor to cause a concerned wrinkle in Raven's brow. He stopped in front of her, tilting his head and weighing his words carefully.

"I'm aware that things didn't go according to plan." He paused for an exceptionally long moment, considering his words carefully. "After your...explicit promise to keep my family safe." Despite years of self-imposed tanning, her face grew to be as pale as Violet's with a quick flash of fear.

"Jalix I-"

"Don't speak." He interrupted, maintaining an even and decisive tone. "When Violet was unconscious, you stood over her body so no one could touch her. Afterward, you kept Amy upright and stood by her side so she couldn't be taken advantage of. You even offered yourself up to the Tortured in Alice's place, putting up a hell of a fight when you realized she needed help." Confused, Raven stared at Jalix with fearful eyes. "Thank you." He concluded resolutely. He extended a hand slowly and waited for her to return the gesture, a feat unmatched in power by Val's bullish strength or the prime of my telekinetic abilities. She was awestruck, and stared warily between his focused eyes and waiting arm. Even Sonya, stoic as she often was, tilted her head and raised her eyebrows in amazement.

"I..." She stammered quietly, gritting her teeth and letting the tips of her fangs poke the top of her bottom lip. "I'm not accepting it." She quickly took a step back, standing near the doorframe and crossing her arms. Jalix slowly relaxed his arm, calmly waiting for her reply. "If protecting other women from that...atrocity is what merits thanks, then you don't trust me yet. I didn't do it for *you*. Or part of any *promise*. I did it because it was decent." She hissed, growing disdainful at Jalix. "You'll have plenty else to thank me for before the day's over. But that isn't one of them." Jalix was accepting of her logic, nodding once and looking to me for approval.

"You went *beyond* what was required of you. For that, we're grateful. Whether you accept it or not…that is your choice. Just know that you have our thanks." I said to her, hoping the words were truly heard. She nodded in understanding, a harmony falling into place between us all.

More footsteps echoed down the hall, and through the open doors I could see my proud daughter walking alongside Tony, her face set in a soft smile as she recognized that we were all in one place. Tony looked healthy, his injuries bearing no change to his gait or posture and he held the same glow of silent positivity that Amy did. We greeted them both in silence, no one clamoring to climb on top of one another to see either or pushing anyone out of the way. Instead, the pair acted as the missing pieces of a puzzle, now completing the image that was our own legacy, forged in fire through battles and scars we had never expected. It forced the lump in my throat to grow harder and made it no easier to stand with composure as the centerpiece of our circle.

"Hey, mom." Amy said quietly, taking two long strides and encompassing me in a gentle hug. I felt so much relief at her touch and knowing that she was safe and sound. I took her shoulders in my hands, holding her at arms' length and inspecting the young woman that stood in front of me. She smirked, knowing very well that I simply needed to satisfy the maternal instinct to see her intact and happy, and the hand she placed on top of mine was a symbol of recognition.

She's so grown. So mature. She takes after her father with her poise, her confidence. It's been two weeks, but I feel like I haven't seen her in years.

"As I had mentioned…" Raven said quietly, pulling closed the conference room doors. "I wanted everyone here so that you could meet the specialist I've been referring to." She swallowed quietly, a sign that was missed by everyone else, but marked an indicator of stress in my own perception.

"And I want everyone on the same page. No confusion, no questions, and no doubts."

"We're going to doubt *anyone* you bring in, Raven. No offense." Violet remarked, glancing at Alice. She now sat in Val's lap on an office chair, cuddling in their own small corner of the room. "We're not big on new people."

"Yeah." Alice agreed simply. "You keep saying *specialist*. That's a military term for the most part. What's this person's background?"

"That's exactly what she's afraid to tell us." Amy interjected, smirking. "She's stalling. Wants him to get here so the burden is on *him* to explain instead of her. Which means we're not going to like it."

"I swear to God-"

"No one came back to life." Raven interrupted Krystal's brief statement, which conjured puzzled looks from Val, Krystal, and myself at the ironic statement. "Well-th…okay, no one *else*. It's not my father or Kilkovf. Both *very* dead. *Super* dead. Beyond saving. Am I making that statement clear enough? Can we stop worrying about it?" Her remarks bordered on sarcastic, but she was genuinely tired of hearing about the concept.

"You're doing the classic Schillinger theatrics thing again." Val motioned briefly with his hand. "You guys have a bad habit of, like…talking. You'll talk for five minutes and say nothing significant, but somehow stroke your own egos. Wanna break that cycle? Let's start with a name."

"Oh, I'd rather-…not." Her startled reaction was enough to have the room on edge, being aware now that it was a name that we would recognize.

"Raven." I enunciated, bowing my head. The room split into two parts, with Krystal, Sonya, and Tony moving toward the conference table and away from the doors where Raven stood. It led to an awkward and symbolic image of divisiveness while she stood alone in front of us. One distant scuff against the floor was enough to indicate that the person in question was approaching, and I stared at the door rather than Raven as she continued.

"We agreed to be partners. He and I are a team, so to speak. I handle some things, and he handles others. Yuri is helpful, obviously, but-"

"If we don't like him, he dies right here. You know that, right?" Tony spoke up, his jaw clenched from stress.

"I kinda doubt that. I know how you guys work." The footsteps grew close enough to be inches from the opposite side of the door, matching the voice that echoed from behind it as the figure pulled it open. The nine of us on the far side of the room sat forward, staring in disbelief at the man who sauntered toward us, stopping next to Raven and gesturing to himself. "I have the cure and the solution to Legacy. Bad idea to kill me until I give you those." No one moved, but a silent understanding started to make its way through our thoughts. Raven waited for us to speak first, and surprisingly enough, kept an even facial expression instead of the cocky smirk we all waited for. Understandably, we looked at Tony for his opinion, who took several steps forward and stood in aggressive confusion.

"Eric?"

***

Violet sighed and ran a hand through her hair, indicating that she wanted to move even further away from the loud conversation taking place behind us. I couldn't blame her, the voices escalating one after another and competing for a dominant volume. Tony was somehow the loudest beyond any doubt, bellowing and emphatically using his hands as he shouted at his brother. I tried to tune out the words and focus exclusively on Violet.

"Sorry." I said quietly. "I just figured-"

"No, I appreciate it." She returned, leaning against a leather chair and running her hand along the projector screen. We were as far across the room from the rest of them as we could be, and it still felt too close for comfort. "Anyway, you were going to ask me something."

"Yeah…" I started, trying not to approach the topic with the motherly trepidation I wanted to. "I heard you…lost control a bit. When Rachel attacked Krystal. Amy had to stop you from killing her."

"Difference between losing control and reacting." Violet defended, glancing downward. "I reacted. I think it was reasonable, considering the circumstances. She would have killed Krystal. If I have a choice, it's an easy one."

"I know. And it's easy to frame it with logic when the moment's over, but is that how you felt in the moment?" She paused, and I knew I struck the exact chords I wanted to.

"Krystal trained me to defend myself. All those years, she spent making sure I felt safe by taking me through the paces in the boxing ring. It was for a reason-"

"But it's deeper than that, isn't it?" I pressed, seeing that she was close to speaking freely. "It felt good."

"It did." She responded. "I felt ready. Not even sure for what, but ready. Like I could have fought all of those Tortured at once."

"And would you have stopped? If Amy hadn't interfered?" I probed. She paused, her eyes flitting back and forth in deep thought.

"No." She said quietly, but confidently. "And I'm okay with that. She was a threat – an immediate threat – to Krystal's life. It's a good reason to kill. The only reason to kill. I'm fine, Kara." She took notice of the conversation's topic and recognized that it was about more than self-defense. "I don't feel bad about it, and I don't feel like a different person. It's what anyone else in the family would have done."

"And that makes it okay?" I countered. "That's what I'm worried about. That you did what you did because we've made violence the normal way of life."

"No, I did it because they made violence the only option." She spoke truthfully and without reluctance. "If Rachel dies, and I was the one to kill her, I can sleep at night knowing I saved Krystal's life. There was *no* other option." She paused. "And I know what happened when you rescued Alice. What you and Sonya did to them, as deserved as it may have been. Violence seems to continue its path in our lives irrespective of our desires to avoid it."

Those sound like my words.

"Violence isn't the reason I'm checking on you. It's your reaction to it that I have to make sure is okay." She lifted her head, free of tears and unburdened of any obvious signs of trauma.

"Kara, I hate that it had to happen. But it did. And I would have gladly continued if it would have saved Alice from-"

"Alice is okay. She's doing fine, Vi." I interjected, not seeing a need to revisit the memory. She looked at me curiously, tilting her head and locking eyes with me.

"From being *raped*." She continued, her words cutting into my soul like a hot knife. "Just because they weren't successful in…doing worse doesn't mean she's okay or that she wasn't assaulted. And trying to avoid the word doesn't help her. She was almost raped. She was stripped and held down as a sacrificial lamb for the rest of us. We need to come to terms with that and provide her with every ounce of support we can." Her voice lowered as she spoke, so Alice wouldn't overhear us. "We can't *begin* to understand what she went through, but every time we avoid thinking about it, we feel a little bit less pain than she does. And that makes us a little less compassionate each time."

"Vi-"

"I'm not saying you don't care. I'm not saying that at all. If I'm saying anything…" She glanced at Alice, still leaning calmly into Val as her husband occasionally bounced in and out of their argument with Eric. "The things you're asking me…you should be asking *her.*"

She's not deflecting from her own situation; she genuinely wants to make sure Alice is okay. And she's right, for the most part. Maybe Violet is beyond needing my moral support right now.

"I'm here if you need me. Okay?" I gripped one of her hands in my own, squeezing lightly. "I'll be here for all of you. I just don't want any of you to feel alone. I think it's…easier than ever right now." She squeezed back, smiling gently and appreciating the gesture. Switching topics, she used my words to create a new context for discussion.

"Yeah. Outnumbered. Outgunned. Fighting a shadow war again that the rest of the world doesn't know about."

"Hell, the rest of the *country* doesn't know about it. They think we're still in charge and just…gave up." I felt wretched at the thought, coming to terms quickly with the fact that we had failed in our previous attempt at protecting the free people of the world.

"We'll prove them wrong." Violet said confidently, staring at Eric. He was rebuking each person that offended him, his previous timidness and introversion entirely gone from the version of him that stood in front of us.

"You're right. We just need to-" I lifted my hand, quickly reacting to a chair that Eric threw and using my powers to lower it gently to the ground. "Get *along.*" I snarled, turning my head to look at him.

"At least *I'm* over here discussing what needs done instead of running from the problem." Eric returned coolly.

Damn. I preferred it when he called me ma'am.

"Easy, Eric. You already have a friend in me; that's why I'm over here. I have nothing to say except to catch up with you personally." Violet and I stepped out of our corner and made our way to the rest of the group. "And that can wait."

"You don't have questions?" He asked, confused and beckoning to the others. Sonya and Raven were the only two that had stood silently in the mix. "I'm being berated for being some kind of undercover shadow operative for the bad guys, but you're okay with the fact that I'm here?" He was genuinely curious as to my opinion of him, so I answered honestly.

"Eric, you left us on good terms. And I felt guilty that you left at all. We expected too much from you. We leaned on you *only* at our hardest moments, and at the end of it all…we were staring at failure. You were always welcome to return to us. And if *this* is how you have to do it…then so be it." His brow relaxed at my words of kindness.

"We know you-" Sonya started speaking, then quickly calmed her attitude as she realized she had picked up the angry tone in the room. "We know you didn't join up with Raven while you were with us. We just have a lot of missing time to fill in. Unknowns are…bad news for us. Fill us in on the story, the whole story, and you'll have less issues to contend with."

"Says you." Tony snarled. "I don't give a *shit* where you were or what you've been doing, Eric. I wasn't worth filling in, apparently."

"I was protecting you." Eric replied calmly. "If I had told you, then everyone-"

"Told me *what,* Eric? That you were alive? That you were *safe*?" Tony was highly aggressive and nearing Eric's face. "Eighteen years I haven't heard from you, and now you show up like nothing happened?"

"In my eyes, I never left." Eric sneered, returning Tony's hostility. "After helping solve Krystal's survival problems and helping Alice with the Factor Five formula, I stepped back for a year and worked a regular human job…until the

Outbreak. The day the CDC declared an emergency, the same day I saw Jalix's face on television explaining what Vampyres were, I told myself I was coming back. But Raven showed up at my apartment with a handful of private security. Gave me an offer. I could go back to you all and watch as you tore each other apart, or I could stop the bleeding from a distance. No emotion. No distraction. Just unlimited resources and a good purpose." He paused, looking back at Raven. "And I figured she had some kind of evil plan, some way to warp this all in her favor. But she didn't. The longer I stayed, the longer I understood what we needed to do. What none of *you* were willing to do." He turned on me again, gritting his teeth. "Create a new order. A new system. One without the human element." My blood chilled, a visible shudder through my chest as I pointed at Eric.

"You sound *dangerously* like Schillinger." I growled. "Choose your words carefully."

"No. I sound like *you*." He spat. My hand fell limp, listening to his words. "It's *exactly* what you did. Your city. Your people. *Your* family, right? Isolated. Cut off, apart from humans. You lived above them and acted as guardians in your *city of light*. You, specifically, were cut off from emotions and went after Schillinger like a mechanical predator. But you can't stand the fact that you and Schillinger agreed on something."

"Eric, don't go there." Jalix warned, joined by Krystal as she went to say the same thing.

"Eric…"

"And you were wrong." Raven chimed in, politely making the statement to Eric. "Within months, we brought people in. Families. Let their vibrancy create the soul of the city. Until then, until the human element, it was just empty space."

"And Vanaheim was born." Eric agreed. "But it didn't start that way. It started with the need for a new beginning. And you all need to understand the distinction of beginnings and endings. Sometimes, to get something worth a damn, you have to agree with necessary evils. No one here can claim otherwise without hypocrisy." He finished, shaking his head.

"The distinction is the understanding that evil actions don't lead to an evil person without the element of choice." Amy attested. "Which choice did you make?"

"Neither." He mumbled, looking at Amy with tired eyes. "I became an agent of vigilance. Of change. And I stayed away from choices. The only decision I made was the decision to work on fixing the world so it can make its own choices."

"And that's all I've ever wanted, Eric." I took a step toward him. "To let humanity make its own choices. We're on the same side."

"We're in a world without sides, Kara. But we do want the same results. Reasoning aside, I can work with that. And believe me..." He pulled a small remote out of his pocket and aimed it at the projector, pressing a button. "We have a lot of work to do."

His soul, his spirit...he's a changed person. Changed by our deaths, by the fall of Aerael. I hope he finds himself again after this is all over.

"Emphasis on the *we*." Raven nodded, beckoning to the table and indicating that we settle in. The projector lit up, flooding the far wall in a bath of vibrant color. "Yuri and Eric haven't been my only associates. We're waiting on two of my chief scientists, as well. They're going to walk us through a bit more of the cure details. More than what I'm familiar with. Should be here any minute." She glanced at the door, giving Alice an opportunity to continue the conversation in a decent direction.

"You seemed to be pretty well-informed during Project Catalyst. How much of that information helped with your cure research?"

"A significant amount." Raven conceded. "My people aren't as experienced as you are, but we were a bit ahead of the curve with the different strains we worked with. The Catalyst data, what little we had left, was absolutely invaluable. We even salvaged pieces from Project Cerberus."

"We'll be splitting this meeting into two segments. The first segment is going to be all hands on deck. Afterward, we'll break off those relevant to the medical staff – and volunteers – for the more complicated parts. Everyone is *welcome* to stay, but…" Eric shook his head and shuddered, making a mild joke at the dryness of the anticipated content.

The group seemed to settle into their places, with Jalix and I each taking seats near the head of the table next to Eric, who stood to present his information. On Jalix's side, Amy and Violet sat next to Krystal, talking to themselves quietly and making subtle jokes. Raven was next to them, closest to the projector screen and clearly disconnected from the others. Next to me, Sonya sat as I did and bided our time in silence. Tony, Alice, and Val all sat to her right and stared at the screen while Eric scrolled through slides of data, looking for the proper starting point. While a certain unease resonated through the air at our mission, our pasts, and our next steps, there was a sense of comfort that was obvious in each of their relaxed faces as they sat idly and felt, for the first time in an eternity, at home.

"So we can all agree that Legacy is a giant pain in our combined asses, correct?" Violet enquired randomly. We collectively shrugged and nodded, waiting for her to make a point. "'Kay, cool. It's just-…we can use that to get along, I guess." Sonya chuckled quietly, shaking her head.

"And getting rid of that pain in the ass is going to be our topic of the day…come on…" Eric shook the remote violently, pressing the same button repeatedly and aiming it at the projector.

"You know that doesn't actually help it, right?" Val added helpfully. "Batteries are prob-"

"Yeah, I *know* the damn batteries are low, Val." Eric mumbled, finally arriving to where he wanted. A swirling logo appeared on the screen, followed by a flicker of jagged frames and a smattering of incoherent audio. Finally, a face appeared on the screen and was centered as if the man on the other end was setting his phone on a hard surface. "Yuri. Hear me okay?" Eric asked.

"Perfectly." The man replied, saying nothing more.

"Alright, then we're all here. So-..." Eric started, briefly walking over to the doorway to the room and dimming the lights slightly. "For those of you that haven't been here, I have been a part of a team of five. Raven, Yuri, and myself, you're already familiar with. The other two are Doctor Brynn Weiss, our director of science and technology, and Doctor Tamara Goodson, our medical director. Doctor Goodson is away right now, but should return to the city in a few weeks."

"Wait, ugh, sorry..." Krystal interrupted, much to the disdain of everyone else in the room. "*Sorry...*" She emphasized, her eyes growing wide. "I was just going to ask why *you* weren't the technology director. Aren't you, like..." She left the question open-ended.

"I have another role." Eric said simply, trying to end the interruption. Krystal grew quiet again, slinking down in her seat by several inches. Amy chuckled and said something to her quietly, shooting her a quick, cute smile.

Does she actually feel ashamed for interrupting? Huh...awkwardness was not something I ever expected to see from Krystal. I'm glad Amy seems to have taken a shine to her.

"Each of us has a full-time staff within the city. Raven has a network of informants and miscellaneous personnel on the surface. Closest to what Sonya used to manage. Dr. Weiss and Tony will have similar prospects for the cure effort, and obviously Dr. Goodson fell into Alice's role. While not everything is going to match up, we're going to do our best to split the upcoming mission into roles for each of you, and give each of those roles a piece of the staff from each department. No one will be working alone, with a few exceptions. More on that later, but something to keep in mind as we go along." Eric clicked his remote, pulling up a spreadsheet of dates and locations. "Let's put some background context on what's going on." He started to pace back and forth slowly, telling a story rather than reading off the information on the screen. "We, meaning *our side*, worked with the government after the Outbreak until it fell apart. Some of you maintained those roles until best decided to leave them with successors to manage our own affairs at home. Others became obsolete." He gestured to Jalix, whose job as a middleman between Vampyres and humans had become less practical as less humans remained. "Our enemy took advantage of this and wrestled the power away in secrecy. What the United States knew as the truth and what the rest of the world knew as the truth became separate. Within the country, our military, our government, dissolved and our people governed themselves well. Outside of the country, the operatives that now lived in our nation's capital gave the impression that we were now a free and lawless nation, and one not to be disturbed. They played a game to buy time, and they've played it well. But we're going to turn the tables on them." Eric clicked to the next slide, showing a series of maps marked with circles indicating search areas. "Legacy has been on the hunt for Kara and Amy since coming into power. Now, we managed to stop several probing attempts and thwart their intelligence for a good while. Unfortunately, as their numbers grew, it was harder and harder to stop them from ultimately realizing that kidnapping you was easier *done* than said. We wanted to wait until Krystal was awake to reveal ourselves so we could immediately bring all of you into Vanaheim. Until then, moving her would make all of you a fragile target. Raven's direct involvement was a result of being so short-staffed on security that we could barely cover all the leads we had." I raised an eyebrow, looking diagonally across the table at Raven.

"Stopped an ambush when Krystal woke up." She explained quickly.

"Saved our asses." Val admitted, much to his own disdain.

Another instance of putting her own life on the line instead of ordering others to do it. Interesting.

"Ah. Sorry, was kidnapped and unconscious for some of this." I remarked. Eric gestured to me.

"Yep. Brings us to that part. So…one of the scouting parties left with Kara and Jalix. This was obviously intended to be Kara and Amy, but they thought they could torture Jalix until he broke and consequently give up Amy's whereabouts. Very, very stupid and ultimately costly mistake."

"Why did Legacy need both of them?" Sonya asked. "Wouldn't one or the other work?"

"No, not at all. Well-…not the way he wants. See, if he has Kara and Amy, he can use one as leverage, a hostage, while the other does the work. He's said repeatedly that one of them would take over."

"I was wondering about that. He kept using the same language when I spoke with him. Kara or her daughter would take the throne." Sonya elaborated.

"Exactly. That's why. Now, if something were to happen to either of them, he knows he still has his threat of killing random people to make the surviving one cooperate. But he wants both, and he wants them badly enough to postpone his plans. Now, we aren't sure how he *thinks*, what his logic really is. Not a hundred percent. But the rescue efforts to grab Jalix and Kara proved a lot of things. First of all, he kept Kara sedated. Which means he wasn't ready for her. And second, he tortured Jalix, which means he still wanted Amy."

"I assume he also wants me in captivity due to my value as a potential cure of some sort. I still haven't been...enlightened as to how that has a part to play." Amy leaned forward, looking at Raven.

"That's part of what Dr. Goodson is going to talk about later. Basically, the virus in your blood is a hybrid. An experimental Catalyst strain that Jalix was infected with many years ago, and Kara's, which is an ability-granting strain. Hence..." Raven beckoned to Amy.

"Ah. That...makes sense." Amy mused. "And thus my powers are explained."

"Yeah, along with Legacy's. The bottom line is that your variant could carry the cure itself. It'll heal itself if it's damaged and survive in harsh conditions, far long enough to spread to everyone. Including the humans. They'll inherit this new, synthetic strain as...basically an immunity. That's why your blood is vital to our cure effort. But if used the wrong way...it could grant abilities to the Tortured. Another reason Legacy wants both Kara *and* Amy."

"Why the hell did you tell me *plant pollen* was how it would disperse?" Alice was puzzled, referencing something to Raven I had no knowledge of. "Back at Krystal's mansion, you said-"

"It...was more about what I *didn't* say. If I had said something reasonable, you probably would have kept me as a bargaining chip until you got more information on the cure. I couldn't risk it. So I said something so insane that you'd have to come with me and see for yourself." Raven responded plainly.

"It worked." Alice agreed.

"We're getting off-topic." Eric stated. "Let's get back on track. We had enough information to start moving, finally. With Yuri as our inside man, we staged the rescue and got everyone out. Yuri was also carrying the tactical information for Legacy's personal military, which gives us an exact layout of his assets from D.C. to Quantico. That part is critical to being able to take him out militarily, because now..." Eric clicked to the next slide. "We know exactly what his capabilities are."

"We've already made adjustments for his loss at Quantico." Raven spoke up, giving Eric a break. "As of right now, he has two fighter jets and a handful of Blackhawk helicopters for air support, two anti-air, short-range missile platforms, and a separate aircraft of some sort for his personal evacuation. This is obviously in addition to a few dozen armored vehicles and about two thousand Tortured. All guarding the White House and his nuclear arsenal."

"That's a *tall* goddamned order." Jalix rolled his neck, sighing.

"It is, Jalix. But that is why I have stayed behind." Yuri chuckled, his face still on the corner of the screen. "We will have our own forces trained."

"That's going to take *months*." Jalix argued gently. "Something tells me we don't have that kind of time."

"We don't. Yet." Eric warned. "I have a plan to buy us the time we need. But that comes last. First, we need to talk about dismantling D.C."

"Is there any other way to take him out?" Tony asked, fidgeting with his pocketknife. "Anyone left on the inside, or maybe a stealthy approach?"

"Nothing to be considered." Yuri said over the speakers. "Between his unnatural abilities and the thick layers of security, every approach will lead to a fight. We must also think about the innocents in D.C."

"Just what I was getting to." Eric continued. "There's still a population of neutral, or I should say innocent, Vampyres living in the area northwest of the White House. He's holding them as peaceful hostages. Basically, their medicine, food, water, everything go through him. He makes sure they have what they need, but they can't leave and they can't cry for help. In return, he gets them as workers and a massive bulwark to his north. We can't cut through them, and the Potomac River makes the west a pretty undesirable approach. Now...we have freedom for the other two directions, but each has its advantages and its drawbacks." He clicked to a set of small maps. "South is defended the lightest, but we have to cross a lot more terrain. It's a kill zone for his defenses. An open no man's land. From the east, we have a lot of cover, but it's where his troops are garrisoned. Heaviest close-quarters fighting but little room for larger defenses."

"Which one are we taking advantage of?" Krystal asked, pointing. "We could go either route, depending on the assets we have."

"Both." Eric replied bluntly. "The south is going to get our ground vehicles and push in as far as they can. The east force is going to come in via helicopters and take one building at a time."

"This is the time for details." Jalix sighed, rubbing a hand across his brow. "This is...honestly, this isn't even something *I* trained for back in the day."

"Aw...you have a back in the day." Sonya giggled. "That's so cute. I remember when you were just a little human." A few of us chuckled, Sonya's lightheartedness breaking the tension for a moment.

"Seriously, though..." Jalix continued. "This is a large-scale battle. Bigger than Fallujah in Iraq and more like D-Day in Germany. We're going to need meticulous planning and backup plans A through Z."

"We have a good outline so far, but yes, we'll be refining the process over the next few months." Eric supplemented his previous summary. "To do that, and to pull this off, we have a lot of logistics to work out. We'll need to prep a chain of command, give everyone their combat roles, and genuinely *train* the people willing to fight. The way we've worked it out was perfectly aligned with you guys taking Quantico." Eric pointed to Val. "It might have won us the war. We had anticipated needing another month or two in order to capture it." Val nodded, trying not to take credit. "We've bussed half the rescued Vampyres here to Vanaheim. They'll be trained on specific jobs. Some as combat medics, some as infantry, some as communications or electronic warfare. I have a rough set of numbers for each. The ones still in Quantico will undergo combat training with Yuri. And as needed, we'll swap them out so that each soldier has gotten both sides of their training."

"Took a play out of the military's handbook? That's exactly how they do it." Jalix commented.

"Might even be for the best." I added. "From what I heard, we rescued a lot of former FBI, a lot of Marine Officers, and a huge handful of candidates who got stuck in Quantico before they could start training."

"Yeah, and to that end, I'd like to request that two of those officers be transferred to Vanaheim as soon as possible." Jalix looked at the screen to talk to Yuri. "Andrea Scott and Layla Goss." Yuri frowned for a moment, tilting his head.

"I've spoken to both of them and I understand why, but I need Layla here to oversee the aircraft. I've already sent Andrea to help develop an air combat strategy. She should be there within the hour."

"That'll be enough." Jalix conceded. "We can always conference with Quantico for updates."

"Well, I picked right, at least." Eric mumbled. Everyone looked at him in curiosity for a moment. "Your roles. Jalix is going to be the Air Wing Commander. He'll be directing the air assault infiltration efforts alongside Yuri, and he'll be directing the airstrikes from our combat craft."

"Thought you said they had anti-*air* missiles." Alice quipped.

"Details we'll work out over time. We'll obviously need them disabled first." Eric explained. "Listen, don't...focus too much on the details. Plans are going to change, so this is a very brief, very rough outline without any of the meaty bits. So don't try and memorize the battle, just focus on your roles. While Yuri moves in from the east, Val will be pushing from the south. Val, you're going to be the Security Forces Commander. As you start making progress and claiming areas, you'll assign defenses to hold them in case of a counterattack. Yuri, you'll be the Air Assault Commander. Pretty straightforward. Cut through their barracks and quarters from the rooftops." Eric turned toward the screen, Yuri nodding in agreement and saying nothing further. "Kara, you'll be the Commanding Officer for the entire battle. What you need, we make happen. What you say, goes. We'll work out how, but you'll be fed data from our resources and make large-scale decisions as the fight progresses. Jalix, Yuri, and Val will have to operate independently, but you'll be able to move, utilize, and reposition everyone else as you see fit. You'll have to be on the ground for that to happen."

"Always happy to join the fight." I smiled.

"Perfect. So...Alice. Chief Medical Officer, obviously. You'll be in charge of the combat medics and keeping casualties to a minimum. Amy is going to be alongside you. Krystal, you'll be our Mobility and Countermobility Officer. You'll look for ways to get us from point A to point B safely while stalling and hampering the enemy's progress." He continued, not hearing any objections. "Violet, you're going to be our Forces Analyst Operator. Most of your work will be prior to the fight with Sonya, but you're going to keep an eye on numbers and make sure we send the right reinforcements to the right place. I don't want our medics going straight to the front and I don't want our infantry trying to repair a cell phone tower. Tony is our Chief Ordnance Officer, in charge of all the mechanics and engineers. Sonya, you'll be our Personnel Operations Officer. Basically…military human resources. Making sure everyone is trained up properly beforehand and handling any personal issues as they pop up. The last thing we need is someone distracted going into the fight because his wife is due with a baby in three days. You'll basically do what you used to do in Aerael. Finger on the peoples' collective pulse. You'll be pretty busy here in the city, but you'll join up with Kara for the main fight to help her coordinate the attack. And lastly, Raven and I are going to be Combat Analyst Operators. We have satellites, overlays, drones, and some technology that'll help us give Kara and Jalix the information they need as the fight goes on." He took a breath after giving out a whirlwind of information and looked around, waiting for an objection or question.

"So…I'm confused, where will I be during the fight?" Violet asked.

"At the rear of the south assault, behind Val's troops. With Krystal. You can work with Kara over the radio to call the shots on shaping the fight in our favor. Once we have a path to the White House, you two are going to be critical. You're going to make sure we have everything we need to deliver the cure and have all possible escape routes covered. We're counting on you *heavily*."

"Won't let you down, Eric." Krystal replied solemnly, respecting her position.

This is…masterful. He mentioned more details to come, so I can't criticize the plan too much yet. He picked out roles perfectly suited to each person.

"Amazing work, Eric." I said, watching as everyone else nodded. "I know you don't need my approval, but you have it. This is…a long shot, at best. A slaughter at worst. But if we have any chance of fixing this, we need to get rid of Legacy and restore our trust in the international community. This is the way to do it." Eric smirked softly, grateful for my honesty and praise.

"Lot of prep work." Sonya said quietly, looking over at me.

"Agreed." I replied. "We have a lot of things to do in advance if we're going to pull this off."

"Krystal needs surgery. We already discussed it. Jalix needs a complete physical, Amy should still have a once-over…we need some time to recover a bit." Alice added.

Krystal finally getting surgery to fix her shoulder? Finally settling an old argument, and an even older injury.

Krystal glanced at me briefly, knowing that I would have acknowledged the comment. Alice continued, unaware of the brief interaction. "Not to mention, if we want this cure ready to go, I'm going to need a *lot* of hours testing and working with the new team. We need time before this attack. A lot of time."

"We do." Eric agreed. "And you guys also need to unwind a bit. Take care of things, sure. But relax during your downtime. Don't forget, we're safe here."

"Quantico isn't." Jalix countered. "As soon as Legacy re-invades that place, we're done. We'll lose half our people and every weapon, every aircraft, everything."

"How long do we have?" Amy asked. "You mentioned buying some time. How much of it are we buying?"

"Uh…it'll be a bit on the open-ended side. I'd like to hope for a few months."

"Open-ended?"

"Yeah. However long we can keep Legacy both gullible and blind."

"And how do you propose we do that?"

"We negotiate with him. Actually...*you*...negotiate." Eric turned to Violet and the room fell into a curious silence. Violet pursed her lips confusedly.

"You want me to do *what*?"

***

I stood with Sonya in silence and solidarity, fidgeting with the stone of my necklace and watching Val work with Jalix to carry out one of the last chairs in the room. Under the circumstances, they wouldn't be needed, but the lack of most of its furniture made the conference room look significantly larger than before. Eric winced as the projector turned on prematurely, a loud beeping disturbing the quiet in the room. The only discussions audible were Amy and Eric asking each other questions about the upcoming process and Raven chatting quietly with Violet in rehearsal.

"I don't like it." I whispered, more to myself than Sonya and barely turning my head.

"Who would have guessed?" She beckoned briefly to my posture, a mix of anxiety and skepticism forcing my stillness in the farthest corner of the room.

"*Everything* about this is a risk, Sonya." My words acted as a reprimand, but my tone was tempered with fear. "We have one thing right now, one thing, working to our advantage. This city. And if we lose that-"

"We've trusted Eric for how long? He knows what he's doing, hon. Always has. He wouldn't let anything happen to us."

"I know." I sighed, looking over at Raven again. "Not to mention putting Violet in the spotlight. Legacy doesn't need another target."

"Well...she won't be, after this. That's sort of the point. None of us will be. At least for a while." I shook my head slowly, not continuing the debate and having no better ideas.

I watched Violet nod, stepping away from Raven and bowing her head in thought. Raven approached us, whispering so as not to disturb the rest of the room.

"She's...getting into character. Getting her thoughts together." She paused, grimacing and exposing the tips of her fangs below her top lip. "She'll be okay, Kara."

"I don't need patronized." I scowled, breaking eye contact. Amy left Eric's side, nodding to me and taking her place quietly next to Sonya. She wrapped her arms around Sonya's shoulders and leaned in, fulfilling the need to both provide and receive some sort of comfort. Although she avoided leaning against the body armor that hung on a low spot against the wall behind her, most of her weight rested on the wall itself rather than her own feet. She was clearly exhausted, equally or more so than the rest of us.

"Alright." Eric sighed, turning to our small group. "Everything's ready to go. We'll start as soon as-..." His sentence trailed off as Val and Krystal walked through the door. Tony lagged behind by a few seconds, buried in his own thoughts. "Now, I suppose." Eric finished, turning to Violet as she approached him. "You good?" He asked quietly. Her face was set in a dark, drawn frown as she nodded once, reminding me far too much of my previous self. "The projector screen is going to be as bright as I can make it. You shouldn't see anyone standing off to the side of the room. But try to avoid looking anywhere but the screen or the camera. We need to sell the concept that you and I are alone, more than anything-"

"I *know.*" Violet hissed, her eyes looking up at him without the rest of her head moving. "Sort of the basic concept, isn't it?" Eric hesitated in response, deciding to walk to the doorway and turn off the lights.

"God damn, you can be scary." He breathed, bringing a unanimous smirk to our group. We all held back any audible chuckling to keep Violet in the mental state she chose.

Please remember this is a game. It's an act. Don't believe it any more than you need to.

"Alright…everything is set up. It's not possible for him to track us. Period. And our connection is…super secure. I'll leave it at that. Jalix should be able to hear us. Make sure you don't mess with that microphone in your pocket. It won't go anywhere, but you'll give something away if you fidget with it."

He learned to leave out the technical explanations. I might miss that.

"Ready?" He looked up at Violet, who took a deep breath and nodded rapidly, stepping in front of the camera and adjusting her hair briefly. "Alright. Positions." Sonya, Amy, and I remained still, allowing Raven to join Val, Tony, and Krystal on the far side of the room and in the darkest corner behind the camera. Sonya used her foot to nudge the small pile of rugs at her feet, fidgeting restlessly as she started to adopt my impatience. I held her hand for a moment in camaraderie, giving her a sign that I believed in them. "Okay. Action." I could hear the faint difference in Eric's breathing at the last word, the weight of our goal once more squarely upon his shoulders. Amy sighed, her prior position now an empty space between them while she stood several feet to Sonya's right.

Eric sat down in front of his laptop at the staged computer desk in the center of the room as a pleasant, musical ringing tone echoed through the speakers next to the projector screen. As if we weren't quiet enough, even our breathing simultaneously paused while we became nothing but ghosts, staring at a bright screen in long wait. After almost a minute, the sound stopped and was replaced by a simple font in pastel colors against a dark background. The light from the screen illuminated the area in front of the camera, showing only Eric's desk and Violet's impatient stance.

"Why isn't it working?" Violet demanded, turning her head slightly. She kept eye contact with the screen, as if something would change in the next few moments.

"It's his personal cell. It's *working*, he just didn't pick up. Trying again." Eric repeated the process, the rest of us letting our heartbeats palpitate as freely as they would in absolute silence. This time, the friendly chime echoed in a repeating pattern twice before cutting to nothingness. The screen of the projector stuttered and struggled to change into pixelated images as the electronics connected to one another. Abruptly, Legacy's face appeared on the screen and quickly changed from an unsatisfied frown to a curious glare. Violet played her part masterfully, taking control of the situation before he had the chance.

"Legacy." She said the words in a mouthing, mocking manner while scowling at the brightness of the light background behind him. "Where are they?" She demanded, her timbre steady and controlled like a talented vocalist.

"Who might you be referring to-"

"I'm on the clock. I don't have time for games, and neither do you. I'm willing to negotiate, but you tell me what you did with them or so help me God-" Her anger was interrupted by his commanding tone, loud and abrupt through the speakers. She was undaunted, barely affected by the disruption.

There you go. Hold strong.

"I *asked* who you're talking about." Legacy returned, his patience starting out on thin ice. "I deal with a great many people." His voice was obviously honest, but his face reflected a great deal of hidden lies that were tucked away behind the disguise of a tired man.

"Your *animals* captured Kara and Amy. Took the woman that was leading them too, Rachel. Think they ended up killing her. Not sure, I got out of there before they could make me bleed the same way she did." She buried the story in small details, letting an aura of truth settle into her voice. "Where did they take them and what did you do with them?"

"If *either* of them were in my possession, I would know about it."

"And you would *lie* to us about it. Obviously. We need more than that." Violet stepped to the side, pacing in slow strides.

She used the word 'we' and put Eric into the frame. Higher chance he'll buy that this isn't a hoax if she's not entirely alone.

"I'm not sure what-"

"*Enough.*" Violet growled, her voice increasing in volume and rasp. It was sufficient for Sonya to shudder next to me. "They...are my family. Do you understand that? And *your* monsters-"

"I know the team you must be referring to, and they have yet to report back to me. I don't even know of their whereabouts, let alone what prisoners they may or may not have." He showed the mildest signs of frustration, growing defensive. "Do you mean to tell me that my own men would-"

"Cut the video." Violet turned, saying it only loudly enough for the camera's microphone to pick it up.

"No." Legacy protested, continuing. "We clearly have matters that need discussed." Eric had twitched, moving to click on something, but stared at Violet as he waited for her command. She stood with her back to the camera, waiting for a long moment before turning to face him again.

"I'm only going to ask you one more time. And I'm going to *pray* that you quit playing stupid."

"You need not ask again. I don't have them. If I did, I would have no interest in speaking with you. The team sent to patrol New York for your family has not returned to me." She tilted her head downward for a second, as if taking in what he said as a valid point.

She's playing him like a piano. And it's a masterpiece.

"Then your men either took them somewhere else...or your men are dead and Kara and Amy are long gone." Violet said conclusively, allowing for no third option. "And if it's the latter, I *may*...know where they went." Legacy chuckled briefly, locking eyes with the camera as if staring into our collective souls.

"I didn't make it this far without being able to smell either a plea or a ruse. My people need nothing from her but ransom, and I reward them far too well. Which means I'm inclined to believe that Kara escaped them and left with Amelia...and you wouldn't give that information so freely-"

"I don't give a damn what you believe. We need the cure as much as you do. We can send soldiers against soldiers all day long, but neither of us wins until we have that cure in our hands. If Amy's gone, so is the cure. If Kara's gone, so is the next ruler of the country. Unless we find them, we *both* lose." She emphasized, leaning into her words heavily. He paused, true and deep contemplation in his eyes.

That was it. The punchline. She's selling this. It's working.

"What do you propose?" He asked quietly.

"Don't touch Quantico. We took it, and it's ours now. So are its people."

"I will not allow you to control a military might-"

"With *what* military? Oh, the people you had in captivity? They'll make a *fine* army, I'm sure. I'm not sending them as fodder to your creatures until my hand is forced."

She let it slip; that was perfectly executed.

"*You*...won't send them?" Legacy enunciated, leaning away from his phone. Violet slid her jaw a fraction of an inch out of place as if she had accidentally let something slip. "Your *timer* is that of your people finding out, isn't it? That's why you're in a hurry. You don't have their approval."

"I don't *need* their approval!" Violet roared, taking a step forward. "Our leaders have fallen into myth. They don't exist anymore. They gave up on our city, on our people. *Kara* gave up on us by running. And if Kara ran, she's as much a coward as her daughter. I don't care about them. I care about the millions of people, *innocent* people in this country."

Oh, the innocent people card. Well done, Violet. And she makes it sound like we're desperate, with nowhere else to go.

"It's non-negotiable. *We* keep Quantico to rebuild. I don't want to smell a single one of your butchers anywhere near that place. This isn't some…term of our agreement. This is a fact. Are we clear on that?" She continued. He stared for a minute, his expression unchanged.

"I won't be listening to a list of demands. Tell me what you want and get on with it."

"That's all I want. An absolute truce across all grounds until Kara and Amy are found. If my side finds her, we'll give you Amy long enough to manufacture the cure. Then we take her back. Kara is yours to install into leadership. When everything is said and done, you disappear. Permanently. If *you*, or your horde, find them, Amelia comes back to us once the cure is made from whatever you need out of her." A faint wrinkle furrowed in Legacy's brow as he listened to her words.

"This is the arrangement I provided previously. The only difference is your control over a…meager city."

He's downplaying his losses and trying to take control back. He knows he's getting what he wants with almost no drawbacks. She has him on the run.

"You provided the agreement to the wrong people." Violet's tone took a somber note, as if she regretted something. "To Sonya, to Jalix…the ghosts of former heroes. The old leaders. And there's no room for them anymore. Not for visions and ashes."

"And I assume *this* is part of your…negotiation? Leadership? That you remain in charge of your people?"

"I don't need anyone else to guarantee or promise me that. I'll take control on my own." She paused, testing the waters of the conversation. "But if you betray our agreement, at any point, all bets are off. I'll pass word along that you plan to kill both Kara and Amy the second you get your hands on them. I'll start rumors that your search teams are kill squads, spread those rumors to every city in the country. Once Kara and Amy find out, they're gone forever. And believe me, if Kara wants to disappear, she will fade into *memory*. You won't get your cure, your control, or your society."

"Betraying you does nothing for me." He said in support of Violet's suggestions. "This is all…amenable. I'll tell my men to remove all current search parties and my commanders will ensure that there are no skirmishes with your own people as they travel. Quantico poses no threat to us. My army in Washington is more than sufficient. We will play your game until Karalynn and Amelia are found. Does this sound appropriate?"

Now's the time, hon. He's going to start asking you the hard questions.

"Perfect." Violet smirked, and I tensed in awareness of the coming moments. "Sunshine and rainbows on my end." She went to inhale, spinning around along with Eric as they looked at the door in panic. There was a quick beat, a pause as they looked at each other. "I thought you said-"

"It's not possible, Jalix isn't even-" Violet and Eric were able to start the beginnings of an argument, interrupted by Jalix and Alice kicking in the door and moving into the room with their guns drawn.

Rainbows. Jalix's old code word.

Alice held her pistol firmly at Eric's head as he sunk to his knees and bowed his head, vanishing from sight behind the desk. Violet's leather jacket rubbed against itself in a scrunching ruffle as she lifted her hands, stepping backward until she was solidly in the frame of the camera with Jalix. Jalix wasted no time, barking as soon as he came through the door and standing in the scene.

"Violet, what the *hell* are you thinking?" His head snapped up to the projector screen, a genuine hatred rolling from his face and through his lips. "Legacy." He growled, turning back to Violet.

"He's willing to look for Kara and Amy." Violet defended, shaking her head. "It's more than you're willing to do-"

"We can't look for them *because* of him!" Jalix shook the gun in his hands, emphasizing his emotions. "You're playing into his hands, Vi!" He roared, shuddering with aggression. His expression suddenly dropped. "What did you tell him?"

"We made an agreement." Violet said quietly. "He'll leave us alone, he won't come after us. Quantico will be a haven for us-"

"Did you tell him where they went?" Jalix growled, inching closer. His pistol made small movements, which would have been invisible to the human eye. I could tell that his attention was primarily focused on his point of aim, carefully choreographing Violet into her proper position as they took small steps around our makeshift stage.

Like puppets on strings.

"Not...yet." Violet stumbled on her words, hanging stress on the forefront of her tongue.

"Don't say another word." Jalix spat, turning to Legacy for his next remarks. "And you. What you did to me-"

"Do we have a deal?" Violet asked, her voice shuddering in fear. It was almost overstated, but I realized that in the context of truly believing she would die, it would have been appropriate.

"Not another word, Violet. I swear to God-"

"What, Jalix?" Her lips trembled, tears falling from the corners of her eyes. "You'll *shoot* me?"

Those tears look...too real. She's genuinely afraid.

"Vi-..." Jalix fed on Violet's fear, his empathy hurting him as much as it did her.

"Do we have a deal?" She asked again, unable to see Legacy's face while staring down Jalix. Legacy watched with anticipation, entirely drawn into the scene and wholly captivated.

"We do." Legacy said, nodding once. "You have my word." Jalix clenched his teeth, wrapping his finger around the trigger and taking a deep breath in preparation. Violet slowly turned her head, an inch at a time, closing her eyes.

"Don't." Jalix whispered again.

"Jalix." Alice said harshly, still pointing her unloaded gun at Eric. "We can't-"

"*You* can't, Alice." Jalix whispered, his voice shaking. "I will if I have to. To keep my wife and daughter safe."

Get ready.

"*Jalix.* You can't shoot Violet for-"

"West." Violet breathed quickly. Jalix twitched, his lips pulling back in a mass of clenched teeth and fangs. "To Oregon. Back to-" Jalix's finger pulled back on the trigger of the pistol carefully, moving in such a straight line that the barrel of the weapon hardly moved as the round was fired.

Our turn to help set the stage.

I closed my fist, pulling my arm back in a tugging motion while Sonya made a similar movement in a direction perpendicular to mine, with a fraction of a second's delay after my own. Violet screamed in very real pain, the bullet grazing the outermost surface of her ribcage and impacting the bulletproof vest hung on the wall behind her. My abilities pulled her chest backward, as if the force of the round had penetrated her heart, and let her fall into Sonya's maneuver off-screen.

Sonya's powers let Violet fall directly into Amy's waiting arms, catching her against a pile of rugs on the floor and beginning to heal the laceration on her side. Unfinished with the act, Violet let her pain out in another scream of agony, watching Jalix move in for the kill. Violet laid on the floor off-screen while Jalix's steps were captured perfectly in composed movements.

Now for the grand finale.

"Salem!" Violet roared, falling silent as Jalix fired two more shots into the wall-mounted vest and let the now-empty gun clatter to the floor.

Amy had her hand wrapped around Violet's mouth, each of them breathing slowly and in synchronization as Amy's healing powers went to work repairing the gash in her side. The room fell into a perfect silence as the scene ended, punctuated with Jalix's convincing howl of unbridled pain. Alice looked at Jalix in a horrified expression, no words able to leave her mouth as she backed away, breaking into a sprint as she and Eric left the room.

Violet out of view of the camera, everything according to plan. Now Jalix just has to seal the deal.

Neither Legacy nor Jalix said anything, Jalix's breathing only coming between forced sobs. Legacy waited as long as he was able, finally speaking to gain control.

"Salem, Oregon. Where she ran from Schillinger centuries ago…I have that memory from him." Legacy pondered.

Dark times for me, for Val and Sonya…I guess it's true. Legacy does have Schillinger's memories.

"I will respect our contract regardless of who holds it. We will not attack you at Quantico if we are left unprovoked…and we will both search for Kara. Violet-"

"Don't-" Jalix growled, moving back into the center of our stage. "She's…she's dead because of *you!*" He pointed at the screen, looking down again as Violet gave him a slow thumbs-up that she was okay. I could see in my peripheral vision that the cut was already healed. Jalix's aim had been flawless, only the lightest break in skin giving Violet a convincing reaction time and cry of pain. Jalix continued the pretense that she was a corpse, averting his gaze and looking back at the screen. "We're done here." He said quietly, moving to the laptop. "You'll get your cure, and then I'm going to find you. No matter where you try and disappear, I will find and kill you when this is all over."

"I could only have expected as much." Legacy murmured, seeming to be genuinely disturbed by the events that had unfolded. "Feel free to try. I just ask that you remember the fact that Kara or her daughter *will* take the throne." His eyes bore a hole into the screen, his deep voice echoing the final words through my ears and into a place I was unable to describe. "It's a shame you had to kill one of them." A pause rumbled through the room, rattling the sense of reality for everyone listening.

No…

A weakness in my knees and chest coincided with the room growing dark again, the same pastel letters on the same black background flooding our room in partial obscurity again as Jalix ended the call and diminished the light from our projector screen.

No, no, no, no.

Sonya's left arm held me upright as an incomprehensible dizziness created a rolling wave of nausea and pain from my unsteady knees to each high point on my face.

No. No, no, no, no…

Whether anyone had spoken yet, I was unsure, as an impenetrable barrier of ringing erupted in my ears and washed over any coherent thoughts.

Not like this. Please…not like this.

The lights came back on and nearly blinded me, unprepared as I was, staring at the ground and taking in deep, uneven breaths. I lifted my head and frantically looked around as I realized I may have been the only one to take notice of Legacy's wording.

Please. Please, anything but this.

While mostly from concern, everyone's eyes were on me and bearing down as I slunk lower against the wall. The room had started dividing into groups as they crowded around Sonya and I in our heartrending huddle.

I can't yet. I can't.

To my left, I watched Krystal, Tony, and my brother stare at me with wide, watching eyes and matching looks of growing distress. Jalix and Alice leaned against one another, Alice quietly exhaling the long sigh of half-century-old fears into his shoulder. Even Raven approached from the side, leaning against the wall in quiet contemplation, but the most prominent face among them all was Violet's as she sat up in Amy's arms and stared directly into my soul. I couldn't look back at her, or any of them, and instead waited for the rain to fall on its own. As if a thunderclap to the storm, Amy – very much taking after her father in the caring tone of voice and calm pressure she placed upon me – was the one to ask.

"What did he mean by that?" I couldn't bear to ignore my silver-haired baby girl, turning my head and letting her watch my watery eyes gaze back at her own in a loss for the right language to illustrate the gravity of the words Legacy poured into the room. "What did he mean...*one of them*?" She held only curiosity in her voice and wandering eyes, inspecting me for any clue or sign of truth, until I did the one thing I thought myself capable of in the moment and locked eyes with Violet as deeply as the silence could bind us. I said nothing, moved nowhere, and felt hollow in our gaze as I watched the chocolate-brown orbs glow and burn as they brimmed with tears.

"You." My lips parted, hurling the word at her and watching it hit harder than the bullet that graced her chest only minutes ago. My throat didn't let me say anything else, even had I borne the words to say the things I felt. All I could do was let hot tears run across my face, red and cold in the room as my friends, my brother, and my youngest daughter made sense of Sorrow's last true secret.

"What?" Violet expressed her confusion, the word barely audible through her wet lips and strained voice. "Hm-" She tried to say more, shaking her head and staring at me with an intensity of unimaginable proportions.

"You're...Kara's daughter." Raven confirmed slowly from her position against the wall.

Please, please no. Not yet.

"Raven-" I whimpered tearily, losing the entirety of my composure and letting myself become totally supported by Sonya's arms.

"But...I..." Violet's incoherent muttering couldn't be fixed with Amy's powers, but the energy created by them holding onto each other was a bond of its own, strengthening the truth they already knew at heart for many years. "Can't." She finished, looking at the crowd frantically. My brother, still in shock, could say nothing at the moment, and instead stood as a statue of marble, equally as pale and nearly as still.

Krystal was torn between being unconvinced and being confused, standing with Val without moving. Alice hid her face in Jalix's shoulder, shedding her own tears and letting out a long-captive set of emotions from our deeply-rooted vow of silence. My husband, long-aware of my many secrets, smiled at me supportively and held Alice with great care.

"That's not everything." Raven shattered the peace once more, causing my slowly rising conviction to falter and ultimately fail. I looked at her quickly in desperation, but was too late to stop her from vocalizing the truth. Even had I lunged, had used my abilities, had drawn a weapon, it all would have been too late, as the pieces were put together by the rest of my family at her first words. Raven was looking directly at Violet, speaking softly and in a manner that was an irrefutable and unquestionable truthfulness.

"You're not her only other daughter." Raven took in a short breath, sighing and running a hand through the long, black hair that was the hallmark feature of the two of them. "You're a twin." She paused long enough to let me suffocate from the immeasurable stress. "Kara had two girls. Born four minutes apart. And that four minutes was enough that your father didn't know you were even being delivered. He whisked me away too quickly in a protective rush...didn't realize Kara was still in labor. Then she gave birth to you. And escaped before your father...*our* father could take you away." She took a breath. "You're not just a twin, Anna. You're *my* twin."

CONCORD
AMY

Alice's face was pained, speaking with unconstrained emotion during the conclusion of the story she had told over the course of the previous hour. Violet had left in a frenzy of anguish and Kara had followed suit so as to regain her composure, but the rest of our group sat in absolute silence as we listened to the regaling of a story Alice felt appalled to address.

"And we got out of there. That...prison. Sonya took Violet – Anna at the time – across the border and got transport safely back to America. Kept tabs on the foster parents as they came and went. Raven – Ava at birth – was gone from the face of the earth and assumedly in the hands of Schillinger until her public appearance some twenty-six years later. Kara...was never the same. It was the reason we started rotations, when everyone was sent to different countries to gather information for six months or more. The same reason she went from being *somewhat* emotionless to being dead inside until she met Jalix. Schillinger violated any hope she had of being normal. He violated a lot more than that...And she pursued him from that day forward with everything she had."

"His version was much the same." Raven finally spoke, jarring us all as we forgot that not only was she present, but she was a major factor in the story. She avoided using her father's name, a fact we all took notice of. "He regretted what he did...realized it much later. Said it was a horrible thing to put someone through. Said that children should never be forced on someone." She paused, thinking back on what we had been through only days ago and the pain that could have been inflicted on her and Alice. "But he was grateful he had me. I didn't realize until later that he was referring to a heritage and a birthright rather than the person I grew up to become. But regardless...the story was the same from his side. The truth. As horrific as it is." Alice nodded slowly, having nothing further to say as her account of the events concluded.

Violet...is my half-sister. So is Raven. It explains so much, at least-

"I'm so sorry I couldn't tell you." Alice wept, turning to Val quickly in a moment of realization. "I feel like I betrayed you, I feel like I-..." She broke down almost immediately after she spoke, sobbing quietly and covering her face in her hands as Val leaned in slowly and took her huddled figure in his arms. He was still in shock, paler than a ghost and sporting eyes that roamed across the floor in contemplative thought. Regardless of how he felt, and regardless of what he couldn't bring himself to say, he held onto Alice supportively and caringly, knowing that his feelings for her hadn't changed.

"I'm...sorry, as well." Jalix started, looking at the group before his eyes settled on me. "Amy, I-..." He paused, grimacing and trying to find the right words. "I *wanted* to tell you. I tried to do everything I could. Before the city was lost, we had you two live together. And then we took Violet in with us when we left for Krystal's mansion. We had her raise you, babysit you…we *wanted* you to be her sister. Just without those words being spoken." While I already understood his reasoning, I listened to hear out what he had to say in his defense. He sounded like my mother, using more of her words than his own. "We couldn't afford to make her a target. To…change her life so suddenly like that. The world already looked at you like an object, and we couldn't change that. So we kept Violet's lineage a secret. Kara…she told me what happened shortly after we got married. After she came back to us from the dead. And we agreed to wait until the world, at least for Vampyres, was a better place before we told either of you."

"Well, it's certainly not a better place right now. I think we can all agree that it's worse than ever." As much as I was bitter to find out how I did, I still tried my best to stay empathetic and understand his perspective. I sighed, shaking my head and watching my hair wobble. "I'm not angry. This is just…a lot to take in."

"Yeah. Especially for *her*." Krystal whispered, struggling to state her feelings. "I can't *imagine* how Violet feels right now." She started. "She's always been confused as to why she was picked to be one of us. And now she finds out that Kara is her mother and Schillinger, the man her mother was trying to kill for centuries, is her father. Through *forced* pregnancy." She paused, panning across the room. "How is *anyone* supposed to handle that with rationality? That she was a child that her mother didn't expect or want, or that her father was a genocidal monster?"

"I think all of us have things to consider." Sonya said quietly, her usual glow diminished to a sad aura. "I mean…if I was *there* when Kara…when Schillinger did what he did…I mean, obviously I don't remember it. I have no memory of it. Why Kara didn't tell me, why Alice didn't tell me-"

"I *swore* I wouldn't." Alice returned quickly, the horror washing over her face as she believed that Sonya would distance herself as a friend. "I made a vow in the deepest, darkest-"

"No, I understand, Alice. I get it, the logic is there. But the emotional portion is what I'm struggling with. Whatever parts of it *aren't* logical. It's like dealing with my amnesia all over again. Having to learn what's real…" We sat again in silence, trying to settle into the facts of the situation. Eric spoke up quietly, deciding to be the one to disturb the peace.

"The medical staff are going to be here any second. We still have a lot of ground to cover. Alice, if you're up to it, we can still brief you." He paused. "The rest of you should get some rest. Go unwind and let everything sink in. Get some real food for a change. We have the time we need, now. Kara and Violet will be around when they're ready. They've always been family. Now we just…have the proof." He summarized, trying to lighten the mood.

"He's right." Val said, looking at Eric briefly. "None of us are in a good condition to think about any of this. We're still tired. Beat up. Drained. And mentally exhausted. One night isn't enough rest to shake off everything we've been through. Raven, is there any place to grab a good burger?"

"Couple of restaurants on the main strip across from the hospital. Open all night, too. So don't worry about the clock. You guys do what you need to while we-"

"You go, too." Eric added, pointing to Raven. "You've been through a lot. And I'm not taking no for an answer. Get out of here and go take care of yourselves." Raven didn't argue, an exhaustion behind her eyes indicating Eric's truthfulness and suggesting that she was as ready to forget the world above as the rest of us were.

"I know I don't exactly have any stake in this…" Tony started. "But it shouldn't change anything." He looked at me, then Val. "We love them. We always have, and we always will. But right now, we need to take care of them while they process these things. Sure, *we* may be shaken by the facts, but *we* aren't the ones struggling with our identity. We don't need to treat them any differently, but we need them to know that we're here. Now and forever." I nodded, feeling exactly the same way and glad to see that the rest of the room agreed. As Tony finished his sentiment, he stood up and left the conference room along with Val. Sonya followed soon after, and was accompanied by Raven while they spoke quietly to each other. I watched my father approach me, lingering and debating which words were appropriate for the situation.

"I love you." I said before he could speak. "And I'm okay." Krystal approached, standing behind him as I tried to allay his guilt. "You made a promise to mom. I'll always respect the love you two share. We don't have anything else to talk about." I grabbed his hand lightly, smiling as he pulled me in for a hug to hold me for a long moment and let himself feel calmed for the first time in a long while.

"Sometimes I forget how much of your mother you are. What a powerful woman you've become." He said in my ear, swaying lightly. He held me at arms' length, nodding lightly. "I'm going to let you go for a bit. Go relax and unwind. If you need to talk...I'm here." I nodded a silent thanks as he departed and left me alone with Krystal. She touched her arm briefly, feeling the sling that bound her shoulder and refusing to look at me directly. Her cerulean hair held the faintest hints of sky-blue strands that made a dance of oceanic depth, touching her shoulders lightly in gentle waves. Her eyes, a slightly darker color, flicked from side to side as she tried to think of what to say.

Violet was her best friend. For all those years, they stood side-by-side, and now Krystal has to watch her struggle alone.

"I want to go see her, too." I said truthfully, speaking on her behalf. Krystal's eyes met my own finally, the depth of them gazing somewhere I wasn't sure existed. "Why don't we give her some time alone and go see her in a while? Once she's...coping a bit better."

"Yeah." She agreed quietly. "I-…thanks. I'm not really sure where I fit in, anymore. Might just walk around with you for a little bit."

"You'll always have a place at my side, if you want. I've been told I'm a good listener." I smirked, lightening the mood and gesturing toward the door. She smiled back, a gentle movement of her lips matching the softness in her brow.

"I don't know if I want to talk or if I want to be the one listening right now. There's so much going on, so much change…and no one that I knew as a close friend is available to do either." I could see in the slouch of her shoulders that she was in need of support. We both turned our heads back toward the center of the room, Alice and Eric talking about something quietly.

"We should change that." I suggested. "I've been excited to know you for…as long as I can remember. I've heard so many amazing stories about you and the things you did in the city. I'd like to get to know the woman behind the legends." I chuckled.

"Definitely don't think I'm part of any *legends*." She winced, leaning against the doorway and adjusting the strap of her sling.

"I can try to fix that, if you want." I offered. "Maybe…I could do it by myself. You wouldn't need Alice or surgery." She stared at me strangely, her hand resting on one of the buckles in a moment of pause.

"You…*we*…haven't exactly had great experiences with your abilities." She offered, trying to decline politely. "I don't want you to have to go through anything else traumatic."

"It needs figured out." I countered, uncomfortable with the idea of trying again but too curious to turn down the opportunity. "Whatever is going on, I'd like to know. I *need* to know, if I'm going to improve on my skills. If you're willing, we can give it a shot." She stood in thought for a moment, watching two women in white coats approach and pass us to enter the conference room.

"Are you sure?" She asked. I could almost feel the concern radiating from her figure.

"Let's do it." I said confidently. "Your shoulder needs fixed either way. So we're getting two birds with one stone." I nodded once, satisfied that we had reached an agreement. "Back to your place?" I suggested, beckoning to the private living spaces that would belong to my mother's close counsel. "I'm assuming that you have a room here if this is a near-replica of Aerael."

"Fair point." She swallowed hard, stepping into the grand hall and gazing at the central arboretum as we strolled slowly toward her room. "This is so bizarre." She whispered, shaking her head.

"Yeah. Almost...creepy?" I offered. She nodded in agreement, but didn't say anything else while she looked around. "Not to mention a bit...coincidental?"

"Auspicious." Krystal offered.

"Ooh. Yeah, that's...that about sums it up."

"Quite a while back, Kara actually *wanted* more cities. It came down to planning and preparation, and we ended up being too distracted with Schillinger and the issues with our war to finish any of them. I'm not surprised at all that Raven had this in the cards. When she lost her company's massive building, she would have needed somewhere to operate. And I'm sure Eric had quite a bit of influence, especially knowing the details of Kara's plans for new cities." She took a breath, sighing and staring at the lights. "Still creepy, though."

We walked in silence for a minute, turning into the short hallway that housed the apartment-style living spaces of the city's elite. Krystal's room was at the end of the hallway on the left side, adjacent to my parents' at the head of the hallway and her sister's to its left. No locks were present on the doors, assumedly due to a lack of need, so Krystal turned the simple silver handle and swung the door open to look inside. A warm breeze indicated that the units had their own air conditioning and that this one was set to aid in any company resisting the effects of Krystal's naturally cold energy. The room was laid out simply, and similar to her old one. I could only faintly remember it from when Violet and I had visited once or twice in nostalgic trips of solemn remembrance. This time, it was much cleaner, and the bed held a large tray full of various wines, cheeses, and preserved meats. A small tag was affixed to the basket, read aloud by Krystal as she approached the bed.

"Welcome home. Heard you like the same expensive shit that I do. Raven." Krystal smirked, chuckling quietly and picking up one of the bottles. "Elé Perión. Girl's got taste." She looked over at me, turning the bottle in her hand. "Your mother and I *love* this stuff. It's from Spain. Near where I was born, actually."

"You're Spanish?" I asked, never hearing that fact about her life.

"Spanish-Irish. Alice shows a more clear Irish descent than I do, but we were both born in Europe. Wait, where did you think I was from?"

"I just never...I don't know. I guess everyone's from somewhere." I shrugged, not caring as much as I would have expected by the answer.

"The rest of the basket is from Eric. Want to break open the wine before we break open my body and soul?" I could tell she was trying to be humorous, but her eyes and tenor implied that she was anxious about the upcoming process.

I'm nervous, too. Each time I touch her...I still think about it. But I have to figure out what's going on and why. I can't do it without her.

"You can help yourself. I think I'll need a clear head." I offered. She gazed at the bottle for a minute before putting it back in the basket and carrying the silver tray over to her dresser. She paused before setting it down, tilting her head and placing her free hand on her hip.

"It's not the same dresser. God, it's the…smallest things." She sighed, walking back and sitting on the edge of her bed. I continued to stand, waiting for an invitation instead of assuming I could occupy a spot next to her. "Everything is only *slightly* different. It's pissing me off. If the world was a radically different place, I could adapt. But I have these expectations of what I'll see, what I'll feel, and then they're subverted by something else. It's frustrating." She ended her rant quickly, not wanting to bother me with what she perceived as trivial issues. I opened my mouth to speak, but stopped as she smirked and patted the blanket next to her, realizing that I had been waiting for an invitation to sit.

"Yeah, I can imagine. You could be developing some anxiety from it. You seem…well, the symptoms fit as compared to what I heard of your old self."

"And what exactly did you hear of my *old self*?" She asked, almost mocking the statement. I smiled, realizing that she was starting to finally relax around me. I nodded to her sling, indicating that she start to remove it while I spoke.

"A lot. Something different from everyone. They all had their own perspectives. Val said you were quirky…strong-willed. I think he said *menace to society* at one point, but I could be mistaken." She laughed at the description, listening for more as she started to undo the buckles that held the sling in place. "Let's see…my mother said you were conflicted about a lot of things. Very emotionally-driven. Passionate."

"Exactly how much did she tell you?" She winced, more at the question than at the pain in her shoulder.

"She told me enough." I snickered, watching her face grow red. "It's *okay*, I don't really care. We're both adults. I can handle the fact that you had feelings for her." She looked at me curiously as the sling fell down her arm and lay on the bed. She held her right arm with her left hand, keeping it in place.

"You say *had*. How did you know my feelings changed? I mean, even I-"

"I had a theory about this long before you woke up." I interrupted, saving her the questions she had. "We all did. We figured if you were completely free of addiction, exposed to a new environment and a new way of thinking...you'd probably realize that Kara was a way for you to cope. She was just a way of tethering you to a harsh reality while you tried to escape it, and it was disguised as love." Krystal stared at me, her pupils changing in size rapidly as my words rolled through her thoughts.

"Oh. Okay, then. That's...a lot to take in." She hesitated before speaking again. "You're not wrong, I don't think...but that's a lot of years I have to think about and realize how much I did the wrong thing. How Kara wasn't...what I thought she was, to me. I think I was in love with...being in love. I wanted the *concept* of love because it meant peace and control for me. Even when I first woke up, my thoughts about her were...different."

"That's addiction for you." I sighed, turning so we were facing each other and I could start to undo her bandages. "I could kinda tell when we were in the same room together. You looked at her...in a different way than anyone else. Almost like you were watching your back. Guarded. I figured the way you were perceiving her was differently than before."

"Yeah, she seems...more normal. Everyone does. Like everyone is part of my daily routine. Before, it was always like they were changing or I was expecting something *about* them to change. I can't really explain it."

"Because you made that happen. How many times did you argue with her? Or with your sister? You felt angry, then sad, then happy, then repeated the process. The only one you could connect with was Violet. The closest to my mother you could get, and someone else who was seeing the world as an ever-changing ball of violence and unpredictability." She laughed again, her head tilting back to the ceiling as she stared at it.

"I haven't known you for more than a few days, talked to you about this for more than a few minutes, and you understand what I've been through more than I do, myself." She looked back at me. "What's the secret? What's the magic?" The last of the gauze was daintily pulled from her wound, a largely scabbed-over line of crushing trauma and bruising exposed on her shoulder. I pulled down the right strap of her tank top, trying not to touch her skin yet.

"No magic. No secret. It's just what I do. I see people, I understand them. And I become a mouthpiece for brutal honesty. Harsh truths don't have to be insulting, but they *do* have to be truths. I'm a very fact-and-information-oriented person. And while I make *some* assumptions, a lot of it is based on my medical or scientific opinion. Which…I would say is an informed one." I pulled my hands back for a moment, willing to talk and being in no rush to get started with the healing process. She noticed my hesitance and commented on it quietly.

"So…what happened last time you touched me? Right after I was stabbed?" She asked.

Blackness. Dark and cold. Then heat, intense and blazing heat. Bright, radiating light. Darkness again. Suffocation. Drowning…drowning long after I was out of air.

"Alice said I was in a daze for a bit. Nonresponsive but on my feet-"

"Not what I meant." She looked directly at me, one of the few times she had looked into my eyes. "What did you…feel? See? What *actually* happened?"

"I think I saw the early stages of your death." I licked my lips, trying to find the right words. "I felt things we can't feel in real life. Things too intense to describe and in environments too impossible to be real. Fields of absolute black, darker than being in the darkest room with your eyes closed. Light brighter than what our eyes should see. Light that would normally be blinding but it just gets brighter. Colors that don't exist. Things that…even when I'm accessing someone's nervous system, I can't feel. And last time, those images, those sensations, they held onto me for a long time after I physically let go of your injury."

"I saw it, too." She said quickly. "Not when you healed me, but right after I woke up. Violet asked me about my death, and I…when I thought about it, that's what it was like. Except I had a seizure."

"Then what happened to me could have been an absence seizure of some sort." I speculated. "It might be why I don't remember…what happened." I grimaced, remembering what Sonya described to us of what we had been through at the hands of the Tortured. Krystal felt the same discomfort, squirming where she sat.

"I guess we should be glad we don't remember it. Alice and Raven, I…*especially* Alice…" She whispered, her eyes glistening.

"She seems to be doing okay. I'm sure it will always be a horrible memory, but she's being strong and willing to face it. Her strength is keeping it from changing her. That's incredibly, impossibly rare, but she's managing to move forward with her life and leave it behind. We'll still give her all of our love and support." I moved to touch Krystal's hand, laying my palm across her fingers.

Screaming, but silence. No vocal cords to make a sound, but the breath is leaving my body regardless. A fight against it, a struggle to hold the last of my air inside. A void of soundless isolation. No dark, no light. Just a colorless, blind vacuum of nothing. Pulling me deep inside, but I can't go. I'm afraid. I'm losing the fight. Wait…a breath-

I jerked back, pulling my arm to my chest and shaking before opening my eyes. Krystal's reaction seemed opposite of mine, a gratified sigh leaving her chest as her eyes wandered in memory of whatever her thoughts had just consisted of. I shook my head, trying to shake out the memory of those thoughts and hold onto the hope that had inched its way into the final milliseconds of the odd vision.

"You first." I said quickly, rubbing my temples.

"I'm so sorry, Amy…" Krystal started, placing a hand on my back. I twitched, but quickly realized that my shirt was covering enough of my skin.

"Don't be, it's not your fault. Just tell me what you saw." She faltered, a slight smile lighting her cheekbones.

"I was…happy. More than happy. It was a version of a perfect life. Just…no stress, no lost friends, no war. A life I wanted. That I want." She corrected. "Impossibly perfect."

"Can you be descriptive? Was there any imagery?"

"Yeah. The same thing happened when you touched me in the van before we got to New York. It was…blissful. This one was a forest. A log cabin lit with a warm fireplace and warm wood furniture. I was lounging on the couch just…watching the flames as a log broke down. Nothing else. I just laid there. But things felt perfect." She chuckled, clearly savoring the emotions within her dream state.

"Mine was the same as last time, but I felt something different at the end." I started, trying to describe it clearly. "It was like holding your breath for as long as possible. And then at the last second, right before it ended, it was like I let it all out and started to take in fresh air. Just enough to keep me alive, but not enough to fill my lungs." I pondered the meaning of it, trying to decipher what part of her could be broken enough to hold such a powerful pain. "It was anguish. And nothing but. Until that last moment. Did anything change for you right before the vision ended, in the final moments? Like it did for me?" She looked away in deep thought, shaking her head after a pause.

"No. Not that I remember. I was staring at the fireplace, then looking around. The last thing I remember was looking at the front door. Maybe…maybe it was opening?" She asked a question I couldn't possibly have answered. "I don't know. It's hard to hold onto, once it's over."

"Yeah, thankfully I agree. It fades after a minute or two. At least, it did in the van." She contemplated my words, grabbing a blanket near the foot of the bed and pulling it open across her lap.

"I wonder why it didn't go away when I was stabbed. Was it because you were also healing me?"

"Maybe." A spark of thought gave me an idea. "Maybe it was because I was *actively* using my abilities that time. I wasn't when we were in the van. Maybe that's how I can dive deeper. Try to get past the imagery and figure out what's causing it."

"Yeah, at the risk of another seizure. Or worse." She scoffed. "Is it really worth it? I mean, I can avoid bumping into you if it means my touch is going to torture you. I'm not sure this is a problem that needs fixed at the risk of-"

"No." I said adamantly. "I need to know. I *need*…to know. There's something about this I have to figure out." I knew I wasn't speaking from a place of logic, but I also knew that she didn't care. She looked at her shoulder, pulling open the blanket further as she laid down on the bed.

"Might as well come over here and lay down. The *last* thing I need is to explain to everyone that you fell off my bed and cracked your skull while passing out after trying to fix my shoulder." I nodded in agreement, wanting to avoid any unnecessary risk, and crawled my way across the plush, king-sized mattress.

"There is *no way* everyone's bed is this nice." I laughed, pressing my hand into the material. "I bet Eric had a hand in making sure you got all the high-end, fancy stuff."

"I guess he does know my tastes fairly well." She noted. "This is the same type of bed I had in Aerael. It was definitely Eric. He was the only one that knew about my mattress."

"Oh. *Oh.*" I started. "Were you two…intimate?"

"What?" She retorted quickly, starting to laugh. "No. Nooo, no, no." Her laughter took over, delaying the rest of the explanation. "This thing had a waiting list of like…two years. They're hand-made." She wiped the tears from her eyes. "He got onto their database and bumped me up the list so I could get it faster."

"Sorry, I was only-"

"No need to apologize." She chuckled. "That's just…funny. He's, uh…not exactly my *type*. If you get my drift."

"I don't judge." I shrugged. She shook her head admonishingly, rolling onto her left side so I could access both sides of the wound.

"You've been through a lot, too, you know." She remarked, her voice diminished since she was now facing away from me. I stared for a moment in confusion, wondering where her sentiment came from.

"Not as much as-"

"Oh, come on, Amy. You know better than I do that you can't compare your pain to someone else's and say it's all okay."

Damn. She's got a point.

"You just found out that you have two half-sisters, and one is your best friend while the other is a previously avowed enemy. Your blood is carrying a virus designed by the man who killed your mother, which resulted in your abilities, and we watched a huge piece of Manhattan disappear from the

Earth. Probably tens of thousands dead all because the world's most powerful man is hunting for you and your mother." She continued. "All while you grew up in a world that's deteriorating and your parents were expected to save it." She rolled over slightly, just enough to look at me again. "You're not okay."

"I'm *absolutely* fine." I expressed, trying to sound comforting. "I may only be nineteen, but I've had fifteen years of adulthood and more life experience than even most Vampyres."

"And that means nothing in the face of trauma." She said pointedly. "Come on, you *know* all of this."

I do. I do indeed.

"So why are you hiding from it? Are you just too uncomfortable to talk about it?" She continued.

"I don't have anything to talk about, Krystal. It…sucks. It all sucks. But we have hope, and that means we have a mission, a task, a goal. We have something to work toward. That's enough to get me through. I see the other side."

"So then what does being happy look like to you?" Her question was plain, but made me recoil and immediately sit deeply in thought. It wasn't something I had ever given too much consideration to; I was always on the move to help the next person in need.

"Seeing all of this end. The war. Getting the cure done-"

"Sure, but then what?" Krystal pressed. "What do you want at the end of the road? What do you want people to talk about at your funeral?" She rolled over fully, in pain but more concerned about our conversation than anything else. "What will matter to you when the war is over?"

"I don't know." I admitted. "I haven't-"

"Then think about it now. Think hard. Because until I found what I wanted, I was lost. And I can see that same thing in you. You may seem like the most put-together person in our group, but you're as lost as I was."

"And what did you magically determine would make your life better?" I snapped, getting tired of hearing her lecture me on what my considerations for the future should be.

"Peace." She said quietly, the blue of her eyes flaring in a slow burst of lightness. A snowy, icy white crept into her irises before disappearing like melted frost. "I just want peace. I want-"

"You want what's in those visions." I realized, feeling the gentle creep of cold air radiate from her body. "Somehow, that's why you keep having them."

"I guess." She mumbled. "That's *your* area of expertise. Shrink." I sighed, staring at the slit on her shoulder and the bruising around it.

"I think I'm as prepared as I'm going to get." I said quietly, kneeling on the bed with both knees and hovering over her body.

"Wait." She called. "Before you start…think about what you want out of your life. Or think about the good things you have now. Maybe…it'll help you stay away from the nightmare you keep having to experience." I chuckled, taking the advice lightly.

"I don't know that thinking positive thoughts is going to fix things. It might take more than that."

"You said it yourself, you felt yourself reaching out to me. Maybe if you have nothing to reach for, you won't be dancing with memories of my death anymore." I ran my hands through my hair, letting it tug on my scalp as I pulled it behind me and held it all in a ball behind my head.

Great questions, Krystal. Bit more pressure than I needed going into this. Oh, just figure out what your entire life goals are in the next fifteen seconds. No big deal. Not a problem at all. I'll just figure out what would make me entirely fulfilled and satisfy my entire existence. Easy-peasy. Why don't we focus on you instead?

"Just take a few deep breaths." I sighed for the thousandth time, taking my own deep breaths and trying to clear my head.

Don't fight it this time. Chase her.

I placed my hands gently on her shoulder, immediately jerking as if hit with massive amounts of electricity. I could only feel my body react for the first split second, everything after a haze of confusing images.

Ball joint. Muscle. Damage. Pain. Darkness. Pain. Sorrow.

Violet's brutal tone cut into my heart as I watched rage and anger fill her eyes.

"Bringing her back won't make her love you, Krystal." She lifted her hand, pointing through the glass wall to the incubator and health monitors that lay beyond it as she spoke to me. "That child is all that's left of Kara. You need to find a way to live with that." My fangs dug deeply into the flesh of my lip, forcing a spurt of blood onto my tongue. I hated her words and I hated that they were the truth, but I hated most of all that the truth I couldn't stand to hear had to come from my best friend.

"There's a fine line between truth and cruelty, Violet." At the risk of my voice cracking, I continued. We were alone in the main hall and I still felt embarrassed for how red my face was growing and how horrible our words had become. "You're young, by anyone's standards. You have a lot to learn about what the truth is, and you haven't begun to scratch the surface. But one day, you're going to find someone that loves you unconditionally. And you're going to appreciate them more and more every day…growing just a little bit more attached to them. And you're going to hope and pray that they lie to you…just so you can hold onto that love. Sometimes, Violet…lies are all that hold a person together." Violet's eyes darted away briefly as Sonya's voice tumbled down the cavern, scolding Jalix loudly as they followed each other to the surface above the city. As her eyes flicked back to meet my own, they were filled with disgust and hatred, and I could barely stand to see her regard me with so much disdain. "And sometimes…it's all that's holding two people together. Sometimes those lies…become what we love." She ran

her fingers through her hair, grabbing handfuls in frustrated moments of rage.

"That's not true! I heard what Jalix said to Kara, and it wasn't a lie! He said that love is something you do, a gift you give to someone. It's not how you feel. And I know I loved you, Krystal. You're the only one I've ever opened up to. Are you saying you've only ever deceived me?" I couldn't believe that she could ask me something like that, having spent more than a few nights together dealing with these same issues.

"No, I-"

"She'll never love you, Krystal! Look at yourself! Face your own lies!" I shuddered, caring less about Kara and her feelings than at Violet's growing distance from me.

"I'm going to get her back, Violet." I whispered, ignoring everything else for the time being and focusing on bringing back to life the core of our family. "What she does with her second chance is up to her, and her alone. If she doesn't love me…then so be it. But that's the gift I'm going to give to her. It's how much I love her…with my life." Violet's eyes grew hazy, realizing that she was fighting a losing battle in her own mind. I could see the detachment with each step backward she took toward the infirmary and the child within its walls.

"You're not lying to me, Krystal. You're not dishonest to Kara, or to Jalix. Those lies? The ones you're so in love with? They're the ones that you tell to yourself."

"Violet, please-" I begged, trying to ask her to stay. I wanted nothing more than to hear her voice calm down and try to understand how I felt.

"Go away, Krystal…go find Kara." She whispered defeatedly, starting to turn away.

"Vi, you're my friend…" I pleaded.

"I thought I was. I'm just one of your lies." She shook her head, accepting the darkness of the hallway in front of her and disappearing to tend to Amy.

"Don't leave me." I whimpered tearfully, "Please come back." I knew she could hear me even over the distance between us, but I couldn't bring my feet to carry me any closer to her. I knew she finally hated me

in the way that I had feared she always would. I knew in my heart that everything I didn't want to turn into, everything I had tried to shy away from was now exactly what I was. Alone. Isolated. Most of all, I was hopeless, and turned to walk slowly through the empty corridor back to my room with sluggish purpose.

I had a moment of clarity, a surge of energy pummeling through my rapidly beating heart as I felt Krystal's body light up in emotional response. Her hormones, her heartbeat, and her twitching movements as we fought off darker thoughts all raced through my mind and were matched by my own body. I fell from my knees onto my side, lying next to her and clutching her shoulder tightly so I didn't lose my grip. I could feel myself slipping away from awareness, joining with her again to fight what was coming.

Despite the fact that it was already loaded, I pulled the magazine away from the bottom of the pistol and pulled out all eleven of the rounds. They tumbled around each other in a display of brass and copper shine as they rolled against my hip, each one being dropped as a name escaped my lips.

"...Alice...Val...Violet..." I continued, each one slipping through my fingers until I held the last one, sitting gently against my palm with a surprising weight. "And me." I whispered, placing it back into the magazine. It clicked into place and spurred my heart as I loaded it into the gun, the beating against my chest combatting the tiredness I felt in every other area of my body. I could see a white layer of frost against the pistol's slide as I pulled it back, exposing the barrel for a brief moment before I released it and chambered the bullet. The synthetic grip was comfortable in my hand, effortlessly held as I lifted the weapon and placed the tip of the barrel against my temple. Even in its freezing-cold state, it couldn't make a difference against the temperature of my skin. I straightened my right index finger, feeling my manicured nail slip into the well of the trigger and rest lightly against it. "I love all of you." I whispered, another tear crawling out of my tired eyes and freezing against my cheekbone. I closed my eyes and curled my fingertip for the few millimeters I was allowed. The rest of the distance before the round

would fire was now prohibited, which I noted in a deep and shocked sigh before placing the gun on the blanket to my right and staring at my feet.

"Why?" I asked, seeing Sonya step toward me in my peripheral vision. Her hand lowered since she no longer needed to use her abilities to keep me from my peace.

"They need you." She knelt next to me, her voice low so the others couldn't hear us if they would walk past my room.

"No. They don't." I shook my head, gritting my teeth. "They don't. I'm nothing but a burden to every one of them. Every last goddamn one." I struggled to speak through the lump in my throat. The roaring pain made further explanation impossible, so I cried instead and let myself heave the emotions out of my chest in shuddering breaths.

"They love you, Krystal. We...love you. She loves you." She put a hand on my knee, knowing my jeans would be enough to keep her from being frostbitten.

"Never the way I want. Never the way she could." I coughed.

"If she could...she would have. But she can't. And neither can you. This has broken you fully, Krystal. Love doesn't do that to someone. Obsession does. Addiction does. Loss does. Not love. And what you feel might look like love...but it's a lie." I took a deep breath and remembered what I had told Violet only minutes ago. "You're going to let a lie kill you."

"No." I mumbled, the only thing I could conjure.

"Krystal...I've been through death. There is nothing there for you. There is no peace in that void." Sonya's voice grew clear, trying to get through to me as her bright green eyes met my own. "You will have your chance to make peace. To give your gift and show your love."

"There's only one way I can do that." I whispered.

In a brief moment, I had the choice to continue chasing the erratic series of thoughts and memories that flowed through my head or release my grip and halt the seizing of our bodies. I felt my fingers nearly slip for the briefest second, my fingertips grazing the top of her shoulder before my hand clamped down again, squeezing the slowly-healing injury with all my strength as both of us started to stiffen, the beginnings of a seizure wracking our bodies with matching bouts of paralyzing stiffness and uncontrolled spasming.

I gently pressed my foot into the brakes, the responsiveness of my expensive car forcing us to slow down quickly next to Jalix's black SUV. I shifted down into neutral and watched Sonya roll down the window on the passenger side as Jalix and my sister watched us.

"What do you think, about a quarter mile away?" I asked, only raising my voice enough that he could hear me. The four of us looked at the chain-link fence at the end of the drive, ten vertical feet of thin metal and floodlights barricading us from my true love's place of rest. I started to count the pacing bodies in front of the building, noting their locations. "How many do you see?" I continued. "I count ten on the outside."

"I see ten." He called, his voice rough and firm in its place of emotional stillness.

"I can do...twelve seconds." I joked, knowing that this would be the last time I would ever feel the roar of an engine with my hands on the wheel.

"I think I can keep up." He returned, avoiding the imminent threat we faced.

"What, in that thing? Not likely." I retorted, the lump in my throat growing and affecting my voice enough that Sonya rolled up the window again and looked at me. I bit my lip, looking downward and remaining unwilling to face the short-lived future.

"We love you." She said quietly, leaning forward and kissing me on the cheek. I was glad the dark silhouette of her head covered my face as I started to break down again, my face fighting a contortion into desperate tears. "You have a place here." She whispered.

"No." I said quietly, lifting my head and shifting into first gear. "I don't."

I could feel my moments of clarity diminishing to nothingness, and held on to the thought of reality for as long as I possibly could. My body was somehow separate from my mind, and while I was aware of the violent shivering, shaking, and jerking that strained my muscles to their breaking points, I became a neutral observer as my brain descended rapidly toward the dark, spiraling blackness of memories that shouldn't have existed.

"Jalix, go!" I screamed in desperation, my fist hitting the concrete pillar to my right in a show of force. He knew I wouldn't pursue him, nor harm him, but the reality of the situation settled in his mind as he locked eyes with me and parted his lips.

"She loves you." He paused, tilting his head downward for a moment. "Know that, Krystal." My stomach heaved a horrific choking sensation into my throat, forcing me to crumple against the wall as he turned and sprinted to his wife and a life I could never have.

I slowly accepted that there was nothing left in this life for me to reclaim, the complete and total loss of everything I cared about having vanished into nothingness. I dwelled for too long on memories of Val, of Jared, and of Kara, each as dead to me as the other in their places of peace. I sat for a moment and watched the red emergency lights flash and strobe, lighting up the room with an eerie glow before I took a step forward and lifted my hands. Although no one in our family with abilities needed to use their hands in a tangible or visual motion, the concept of motion, of movement, and of creation helped facilitate colder and colder energies around my hands. I watched the walls quickly succumb to white frost, layers of dense ice growing to close off vents and doorways as it thickened to a protective structure of hard layers. As they grew, the size of the room shrank until I barely had the space to stand at my full height. The movement of my hands slowed, and I let thoughts of Kara energize me and fight the fatigue that saturated my physique from the extended and intense use of my abilities.

Nothing felt more real than the escalating, frigid cold that touched my skin, and while real, felt miles away from my thoughts. In my own waking dreams, Kara and I danced for hours in the empty halls of Aerael. We wept together at the loss of her brother and of Jared. We sat for long hours in her room, holding each other and appreciating the simplest form of touch. Afraid, I ignored the deafening sound of explosions that cracked the ice and shook the floor. I persisted, the cracks sealing quickly as my body continued to push my abilities to their limits and encase my form in a self-made grave. Flames and debris smashed into the tomb and threatened its integrity, but was kept at bay by the wedding in my daydreams, the early morning breakfasts in my fantasies, and the daytime naps in my deepest desires. I allowed myself to drift into a deep sleep, Kara's image burned into my closed eyelids in my final thoughts.

I was asleep, I was in pain, and then I was dead. And death, it seemed, had its own way of inflicting thought on a mind that ceased to perform its duty. I awoke, challenged by a black void with a deafening voice that said nothing. Without a body or form, I could do nothing to avoid the terror that stared at me without eyes or structure of any kind. It wanted nothing, I could tell, but stood in horrifying scale beyond the scope of comprehension and waited for my acceptance. Into its darkness, I stared for eons and waited for something to change. For centuries, millennia, and beyond, I was terrorized by an all-encompassing shroud of black that did nothing to end my suffering and refused to leave my side. Despite the hazy, detached concept of fighting against it, I grasped nothing of its belief and only stared until I was allowed the privilege of a single, unified, and coherent thought that emanated from a voice I no longer had.

"Why?" The whisper went unanswered, growing in volume and resonance exponentially, until my own word deafened my ears to scales of pain beyond human imagining. I could do nothing as the sound battered around me, forceful in its screaming hisses and relentless questioning.

And then everything abruptly stopped. There was no fear, no shouting whispers of unanswered questions, and no clutched paralysis of my own senses. For the briefest flash of a remarkable second, I was lucid enough to hear the void in its reply before it rapidly descended into a more powerful and incomprehensible nothingness.

"Sorrow." There was no voice to sound the reply aloud, but the word was granted directly in answer to my question before I was dropped into the emptiness of pure nothing where even the darkness I faced had disappeared. There was a moment of fear, and in that moment my spirit

was granted the power to feel fear's true power. As I began to fall, I quickly wished that any sense of suffering be ripped away along with whatever was left of my soul.

There was a long pause, like the deep breath before a plunge into frozen waters, before the pain finally came to infect my body. All my long life, I had not known true pain until the certain fact came to my mind, despite its madness in my state of apparent death: I was, in some form, alive. The darkness that shrouded both my eyes and my sense of awareness was unparalleled by even the blackest night, fading all rational thought from becoming useful and only serving to keep me aware of the same burning torment I felt that I suffered for eons.

Time passed. Whether it was seconds or millennia, I was unsure, but the trickling grains of each blistering surge of agony kept the sands of my internal hourglass moving forward, and until the pain would subside, I knew I was still alive. Ghosts of images formed themselves in front of my eyes: fading and fleeting pictures of nonsensical environments, irrational surroundings, and impossible atmospheres. In my comatose slumber, I was torn apart and repaired time and time again until I was sure that it was nothing more than a terrorizing nightmare. This was my hell.

Repeatedly, I found myself nearly lucid, flailing without hands to grab some imaginary support or take hold of consciousness, although both eluded me. I thrashed, screamed, felt my hands on cold metal bars without end or purpose. I cried. I fell. Until I was spent of my life's energy, I fought and confronted these twisted visions of nightmares, until at long last, there was a convoluted, isolated semblance of thought. I was…cold.

***

I placed the bowl in our sink at a precarious angle, perching it atop other dishes as I pulled back the curtain to look at the small garden just outside the window. While my tomato plants hadn't yet reached maturity, I was excited to see the small fruits of peppers begin to litter their stalks in an array of bright green. I slid the lace curtain into place again, keeping out the harshest rays of sunlight that glinted off the windshield of the car in the driveway. Before I could flood the pile of dirtied plates and utensils with soapy water, I felt cool hands slide onto my hips and move around my body to cradle my stomach in the gentlest of touch. I smiled, moving back only far enough to press our bodies together in a moment of peace. The silver hair on my temples, free from the rest of my ponytail, danced against my cheekbones as I looked down to lace our fingers together and sway gently in the morning sun. Her painted fingernails gently stroked my palms in contemplative thought before she opened her mouth to say something.

Groggily, I opened my eyes and regretted deciding to exist in the reality I lived in. Every muscle in my body ached, including some near my joints that I hardly knew existed. More so than physical pain, the toll on my mind provided a form of friction to my sense of alertness as I sat up and looked to my right. Krystal let go of my hand, which she had apparently been holding, and backed away a few inches to look at me. She looked the way I felt: sweaty and exerted in spite of being essentially unconscious.

"You okay?" She asked cautiously. "How do you feel?"

"Mm. Fine, I guess. Tired. Sore." I mumbled, yawning at the end of my statement. As I stretched, I could feel the tension in my joints begin to ease. "What about you?" I continued. "You okay?"

"Yeah, I've...*been* okay. For like, two hours." She stared, nodding to my hand. "I woke up before you and watched you keep...sleeping. I went to get up and walk around, but you would convulse unless I was touching you. I tried calling Alice, but she didn't answer. You seemed okay, all else aside." I hesitated, lifting my hand slowly and reaching out as she winced in preparedness. Almost lightheartedly, I poked the healed portion of her exposed shoulder to see if the physical contact would have the same effect as before. While I didn't dip into an illusory or hallucinatory state, I could feel a unique energy from her body in the form of emotional influence. Each time my finger touched her skin, it was as if I could catch brief glimpses of emotional states without completely embracing them as my own.

Anxiety. Contentedness. Calm. Serenity.

"Yeah-…Just-…please stop doing that." She chuckled, rubbing her arm. "Shoulder's good. Still a bit…odd with whatever's going on emotionally. Not sure that'll ever fully go away. I still get…glimpses when you touch me. Not hallucinations anymore, but… reactions."

"So do I. At least I'm not having night terrors in my waking moments." I rebutted, pleased that we had, at least, made some form of progress in changing things for the better. "I'll take what I can get." I rolled off of her bed and stood, stretching again and looking around her room. "I'll save you the questions." I started, hearing a silent tension build between us. "I *experienced* your death. It was…traumatic, to say the least. But imaginary. So I can handle it like a bad dream and brush it off, I think. You went through more than you're aware of, and I'm not even entirely sure how I managed to make sense of it. It was nothing like I've ever been able to sense in anyone else."

"Are you okay?" She grew concerned, pulling the cell phone from her pocket and placing it on her lap. "I'm going to try Alice again-"

"There isn't anything she can do. I think all of this came from your lack of recovery from everything that happened. You didn't get a chance to fully deal with things before *or* after your death…and I think it finally caught up to you. I have no idea where my abilities fit in, but I was able to access that emotional damage, the psychological trauma, the same way I could for a physical injury. I wasn't prepared for it the first few times I touched you, and I wasn't doing it on purpose." She paused her pacing, rolling her head in a small circle as her brow furrowed. "I think the reason I was having those issues is because I was *sharing* your seizures. Taking some of the toll off of your body and onto mine. Healing you as it was happening, maybe. It explains the state I went into when you got stabbed and I tried to heal it." I clarified.

"And now?" She stared from across the room, afraid that she had done something wrong. "I can't believe I put you through all of that-"

"Hey, no-..." I started, quickly closing the space between us to speak as honestly as I could. "I told you I wanted to figure this out. I *asked* for this. I wanted to explore what was going on. Don't apologize for...what, for going through what you did? For sitting on the brink of death for so long?" She shook her head, either in disbelief or in remembrance. "You are the strongest person I know." I confessed, tilting my head as she looked down at her shoes. "To go through something like that and come out on the other side intact? Whatever anyone says about you being *changed* is nothing compared to how anyone else would have ended up. No one else would have been resilient enough, intense enough to face down what you did and challenge death itself." She smiled genuinely, her eyes softening as she looked up at me. "The things people told me about you don't even come close." I chuckled. "You're infinitely more of a badass than you know. I'm glad to have you as a friend."

"You, too, Amy." She nodded, her eyes alight with happiness. "Whatever you did...it helped. I feel more free now. A lot less chased by whatever was nagging at me since I woke up. Oh, and the shoulder feels *amazing*." She emphasized, rotating her right arm.

"I'm glad. Just...be careful, okay? You're suppressing a lot of emotions. Even after all of that." I added.

"I will." She chuckled.

"Good." I said, pulling her in for a hug. I stopped as her arm met my back, hearing footsteps down the hall and stopping a few feet from Krystal's door. While I was simply distracted by the knocking on someone's door, Krystal felt awkwardly rejected and ran her hand through her hair, letting out a long sigh. "Sorry." I mumbled, not meaning to make her feel even more offended or uncomfortable. I listened to the voices outside, responding in kind.

"Amy? Miss Kane?" One of them called, knocking on what I could only assume was my assigned living space.

"I *thought* that was my room." I confirmed, opening Krystal's door and gaining the attention of the three women that stood in front of the door across the hall. "Hi." I said awkwardly. One of the women was Raven, who had changed into a boutique set of black, athletic-style leisure wear.

Right, I was out for more than two hours. Everyone is probably getting changed and trying to deal with reality.

I didn't recognize the other two, but one was carrying a white lab coat as if it had been worn recently and the other was an out-of-place-looking short woman with a sharp, clean appearance. The woman holding her lab coat extended her free hand and introduced herself.

"Great to meet you. I'm Doctor Brynn Weiss. I'm overseeing Project Starlight, the cure project. I guess you already know-...um, are related to...Raven, I suppose..." She stumbled over her words awkwardly as Raven shrugged lightly and leaned against the wall as if very little in life mattered to her in the moment. She seemed almost inconvenienced by being there, but gave me a small nod as a sign of respectful acknowledgment. "And this is Andrea Scott. She's a pilot from Quantico and is going to be working with your father on some of the plans for our attack against Legacy." Andrea leaned out from behind Dr. Weiss and shook my hand, as well.

"Good to meet you both. Can I help?" I offered, still unsure why they were present. Although Raven seemed distant, her eyes roamed around the inside of Krystal's room, watching as she moved behind me into the bathroom to assumedly get changed.

"Alice suggested that Raven and I debrief you on the cure information, since we already went over it with her. But I take it you're...busy." She looked over my shoulder as Krystal threw her sweat-soaked clothes and sling from inside the bathroom, across the bedroom, and into her bedside laundry basket.

"I...had to fix her shoulder. Stab wound. Healing powers." I pointed to my palm as if it explained anything. Her eyebrows raised in remembrance, her curly, brown hair bouncing as she nodded.

"Oh, right! You have that thing. Regardless, we can come back-"

"No, it's fine. We can chat. Are you a part of the cure project, too?" I pointed to Andrea, confused as to why she was part of the group.

"Nope." Andrea said simply, shrugging. "I'm a tourist for today, learning my way around the city and meeting who's who. Just got here, trying to meet people since I'll be here awhile with your father and coordinating the aerial combat side of things."

"Oh. Well, come in. I'm sure Krystal won't mind." I offered, allowing them to step inside. "I think we'll have to wait on the technical information for a few hours. My brain is a bit frazzled at the moment. I'd still like to meet you both, since I'm sure we'll be working together." Still unaware as to the layout of each of the rooms, I guided them around the corner instead of back to the bedroom and gestured to a well-lit dining area that resembled a small bar. While there were cooking appliances behind the counter, the majority of the space was occupied by a slab of black marble with bar stools placed around it. Raven took a seat closest to the door, hardly making eye contact with me as she stared at the refrigerator. Dr. Weiss and Andrea sat across from her, leaving the spot next to Raven open for me.

"So..." I started awkwardly, taking a seat.

"I met with your mother." Andrea commented. "Powerful woman. The way she speaks, the way she looks at you, holy crap." She chuckled. "Makes the stories pale in comparison. Your parents are the poster children for a power couple."

"She's very kind, though. Like your father." Dr. Weiss added. "I feel terrible for…well, what you're all going through right now with Legacy. I hope there's some resolution to it all soon."

"I'm surprised she was taking visitors." I returned, shocked that she had allowed anyone but my father near her presence during her state of hasty retreat to tormented solitude. "How is she?"

"She's…" Raven started, still refusing to look at me. "She's the way she always has been. Poised. Confident. Deadly. She wasn't expecting Legacy to say anything about Violet's or my lineage. I think it took her by surprise, but I could tell that she wanted you two to know." The left side of her head was freshly shaven, a Viking appeal gracing the angle at which I watched her.

"She seemed in rough shape after leaving that meeting with Legacy. She's okay though?" I reinforced, wanting to hear more about her mood and demeanor.

"We had just been visiting with her in the infirmary before coming here. She wants to see you. And Violet. But she wants you both to come on your own terms, not by her request. Even your father is afraid of what you two will think of them, now." Raven tapped her black nails on the countertop, a clear nervousness in her posture. "I think it's the *only* thing they're afraid of. Your dad talks about Legacy like he's a ragdoll with a bullseye on its back. But when he mentioned Violet…" She let the sentence hang, shaking her head slowly.

"I hope we're not bothering you." Andrea said suddenly, leaning forward. "I mean, this is…I don't want to sound like an asshole, but it's family drama. Your business, not ours." I laughed at her naiveté, a clear misunderstanding of the role of our family. Raven joined me in a light chuckle.

"We're unique. Our business is the world's business. Always has been. So don't worry, you're not bothering anyone. Just maybe avoid Violet for a bit." I added, the thought of her reaction too somber to elaborate further.

"That...won't be an issue." Raven's smirk fell away very suddenly at the mention of Violet's name. "She locked herself in the nightclub. Sonya and I tried checking on her, and...all we could hear was crying. Just...weeping. There was...a short conversation, but it won't be enough."

My poor sister...I need to go see her. If anyone can break through, it'll be Krystal and I.

I let the thought linger for too long, staring at the wood cabinetry behind the counter and contemplating the idea of food. I wasn't sure how long it had been since I had taken any medicine to keep away cravings for blood, but the doubt lingered as Dr. Weiss asked a hesitant question.

"How are you all holding up? I mean, after...I heard you all went through a rough time before arriving at the city."

"A rough time?" Raven growled, her eyes darting up to look at Dr. Weiss. Andrea twitched at Raven's voice, an intimidating snarl of hateful remembrance. "It was a *bit* more than that."

"I'm sorry, I-"

"Hey." I said softly, nudging Raven. "Not her fault. She wasn't there."

"Neither were *you* in any practical sense." She returned, leaning forward in her seat and resting her arms on the bar. "Sorry. I'm...relieved. That you and Krystal, Violet...none of you were there to really see it. But it doesn't make it easier."

"We can change the subject." Dr. Weiss quickly defended, shaking her head. "I had no idea-"

"It's fine." Raven said softly, shaking her head. "Amy's right. Not your fault. I'm just...I think Alice and I are going to need time before we can talk about it. Alice had it worse than I did, but...they weren't going to wait until they finished with her. I started fighting back. I tried, I really did. I was..." She stopped suddenly, closing her eyes and inhaling sharply, a shudder hindering her breath. "Sonya and Kara came in at the right time. So did Tony. He...he was helpful in snapping me out of it. I wasn't exactly *pleasant* at the time. Thank him if you see him again before I do. I didn't have time at the meeting." She commented to me. I nodded, starting to change the topic before the sounds behind me attracted our attention.

"Hey." Krystal's voice emerged from the bedroom, leaning in as she approached the kitchen and rapidly rubbed a towel through her hair. "Two questions." She whispered. "First of all, is long hair always this much of a pain in the ass to dry?"

"Yes. My hair takes forever, so does mom's. Long process. Try blow-drying with a conditioner."

"Ooh. I wonder if I have a blow dryer. Second question, why is there a party in my kitchen and I wasn't invited?" Her whisper elevated to a soft question to the group as a whole.

"Alice and Jalix's second-in-command people. Dr. Weiss, Andrea, this is Krystal. Krystal, Andrea and Dr. Weiss." Raven introduced them quickly.

"Pilot. Hopefully to blow up Legacy."

"Doctor. Hopefully to fix the virus." They each added, giving Krystal a small wave.

"Oh, and speaking of roles..." I started, looking at Andrea. "How much have you been told about everyone's place in the city?"

"Everything, as far as I know." She answered, her eyes flaring open at the thought of the scope of our endeavors. "Which was a lot to handle all at once."

"You're not alone." Krystal added. "Eric had some bad timing with telling us all of that. We *just* arrived, beat to hell, injured, traumatized, and exhausted, and he needed to dump the world's problems on our shoulders immediately?"

"I was the one to come up with the theory of choreographing the video call with Legacy, and even *I* had protested that it was moving too quickly." Raven quipped. "But...he wanted to get it out of the way so there was nothing looming over our heads. No fear, no watching our backs until that was done. And I can't say I disagree with him."

"Well, when you put it like that." Krystal nodded, accepting Raven's reasoning.

"Got any wine?" Raven asked casually, pointing to the refrigerator. "Specifically the rosé I left you on the bottom shelf?" Krystal chuckled, throwing the towel back into the bedroom and approaching her fridge. She whipped the length of hair over her shoulder, a partially-wet mass of blue sticking to her ribcage over a designer crop-top.

Damn, she cleans up nicely. Looks like a supermodel with the attitude to match. Oh crap, I probably look terrible.

"Sorry about..." I gestured to myself, suddenly becoming self-conscious about the apparent layer of oil on my face and messy hair. "Healing takes a toll sometimes." I tried to justify my appearance, apparently not a consideration by anyone else as they shrugged passively. Krystal opened her refrigerator and let out an elated gasp at the array of wines and liquors on its shelves.

"Stocked it for you." Raven mumbled. "Figured you'd be happy."

"*Very*. There's enough wine in here for a new bottle each day of the week. Why the extra effort?" Krystal humorously glared at Raven, accusing her of goodwill.

"I moved my private collection from my old home in Boston to here in Vanaheim. There's...*much* more in my room. Figured I won't live long enough to drink it all." The sour note of her statement left us all in an awkward silence as Krystal uncapped one of the bottles and poured glasses for each of us.

"Well, I can always grab the tray of prosciutto and cheeses that Eric left me. Since it's already a party." Krystal suggested. Dr. Weiss lifted a finger and grimaced.

"Does it...happen to be kosher?" She asked uneasily.

"Oh, you're Jewish?" I asked quickly. She nodded. "Why the embarrassment? That was a reasonable question." She shrugged lightly, scratching her head.

"Not many people are big on religion around here. Too much logic, too much focus on the present. It's not so bad in the residential part of the city." She elaborated. "Down there, I have a great group to study with and spend time around. But working with the other researchers...it gets a bit spiritually lonely."

"I think spiritual practices are fascinating. When I used to do counseling, I helped a lot of people overcome that same mentality that you have. That isolation? You're definitely not alone." She smiled as I tried my best to comfort her. As Krystal slid me an overly-full glass of wine, I took a long draught and looked at Andrea while she spoke.

"Counseling? You're a shrink?" Andrea seemed surprised, and I quickly realized that she wasn't familiar with the dynamics of the city's history yet.

"Yep. I'm trained in psychology, psychiatry, neuroscience, and physical medicine. Not too many places to get degrees once the world went to hell, but I studied with the best that Alice and the city had to offer. Counseling and therapy was my own way of relaxing. Helping others solve their problems made for the city to be a friendlier place."

"And now *we* need therapy." Raven retorted before taking a sip from her glass.

"Jesus." Andrea returned. "I felt an IQ jump when I got infected, but I'm not *that* smart."

"Amelia is a clinical genius." Dr. Weiss explained.

Oh, no. Please don't do that. I'm not good with compliments.

"Alice told me quite a bit about Amy's upbringing and training. Her IQ was tested at around a hundred and sixty-five if I remember correctly." She looked at me for reassurance and I shrugged, unwilling to admit that she was right. Krystal stared at me inelegantly and chuckled.

"You didn't mention that one." She admonished gently, refilling her already-empty glass. As she passed the rest of the bottle around the table, I recognized that I was the only one drinking slowly. "What else are you hiding?" Krystal's smile was a mix of teasing and curiosity.

"Numbers are numbers. I take pride in my abilities, and much less so my test scores."

"Says the nerd." Raven mumbled curtly. The table laughed, myself included, and I started to feel relaxed within the dynamic of the group. There was a moment of silence, filled quickly by Krystal.

"Dr. Weiss, I'll make sure we get some kosher snacks for next time."

"Please, just Brynn." She requested. "And thank you. A next time would actually be nice. You all seem like interesting people."

"Maybe Violet can join us." I said softly, thinking of her again. "She would love this. Quiet, no interruptions, no noise. And wine."

"Wine and bitches." Raven raised her glass briefly, an unintentional toast as the rest of the room raised their glasses and took a long drink. In the silence, we could hear growing voices in the distance becoming both closer and more alarming. One was a female and I recognized it as Violet's in the few vulgar words I could make out. The other was softer, a man's, and as they both became audible in the hallway behind us, I could make out that it was Val. We tried to ignore the chaos, but the volume was too much to avoid hearing.

"She's your *wife!*" Violet screamed, audibly stopping outside of her room down the hall.

"I know." Val said quietly, defeated in his tone and energy.

"How the hell could she not *tell* you? I'm your *niece!* And she doesn't think I deserve to know who my own *family* is? That *you* don't deserve to know? I'm going to punch her in the goddamn face the next time-"

"Vi-"

"Don't *Vi* me! It's not even my name! It's literally some shit I made up when I was a kid! You think I liked hearing my foster parents scream *Anna* at me for fifteen years?" I cringed at the argument and the disruption it brought to the group. My sister's anger was palpable, and while I understood where she was coming from, I felt horrible for Val in standing next to her and accepting the onslaught. The rest of the table felt much the same way, although Krystal was the only one who seemed to feel the level of pain that I did.

"Vi, this is a good thing. It's just going to take time for us all to adjust." Val tried to be soothing and was largely unsuccessful. Violet breathed a loud sigh and opened her door.

"What I realize is that I was lied to. I'm starting to think those lies are all that was holding us together."

Oh, no. Those are Krystal's words.

As the door slammed shut in the hallway, I watched Krystal's face grow red while gentle tears crept into her glistening blue eyes. There was a moment of silence, broken by a quiet comment from Andrea.

"Once again, I feel like I probably shouldn't be involved in any of this." She finished her glass, looking across the table at Raven. "You guys have a lot going on."

"Oh, you don't know the *half* of it." I returned. "But she'll be okay. We all will. And I think it's high time we pay her a visit. What do you think?" I looked up at Krystal, who nodded gently.

"The Wine and Bitches club will resume at a later date." Raven sighed.

"Let's get together again soon." Krystal suggested. "Honestly, I need some normalcy. And this…well, it's as close as I'm going to get."

"Getting out of the lab would be nice, as long as we're not intruding." Brynn added.

"I'm literally just along for the ride." Andrea emphasized, stating her neutrality in the situation. I nodded once, patting Raven on the back once as she stood up.

"We'll do this again. Maybe get to know each other all as people." I looked directly at Raven as I made the statement, who finally returned eye contact and realized that I was talking about the two of us.

"Yeah." She paused, brushing me off after a moment and walking toward the door. "Maybe."

"Good luck." Andrea said as she departed from the room. "I think you guys might need it." After a moment of shuffling and the sound of a closing door, Krystal and I were left alone again. She sighed, a shudder running through her chest as the breath left her lungs.

"I'm not looking forward to this, either." I said quietly, leaning against the bar top and expressing what she was feeling. "I'm afraid that Violet's going to bring up points that I agree with and I'm going to end up on her side. I was lied to, as well. And I know that I'm not angry at either of my parents – or Alice – for not telling me, but I still wonder what would have been different if they had. It's confusing. And for her to be put through the foster system first, only to be picked up and brought to the city at the last minute before adulthood…it's not ideal. I can understand her frustration." Krystal nodded slowly, finally locking eyes with me.

"Then let's go tell her that. Maybe she'll feel better if she knows what you're going through, too. Plus you're a therapist. That'll help." She chuckled. "With an IQ of a hundr-"

"Don't." I interrupted. "It gets annoying. People develop expectations." I went to take a step forward, stopped by a sudden cramping in the back of my stomach. "Oh, that sucked. Ow. We have any medicine in here? Maybe try the fridge?" I leaned against the wall, wincing as a craving started to set in. Krystal whisked over to the kitchen again while I fought the odd combination of itchiness in my jaw muscles and sense of mixed hunger and thirst.

"Here. Plenty in there, apparently. I actually needed some, too. Thanks for saying something." I hastily uncapped the needle and slid it into the faint blue vein in the center of my arm, pressing just slowly enough that the feeling went away with a gradual decline before disappearing completely. "Thank you." I sighed gratefully, leaning over and disposing of the re-capped needle into her garbage can. I held it open as she did the same. "Kind of wish I had gotten *that* superpower. Not needing our medicine." We left the kitchen and walked past the bedroom into the small foyer area. "But that would be fairly impossible."

"Eh. Maybe someday, who knows? My friends have a habit of doing the impossible." Krystal shrugged, opening her door.

"Aww. We're friends." I taunted, leaning my head into her shoulder. "And here I was told you were antisocial."

"Don't get used to it." Her tone was intentionally bitter, but her ear-to-ear smile lit up her eyes with an unmistakable glow of happiness. We both stopped before reaching Violet's door, our phones vibrating at the same time. Krystal got to hers first, opening the text and groaning.

"Eric." She explained, looking over at me. I stared at her for a moment and shrugged.

"And…"

"Oh, right. You weren't around back when we were at war the first time. Eric does this thing where *anytime* I need a damn break, we all have to meet for something important. He has the worst timing you can imagine." She put the phone in her pocket again as I did the same, staring at Violet's door.

Maybe she needs some more time.

"We should probably take care of the urgent things first." I nodded, gesturing to the end of the hallway. Krystal hopped a few inches off the ground, puffing out her chest and putting her fists on her hips.

"To the conference room we go." I laughed at her silliness, shaking my head at her and being infinitely grateful that there was a drastic change in her level of positivity. As much as I could still feel the lingering effects from our exchange, I couldn't shake the now-visible traits that no one had ever adequately explained. Her strength, her tenacity, her compassion, and her resilience were all exposed and a part of how I saw her. She chuckled with me, walking alongside me down the hallway.

"This meeting…it's the first of many." I started quietly, looking over at the gentle glow of her face. "We have a long way to go, I think."

"We do." She said, her chin lifted and held high at the prospect of our upcoming challenges. She looked back at me, her deep blue eyes alight with fire in spite of the cold I could feel from her skin. "But we're back. And we're going to win this war."

"Desolation has left us unbroken."

Reverent in the way I viewed the majesty of our city, I had never taken counsel in the ways of my own leadership. Too many times had I failed to inform and protect those under my aegis, and to my own misguided ways, my people fell into despondency. And then they were gone.

As easily as my family had come together, we were disbanded, separated, and isolated from one another. We had forsaken the thought of returning to a glory we believed we had. But in my ignorance and blindness, I had forgotten the very reason for our society's collapse. In the splintered glass of my own reflection, I saw too clearly the allies standing behind me and could only then realize their potential. In both unification and division, they had proven time again that their place was at my side, and had shown me that even through the darkest time of our long lives, death would not stop the one thing that brought us back together.

Hope.

Acknowledgements:

I could fill another book with people I'd like to thank by name, but I have to stick with only a few because my editor said so.

First and foremost is my family, beyond a doubt. On a daily basis, I tell myself I couldn't possibly be any prouder of my younger brothers than I already am, but they have proven me wrong at every turn. I commend you both for always following what you love so deeply. I'll always be there for you.

The same goes for my supportive parents, watching me struggle to write during a military career, graduate school, and painful diagnoses; Your steadfast support is not forgotten. My grandmother, a best friend since infancy, is also worth a book in her own right, and for the guidance she's given me through hard times and challenges, I credit my success in large part to you.

To all those mentioned and to the incredible extended family who is equally supportive of my path (but I'm out of room for), I thank you deeply.

To my wife: On a serious note, which we both hate, your love and support has always been treasured. I'm lucky enough to consider you a centerpiece in my life, and I'm proud of the woman you've become.

To all of my friends and mentors, close and distant, near and far, from military, work, school, or fate, I don't forget the experiences I've had with all of you and the ways you've helped me grow.

And, perhaps most importantly, to my readers:
You are the core of the Sorrowverse. This series is full of pain, suffering, loss, addiction, trauma, and more, and it's not written blindly. For every reader who finds a personal connection with a character, a theme, an event, or one of its volumes, I hope you no longer feel alone in knowing that others have been where you are and have conquered their worst nightmares. My goal in writing is to create a connection between you and myself through the world I've created. Enjoy it, cherish it, and support it as it grows to help people escape reality or understand its consequences within these pages.
You are my legacy.